ONE
NIGHT
with the
DUKE

JODI ELLEN
MALPAS

FOREVER

New York   Boston

Forever
Hachette Book Group
1290 Avenue of the Americas, New York, NY 10104
read-forever.com
twitter.com/readforeverpub

Originally published in 2022 by Orion Books in Great Britain
First U.S. Edition: April 2023

Forever is an imprint of Grand Central Publishing. The Forever name and logo are trademarks of Hachette Book Group, Inc.

The publisher is not responsible for websites (or their content) that are not owned by the publisher.

The Hachette Speakers Bureau provides a wide range of authors for speaking events. To find out more, go to www.hachettespeakersbureau.com or email HachetteSpeakers@hbgusa.com.

Forever books may be purchased in bulk for business, educational, or promotional use. For information, please contact your local bookseller or the Hachette Book Group Special Markets Department at special.markets@hbgusa.com.

Library of Congress Cataloging-in-Publication Data has been applied for

ISBN: 9781538726174 (trade paperback), 9781538726198 (ebook)

Printed in the United States of America

LSC-C

Printing 1, 2023

ONE
NIGHT
with the
DUKE

To Charlotte and Leah, my editors. Thank you for pushing my imagination into the past and believing in me. So much appreciation for you both.

JEM x

ONE
NIGHT
with the
DUKE

Chapter 1

The view from the drawing room window is not one that I am accustomed to. I don't see the rolling countryside and crops growing aplenty. My favorite mare, the blackberry bushes, the cowsheds.

The smell.

I sniff, getting a whiff of the new aroma. It isn't horse manure or grass, but instead an odd earthy smell. Bricks, mortar and paint. It's the smell of our new house. A grand new house that sits beside many more impressive dwellings, looping the lush green gardens of Belmore Square, where a fountain, a few benches and rose bushes are all closed in by cast-iron railings beyond the cobbled road. There's not a farmer to be seen for miles. Instead, here in London, we have affluent members of the ton strolling with no urgency, the fancy, gold-trimmed clothes of the gentlemen and the intricate lace-trimmed garments of the ladies providing an eclectic color palette I'm not used to. Top hats, canes, and carriages. Money leaks from every brick, cobble and pruned bush. It's another world, one I am not entirely certain I can fit into. Or *want* to.

It's the start of a new season, and my very first. The politicians will do their work in Parliament and the businessmen will conduct business, while their wives update their wardrobes and plan their social calendars for the next few months. There will be parties galore, dinners, and gossip to be had. Now, I am a part of the circles I had only ever heard of. Not dreamed about but *heard* of. Perhaps even dreaded. I can't say I'm all too keen on what I have experienced of London so far, and, worse, I am without the freedom I was once blessed with in our old life.

I grimace.

And I can hardly breathe in these fancy frocks.

On top of that, my inspiration is lacking, and I have absolutely nothing to write about, unless, of course, I should like to indulge in the unsubstantiated nonsense that Father's new business partner and financial backer, Lymington, Duke of Cornwall, thrives on. Which I don't, and it is a good thing, because I am not allowed to write for Father's newspaper in London.

I pout to myself, remembering the times I would take a story to Papa and he would sit in his chair by the fire smoking a cigarette, humming his interest. And his wry smile when he would say, every time, "You know, my dear Eliza, this is really rather good." Then he would dip, plant a kiss on my cheek and send me on my way. The fact that each and every story I penned and that was printed in Papa's newspaper was credited to my brother, Frank, was a small price to pay. Recognition wasn't something I sought, even if, admittedly, I would have liked it. It was more the freedom to write what I desired and not what I thought people would want to read. I wrote factual, informative pieces meant to educate people with the truth.

Alas, now Father's newspaper only has space for censored news and advertisements, and Lymington doesn't mind reminding Father, at any opportunity and sometimes without opportunity, that it is his name and backing that allowed my parents to buy the final plot on Belmore Square and build this sprawling, beautiful cage.

I am surely not the only young lady around these parts that feels suffocated. Or perhaps I am. The residents here are a peculiar bunch of humans, who do not seem to care for the world, but rather their position in it. The men must be successful, wealthy and loud. The women must be compliant, well turned out and unopinionated. Image is everything. Money is power.

My father is now a very wealthy man, and, as a consequence, also very powerful. I'm not at all certain that I like power on my father. Being powerful seems to take up all of his time and makes him appear persistently exhausted.

How I long to return to a time when his business limped along and mother baked all day. It was of little consequence that I liked to indulge myself in words, whether reading them or writing them, or that I perhaps spoke up too often in matters of no business of mine. There was no one to impress, therefore lectures were a pointless task my father rarely wasted his time on. In fact, I think he enjoyed me biting around his ankles, squeezing him for all the information I could get. He let me sit on his knee while he worked. Answered my questions when I asked. Gave me more books to read, perhaps to keep me quiet. And Frank would always creep up on me whenever I was lost in those books and flick my ear. I'd punch his bicep. He would scowl playfully. Father would grin down at his quill. I would stick my tongue out. Then Frank would chase me around our father's desk while I screamed to high heaven and Papa laughed as he dealt with the poor state of his finances.

Now?

Now our address is Belmore Square, Mayfair, London. Father's newspaper is on course to become the biggest in England with the help of steam printing, and I long for the days when Papa laughed, even though we struggled to make ends meet. These days, all I have to look forward to is Latin and piano. Playing piano bores me to tears, and learning Latin seems like a pointless chore, since I am not permitted to travel to a place where I may have an opportunity to speak the language.

I scowl at the pane of glass, looking across the square to the corner of Bentley Street, where a house, individual in its architecture, stands alone, starkly separate from the rest of the homes on Belmore Square. It's fascinated me since I arrived here in London. It was once the Winters residence, until it burned to the ground a year ago and the family perished. I read the report that was written by Mr. Porter, a journalist who works for Father, about the tragic accident that wiped out the Winters family. Rumor has it that it was not, in fact, an accident, and it was the eldest son, Johnny Winters, who started the fire. That he acted in a fit of rage after a disagreement with his father over...what? No one knows. It's easy to fill mindless people with thoughts and conclusions when the accused is dead and unable to defend himself. Except, Mr. Porter is a journalist, and, oddly, a respected one. I say *oddly respected*, because how anyone in their right mind could possibly trust a man who lives such a promiscuous life I do not know. He is loud, abrupt, egotistical, and dare I say it, a monster. And a power-hungry one at that. He mistreats his wife, ignores her in public and beats her in private. He's also a raving Conservative.

In any case, the Winters house has been rebuilt and some-one is moving in.

But who?

Someone audacious, I am sure of it. Bold and unapologetic. There are thirteen houses here on Belmore Square. The old Winters residence is the only one that hasn't followed the uniform exterior so as to keep the rows of homes looking as pristine and neat as the gardens they circle. In fact, the new owner of number one Belmore Square seems to have gone out of their way to make the old Winters residence as differ-ent as possible to every other home. Better, actually. Bigger and grander in every way. It's a statement. A declaration of supremacy. Over the past few weeks since we have moved in, I have watched huge, exotic plants being off-loaded and taken into the property, along with the biggest, most spark-ly chandeliers you ever did see, and beautiful, heavily carved pieces of furniture, which, after I had asked the men trusted to transport the pieces, I discovered were from India! So, whoever is moving into number one Belmore Square, I assume they are well traveled. How thrilling, to have traveled further than England.

So the finishing touches are being added, the wooden branches held together by hemp coming down from the exterior of the building, and now I, along with the rest of Belmore Square, wait with bated breath to see who will be moving into the sprawling, opulent mansion.

Hmmm, royalty, perhaps? Time will tell.

My attention is caught by the Duke of Cornwall, Lymington. His gray powdered hair is a beacon that could light the street better than the new gas lighting I have seen down in Westminster. He also happens to live at number two Belmore Square, with his son, Frederick, who I am yet to meet, which isn't such a hardship as I have heard he is an eternal bore. Lymington stops rather abruptly, and I follow his eyes to Lady Dare—she lives at number six Belmore Square and was widowed at the age of twenty after being married off to a decrepit lord at nineteen —breezing toward the gardens in a beautiful coat dress and an elaborately decorated bonnet. The woman does not walk, but floats. Her chin is constantly raised, her lips persistently on the verge of a suggestive, knowing smile, as if she is aware of the unspoken disapproval of the ladies of Belmore Square and the silent awe of the gentry who try and fail to ignore her beauty. Like Lymington right in this moment, who is still motionless, apparently caught in a trance, as he watches Lady Dare go. She is supposedly an exhibitionist, winning genuine disapproval from the ladies of the ton and false disapproval from the gentlemen. This rumor I know to be true, for I have seen the many men come and go from number six in the dead of night when I have been unable to sleep and have sat in my window wishing to be back in the countryside. Lady Dare is a ladybird, set free from the constraints of an arranged marriage by the fortunate death of her ancient husband, and now she will not bow to expectation, and yet she will also not flaunt nonconformity.

I purse my lips and peek down at my morning dress, an elaborate button-down piece trimmed with endless lace and sporting needlework that's really rather impressive. It's a status symbol, that is all. Along with this house, the staff, and the parties thrown most evenings by various members of the ton, this dress is merely here to demonstrate our wealth and standing. It's ironic, since no one will see it while I'm hanging around the house.

I lift the endless material so I can walk without tumbling, hearing the clanging and clattering of pots coming from the kitchen. Lunchtime. It has been only a few hours since breakfast, and it will be only a few more hours until dinner, and then tea, and finally supper. Eating five times a day is, apparently, a necessity when one is stinking rich. Because what else is there to do but hang around our mansion in a fancy dress constantly stuffing my face?

I pass the dining room, where one of our staff is laying the shiny mahogany table, and divert down the stairs to the kitchen. The smell of freshly baked bread is strong, the constantly raging stove and ovens making the underground rooms bordering unbearably hot. But it reminds me of home. I find Cook hunched over the flour-dusted table kneading more dough, probably in preparation for any one of the other three meals we will eat today. I release the bottom of my dress, not at all bothered by the mucky floor that will most likely dirty the crisp white muslin material. My hands are itching to sink into the mixture and get dirty.

"Miss Melrose," Cook cries, her doughy hands held up. "You mustn't be down here."

I pluck a plum out of the basket and sink my teeth in, something catching my eye. I slowly move around Cook's table. "*The*

Art of Cooking," I say quietly, looking down at the open page. "Mama had this when we lived in the country."

Cook wipes her hands on her apron, rounding the table, shooing me away as I sink my teeth into the ripe fruit. "I believe it is Mrs. Melrose's, Miss Melrose."

My chews slow, a sadness that feels perpetual since I left the countryside overcoming me. Mother doesn't have time to bake for us anymore. She's too busy being a lady in her new shiny manor. "Off you go now," Cook says. "We must serve lunch."

Silently, I leave Cook behind to finish her bread and climb the stairs, one hand holding up my dress, only to stop myself tripping and tumbling flat on my face, the other holding my fruit. By the time I have made it to the dining room, I have a band of grime around the bottom of my white day dress and a juice stain on the bust. "Oh dear," I murmur, brushing at the mark on the perfect dress.

"Eliza, you look like you belong in a slum terrace," Frank muses, looking up from the newspaper he is reading, seated at the far end of the table. "Perhaps even a gutter."

"I am not worthy, brother," I say, nibbling around my plum, eager to get every last piece of the juicy, sweet flesh as I present myself to the wall-hung mirror. I wipe my mouth and lean in, staring into my eyes that have always been described by my father as amethysts, and feeling at my hair that he says is rich like cocoa beans. I get both from my mother. And today, both seem significantly less… alive.

"I trust your mind is being suitably entertained by high-energy, top-quality, highly substantiated, educational reports about London and its residents," I say, looking away from my reflection and back to Frank, who, ironically, has blond hair and blue eyes, like our little sister, Clara, which they take from our father.

Folding his newspaper, he sets it aside. "Of course, since it really is I who writes the high-energy, top-quality, highly substantiated, educational reports which grace the pages of Father's

7

newspaper these days." He cocks a brow, as if challenging me to challenge him. I would not, and he knows it. Frank wants to be a journalist about as much as I should like to be here in London. Not at all.

"And how are sales?" I ask.

His eyes narrow. "Sales are not something you should concern yourself with."

"Could be better, then?" I ask, feeling the corner of my mouth lift as I sink my teeth back into my plum. "I know a great writer who may help increase readership. Not everyone wants to read censored, political and religious nonsense."

"Will you please sit down while eating?"

"Now if I did that, brother, I would be on my backside permanently." I lower to a chair, my back as straight as it is expected to be, my neck long. This is not through practice, but more my natural posture through years of horse riding. "What treasures will I find in today's edition of *The London Times*?" I ask, reaching for the newspaper. "Are the Catholics threatening to take over England?" I gasp, and it is wholly sarcastic. "Are they plotting to assassinate King George III?"

Frank scowls, unamused, pulling the newspaper out of my reach and standing, wandering over to the glass cabinet under the window. "You are caustic, Eliza," he breathes, unlocking the door and resting the latest edition atop the pile of newspapers, one copy of every edition since Father invested his last seven hundred pounds on a steam printing machine. The average and underwhelming two hundred copies per print are a distant memory, although, I hasten to add, Papa always sold more when I had written for his newspaper. Accepting my brother was named as the author was a small price to pay. I wanted not the accolades, only the satisfaction, fulfillment and purpose. Now *The London Times* is slowly building, although I cannot help wondering if it is growing fast enough for Father and Lymington's liking. There are other newspapers biting at their heels, all trying to get their hands on one of those fancy steam press machines.

"Papa should let me write." I pluck a bread roll from the basket in the middle of the table and begin tearing it apart, popping bits past my lips. "I don't mind if you have to take all the credit."

"You know that can't happen," he says, settling in his seat, his arms folding over his single-breasted frock coat. It's a new one. *Another* new one. While I have struggled to learn my place in this world, Frank has fallen seamlessly into upper class living —shopping, drinking and socializing with ease. And, I know, indulging in the fresh selection of women in between writing for Papa's newspaper. I know the latter pains him, which makes this whole situation even more ridiculous. I could free him of the burden.

"Have you been to see your new best friend at the Burlington again?" I ask, chewing slowly, keeping my smirk concealed.

Frank dusts down the front of his new piece. "Perhaps."

"Another twenty shillings on *another* coat?" I tut and sigh, rubbing the tips of my fingers together to rid them of flour dust. "Why, brother, you are becoming rather frivolous in your old age."

"And you, dear sister, are becoming rather cynical."

"I'm a realist."

"A real pain in my backside," he muses, peeking up at me with a wry smile. "Please, can you keep your world-saving, pioneering ambitions in check tomorrow evening?"

"What is happening tomorrow evening?"

His head cocks, his look uncertain. I know it's because whatever it is I have neglected to remember, I should not have forgotten. "Only one of the biggest events of the season."

My shoulders slump, but I soon correct them. "Oh yes. How could I have allowed that, of all things, to slip my mind?"

"Easy. Because you, dear sister," Frank chirps, "do not want to go."

"I don't want to be paraded around the palace like a fat, delicious pig waiting for Mama to give permission for some greedy, rich lord to sink his teeth into me. I wish to remain a spinster." I frown to myself. Do I? I've never really given much thought to it, because I never had to.

Frank balks. "A spinster?"

I square my shoulders, deciding in this moment that I am wholly invested. "Yes. I don't know why the word arouses such dread in women and pity in men."

"Over my dead body will my sister become an ape leader." Frank laughs, but quickly reins himself in, clearing his throat as I smirk across at him. "And there will be no teeth sinking into anything."

"Oh damn," I whisper, and he shakes his head, exasperated. "That's a shame, since with all this eating and nothing else to busy myself with, I am gaining some extra flesh to bite at."

"Your mind needs a wash."

"My mind is fine. My spirit, however, is slowly dying." I reach for Frank's hand and squeeze, my expression turning into one of pleading. If Father listens to anyone—which isn't many people since he became a magnate—he listens to his oldest child, his most reliable, abiding offspring. His heir. "I don't want to go. Please, please, please tell Father I am unwell."

My brother smiles fondly, turning his hand over to clasp mine and leaning toward me, pushing one of my dark curls back. "Not on your nelly."

"What a silly expression. What do you even mean?"

"I don't know, but I think I shall coin the phrase."

"You do not need to coin anything, brother. You are now the heir to a growing empire, and I shall wither and die of heartbreak for the life I have lost in the arms of my suitor, whoever he may be." I snatch my hand back. "You never know, if I'm lucky, my first season may pass without even a sniff of interest from any eligible bachelors." I know it not to be true; Father has been flexing his matchmaking muscles even before we arrived on Belmore Square, and I know he's been prepping Mama for the part she will play in the Demise of Eliza Melrose too. I'm doomed, but only if I allow it, which, of course, I absolutely will not. "I just need to survive the season and the ton and escape back to our home in the country," I say quietly.

I catch a look of guilt that passes over my beloved brother's face, and I find myself leaning back in my chair, wary. I can hear Mama in the distance, singing orders to the staff, and Clara, our little sister, playing piano. "Why are you looking like that?" I ask.

"Like what?"

"Like you know something you think I should know."

"I must be going—reports to check, and Porter is due imminently to meet with Father and me in his study about the next edition."

"You mean talk about what rubbish he'll be putting in Father's newspaper tomorrow?" I ask, getting a tight smile in return, which tells me my brother understands me, even if he cannot admit it. I lean forward. "Oh, Frank, please speak to Papa. Convince him to let me write again, I beg you. I feel utterly misplaced and without purpose."

"What will you write about, Eliza? We are in a different world now." He motions to the table that's laid with silverware and bone china, and I sigh. Perhaps Frank is right. What would I write about, because I'm certainly finding no inspiration from these surroundings or the people? But imagine if I could travel. Imagine if I could bring back stories to London. *Imagine, imagine, imagine.*

Frank rises from his chair as he pulls his jacket in.

"Wait!" I seize his arm, and his backside plummets to the seat. I narrow an eye on him, and once again he cannot look at me. I gasp and sit back. "My God, he's done it, hasn't he?"

"Done what?" Frank asks, wincing, as if regretting opening his big, fat mouth.

"Found a man. A suitor."

Frank's eyes drop as he rises. "Have a good day, sister."

Once again, I seize him, making him sit. "And you know who it is," I say, sounding rather accusing.

"I know no such thing."

"Oh, God, Frank, we've been here just a few weeks."

"Think yourself lucky," he says, close to a hiss. "This is Esther Hamsley's fifth season. There's talk of Lord Hamsley now offering money."

I roll my eyes. Perhaps Esther, like me, doesn't want to marry. Good for her. "Did you accept?"

"Eliza," he warns.

For pity's sake. It's preposterous that credit and acceptance comes only through giving yourself up. I will not. I can only liken this whole ridiculous situation to a sandwich. I like beef sandwiches. Have always been partial to one. But, and it's a surprise to me, if indeed worrisome, I have recently developed an aversion to the meat. Yes, I have gone off it. Perhaps because now, here in London in our fancy new home complete with servants, maids and cooks, we have been scoffing the rich meat in abundance. I'm bored of it. What was once indulgent is now tiresome. I crave variety. Like when I write, I like to write about various subjects, because one would surely become bored if their mind was eternally focused on one matter. I imagine the same can be said for a man. I might like a man. Become partial to him. Even marry him. But what about when boredom strikes? I'm then stuck with him? No. Lord above, it would be hell.

But, really, do I have a choice? To be impervious would be to tarnish everything my father has built. Destroy it. I am defiant, but I am not wicked. I know his intentions are admirable. That a good life is all he wishes for, for Mama and Frank, Clara and me. But a good life is what we had before the newspaper started growing. This?

This is hell glossed over with fancy food, drink and frocks.

I sink into my seat, despondent, my life as I knew it in ruins.

"Frank, Eliza," Mother chants as she flounces into the room, happy to see us, like this lunch is a rare family event and does not happen five damn times a day. She swishes her way round the table to her chair, followed closely by Emma, her maid, because since Father became stinking rich, our mother suddenly cannot do anything for herself.

She lowers herself like a lady to her chair, and Emma pours her tea.

"Where's Papa?" I ask. Perhaps he's been forced to abandon lunch with his family in favor of a breaking story. Something outrageous and also probably untrue. *Let us not get sticky over minor inaccuracies*, Father had said last week when I read the article Mr. Porter had written claiming a vagrant ransacked a home and murdered a lady while she slept in her bed. Bypassing the matter of one violent husband who I had personally seen manhandling said lady into their fancy, gated home off Grosvenor Square on more than one occasion did not seem like a minor inaccuracy to me. *Your imagination will get you into trouble, Eliza,* he'd snapped after I'd pleaded for him to let me re-write the story with the facts I had and knew to be true. But no. The vagrant will be hung. The husband will mourn his wife for a few weeks and then find a young bride who will face the same fate.

"He's indulging himself in Clara's latest piece." Mama motions to the china bowl of sugar and Emma is quick to fulfill.

"How delightful," I mumble, unheard. Or ignored. But Frank hears me, and he nudges me under the table for my trouble. I scowl at him, giving him a look to suggest that I will not be abandoning our previous conversation. He knows who my suitor is. *Suitor.* It's a ridiculous word to use, especially for me. Every member of my family would admit—not publicly, mind you—that there is possibly no man alive *suited* to me. The world outside these doors is led to believe that I am a perfect example of a lady. God help the poor gentleman who has been handpicked by Papa to take me on. I suspect he'll expect a subservient female. Am I capable of that? *Who is he?*

"It was wonderful, darling," Papa says, leading Clara into the dining room. "A beautiful piece."

"Thank you, Papa," she replies, indulging the world's need for politeness and compliance. "Next week, I will learn Beethoven."

"Marvelous! Did you hear that, dear?" Father beams at Mother. "Beethoven!"

I roll my eyes and sink into my chair.

"Do sit up, Eliza." Papa directs a warning, albeit soft, look my way as he lowers himself to the chair at the head of the table. "You are all scrunched up."

My brother's persistent half smile is kept in check, naturally, as our staff serve lunch.

"And what delights are we being blessed with today?" Papa asks.

"Beef sandwiches, sir."

I look down at my plate. "I don't feel like beef today."

Papa laughs, Mama and Frank joining him. "Do behave, Eliza," he says, helping himself and sinking his teeth into a wedge of bread. "Everyone feels like beef."

Do behave? I'm not in the least bit hungry. Not for food, anyway. "I don't feel at all well," I say quietly, more to myself than to my family. I honestly don't, my stomach is churning terribly. I'm unsure whether the constant sickly feeling is me mourning the carefree life I have lost, or dreading the stringent, shallow one I have gained.

"Eliza?" Mama says, and I look up.

"Can I please be excused?" I ask, standing before I am granted permission to leave the table. I do not relish the concern on Mother's face. She may have become a little rigid and blinkered since becoming a member of the ton and feeling like she needs to fit in, but her love for her children has not been misplaced.

She wants contentment for us all, even now when she knows contentment must come second to status. My father worked like a dog for twenty years, and that commitment has finally given him everything he ever dreamed of. He dreamed of money, respect, power, and a guaranteed comfortable future for his children. Sadly, our dreams are not aligned, for I dream simply of freedom. Even more so now that I no longer have it. I wished to travel and write tales of those travels. To educate readers of the world beyond our little island, although I always knew that dream was out of reach. Money, and a lot of it, would be required to travel to lands far and wide. Only the richest could indulge in such a luxury. Now, ironically, my family has the money that could see my dreams become real, and yet now I am a prisoner in my new life.

I turn and leave the dining room, feeling suffocated in this enormous house. This dress suddenly feels like one of those garments described in a book I have read. A *camisole de force*. And yet I am not insane. And I definitely do not want to be restrained.

I arrive in my bedroom, go to the window, and look out, seeing more beautiful objects being carried into number one Belmore Square, this time paintings. One is of a landscape of the rolling countryside. I tilt my head, the rugged terrain similar to where I often rode, galloping through the unspoiled land, free as a bird, as happy as a pig in muck.

The painting is a cruel reminder, so I divert my attention to the other piece, before it can torture me for a moment longer. I find a coat of arms, albeit indistinguishable from this distance, so I squint, moving closer, until my face is practically squished against the pane of glass. I finally make out two beautiful silver unicorns up on their hind legs, looking all noble and mystical. "Oh my," I whisper, my head tilting, my curiosity exploding. And to which family does that belong?

I look over my shoulder, hearing the front door close. Porter must have arrived, which means they will be in my father's study.

Which means I will have to wait until later to raid it.

I waited for the rest of the day. Porter came and left, Frank was in and out, and my father only left his study for meals and to relieve himself, which left no window of opportunity. By nightfall he still hasn't appeared, so I ready myself for bed, but sleep eludes me. I'm up and down, listening and waiting for Papa to finally leave his office. It's the day and night that feels like it might never end.

He finally staggers out of his study, full of Scotch, at three in the morning, and I watch as he practically crawls up the stairs. The moment he closes his bedroom door behind him, I hurry down to his study and let myself in, closing the door as quietly as I can behind me. I walk the foot of the bookcases, my eyes scanning the spines until I find what I'm looking for, and on a deep breath, I pull the thick, leatherbound book out, having to use two hands, for it is as heavy as it looks. And dusty.

The fine particles get up my nose, and, in a panic because I am not known for my quiet, ladylike sneezes, I rush to Father's desk, drop the book to the leather top, and quickly block off my nose and mouth with my hands, squeezing my eyes closed.

A-choo!

My shoulders tense, and I screw up my face, slowly releasing my hand, listening for any signs of anyone coming to investigate the noise. A few seconds pass before I deem I am safe and undetected, and I start flicking through the pages of the book until I find what I am looking for.

I stare down at two silver unicorns up on their hind legs, except now I can see them perfectly clearly. With the utmost anticipation and with my heart thumping wildly in my chest, I read the piece that will tell me which family this coat of arms belongs to, therefore who will be moving into number one Bel-more Square imminently.

"What?" I blurt, reading it again, just to make sure I'm seeing right.

I am.

I am looking at the coat of arms for the Duke of Chester.

The Winterses.

I frown, resting back in Papa's chair, my mind racing.

But the Winterses are dead.

What in the devil's name is going on?

Chapter 2

After discovering the coat of arms belonged to the Winters, I was a woman on a mission, trawling through every book in Father's study searching for anything I could find on the family. I wouldn't rest until I found at least something to substantiate the wildness of my thoughts, and, actually, if I am to do what I plan on doing, I need that little thing everyone else seems to think is unimportant.

Evidence.

At exactly fifteen minutes past six o'clock, I stumbled across an entry in an art book detailing the buyer of a beautiful land-scape painting depicting the English countryside. The painting I saw being carried into the Winters residence. The buyer being the dead Duke of Chester.

I spent the next two hours writing fast, my hand struggling to keep up with my brain, my task tricky, only because I was trying to disguise my handwriting. I finish in the nick of time, hearing our butler, Dalton, rise. I fold the parchment and run out to the front door, pulling it open and holding the handle. And the moment I detect our butler behind me, I push it closed and turn, waving the paper.

"Mr. Porter left this for Father on his way to the printworks," I say, stretching on a yawn. "Would you mind leaving it on his desk, Dalton?" I hand the paper to him as I pass, not giving him a moment to question me. "I feared his knocking would wake the entire square." I press my lips together, knowing Dalton will be mortified that I was forced to leave my bed prematurely at this ungodly hour to answer the front door to a visitor. "I think I need a few more hours." I hurry up the stairs, smiling to myself.

Gosh, I have never been so intrigued.

After a few hours of restless sleep, I spent the remainder of the day trying to keep my whirling tummy under control. Tomorrow, possibly, people will be reading my words again, and as I sit before the mirror now, looking at a polished, painted version of myself, while Clara twirls, skips and pirouettes around our bedroom as fast as my mind is racing, I wonder if Papa has yet read my story, or even discovered it.

I try to pat down the short puffy sleeves of my dress before wriggling and pulling at the bottom of the stay that seems so pointless under my new high-waisted silk garb. I peek down at my generous chest that's suitably concealed behind a dignified square neckline. I preferred the V-neck version of this particular dress, the one similar to those I have seen in fashion magazines, the more risqué garment. Who knew I would have a preference on fashion? Alas, it was vetoed in favor of this… ladylike piece.

I push my jeweled hair comb further into the mass of mahogany curls adorning my head, wincing as the sharp metal prongs scratch my scalp. "Clara, be still," I warn, speaking through my teeth, the comb starting to give me a headache already.

"Are you not excited?" she asks, not listening to a word I have said, still skipping, still pirouetting, still twirling. She's making me dizzy. "A party at the palace, Eliza!"

Excited? No, I can't say I am. "Thrilled," I murmur. Poor Clara. My innocent, oblivious little sister. Does she realize that in a couple of years, she, like me, will be thrust into society and showcased to all potential suitable gentlemen? Although after yesterday's lunch and Frank's shifty mood, why I'm even attending this ball is a mystery. I'm not so much being launched into society, more introduced. Perhaps Papa snapped up the offer of the first notable nobleman. God, what does my future have in store? Frank knows exactly who I will be thrust upon—thrust upon someone and expected to smile, swoon and speak only when spoken to. I grimace at the stark reality of my new life and swallow down the lump spiked by the reminder of my lost one. The life where the possibilities were endless. My dreams were big. My imagination nurtured.

I look down my front, wriggling again. And my garments were comfortable. I know not of one married couple on Belmore Square who are *happily* married. I pause for thought. No, that is not true. I know of one. Mama and Papa, although they were matched through choice not expectation. Neither were launched into high society because they were not part of high society. Until now. I cannot help myself from worrying that perhaps their happiness may not last. Papa seems so absorbed by the constant accolades from his new gentleman friends. The high praise, each edition of his newspaper providing the perfect topic of conversation at each of the many social events while they drink and smoke. And Mama? Her new status pleases her. My ever-increasing despondency does not. And yet with power for my father comes compliance from his wife. She cannot be seen to challenge him. Not now. So my fate is sealed and to fight my fate would be to fight with Mama and Papa, and I would enjoy nothing less. I wriggle and wrestle with the neckline of my dress again, my bust desperate to break free. Not that I am capable of much fight in this ridiculous garb.

I give up and let the constraints win. My acquiescence doesn't bode well.

After sitting patiently in a line of carriages that stretched for what seemed like miles, we roll to a stop outside the palace and the footmen approach. My hand naturally reaches for the door, but Father stops me. "There are servants, Eliza. You are not one of them."

I nod, feeling Mama's wary gaze pointing my way. I look at Frank. He appears completely unfazed by the night ahead. My brother is a handsome man. Tall, athletic, charming. Tonight, he will have the pick of a thousand suitable ladies who will be eager to impress. How will he deal with that, I wonder, because Frank, for lack of a better term, is a terrible flirt. One flash of his boyish grin would have every female within five miles of our home in the country flocking, desperate to win his affections. None did. But they may have won a kiss or two. May have? They most certainly did. I caught him in the woods on more than one occasion. The first time I was unfortunate enough to stumble upon him, I honestly thought he was murdering the daughter of the ironmonger. No one could blame me—she was crying out, after all. It was then, after Frank had pulled up his trousers, chased me down and calmed me down, that he explained she wasn't yelling in pain, but in pleasure, all while looking rather uncomfortable. I had stared at him with wide eyes. Frank had paled further. Then he'd given me a thorough good talking to about all the things I *shouldn't* know about, finishing by warning me of the consequences for a young lady should she succumb to the sin of desire like the ironmonger's daughter had. Ironically, she became very ill just a few weeks later and died. I spent two years believing she was dead because my brother kissed her. Then I found him with another woman in his arms. And another. And another. None of them died, but all smiled when I warned them they would. The last woman, the butcher's daughter, obviously thought it kind to sit me down and give me the truth of it. The ironmonger's daughter died of influenza. I always thought it seemed too tragic to experience such a thing as a kiss and then pay so drastically with your life. Bless Frank for trying. He still believes I think I'll die if I let a man ruin me before marriage.

Stepping down from the carriage, I gaze up at the front of the palace, inhaling deeply as I do. I can hear the bustle from here, the laughter and chatter.

"Can you believe we are here?" Mama says as we follow Father and Frank toward the arch that leads into the center of the palace. "The Prince's royal party, Eliza," she gasps, so enthralled, so excited. I'm awed, no doubt, but I am also dreading the evening ahead.

"Wonderful," I murmur, as we enter a grand hall. I have never seen so many people. Hundreds, if not thousands. It appears every lord, lady, duke, duchess and anyone who is anyone is here. "Oh my," I breathe, remaining behind Papa and Frank as they are welcomed by the Prince himself. His cheeks are red, his demonstrative moves making his wine splash across the elaborate velvet material of his jacket. He doesn't seem much perturbed by the mess he is making. In fact, for such an early hour, he appears rather intoxicated. So the whispers of his indulgent lifestyle are true? The party prince. I bet that would be an interesting story to pen.

"Melrose, yours is the only newspaper I will read," the Prince declares. I inwardly roll my eyes. Of course it is, because Papa's newspaper will only print political and religious pieces to please the Prince and his mad father.

A few words are exchanged, and the Prince laughs, jolly as can be, then music starts to play, he gasps, and he is off toward the dance floor as his guests start to clap, thrilled.

"It's his favorite," Mama whispers, joining Papa.

"You could at least appear pleased to be here," Frank says, prompting me to smile. "Well done." He backs away on a bow that is sarcastic. "Enjoy your evening, sister." A cheeky cock of his head, a peek around at the abundance of women. "I think I will."

My eyes narrow. Off he goes, dragging no chains along with him. "Eliza," Father says, pulling my attention his way. His smile is hesitant, his eyes pleading. "I would like you to meet someone." He motions with his hand for me to come.

"So long as it is not a man I am expected to marry," I say on a sweet smile, making his expression drop, his complexion turning ashen. *Oh, please, no.*

"Eliza," Mama hisses, laughing, checking for listening ears and the faces of the gentlemen that I cannot see past Father. There are two of them, though. One taller than the other. I can only see the taller gentleman. He looks utterly boring. The shorter one, I can't see his face, but I see a cane suggesting he's older. Mother is worrying over nothing. I hardly heard myself.

I step forward, searching the crowd for Frank. The scoundrel. He knew of the introductions about to transpire. "May I present my daughter," Papa says proudly, stepping aside and revealing the gentlemen. *Oh no.* The Duke of Cornwall, Lymington, scans me up and down, his face crabby, his quizzing glass dangling from a piece of ribbon, as who I assume is his son, Frederick, the apparent bore, stands like an unripened, hard plum to his side, showing no signs of softening. This is my suitor? The silence stretches to a point where I become extremely uncomfortable, and His Grace looks as if he's preparing to feel down his chest for that quizzing glass to inspect me with it.

I look at Father, somewhat confused. "Are they mute?" I ask, and his eyes widen as the Duke coughs, recoiling, nearly dislodging his gray wig and sprinkling me with hair powder. That wig speaks volumes, for no one in their right mind would cough up the outlandish tax now demanded for such a luxury item. He must have more money than sense.

Father, mortified, rushes to intervene. "Eliza, you have met His Grace, Duke of Cornwall, and this is his son, Frederick Lymington, the Earl of Cornwall."

I fail to curtsey, my etiquette further abandoning me. *Damn it.* My father crumbling in humiliation gives me no pleasure at all. "Your grace," I say, lowering my head. "How lovely to see you again."

The Duke looks at Father, who quickly gets his confusion under control and smiles brightly. "We have a rather interesting story releasing in the morn," Father says, and I freeze, my inhale sharp. He found it? "I'm sure it will spike the interest of many. Porter hand-delivered it himself at the crack of dawn."

My throat becomes thick, and for a moment I wonder just how guilty I must appear. Is my father even looking at me? "Tell me more," Lymington says, moving in closer.

"I met with him this evening before our carriage arrived, to clarify some of the content," Father goes on, as I try in vain not to look surprised. Father spoke with him? Why? It's not uncommon for Porter to deliver stories for Father's approval. Father has never, not once, needed clarification on anything. Oh, bugger it all, has my cover been blown already? "He was very insistent that we run the story."

He was? I smile to myself. Of course he was. I knew Porter's ego would help me in this instance. I hope it continues to help.

"And what is the story?" Lymington asks.

"About the Winters."

"The Winters?" Lymington blurts. "But they are dead."

"Perhaps not," Father muses, increasing the curiosity of Lymington, which, of course, is the whole point, isn't it? But this is not gossip. This is a mystery to be solved, and everyone loves a good mystery.

Lymington points his cane and walks on, and without a second glance, Father follows, leaving me alone with...Frederick. This here, this stoic, rigid, unfriendly looking *gentleman* is my suitor? God forbid, I will not have it. I watch my father lead Lymington away and my mother move in closer with Clara, who looks persistently and annoyingly awed by her surroundings, as Mama's attention is split between me and various ladies she's conversing with. I catch Clara's eye and blow out my cheeks, a sign of my exasperation, and despite her blissful ignorance, she manages to appear as disappointed as I feel. What am I to do with this? I look at Frederick, and an unbearably awkward silence falls. A whole minute of silence. I smile, he smiles, I look around the hall, so does he, and I smile again. So does he.

"How old are you?" I eventually blurt, unable to bear it a moment longer.

He blinks rapidly. "Twenty-four."

Twenty-four? Why on earth isn't Frederick already married? Good heavens, my stark reality is becoming starker. "I am nineteen." I look over my shoulder, seeing Mama still watching over me, and she smiles the kind of smile that tells me she's in as much pain as I am. *Then why?*

"Would you like to see the gardens?" Frederick asks.

I whirl round far quicker than I mean to and lose my footing, the stupid dress hindering my attempts to save myself. I stumble toward him, but rather than catch me, he moves aside and lets me fall to the floor in a heap. The gasps of shock ring loud, even over the music, and I stare down at the beautiful mosaic detail of the grand hall floor, feeling shame creeping up on me.

"You let me fall," I say, sounding as accusing as I meant to. He could have saved me this potential humiliation, but he did not. He let me tumble because, God forbid, he can't be seen to touch me after we've barely been introduced.

I peek left and right, finding all eyes on me, and, my jaw tight, my throat thick, I get to my feet in as ladylike a manner as I can and brush myself down. "I think I will take that walk," I say, my eyes low, my feet moving fast to remove me from the attention. "Alone." My heart pounds as I make my escape, the pressure on my chest unbearable. I can hardly breathe, and this stupid dress is not helping.

A few ladies jump from my path, shocked, and I arrive outside, dragging in air urgently. I am a lady hurrying, and I am alone, and every footman, servant and guest is looking at me in alarm. My humiliation grows like unwanted, out-of-control ivy.

Someone stops beside me, and I look up. "Let us walk," Frank says quietly, nodding at my audience and leading the way. I fall into stride beside my brother, my eyes flitting, ensuring we are alone before I speak.

"I will run away," I say surely, clasping my hands in front of me.

"And join the circus?"

"If I must," I retort. "Being caged with a man-eating lion somehow feels more appealing than enduring the simplicities of the ladies and lords."

"Must you always be so unreasonable?"

"Must you always be so upbeat?" I ask, shifting my stays again as we wander through two lines of trees, all the same size, same shade of green, and all equally positioned. They are nothing like the woodlands I cantered through daily. Messy. Unpredictable. Wild. "Did you see him? My suitor?"

"I think every guest in the Grand Hall saw him, Eliza. He was the man who appeared frozen by embarrassment while you glared at the poor fellow."

"Poor fellow? What about me? It was me on my knees. He could have saved me, and he did not. I hardly want to be married at all, least of all to a man who won't save me if I fall."

"I know not a lot, but I know my sister does not need saving by a man." Frank turns a small smile onto me. "We must do what we must do."

I sigh. "I want the right to say no. I want to be taken seriously, Frank." Imagine that. A world where we can say no.

Frank chuckles. "Your imagination is wild."

I snort. I could show him. Show *everyone*. But I know I am living in a time when, really, my dreams are quite laughable. Pity for me.

*

26

I found the courage I needed to return to the Grand Hall. I did not really have a choice. We are an hour by carriage from home and it is already past midnight. I stand on the edge of the room, and Papa and Mama catch my eye, dancing the minuet. It's all very old-fashioned. They should be waltzing. But the choice of music and the outdated dance that complements it pales when I look at their faces. Delighted faces. They were born to be in this world. They have found their place, and despite Mother's concerns for me, I can't deny she is glowing. In her element, along with Father. They deserve the recognition being bestowed upon them. Me, however? I resent having to join them, but do not appear to have a choice. I simply cannot ruin this for them.

I swallow, despondent, as Clara finds me. "Eliza, you fell."

"How very observant of you, Clara."

"Are you all right?"

"No, I am in agony," I reply quietly, sighing loudly but smiling when she grows concerned. "I am fine," I assure her. "Just promise you will not grow another year older." Poor Clara has all of this to come, and I know she is wholly unprepared for it.

She laughs, the sound young and sweet, despite her being only three years younger than I. "That is quite impossible."

"Sadly, you are right, sister," I muse, rubbing her gloved arm. "You look very pretty this evening." Her blonde hair is coiled into perfect ringlets and her blue eyes are sparkling. I bet she is already capturing the attention of many.

"I thought so too." She smiles cheekily. "Do you like Frederick?"

"Do you think I should?"

"He's a bit…" Her lips purse. "…bland, isn't he?"

I laugh. Yes, bland. That is the perfect word to describe Frederick. A gormless fool.

I overhear a conversation from some ladies not too far away and instinctively move one step toward them, tugging Clara along with me.

"What are you doing?" she asks. I hush her, listening carefully.

"It should have been demolished," one lady says. Naturally, my ears prick up, and I discreetly take one more step closer, again pulling Clara along with me.

"Eliza, what on earth?" she hisses.

"It spoils the symmetry on Belmore Square," the lady continues.

"Who do you imagine would ever want to live there after the Duke's son burned them all alive."

"The Winters residence?" I say without thought, pulling the attention of all three women my way. The shock on their faces. Oh, the shock. "You are speaking of the Winters residence, are you not?"

One of the other ladies' lips pucker unattractively, her eyes taking me in, up and down, like I'm a street urchin polluting her posh space. Her face is thick with powder, her eyebrows shaved off and replaced with what looks like the fur of a dead animal. "And *you* are?"

"The Melrose girls," another says, casting her eyes from me to Clara.

"Oh," she croons, like our identity means something to her. Of course, it does. "New money." She looks to her snooty friends and grins, revealing teeth that have been indulged with too much sugar. "Did you see that one tumble?" She laughs, the sound cutting, and her friends join her while I stand before them at the mercy of their judgments and the subject of their amusement. "God help His Grace and Frederick."

My inhale is sharp and unstoppable, my hurt great. How is it that these wenches know of my fate before I do? God help *me*.

"If you should like to know who has rebuilt number one Belmore Square, I suggest you read tomorrow's edition of *The London Times*," I retort, making them all snap their mouths closed. Good. I bow my head and wander away, dragging a bemused Clara along with me.

"Who has rebuilt one Belmore Square?" she questions as we move toward Mother.

"Read the newspaper tomorrow."

"I don't read Father's newspaper. Since you don't write for it anymore, it's become utterly boring."

"Hmmm," I hum, trying not to look as guilty as I am. I must not reveal to anyone that I am responsible for tomorrow's story. Never. That luxury will be whipped away faster than Papa could even think to defend me.

Chapter 3

WINTER RETURNS TO BELMORE SQUARE

Imagine if the new resident of the old Winters house on
the corner of Belmore Square, was, in fact, a Winters...

The next day, Father's newspaper sold fifty percent more than
the average day, which, these days, was a handsome amount
anyway. Naturally, the speculation of which long-lost member
of the Winters family would be moving into Belmore Square
reignited the rumors as to what exactly happened to the
Duke, his wife and their children. Now, a week has passed since
my story was printed, and while the buzz on the square has
increased greatly and remains, my knowledge of the Winterses
has not, therefore eliminating the possibility of writing anything of any gravity. I have learned that the Duke of Chester,
Joe Winters, was a renowned inventor, though I couldn't find
anything about what he invented and not one person I have
encountered this past week appeared to know either when I
subtly pried. His wife, Wisteria, was the daughter of a dead viscount who was on the verge of ruin, and their children, Johnny,
Sampson, and Taya were supposedly as beautiful as their mother was famed to be. The eldest, Johnny, the Duke's heir, was
rather wild, by all accounts. Wild and rebellious. Hotheaded
and partial to a few too many Scotches. And a rake, to boot.
A famed lover.

All rumors, of course, and nothing at all new for me to

enlighten potential readers on. Yet still I have scribbled down my thoughts, penning endless theories while wondering if perhaps one day someone may invent a quill with a never-ending supply of ink, because it is utterly tiresome having to constantly dip the damn thing.

Unfortunately, today I cannot write, ponder, or dip my quill endlessly. I must meet Frederick Lymington in the royal park with my mother and we must promenade. Courting begins, as does my imminent death. I have never imagined being in love, and I certainly have never imagined *pretending* to be.

In my finest, most uncomfortable dress coat and an understated hat decorated only with a few pleats, I join Mother and Clara downstairs at just past noon. Emma hands Mama her gloves, and she pulls them on as she takes me in from top to toe, ensuring I am suitably dressed for a lady who is about to promenade in the royal park. Unlike my own, Clara's bonnet is embellished with an array of colorful dried flowers, and Emma is staring at it adoringly, her own mobcap lacking shape and interest. I should offer a swap. I feel heavy with the burden of this frock.

Stepping outside the front door, I'm immediately hit with the constant and consistent bustle of Belmore Square, but my attention falls to the lone building across the gardens. Still with no occupants. I am, as the rest of the square, positively bursting with curiosity.

"What's got your sharp interest?" Frank asks, joining me at the top of the steps.

"Nothing." I quickly divert my eyes elsewhere. "And where are you off to?"

He looks at me in a way I do not like. With suspicion. Has done since the story I wrote and accredited to Porter was released last week. It's exactly how my brother would look at me whenever I denied having a sneaky sip of Papa's wine while he wasn't looking.

His head tilts, and I tilt mine in return, fighting to maintain my stoic expression. "I am off to meet Porter."

"How lovely."

"Perhaps to see if he has another compelling story to tell."

I clear my throat. "Wonderful for you."

"Or to learn where he sourced the facts that substantiated last week's news."

"Good for you." I nibble my lip, looking away from Frank, no longer able to sustain his scrutiny. Of course, Porter never confessed to not being the author of my story. His ego was swelling too much.

"Eliza, I—"

"Come along, girls," Mother calls.

"Must go." I dash down the steps and follow Mama as she floats her way down the street, Clara by her side. I fall behind, in no hurry to wander pointlessly around the royal park, or, more to the point, simply be seen in the royal park wandering pointlessly, but most certainly in a hurry to escape my brother's inquisition.

At the edge of the square, Mother takes a right, and we arrive on Piccadilly. Carriages rumble up and down and men on horseback trot past, and just like Belmore Square, but on a larger scale, there are gatherings of people everywhere. I follow Mother's path as she weaves through the people, increasing my pace to keep up, grimacing at the pinch of my toes from the horrid booties I must wear.

"What is the hurry?" I ask, moving aside to let a young woman pass, whose arms are full of hatboxes.

"Pardon me," she says politely, her chin resting on top of the pile.

I stop abruptly because a name on one of the boxes catches my eye. "Just a moment," I say, making her slow to a stop, my eyes rooted on the handwritten label that says, quite clearly in an elegant script, *Winters, Duke of Chester.*

Looking alarmed, the woman withdraws, and the young man I now notice following her, a scruffy-looking boy with a dirt-smeared face, steps forward, looking both threatening and unsure. Her security, I expect, for a young woman, transporting expensive hats like this is quite a treacherous job, what with, as I have heard, although perhaps simply more whispers, highwaymen on the loose. I smile my reassurance at the boy, feeling quite reminiscent. That was me only a few months ago, smeared in dirt.

I motion to the hatbox. "You are delivering this?"

"Yes, my lady."

I smile. "I am not a lady. Only by default." The poor thing looks mighty confused. I cannot lie, I am too. "Delivering to the Winters's residence on Belmore Square?" I go on, and she nods. "But the house stands empty."

"I do what I am asked, my lady." She bows her head and scurries on her way, and the boy follows, while I stand, thoughtful for a few moments, watching them take the turn toward Belmore Square. Winters. A long-lost cousin, perhaps? But what with the rumors shrouding the family name, I am confused as to why one would want to return. Like the house and the furniture being put inside it, I can only imagine the new owner, the new duke, is quite indifferent. The mystery deepens, and with it I have my next story.

WHO IS THE NEW DUKE OF CHESTER?

I smile to myself, writing the story in my mind.

New hats for the new Duke of Chester were being delivered only yesterday to his newly refurbished house on the corner of Belmore Square. Imagine if today we finally discover who the new Duke of Chester is.

"Eliza, come along now," Mother sings, snapping me from my thoughts, unceremoniously tugging me toward the park entrance. "We have an engagement to keep."

And my smile falls, my mind swiftly reminded of my obligations. A few more paces down the road has us at the entrance of the royal park, where lush meadowland awaits us, replacing the dusty, dirty ground of the street.

Mother breezes through the gilded gates, visibly relaxing, her shoulders no longer high and tense, as if she is running the gauntlet. Now, it is I who will run the gauntlet. I should perhaps *throw down* the gauntlet instead. *I challenge anyone to force me to marry a man I do not know, least of all love.*

"Ah, look, it is Lady Tillsbury," Mama sings. "She's a patroness of Almack's, don't you know."

"I do know," I assure Mother. I know of every resident on Belmore Square, and Lady Tillsbury is quite a fascinating one. The Baroness of Shrewsbury, widow to a dead baron, and quite a force to be reckoned with, everyone wants to be friends with Lady Tillsbury, because being a patron of Almack's, the lavish ballroom where the best of the best party and find husbands and wives, she has a say in whether you will be honored with an invitation to enter. Not many are. I have a feeling Mama is fishing for one.

"Such a lovely lady, she is."

"I expect she is."

"Oh, there's Mrs. Fallow too." Mama waves to Mrs. Fallow, who happens to have a daughter the same age as me, Lizzy, a blonde-haired, blue-eyed, sultry-looking creature whom I've seen Frank admiring on a few occasions.

I watch as Mother breezes across to Lady Tillsbury and Mrs. Fallow and they start ambling down the path together toward the one and only lake in the royal park, while Lizzy, Clara and I follow, me bored to tears and Clara frowning at Lizzy Fallow, who is pouting at any man who passes.

"How is your brother?" Lizzy asks, appearing as coy as she is trying to be.

I look at Clara out of the corner of my eye, smiling as she purses her lips, a veil of warning falling. Clara doesn't know of our brother's rakish ways, or that he would give the sultry Lizzy here a run for her money in the flirting stakes. Clara is blinkered by her adoration for Frank. Make no mistake, I adore our brother too, but I am not deluded. He is a rake, and I know that not to have changed just because we are no longer in the countryside, and the ladies are not like the ironmonger's daughter or the butcher's daughter. It seems wholly unfair that my brother can continue as he did, except wear fancier clothes while he continues to do it, and I have to change...everything about myself.

"Our brother's affections are taken," Clara says, her jaw tight.

"By whom?" Lizzy inquires not too subtly.

Everyone. "We are not at liberty to share," I say, placing a hand on Clara's hand to pacify her. I can see the fire in her eyes, and despite it being quite delightful, I must not let that fiery temper of hers emerge in the middle of the royal park while we are promenading. Lizzy must see it too, because she excuses herself and joins the Hamsley girl—the one who is on her fifth season. This for five more years? Or marriage. God, life is unfair. Lizzy Fallow has probably gone to gloat to poor Eve Hamsley that this is her first season, and it will most likely be her last, especially since Mrs. Fallow will have her in Almack's without delay, taking offers to wed her from lords, dukes and any other man with a title and money. "It is a rather bland park, don't you think?" I say, motioning to the endless green. "Just grass, no flowers." Clara scowls, and I smile, pointing to the grass ahead, distracting her from her grievance. "One hundred years ago, when the Prince Regent's great grandmother was queen, she discovered her lover had a lover."

"Did she not have a husband?" Clara asks, shocked.

"She had a husband, of course. But she also took a lover."

"Whyever would she do that?" she asks, truly astounded, and maybe a tad confused. "A queen of all ladies must behave properly."

"I agree. Aren't you glad we are not queens?"

"I don't know," she says on a sigh. "I'm quite enjoying being a lady."

"Pretending to be." We are all but frauds.

"So why would a queen take a lover if she has a husband to fulfill her every need?" she asks, pulling me to a startled stop.

"Every need?" What does my sixteen-year-old sister know of ladies' needs?

"You were not the only one to spy our brother getting up to no good in the woods, you know." Clara smiles wickedly as two elderly ladies look at us in nothing short of horror.

"Clara," I hiss.

"Oh, please. Are you being a prude, Eliza?" she asks, her cheekiness making way for the true Clara buried beneath fancy hats and dresses.

"I am not a prude."

"You are acting like one. Anyway, what has this got to do with the barren land before us?"

I take Clara's elbow and encourage her onward, away from the disapproving ladies still gawking at us. "She discovered her lover had hand-picked flowers from her royal garden and given them to his other lover." I motion to the park that lacks any color past the green of the grass and trees and the brown of the thick trunks. "Blinded by jealousy, she ordered every flower be dug up and her lover was imprisoned in the tower."

"Blimey."

"Blimey indeed."

Clara shudders, pulling at her dress, and I smile. "What?" she questions.

"Nothing at all."

Her shoulders drop. "Yes, I am uncomfortable. Is that what you want to hear?" She wriggles and grimaces. "And if I am forced to eat one more beef sandwich, I swear it, I will scream."

I laugh loudly.

"Oh shut up," Clara snaps. "And what of her lover's other lover?"

I look at my sister, my eyebrows high, and draw a line across my throat. "Jealousy is not an emotion one should toy with." Especially when a queen with all the power is involved.

"Chr—"Her attention is pulled across the grass. "Eliza, look," she says, pointing. "Over there."

On a frown, I follow her gesture to a boy tying his horse to a tree trunk. "Who is that?" I ask her, just as the boy glances over. He smiles when he finds Clara, his cheeks turning a fetching and telling shade of red.

"I don't know." Clara forces me to continue walking.

"We must say hello," I insist, breaking away, resisting her attempts to stop me. She looks between Mama and me, torn. Our mother is far too engrossed trying to win the approval of Lady Tillsbury, and therefore be granted access to the world of Almack's, to notice our absence. It's a blessing. "Come now, sister, we would not want him to think us rude."

"But…"

"But, what?"

"He—"

"Are you flustered?" I ask, frowning at Clara's cheeks, which are now matching in color to the dried roses on her bonnet. I make it to the tree, Clara not far behind, and motion to the impressive horse. "He is a handsome beast," I say, causing untold shock from the boy as he glances around. "Don't look so surprised." I stroke his horse's nose. "We can just say we have been previously introduced."

"By whom?" he asks. "I am a stable boy, my lady."

I feared as much. "Anyone you wish. Is he yours?"

"No." He smiles up at the thoroughbred mare. "I am merely taking him to my master."

"And who is your master?"

"Mr. Fitzgerald."

Ah, the architect who designed the houses on Belmore Square. At least, all except number one. He lives on the square too. "I know of him, so we are fine. Have you met my sister?" I ask, reaching back and pulling Clara forward.

He eyes her cautiously. "I have seen her on Belmore Square."

"Clara, say hello."

"Hello."

"Hello," he replies, nodding. "I am Benjamin."

I look over my shoulder and groan, forcing a smile when Frederick finds me, his eyes jumping between me, Clara, and the boy. I suppose I ought to get this over with. I am keen to get home and pen my latest story. "We must go," I say, backing away from Benjamin, dragging my sister with me. "He was a nice boy," I muse, looking at my sister, who is looking back at Benjamin. "But a stable boy," I add, reminding her that now, here in our new world, stable boys are not acceptable boys.

"Yes, yes," Clara moans. "And Frederick is a bore."

"But acceptable," I mutter, seeing Mother frown at us as we wander across the grass, probably wondering where we've been. Clara joins her, and this time, when I find myself in Frederick's company, I wait to be greeted, as is expected, before nodding. His father, the Duke of Cornwall, does not approve of me, that much I have established, and while I should not care, annoyingly, I do. As a matter of fact, I do not approve of him, either, so we are, as one might say, on the same page. I talk too much for the old duke, ask too many questions, and I fall over at royal balls. "Should we promenade, Frederick?" I ask, and Mother laughs. It's quite the nervous laugh. "I apologize," I all but grate. "Should we promenade, my *lord?*" I correct myself.

Now, Mother closes her eyes briefly, mortified, and the old

duke shakes his head in despair, making a few specks of white powder from his wig dislodge and settle on the shoulders of his brown coat. Frederick steps forward and sweeps an arm out toward the pathway, and I go obediently, leaving Mother to build our bridges with his father and Papa's business partner. It is not the first time, and I highly doubt it will be the last, for I am, without intention, a constant and consistent form of despair for my newly wealthy, respected parents.

Frederick and I walk in silence for an age. I swear it, he has the personality of a snail. "What do you like?" I ask, keen to kill the silence. If Frederick could only learn to converse with me, then perhaps we might get along. It would be nice to have *something* in common with my betrothed.

"Pardon?" he says, looking at me like I am a halfwit.

"Do you ride, my lord?" I am somewhat taken aback when he laughs. Not because Frederick has shown a hint of a personality, but because, actually, and much to my pleasant surprise, his looks improve enormously.

"I'm afraid not, Miss Melrose."

I frown. Don't all men ride? "Why not?" I ask, and he looks at me, startled. I seem to constantly surprise this man.

"I prefer a drawn carriage."

"Oh." I return my attention forward. "It is not as much fun, though, is it?"

"You've ridden?" he asks.

"Yes, I used to ride often." Before I was forced into a world where riding astride one's horse is not a dignified pursuit for the *fairer sex*.

"Alone?"

"Yes, alone." When we lived in the countryside, I could ride every day on our land, with no one to ridicule me for it. "It was quite exhilarating." I pout, once again mourning the loss of those carefree days, where I could be anyone, anyhow I chose. "What do you do to feel exhilarated?" I look up at Frederick, silently begging him to give me a scrap of excitement, just something to build my hopes on.

"Well, attending any one of the Prince Regent's balls is quite exhilarating, wouldn't you agree?"

Every muscle in my poor, squished body deflates, shrinking me. Exhilarating? My time at the royal ball was torture. I slow to a stop, and Frederick looks back, frowning. "Is something the matter, Miss Melrose?" he asks, coming to a standstill.

"Yes, Frederick, there is."

Poor Frederick. He simply does not know what to do with me, how to handle me, how to react. He looks around, cautious, and I sigh.

"Would you expect me to address you by your title if we were married, *my lord?*"

"Well, it is how my mother addresses my father."

"It is?" I ask, stupefied. That would be like Mama calling Papa Mr. Melrose. What is this madness? "Frederick, I fear we are a complete mismatch," I confess, though it is hardly a confession. Anyone with adequate eyesight must see Frederick and I are incompatible. Surely he is not happy with this arrangement.

"You do?" he asks.

"Yes, I do, Frederick." He needs a "yes" lady. Actually, he just needs a lady. A true lady. A lady who is born a lady, title and all, and not a manufactured lady. And a pitiful example of one at that. And, come to think of it, why would a man of the Duke of Cornwall's status settle for a girl like me? I have no title. Not even much decorum. "I—"

We are both interrupted from our debate on compatibility when a horse neighs and a few ladies scream in shock. I turn quickly and see a man on horseback galloping toward us, everyone shuffling hastily from his path. "Should he be riding so carelessly through the royal park?" I ask, remaining where I am, slap-bang in the middle of the track, while Frederick flees with everyone else and makes way for the reckless horseman.

"Miss Melrose," Frederick calls, trying to encourage me away with a quite deranged flailing hand. "Miss Melrose, please!"

The pounding of the horse's hooves on the dirt seems to travel up my legs, my body vibrating. The ground moving. "He cannot canter through a public park," I declare, outraged. "Has he no regard for public safety?"

"Miss Melrose!" Frederick calls, and I turn to find him on the edge of the crowd lining the path. "You must move."

"I must do no such thing." I return my attention forward, finding the horseman is nearly upon me, and lords and ladies at every turn are yelling their orders for me to get out of his way. This is utterly preposterous. Why isn't he slowing down?

"Johnny Winters," someone gasps.

Those two words finally have me taking a cautious step back. Johnny Winters?

"Yes," another exclaims. "It is he."

"What?" I breathe. The eldest son of the Duke of Chester? But…he's dead. Johnny Winters. The rebellious, drunk rake? The man rumored to have set his home alight and killed the entire family, including himself? I swallow, the horse coming toward me at a rapid speed.

"Eliza!" Clara yells. "Move!"

But I cannot, my legs failing to act under instruction. I am frozen, not by fright at the horse racing toward me, but by the news of who is upon its back. And suddenly the horseman is before me, dust being kicked up, people screaming, and he goes up onto his back legs, neighing. I look up in shock at the enormous beast towering over me, and when his front hooves crash back down to the dirt, the ground shakes.

I blink rapidly, my heart pounds, my eyes falling onto a pair of black leather riding boots. My rapt stare travels up, across the material of his cream breeches and over his thighs. Thick thighs.

Long legs, thick thighs.

I swallow, continuing over a broad torso, across a black wool waistcoat and high cut jacket in matching material. His shirt is white, the whitest I have ever seen, with no puffs or frills. Just a neatly knotted cravat.

And then I'm at his face and all air seems to drain from my poor, labored lungs. My God, have I ever seen such a handsome man? Will I ever again? I swallow, my eyes burning, refusing to blink and deprive me of even a moment of the beauty before me. His dark blond, messy hair finishes before it can creep onto his cheeks as one would expect. It's as if he's rebelling against expectation. *A bad boy.* His skin is dark, he must have been abroad and spent time basking in the sunshine, his nose is so perfectly straight, his jaw chiseled, his brow heavy, his shoulders wide.

And then our eyes meet and the ground beneath me shifts. Or was that the earth? And my breath? Where has that gone?

Shrewd, muted green eyes stare back at me as the horse pads the ground and its rider watches me intently as I search, with little success, for my equilibrium. I fear it may be lost forever. I am unashamedly staring at this man, an audience of hundreds surrounding me, all silent, all watching. I care not. I have taken in, studied every inch of him, from the toes of his riding boots to the eyes gazing back at me. It is as if I have been placed under a spell.

I break eye contact—I probably should have many seconds ago—and admire his hair again, that is too long to be considered acceptable.

Rebel.

I exhale as my chest pumps dangerously, finding his eyes again. They are narrowed, scrutinizing me, but I still see them burn. And in this moment, this monumental moment, because I have been rendered useless by a man for the first time in my life, I suspect the rumors about Johnny Winters's reputation were true. *Are* true. He's not dead? Johnny Winters, *Duke of Chester*.

I am staring at a man who I am sure could send every woman from here to Scotland into a fluster with just one brooding look. "Your Grace," I whisper absentmindedly, swallowing as his head tilts and a slow smirk forms. A devilish smile. I inhale deeply and let it all stream out on a little whimper.

And then I remember myself and blink, clearing my throat as I fight with no success to steady my wobbly legs and move myself from his path, since he seems unwilling to round my static form. His green gaze seems to become amused, and I hate that he's detected my stupor, though, admittedly, it cannot be hard to see. So I scowl and cock my head, challenging him to…what? What in the devil's name am I doing? And I'm frozen once again when his stare takes a leisurely, unapologetic jaunt down the entire length of my body.

I find my chest pulling in, as if I can escape the scrutiny. "My lady," he says, his voice low, deep and—my God—tingle-inducing. I am not at all comfortable with the odd sensations between my thighs, and I clench them together, further preventing me from getting my useless body out of his way. His smirk is wicked and knowing—of course he knows, the rumors are definitely true —and he kicks his horse into action, starting a far safer leisurely trot past me, his eyes not freeing me from their hold, therefore keeping me from breathing easily. I turn with him, lost in his attention, the world around me still and quiet.

Until I am ambushed from the side, physically knocked out of my stupor.

"Miss Melrose," Frederick gasps, holding me in place. "Are you all right?"

I gasp, grappling urgently for air. No, I am stunned, and not because Johnny Winters just undressed me with his eyes in public. *In public!* I am stunned because Frederick is touching me. Perhaps one hundred crashes of my poor, deprived heart too late, but still. We're in public. And as if he too has just realized, he drops me like a diseased pauper and moves back, looking around the crowds. I, too, take in our audience. Every lord, lady, duke and duchess, and even their servants, are watching me. Not Frederick and his wandering hands. They are watching *me*.

Oh dear me.

"He should be reported to the Prince Regent," I say over an exhale, clearing my throat and moving into the crowd. I am so incredibly hot, my underclothes sticking to my clammy skin. My goodness, I am dizzy with shock. Well, I suppose that answers the burning question as to who will be moving into number one Belmore Square. Damnation, my next story has just ridden away on his steed and taken the mystery of it all with him for the whole of London to see.

"Are you all right, Eliza?" Clara says, joining me as the crowd disperses. Thank goodness.

"Yes, I am fine." I laugh, and it is a shockingly terrible *fake* laugh. "What an awfully rude man." *And unfathomably handsome.* Tall, broad, manly. I bet the Duke of Chester would not think twice about having his hands on me in public. Saving me from a runaway horse. *Or* man. I wince at my own filthy thoughts, getting them straight. And my breathing under control. And my mind clear of the vision of such an impressive male upon such an impressive stallion.

A man who isn't dead after all. A man who apparently murdered his family.

Goodness, Eliza. Perhaps I should visit a doctor.

"Mama," I breathe, seeing her coming toward me. "I am fine, be assured."

"Why did you not move?"

"I think I must have become frozen." I look back down the track, seeing the Duke on his horse clip-clopping along leisurely toward the gilded gates, now seemingly in no rush at all. He has the attention of every person in the park, the women looking somewhat breathless and giddy, the men looking somewhat wary.

When he arrives at the gates, he stops and gazes back.

At me.

My breath is lost again, and I quickly look away from him before Mother becomes privy to my peculiar behavior.

"Is this a joke?" Lymington says, joining us, taking his quizzing glass and looking toward the gate.

"I don't see anyone laughing."

He falters, his crabby face wrinkling as he turns his eyes onto me. Accusing eyes. Disapproving eyes. I have not the faintest idea what comes over me, but I bow my head in respect and apology, moving away before my runaway mouth gets me into trouble. Or even *more* trouble. The whole town will hear about this, I am sure. In fact, it will be written and published in Father's newspaper by sunrise tomorrow. Except the story will not be embellished, it really doesn't need to be. It was rather dramatic and heart-stopping without exaggeration.

I look back toward the gates.

The Duke is gone.

But my rickety body, goose bumps and crashing heart remain.

Chapter 4

The moment I arrived home, I hurried to my room, penned my story about the shocking return of Johnny Winters to London, detailing every moment, except, of course, the obvious tension between he and I. I slip into Father's study and pop the story on his desk with a note from Porter.

"I bloody well knew it."

I whirl around. Caught red-handed. Bugger! "Oh, Frank, please don't tell, I beg you." I go to him and fist the front of his coat—another new coat, I note—and give him my most pleading expression, my lip jutting out, my eyes big, round and, hopefully, irresistibly adorable.

"You can't get away with things here in London like we did in the countryside, Eliza."

"Then don't tell!"

"How long do you think it'll be before Porter makes a point of discovering who the mystery writer is?"

"He doesn't care," I grumble. "So long as he's getting the credit."

Frank detaches me from his new coat and shuts the door. "No, Eliza."

I scowl and bump him on his bicep. "It is the only thing keeping me sane. I cannot travel, explore, write about my experiences. At least give me this if I am to be controlled." I quickly think of something, a bargaining chip. "I have a proposition."

"No." He turns away and marches to the window. "This sounds like it could be similar to the time you promised silence in exchange for twenty shillings."

"I was silent, was I not?"

"Yes, and you bankrupted me at the same time. Took all of my savings."

"Don't worry, I won't take your coat fund." I smile sarcastically. "But I will give you something you desperately want."

He cocks a brow, nervous. "What?"

"Time."

"Huh?"

"It'll be our little secret. I know you hate writing for the newspaper. I know it takes up so much time because you're a terrible writer."

"Charming, you are, sister."

I won't apologize, I am right. "What do you say? I write the stories when inspiration strikes me, and you can be the reporter. Papa need never know." I've got him. I can tell by the way he's rolling his jaw in contemplation. "Call it delegation."

"Fine."

I laugh. "Why do you speak as if you're doing me a favor with no gain."

"Shut up."

"All right." I watch as Frank goes to the desk, takes a seat and picks up a quill, ready to rewrite my story in his own hand. "Watch the door," he orders.

"Anything you say, brother dearest."

"Where should I start?"

"The headline," I say, pressing my back up against the wood, "should read 'A warm welcome for the cold Duke of Chester.'"

"Ironic," he says, head down. "I like it."

"Thank you. Ready?" I ask, and he nods. "Imagine if," I go on, falling into thought, "you were to see a ghost…"

My report was in the next day's edition and the newspaper once again topped previous sales.

*

Since that exhilarating afternoon in the royal park, I have not yet succeeded in forgetting about my encounter with the Duke of Chester. I have been on many walks with Mother and Clara, eager and excited, even hoping, perhaps, that I would see him again. Alas, there has been no sign of the Duke on any of my forays, and it was rather hard not to allow the disappointment to reveal itself on my face each time. The thrill I experienced in the moment when he merely let his eyes rest upon me was like nothing I have felt before. The exhilaration I dream of, excitement and anticipation, was mine in that tense moment in the park under the Duke's watchful green eyes. I realize it is utterly preposterous that I feel such fascination toward a man whose reputation is so smeared. But still, I feel it, and I cannot stop it.

But I must. *I must, I must, I must.*

Today I am to meet with Frederick in the gardens of Belmore Square. We will promenade, talk, and I will continue to let him woo me. The truth is, each time I have been in Frederick's company, I haven't much heard a word he has spoken. I would like to think it is simply a matter of distraction on my part, but I know in my heart it is a case of sheer and utter boredom. Perhaps a bit of both. Either way, Frederick and I are not destined to fall in love. I am merely going through the motions of courtship, for if I refuse to see Frederick, I will be stuck in our house too often, or, worse than that, thrust upon many other potential suitors. He is the perfect reason for me to be permitted to venture into the outside world, and, after all, he is perfectly harmless. God forgive me, I have become aware that I am taking advantage of the fact that Mama is distracted by her mission to fit in and be accepted, and Frederick is oblivious to my wandering eye and mind.

"Eliza," Father says as I am following Mother out of the door. I look back and find him hovering on the threshold of his study, a rather thoughtful look on his face that I can't say I like. It's the look he used to give me—one of both suspicion and pride

—when he knew I was up to no good. "How are you recovering after your run-in with that rogue Duke?"

I gulp and try my very hardest to hide it. "Very well, thank you, Papa." I turn on my heel and escape his scrutiny, and it is the worst thing I could have done. Guilty. Damn it to hell, does he suspect it's not Porter or Frank penning the articles? I would like to think it true that my father knows me to the core, knows of my passions and dreams, of my thirst for life, therefore would know my writing, but I can quickly dismiss that fear. He doesn't know me. He can't possibly, not if he has paired me with such a discordant personality as the Earl of Cornwall, Frederick Lymington.

"Miss Melrose," Frederick says, bowing his head. I return the gesture, my eyes naturally falling past him to the house on the edge of Belmore Square. "Shall we promenade?" he says, motioning toward the gates that will lead us to the royal park.

"How about a change of scenery, Frederick?" I ask.

Failing to hide his recoil, he glances around nervously. "Miss Melrose, we have discussed this many times. You must address me in the proper manner."

I breathe in. "My apologies, my lord." For heaven's sake, I'm to marry this man, and yet I am expected to bow to him? "I think I would like to walk this way today."

Frederick frowns, utterly confused. "But we must be seen promenading in the Prince's park."

"Imagine if," I whisper, smiling mischievously, "we were not to be seen in the park. Imagine promenading somewhere else today."

"I don't understand."

My shoulders drop. "Frederick, we have wandered every square inch of the Prince's park. Across every blade of grass."

"I'm certain we haven't, Miss Melrose." He laughs a little, like I am a jester, and my heart sinks along with my shoulders. Frederick just does not understand me, and with each day that passes, each walk, each conversation, my spirit dulls a little bit more. It's not his fault, so I cannot possibly be angry with him. I'm finding it hard enough to be angry with Papa, and I'm certain this is most definitely his fault.

I pick up the bottom of my dress coat and pivot, heading back toward Mother, who is chatting with Lady Blythe, which, I'm sure, will place Mama in a fine mood. After all, not only is Lady Blythe the Marchioness of Kent and a well-established author, but a patroness, like Lady Tillsbury, of Almack's too. Mother is increasing her odds of gaining access to the exclusive establishment. "We shall walk this way today," I say, motioning to the glorious gardens of Belmore.

"Yes, yes," Mother says, hardly looking at me, her attention firmly on Lady Blythe. "Your new novel is simply sublime."

I roll my eyes on a little laugh. Mother is not a fan of reading; she prefers cross-stitch and playing the harp these days. And before these days, she baked, taught her children, and chased her tail trying to control us. My smile widens. Such wonderful days were they.

"Miss Melrose!" Frederick calls.

"Come along, my lord," I sing. "Let us go on an adventure."

"We must not!"

"Says who?" I ask, looking back, seeing Frederick is still in his state of consistent uncertainty, his head swinging back and forth between me and my distracted mother.

"Well...everyone."

Not true. "*I* don't."

"You're just a lady."

I slow to a stop on the edge of the gardens, scowling at the gilded gate. *Just* a lady? I will not be able to marry Frederick, because Frederick will not have a head after I've bitten it off. Besides, he is incorrect. I am *not* a lady. If Frederick hasn't yet realized that, then his ability to observe is lacking as much as his thirst for adventure. I ignore his insult, for challenging it would be a pointless endeavor, and, really, as I keep telling myself, he is a harmless fellow, and continue on my way through the gardens. I look back and find Frederick motionless, his expression still torn. "Do come along, Frederick," I sigh. "Rigor mortis will catch you soon."

Exasperated, he follows, joining me on the threshold of the gardens. As we take our first steps in the opposite direction of our usual route, I look up at him. "See," I say, linking my gloved hands, smiling. "We are still alive."

He rolls his eyes, it is rather endearing, and we fall into an unhurried, steady walk, Frederick keeping his usual respectable distance of one whole very large body-width away from me, and like each time we have promenaded, I hear him talking but fail to listen. My eyes remain on one corner of Belmore Square. It has been over a week since the Duke of Chester made his dramatic return to London, and I have not been blessed with even a little peek of him since, which makes me wonder with increasing disappointment whether he has remained in London or galloped off on horseback to wherever he has been playing dead this past year.

Our stroll brings us gradually closer to the Winters residence, and I unwittingly slow to a stop when I see the silk and taffeta draperies in one of the windows move ever so slightly. My skin prickles, and my body is quickly awash with many of the sensations that bombarded me the day Johnny Winters nearly trampled me with his horse.

"Miss Melrose?"

"Yes, my lord?" I say, lifting a heavy foot and stepping closer, my eyes unmoving from the window. He *is* still here. I silently beg for more movement. For more of these sensations.

"We must walk on."

"Indeed, my lord," I whisper, inhaling quickly when I see another move of the draperies. He's there. Watching me.

Another step closer.

I observe, waiting, pleading.

"Miss Melrose!"

I jump, being wickedly snapped from my moment, my heart pounding from fright rather than pleasure. "Frederick, you gave me a scare!"

"We must not be seen loitering around here." He glances around, nervous.

"Why?"

His eyes shoot to mine, surprised, not only because I have once again questioned him. "It is not one of the most desirable corners of Belmore Square."

"But it is such a beautiful building," I say, looking up at the impressive front of the Winters residence. One can't help but wonder if Mr. Fitzgerald despaired as he watched the renovations, because the homes he has designed sadly pale against it. My eyes naturally and greedily fall to the window where the silk and taffeta draperies hang. I bet it is wildly wonderful inside.

"Miss Melrose," Frederick calls, prompting me to lift a foot, ready to follow, but before I can, something on the cobbles catches my eye. I dip, picking up the paper. A letter? Addressed to the Duke of Chester. On a bite of my lip, I search the window again and slowly slip the letter into my pocket, for I am unable to knock on the door and hand it over. I would like to though. To see him again. Feel those feelings again. Unfortunately, that might make Frederick's heart stop with shock. And, truly, should I be entertaining such thoughts about such a man? *So put the letter back on the ground for the Duke to find!*

"Coming," I murmur, leaving the letter in my pocket and walking on, looking back often. "Do you know what happened to the Duke's family?" I ask.

"Unfortunately, yes."

"Why unfortunately?"

"Because it must give even the bravest of men, and I am a brave man, Miss Melrose, nightmares."

Brave? Oh, Frederick, you dear man. He, like the rest of the ton, have avoided this corner of the square like it is hell since the Duke arrived back. "Do you believe he burned his whole family alive?" I ask as I glance back again, the question slipping past my lips carelessly, my intrigue getting the better of me. I may not believe Frederick to be a solid, dependable man who might indulge my desires rather than squash them, but he is not stupid. I must stop with these crazy, misplaced questions at once.

"Johnny Winters murdered his family in cold blood, Miss Melrose, and," he goes on, looking back at the house on a shudder, "he has shown not one bit of remorse."

"How would we know?" *Shut up, Eliza!* "We, and no one else around here, for that matter, has seen him for a year."

"There is no smoke without fire."

"That is terrible terminology to use when we are discussing the tragic death of a family who perished." Besides, I saw Johnny Winters. Yes, he was cold, almost ruthless-looking, but a murderer? And what evidence is there apart from the careless chattering of a few noblemen and a report in my father's newspaper?

"My father is well versed in the history of the Winters."

Oh, well, of course. I should have known Lymington would be one of the noblemen. Ironically, there is nothing noble about Lymington. "Would you care to share so that I may conclude for myself if the new duke is a coldblooded murderer?"

"Why, are you planning on becoming acquainted with him?"

I laugh, although it is nervous. "Of course not! I am merely enquiring."

Frederick looks down at me, his exasperation at my endless questions unconcealable, but he indulges me. Perhaps he is hoping feeding me the information I am desperate for will shut me up. "You have encountered the Duke, have you not?"

My heart leaps. "I have." He was mysterious, yes. Unlawfully handsome, yes. Aloof, yes. But, again, a murderer? "Where is the proof that he murdered anyone? Before last week, he was rumored to be dead himself!"

Frederick rolls his eyes.

"So, Frederick, I ask you again, what proof is there that he committed such a crime? And how do you know he is the Duke? His father could still be alive. Everyone thought Johnny Winters was dead, after all."

"*Assumed* dead."

"Yes, but—"

"Why do you talk so much?"

"Pardon me?"

"Oh, never mind. I believe we are done promenading for today." And with that, he marches on, bristling terribly, while I stand like a statue, as indignant as I know I *shouldn't* be. I must learn to curb my inquisitive nature.

I pick up my dress coat and go after him. "Frederick," I call, making him stop on the edge of the gardens. "If I have upset you, I must apologize." *Play the game, Eliza. This man is both your prison and your freedom.*

Turning toward me, Frederick stares at me in bewilderment. I believe we are in the midst of our first lovers' quarrel. Except we are not lovers. "Miss Melrose," he breathes, checking our surroundings. A carriage slows to a stop on the cobbles and Frederick bows his head. "My lady."

My eyes move from Frederick, and I find Countess Rose—resident of number nine Belmore Square, our neighbor, and an old, haggard, horrid gossip—flouncing across the cobbled road toward her carriage, the plume of feathers rising three feet from her cap swaying precariously in today's light breeze. She obviously has not yet heard that a peacock perched atop one's head is no longer in vogue. And, God, her eyebrows are as wild as the animals they have undoubtedly come from.

"Miss Melrose," the Countess drones, smiling widely at me. I am quite taken aback. She has never paid me the time of day on the few occasions our paths have crossed, and here she is ignoring the Earl of Cornwall in favor of me? She swishes her way to me, and the closer she comes, the more alarmed I am, for her face is downright disturbing, her old skin rutted and mangy. She is a victim of too much paint and powder, her face ravaged by the toxic concoctions. The Countess's voluntary attempts to cover minor blemishes have resulted in a compulsory need to conceal the disfigurements the paint and powder have caused from too much use. Frankly, close up, the Countess is ghastly.

I find myself leaning back, away from her, and she smiles. It is quite insincere. "Where is your mama?" she asks, her dry rouge lips twisting as she looks between Frederick and me.

"I am here," Mother sings, appearing from nowhere and saving us from the disapproval of the Countess. "Lady Rose," Mother smiles, and the Countess sniffs.

"Lady Rose," Lady Blythe purrs, joining Mother. "Mrs. Melrose was just saying how much she enjoyed my latest work."

Lady Rose's nostrils flare, and I watch with amusement as she fights to prevent her face from creasing even more. "Enchanting, I'm sure."

"You must read it!" Lady Blythe insists, moving in and linking arms with the Countess. "Come now, I have a few spare copies in my drawing room."

"Ah, I must visit with the Duke of Cornwall." Countess Rose quickly detaches herself and waves a hand flippantly before flouncing away, leaving Lady Blythe grinning at her back. "I'm new money, you see," she says, turning back to Mother. "Well, I'm new and old, but you, Mrs. Melrose, are new, therefore your chances of winning the approval of such prehistoric members of the ton is not likely." She links arms with Mother and walks her onward. "A crying shame, don't you think?"

Mother chuckles, and Frederick and I are alone once more,

the poor man looking lost amid the irony. "Thank you for escorting me home, my lord," I say, making a quick escape, crossing the cobbles toward our house.

When I arrive in the hall, I listen for sounds of chatter as I remove my gloves but detect none. I'm relieved. Clara must still be with the governess, and I expect Father and Frank are now on their daily ride, which leaves me to do what I have become rather fond of doing.

Spying.

I gather up my dress and dash up the stairs to my room. "Miss Melrose," Dalton calls, scrambling to keep up with me. "Your coat! Your gloves!"

"I am fine, Dalton," I call, slamming my door behind me. I drop my gloves on my bed and start to wriggle free of the constraints of the endless layers of clothes, breathing easy again for the first time since I dressed for my promenade with Frederick. In my drawers, my palms covering my breasts, I go to the window, tucking myself up close to the draperies, and look out across the square.

Was it him there concealed in the shadows?

I should shudder.

Instead, I bite my lip, forcing myself away from the window before I am seen in my indecent state. I slip on a morning dress, remove my bonnet and sit at my dresser, combing my hair. Perhaps I have not seen the Duke because he is afraid to venture outside. After all, the residents of Belmore Square have not exactly given him a warm welcome. How terrible. He could never have murdered his family.

But he could have.

The comb comes to a stop halfway through my dark curls, and I look back at the bed, lost in thought.

I shouldn't.

I inhale.

And yet I simply cannot resist.

I creep across my room to the bed and rootle through the pocket, pulling out the letter that I picked up from the cobbles outside the Duke's house. The seal is broken, therefore it has been read. Does that make me reading it all right? "Bugger it," I whisper, tossing it onto the bed and beginning a frantic march around my bedroom, biting down on my teeth, forcing my eyes away from the temptation. "Just return it," I say to myself, stopping, my eyes turning onto the enticing piece of paper. This is not a matter of curiosity and lust, but one of public service. I nod assertively and, biting my lip, I grab the letter and ease the seal open, holding my breath.

I only release it when the paper lifts, revealing just a few lines. Anticipation whirling in my tummy, I hurry across my bedroom, sitting at my dressing table and unfolding the paper.

J

It is with sincere sorrow that I must send to you this letter. I am afraid it is being speculated and so printed in The London Times, that the Winters family, or at the very least a member or descendant, will be returning to Belmore Square. What you must do with the information I do not know, for I am certain you have no desire to grace the new residents of the square with your presence. Alas, I felt compelled to inform you of the awakening mumblings of the ton.

Yours, A

I exhale over the letter, noticing it trembling in my hand. He had no desire to return to London.

And yet, he has.

Why?

To my utter annoyance, supper is delayed significantly because Papa is late getting home from the gentleman's club. He blames it on a mechanical issue with the coach. "I wasn't aware our horses are steam-powered like your fancy new printing machine, Papa," I say as he works his way through Cook's scrumptious chestnut soup. I could smell the Scotch the moment the door swung open. Father's meetings at the gentleman's club with Viscount Millingdale, cousin of the Prince Regent, no less, and owner of Millingdale Bank, and, it must be mentioned, a dinosaur in both age and beliefs, are becoming too frequent and too long. I cannot even begin to fathom what gentlemen do for such stretches of time. Well, that's not true. What they do is swaying before me at the head of the table.

"When did your mouth become so sharp?" he slurs. "Why must you pain me so, Eliza?"

"Why must you pain me?" I retort, doing a fine job of disregarding the pleading look pointing my way from Mama. "Frederick Lymington, Papa? Of all the—"

"He is a fine match." He aims a fork at me, but I refrain from pointing out that such a move would be frowned upon by his fancy new friends. *No, father, we are no longer in the countryside.*

"I beg to differ," I breathe, glancing around the table at Mother, Frank and Clara, who are all silently, and quite carefully, spooning soup into their mouths. I shrug and Mother shakes her head.

"He's worried," she explains.

"About what?" I ask. "He has everything he's ever wanted." Money. Power. Recognition.

"All at a price, my dear," she says, so quietly, as if she didn't want me to hear. But I did hear. Father didn't, however, as he has fallen asleep in his soup.

"Oh, Papa," I say over a sigh, shaking my head in despair along with Mother.

Dalton gallantly and patiently coaxes Father up and supports him while walking him out of the dining room, and Mother is silent and contemplative as she follows. When we lived in the country, if our father overindulged at the inn down the lane, she would give him a piece of her mind and make a point of clanging every pot and pan in the kitchen at the crack of dawn while encouraging us children to be as raucous as we should like. Our lives have changed beyond measure, and I hate it. I think Mother secretly hates it too, Clara is too young to understand the ramifications of this move, and Frank? He is too loyal to our father to speak up. To me, this house is a beautiful cage, and the moment I marry Frederick, I will be transported to Cornwall to live in another cage. Dread engulfs me. I try for a moment to reason with myself. At least I do not hate Frederick. At least he is somewhat kind.

All at a price, my dear.

"What do you think Mama meant?" I ask, looking to Frank. "All at a price."

"Why is it you ask him and not me?" Clara asks huffily. "I may be the youngest, granted, but I am not daft. It is obvious."

"What is?" Frank and I ask in unison.

"The price." Clara stands, exasperated. "It's freedom. I found Mama in the kitchen baking bread at four o'clock this morning." She points her eyes to me. "I know you're writing articles again for the newspaper, and you," she says, turning her stare to Frank, "are cavorting with too many females. Everyone is hiding." Leaving her chair messily away from the table, like she would have in the countryside, she departs, making a point of stomping her feet.

"Well, that told us," Frank says on a laugh, getting up from his chair too, leaving. "What she didn't mention is what *she's* sneakily doing."

I hum, pouting, and as soon as I am alone, I make haste, escaping to my room, dressing for comfort and, more importantly, disguise. To be recognized would be disastrous, especially after dark, especially alone. I pull the hood of my cape over my head and check myself in the mirror in the dim light. The shadows across my face are perfect.

I creep through the house like a mouse, holding a finger to my lips when Cook spots me, and leave the candlelit space in favor of the outside darkness, with not even a lantern to help me navigate my way to the other side of the square, but the sky is clear, blessing me with moonlight.

I cut through the gardens, thinking it wise—no sensible person would frequent such a quiet, dark space at this hour. So perhaps I am not sensible. I should laugh at myself. My lack of sensibility in this moment is discernible. In fact, I must be stark raving mad like the King himself.

As I exit the gardens on the other side, I hear the distant sound of horses trotting and the wooden wheels of a carriage bumping across the uneven cobbles. I stop just shy of the gates, waiting, my breath held, as a coach rumbles into Belmore Square and comes to a stop in an extremely unfortunate place, right outside the gardens.

"God above," I mutter, stepping back into the shadows, out of the moonlight, pulling the hood of my cape in some more. I very nearly take a tumble when I see Lady Dare stepping down from the coach. Why on earth is she stopping here, when she lives on the other side of the square? This is a far safer place than most areas of London, but still. No lady should be out alone at this hour. I pout. "You are not a lady, Eliza," I say to myself.

It is dark, yes, but it does not lessen the vividness of Lady Dare's dress, a pink silk affair, that is, quite honestly, jaw-dropping. And the elegant, long, willowy body of Lady Dare carrying it?

Striking.

She's the epitome of wild and carefree. She's out alone after dark unapologetically in a dress that could light up the entire square. I'm jealous. I hardly want to admit it, but I am.

I watch, my breath held, as she walks with confidence across the cobblestones and the hackney coach leaves. My back straightens when I notice in which direction she is heading. She opens the gate, it creaks a little, and then she breezes up the path to the front door of the Duke of Chester's home with confidence and poise I am not sure I like. I find my eyes scanning every window, looking for candlelight beyond. I discover it in the bottom left-hand window. The window with the silk and taffeta draperies that were twitching earlier. Whatever could Lady Dare want with the Duke at this hour?

She takes the door knocker and hits it once. Just once. Then she steps back and waits, fiddling with her hair. My chest starts to squeeze, and I release my held breath on a rush, watching, waiting, and after a few tense moments, she steps forward and knocks again.

Again, only once.

I jump back when she looks over her shoulder, worried I'll be seen. Will the Duke answer her late-night call? Is he home?

And again, what could be so urgent as to warrant a visit at this hour?

I know the answer to that question. Lady Dare is an adventuress. The Duke is, apparently, a libertine. They are perfect for each other. Unlike Frederick and me.

She knocks twice more—once each time, a secret knock?—before picking up the endless material of her skirt and spinning on a huff, leaving the Duke's house sounding less than pleased.

So he is not home tonight? I should not be surprised. I imagine the night is young for the wily Duke. *Exciting.* I sigh down at the letter in my hands. Lady Dare delivers sensual promises. I deliver a letter that I stole. I quickly correct myself. I found the letter. That is what I shall tell him. I found the letter and I did not open it and read the contents. *Who is A?*

"Oh, Eliza," I breathe, leaving the gardens and crossing the road, more confident now that I know he is not in residence, therefore I have no need to even attempt to explain myself. I can leave the letter and be on my way and he need never know it was I who returned it. If he's realized it's missing at all.

I open the gate, walk up to the door and place the letter down. The knocker on the door is a gold lion with an impressive mane and a stare as shrewd as the Duke's. Deliberate? I expect so. But whereas the lion's surface is shiny and polished, the Duke's reputation is tarnished and spoiled. Dirty. And there is no space for dirt in my world, only, I must admit, in my father's newspaper. One must remain as squeaky clean as this gold lion here. This handsome, proud, fierce lion. "Imagine if one was as brave as a lion."

I shake my head and my wild thoughts away, and turn, taking precisely two steps, before I become still again when I hear the sound of a bolt sliding.

Oh blast.

My shoulders rise, my eyes darting in the darkness, ice gliding across my skin, as the door creaks open. I deliberate for an age, tussling with my conflict. I want to turn around. I also do not, because that would be to reveal myself, therefore reveal who is returning something personal to him.

But I am fighting a force far greater than my restraint or sensibility, my body tense, trying to resist the magnetic pull. I want to see him again. I'm shaking terribly, bracing myself for what I might find.

I spin around, just as the door closes, and disappointment envelops me, for the opportunity to melt under his devastating green stare has been lost. The letter is gone. So is he.

He ignored Lady Dare's call, a woman who would undoubtedly bend to his will, if he so demanded it.

But answered mine.

I slowly back away from the door, my wide eyes darting.

What does that mean?

I pause for thought for a moment, turning away from the house and pulling my cape in closer. I am assuming he saw my face. Knew it was I.

Or perhaps he did not.

Chapter 5

I did not sleep one wink that night. Nor the next. I expect I will fail to fall into a slumber on this night, too, for my mind is racing. After breakfast, Father, suffering the aftereffects of *another* excessive night at the gentleman's club, leaves the breakfast room with Frank, retiring to his study to read his newspaper and discuss business, and Mother announces that she will be hosting a dinner party tomorrow evening. "I must buy a new dress," she declares, finishing her coffee. "And a hat. Perhaps some boots too." With that, she stands and leaves with Emma following.

I look at Clara, who seems lost in a daydream. I pick up my silver spoon and tap the side of my teacup. She blinks rapidly and looks up. "Are you dreaming of the hero in your latest read?" She does it often. A true romantic. While Clara reads Austen, I read encyclopedias and books on adventurous travels. I'm not foolish enough to believe the elaborate tales of burning love truly exist.

Clara smiles, but it is meek, and she plucks another muffin from the pile. "I'm not indulging in any sort of book at this time."

"Well, that's not true," I say on a laugh. "Only last night we sat together in the drawing room in front of the fire and read together."

"I am not reading, Eliza," Clara reiterates, sighing heavily. My usually upbeat, enthusiastic sister looks forlorn. And it occurs to me…

Oh heavens.

Frank was right to be worried. "The boy in the park," I say, sounding a trifle accusing.

"I am in love," she blurts, letting her hands fall to the breakfast table with a thwack. The muffin jumps up and bounces onto the rug, and my eyes follow it as it rolls under a chair. "Oh, Eliza, he is wonderful."

"You hardly know him, Clara." I laugh, this time sounding a trifle patronizing. I mean not to belittle her, I really don't, but...in love?

"I know him well enough to know I am in love." Clara stands, offended, her chin raised. "I would not expect *you* to understand."

Said with such emphasis on *you*. I breathe out as Clara marches away in a foul mood, and I consider just how terrible this is. It does not take much of my time to conclude that it is *awfully* terrible. Clara is no longer free to fall in love with anyone who has not been handpicked by Papa. And a stable boy? Did she not hear me when I pointed that out to her in the park? I rub at my forehead, feeling unspoken worry for my dear, naïve little sister. I fear she is going to be left gravely bereft. How silly to fall in love with a man she will never be allowed to marry. How silly to fall in love at all!

I am not partial to fashion, but a good coat dress and fancy bonnet is a necessary disguise, that much I have come to know. To be seen in anything but fine threads would draw more attention to oneself than my preferred, comfortable attire. So I will wear what is expected of me, and I will do it quietly.

Taking the stairs, I pull on my gloves. I shall accompany Mother to buy her new...everything, and if luck is on my side, I will find a moment to slip away and indulge my curiosity with a wander through the gardens.

I come to a stop at the bottom of the stairs when I hear the enthusiastic chatter of many men. The door to Father's study is ajar. I recognize one voice in particular and approach, my eyes unsurprisingly narrowing.

"I believe the courtship is going quite well," Lymington remarks cheerfully. "Isn't that right, Frederick?"

"Yes, Your Grace, very well indeed," Frederick agrees, sounding confident of that. Naturally, I beg to differ, and if I expected there to be even a remote possibility of being heard, I would speak up.

"That is comforting to hear," Papa says, getting up from his chair and joining a rather pleased-looking Mr. Porter by the fireplace, roaming up and down with a glass of Scotch in his hand.

"It is a shame it is not true," I say quietly, reaching for the ribbon of my bonnet under my chin and loosening it.

"Eight thousand copies, Melrose," Porter sings.

"Let us make today nine." Lymington seizes a copy of today's edition from Dalton's hand and starts fingering through the pages. "Any news on that rogue Winters?"

My eyes naturally shoot to Porter by the fireplace, whose back has straightened. "Nothing new, but in the works," he says over a cough. I quickly find Frank, who has turned his back on the room. I know his game. He never could lie, so he's hiding his face and the guilt that I know will be emblazoned across it.

"The workers will need to work longer hours if sales continue to increase so rapidly," Papa says as Lymington inspects the broadsheet. I look at Father, seeing an interested stare pointed at Frank's back. Longer hours? They already have their fingers worked to the bone. "Everyone is apparently buying the paper now primarily to see if there is any update on Johnny Winters's return and his family's demise," Father continues, making me come over all hot and sweaty. "Now which of the two of you will be reporting this time?"

Porter coughs, as does Frank. "Me," my brother interjects quickly. "Just as soon as I have further news."

"Get to it, then, Melrose," Lymington adds. "The workers can cope with the extra workload."

"I believe you will find," I say without thought, my mouth running away with me once again, "that slavery was abolished in 1807." I must learn to control myself, for I am sure I am on the verge of being sent to the Tower and whipped into line.

All the men in the room turn their attention toward the door where I stand, their mouths hanging open like fish. Poor Papa. He of all the men is the most shocked. Or could that be horror? I suspect it is a mixture of both. God, I hate the disappointment on his face.

Frederick jumps up from his chair and nods. "Miss Melrose."

"My lord," I murmur, hatching my plan to escape the downright dreadful silence. "Perhaps you should up the wages of your employees, Papa." *God, Eliza, this is not the plan. To run is the plan. Please, I beg you, do not utter another word.* "I expect you will evoke the greatest of morale which will, in turn, increase productivity to a very satisfactory level."

"I pay well," my father splutters.

"Ten shillings, Papa?" I question on a laugh. "It is hardly a job paid well." That is it. I am well and truly done for, but I have started, so I may as well get it all off my chest. "And whilst we are on the matter of the company, perhaps also, since you are becoming rather flush"—I nod at the well-appointed bar, the cigars, the fine threads he's wearing—"you would like to hire another journalist." I smile and stand taller, thinking it is high time I claimed my own words, since they are so very popular, and, frankly, I have now realized I am tired of a man, whomsoever he may be—brother or egomaniac Porter—taking the glory for my hard work. "I know of just the person, as it happens."

Father laughs nervously.

"Wouldn't that make an exciting change?" I simply cannot help myself. The looks on the faces of these men are maddening, and Frank is quite clearly begging me to stop.

"You?" Lymington splutters.

"Don't look so shocked, Your Grace. I have penned many interesting tales of truth. In fact, Papa used to read them with the greatest of interest, didn't you, Papa?"

"Eliza, please," he whispers, but I am just too mad at Lymington's dismissal. I am mad that I am here. I am mad that Father expanded the business and made heaps of money. I'm mad I can no longer read all day and write all night. I'm mad that I must now marry a man I feel no love for. I'm mad.

I keep my serious eyes on a horrified Lymington, who I am sure is full of regrets in this moment. "I would be thrilled to accept such a position," I say joyfully, "subject to salary, of course." Picking up the bottom of my dress, I pivot. "Now, please excuse me, I have dresses to buy and a dozen invitations to social events to accept. The life of a lady is quite busy, don't you know?"

I step outside the house and pull the door closed with a bit too much force, causing the knocker to knock. "Damn it to hell," I mutter, my angry gaze finding the Winters residence and focusing, not too intensely, on the window. I do not expect the Duke to be any different. *Men!* "Imagine if men were not bigoted pigs."

"Pigs, you say?"

My inhale is sharp at the sound of his voice, and my heartbeat speeds when I find his tall, well-built form standing on the cobbles. He's swinging a walking stick casually, his stance relaxed, his spare hand resting in his pocket. My God, has a man ever appeared so confident and self-assured? And handsome. And mischievous. And…interested.

I work so very hard to gather myself, worried all the odd reactions happening inside are as plain as daylight for him to see. "Your Grace," I say, nodding but keeping my eyes on him. Will he question me about the letter? Does he even know it was me who returned it? Would he think I would be so rude as to read it? The questions! And, again, who is A?

"Miss Melrose," he says quietly, carrying on his way. It's only once he's disappeared through the gates into the gardens that I breathe easily. The man is clearly bad for my health. And how in God's name does he know *my* name? I don't know, but I know, terribly, that it thrills me.

I find Mother and Clara at the bottom of the steps waiting for me, Mother following the path of the Duke, Clara pointing a curious frown my way. "Is everything all right, Eliza?" she asks.

"Yes," Mother returns her attention my way. "You look rather anxious."

Is that because of my grievance with Papa or my encounter with the Duke? "I am feeling stifled, Mama," I admit, looking back at the house. Trapped. Helpless. Unfulfilled. I know there is little my mother can do about this. But still, she comes to me, taking my arm and leading me down the steps. "I have something that will cheer you up."

"What is that?"

"You'll see."

"I found it on my walk back from the royal park last week," Mother says as she pushes the door open, revealing a cavern full of...

"My God," I breathe, wandering in, my mouth agape, my eyes high and low trying to take in the sheer amount of books before me. "There must be every book ever written." I turn on the spot, awed by the sight.

"Not quite *every* book."

My eyes drop, and I find a man behind the wooden counter with piles of books stacked around him—on the floor, the counter, even in the window. "This is wonderful."

"Thank you." He nods his head, looking over his spectacles at me. "Romance?"

I smile, enchanted, starting an unhurried wander, dragging my gloved fingers across the spines as I go, relishing the light thrum. "I like anything about travel or exploration, sometimes history too."

"Then you must venture to the very back of the store, dear."

"Thank you, Mr...."

"Fuddy," he replies, going back to stamping the books on the counter. "I shall be here if you find you should require some assistance." He points to the opposite side of the store. "You'll find all of the works of Austen on that shelf." He peeks up at Clara, who rolls her eyes but does not refute Mr. Fuddy's conclusion, going to the shelf and pulling out a book.

Mother gives me a nod, joining Clara, and I venture further into the store—or more through a tunnel of books—the smell simply magnificent.

When I have ventured as far as I can possibly go, I find the entire back of the shop, floor to ceiling, a wall of books, not one tiny piece of the plaster beyond exposed. Holy hell, where do I even begin? I inhale the smell once again. "Imagine if I could live here," I whisper to myself.

"Just imagine."

I gasp and whirl around, my poor heart shocked into a gallop. "Good heavens," I blurt, coming alarmingly close to a man's chest. I quickly take a step back and look up to his face, despite being quite sure of who is before me. I have the exact same crazy trembles happening all over my body. I make it to his green eyes, his handsome face, his unconventional messy hair, and breathe back my awe as he rather unapologetically takes a long, leisurely look up and down my body, which feels utterly naked under his burning gaze. I have to move back to win some breathing space, but I do not find it because he quickly closes the gap I have made. One more step, and another, until my back is pressed up against the bookcase. He moves with me, watching me, the semblance of a knowing smirk tickling his lovely lips. He is very aware that my chest is not pumping because I am scared. "Your Grace, what are you doing?" I whisper raggedly.

He reaches past me, his eyes stuck to mine, his face coming so close I can smell him. The rush of something unrecognizable overcomes me, but while it may be unfamiliar, this feeling, I know, is unquestionably forbidden. I swallow, silently demanding my body to wake up and move, and yet it refuses to hear me. Probably because it is all too fond of these thrilling sensations pitter-pattering all over me. And still, he stares down at me, almost in challenge, as if he is waiting for me to break and beg him for space.

I will not. I refuse.

"Won't you speak?" I ask quietly.

His eyes fall to my lips, and I hold my breath, his mouth coming closer to mine, his eyes jumping across my face, his expression somewhat curious. My God, is he about to kiss me? *Stop it, Eliza!* "Your Grace," I whisper.

"Miss Melrose," he says softly in return, and I gulp, feeling like his lips could be magnets, pulling me in. I feel his breath. The heat. My heart races faster. And when I am sure his mouth is just a hair's breadth away, he jerks, frowns, and pulls back. "You want me to speak? And what would you have me say?" His voice is velvet and all things illicit. My God, how many sweet promises has he whispered into the ears of ladies far and wide. I can hardly breathe.

"I would have you apologize for crowding me."

He steps back, a book in his hand. "I apologize for crowding you."

I look away from him and clear my throat, brushing down my perfect dress. "You hardly sound sorry."

"Because I am not."

I glance up and notice a copy of Father's newspaper tucked under his arm, and he pulls it out. It's then I notice it is not the most recent edition, but an older one. He opens it, browses casually, hums, and quite curious, which I'm certain is his plan, I crane my neck to see what he's making an elaborate point of reading. It's my story. My story detailing the Duke's grand arrival back in London. "You read the news, did you?" he asks.

"I did not need to because, most unfortunately, I was there on that day."

"Unfortunately," he murmurs softly, and then, in stark contrast, he snaps the paper shut and tucks it back under his arm. I swallow, and his eyes narrow accusingly. Damn me, I look away, feeling my cheeks heat. "Was it unfortunate, Miss Melrose?" he whispers, dipping, coming closer again, forcing me to peek up at him. He scans my face, every little bit of it.

"Most unfortunate," I say quietly, and he smiles a little.

"How so?"

"You are quite rude."

"And you are quite bold. I don't think London quite suits you."

I laugh a little, and it is unstoppable. "I think you are perhaps correct."

His smile is almost cheeky, and in this moment, I consider the fact that I am seeing a very different man to the rest of the world. A murderer? It's obscene. I cannot believe it. My eyes drop to his lips again. Full, lush lips. Lips that were so close to mine just a moment ago.

Eliza!

I shake myself away from those forbidden thoughts and straighten. "You are still crowding me." *And I like it.*

"So I am," he whispers, moving back and pushing something into my chest. The book he pulled down.

"Good day to you, Miss Melrose." He turns and meanders slowly away, and, God save my treacherous soul, I admire the sway of his walk and the fine form of his long, sturdy legs. He is perfect. Perfect but tarnished. And suddenly, being in London doesn't feel at all like a hardship.

He looks back but not enough to give me his full face, just his profile, and what a fine profile it is. I could puddle to the floor, for I certainly need to get off my feet for a moment to gather myself. I raise a hand to the bookcase and cling on, my heart honestly feeling like it could burst right out of my chest. Goodness. And once again I am asking myself how he knows my name. Perhaps one day I will remember to ask when I'm in his company, if I can locate my composure in the moment.

I hear Mother calling me, forcing me to try harder to find my poise. "I'm here, Mama," I call, my voice shaky. I breathe in and out a few long times, checking myself over and patting at my burning cheeks.

"My goodness, it is like a maze in here," she says, appearing round a corner. "What have you found?" I look down at the book in my hand, but before I can tell her what it is, because I do not yet know, she takes it and reads the cover. I am unsure what to think when I see her body shrink a little. "Oh Eliza," she sighs, shaking her head. *Oh, Eliza, what?* I dare not ask. She places the book back in my hand, strokes my cheek, looking at me with a heavy sorrow. "Cook will have lunch ready." Mother leaves, calling for Clara, and I look down at the book.

"*Gulliver's Travels,*" I murmur, biting down on my lip, contemplating. I know it well, I have a copy in my nightstand. A coincidence?

As we arrive back in Belmore Square, I see Frank and Papa boarding the family coach. Mother breezes up the steps to our house, turning at the top and gazing around the square. I expect she is looking for Lady Tillsbury or Lady Blythe so she can continue with her incessant attempts to get into Almack's.

Deciding I am not ready to return to my gilded cage, I hurry across the cobbles and enter the square at the bottom right-hand corner. I follow the path to the middle, and the fountain that marks the center appears. I pass it, treading carefully over some lavender bushes, arriving in one of the few nooks where cast-iron benches are nestled amid the foliage. I take a pew, resting my tired feet for a few minutes, and pick up the book that the Duke gave me, starting to flick through the pages. I browse tales of travels, of lands far and wide, of places only reachable after months on board a vessel enduring the unpredictable high seas. Only the bravest would attempt such a journey. An excited thrill courses through me, and, just as quickly as it appeared, it disappears, starkly reminding me that I have no place onboard a ship upon the high seas. Perhaps I should run away. I would not get very far as a lady, even a fake one, perhaps to the port. Then I would be laughed back to Belmore Square. I wilt and snap the book closed. Why would he tease me with such luxuries I may never have? Has he visited these places?

I stand but falter, bending over when I see a quarto paper. On a frown, I reach for the folded sheet and turn it over, and my heart very nearly stops beating when I see a seal with the initials "JW" embossed into the wax.

I inhale and quickly slip the paper between the pages, glancing around nervously. I always found the purpose of seals quite irritating. How was it possible that someone could act so dishonorably and endeavor to discover the contents of a letter entrusted to their care and protection. Now? Now that I have behaved in such a dishonorable way? I shrink. But this letter was meant for me.

I hurry home, enter quietly, creep up the stairs, and go straight to my bedroom. I place the book by the bedside, remove my bonnet and coat dress, for I am sweating like a pig, and light a candle before slipping into my morning dress, taking the paper, and lowering to the rosewood chair in the window. Lord above, my heart, my poor useless heart, is pounding relentlessly, my eyes burning from staring at the seal. Or the initials on the seal.

JW.

I have not the room in my absorbed mind to wonder what is contained in this letter or why he has given it to me. I carefully break the seal and unfold the paper, and as soon as I am confronted by the elaborate scripted handwriting, I exhale. I must concentrate on breathing, for I may lose consciousness soon, and that would be quite unfortunate, if only because the loud thud of my body hitting the floor would alert someone and bring them to my room where they would find me unconscious with this note lying beside me.

But it would appear the Duke is not a man of many words. There is no cross writing. And, of course, no concern of the cost to send by the postal service, since it was given to me in a book by the man himself. So whyever has the Duke been so exceedingly mean with his words? I huff, feeling more indignant than I should.

Just imagine...

"Just imagine what?" I mutter, slipping the note between two of the mattresses on my bed. I go to the window and look across the square, my mind working as hard as ever, except I am less frequently dreaming of a world where I must hide, and instead fantasizing about a man I should undoubtedly hide *from*.

Chapter 6

I endure the simplicities of Mama's and Papa's dinner party this eve, compliant, polite, and I only speak when I am spoken to. I'm endeavoring, and succeeding, if the lack of attention pointing my way is a sufficient marker, to avoid too much attention, so that when I disappear to my room, my absence may not be missed. I have squirmed my way through dinner, listening to the mindless words of the members of the ton who are seated around our mahogany dining table as they have scoffed their way through all the courses set across the table, although, and I feel somewhat contrite about it, I have held my tongue and not spoken up on matters that do not concern me. Besides, I have other chores on my mind today, chores far more distracting than the claptrap being spilled across this table.

Has the Duke a small mind?

Is it terrible that I *must* find out?

Or must I, for the rush of pleasure may be lost with the enlightenment that Johnny Winters is merely a man like all others?

Dreadful.

Still, he is rather pleasing on the eye.

Rather?

Oh, Eliza, must you be so coy?

"Yes, I must," I say into my wine glass, suitably satisfied with the volume of alcohol being consumed this evening. My eyes fall to Frederick, whose wine has hardly been sniffed, least of all drunk, and that will not do. I lift my glass and smile when he gazes at me, and he follows my gesture, joining me in a sip. I will be intoxicated if I keep up this pace, and I cannot be. Not when...

My tummy flutters, my heart booms and...

Lord above, what was that?

My back straightens, my thighs squeeze, and tingles attack me between my legs. I swallow, darting my eyes around the table, certain my condition must be written on every inch of my face.

How is that possible with merely a thought?

"I look forward to promenading with you in the morrow," Frederick says. "After my ride with my father, of course."

"Of course," I reply, trying to look thrilled when I feel nothing but dread, tussling with the sensations between my legs. They swiftly fade, and I purse my lips around the rim of my glass as Frederick gazes at me. He is not only somewhat unexciting, but a tingler killer. Frederick really doesn't have much going for him, which would explain why this is his fifth season. *Fifth!* Perhaps he would gaze at any woman that he was promised in this way, even if she was ravaged by age or disfigured by disease. I feel somewhat insulted that Papa has seemingly bitten off the hand of the first offer made to him but, of course, I am still wondering why Lymington would settle for anything less than a titled female. I can only surmise that pickings are slim for him and his son after five seasons. Lucky me. And for the very first time since being introduced to Frederick, I wonder what it is exactly that has been brokered for my hand. Father must have known I would spend one second with Frederick and possibly run away screaming my protests. Mother would have undoubtedly raised her concerns, in private, of course. So whatever Lymington offered my father must have been wildly attractive, because Frederick certainly isn't. And I mean not looks, but personality. Although neither are shining. Simply put, Frederick is quite the opposite of a man I would desire, *if* I desired a man, which I do not. I desire so much more than that.

"Miss Melrose?" he says, and I blink, my glass still resting on my lip. I look down at it feeling my forehead wrinkling.

"My apologies, my lord," I say. "I was caught in a daydream."

"And may I ask what you were daydreaming about?"

The Duke.

How I wish he had kissed me. Would I have liked it? Would he? God, would I know how to? I expect ladies such as Lady Dare titillate to their heart's content.

How…delightful.

And yet the Duke ignored her late-night call. One could assume he is not a man easily manipulated, or, indeed, led by a ferocious sexual appetite, but I have heard the rumors, and now I have met the man. The Duke is a rake. An intense, handsome rake, and while his focus was set solely on me in the bookstore, I could not control my overwhelming curiosity. If he were to kiss me…

I jump, knocking my knee on the underside of the table, and the flash of pain jars me from the inappropriate direction of my thoughts. My interest in the Duke is merely professional, for he has been wronged by society. And the letter, who was it from? And the book, why would he give it to me? And the note? *Just imagine…*

The Duke is a conundrum. A puzzle.

And I want to solve him.

When the clock strikes midnight, it would be fair to say that my father, mother and half of Belmore Square who are seated around the grand table of our dining room are as drunk as sailors. Even Frederick is somewhat, and very annoyingly, I might add, tipsy. He looks less uncomfortable now, but his cheeks a not-so-fetching shade of crimson. Alcohol may be aiding.

I watch as Papa rises from his chair and invites the gentlemen into his study. Lymington rises too, struggling with his stick while holding the table, the whole process quite messy. I hear the thud of something hit the rug and push out of my chair, looking beneath the table.

"Eliza?"

I shoot up and find Frederick frowning down at me, and I wave him off, remembering that I have somewhere else I want to be, and I'll get there a lot sooner if everyone's attention is elsewhere. The men retire to Papa's study to drink, smoke and discuss business, and the ladies get deeper into conversation, or, more likely, gossip. I choose my moment carefully and leave the table to ready myself for the dark and cold, draping my cloak around my shoulders. When I reach the top of the stairs, I see my escape is blocked by Dalton, and with only a moment's thought, I go back to my bedroom and shove the window open, poking my head out. I smile when I see the drainpipe. It's been too long.

Checking the coast is clear, I get up onto the ledge and stretch my arm, grabbing the iron and easing myself out, reaching to pull the window down into place, but not all the way. I shimmy down with relative ease—clearly I haven't lost my touch after years of practice climbing trees in the countryside—and point a toe to reach the wall, pushing myself away from the pipe and finding my balance. I exhale and hop down to the cobbles. The wind whistles, gusting, whipping my cloak around my legs. It is less than appealing to be exposed to such unkind weather, but it would seem my infinite curiosity refuses to allow me respite from both that *and* the elements.

Cutting through the gardens, my pace measured but not rushed, the closer I come to his house, the greater the swirl of anticipation inside of me. How gladly I take this joyful reprieve from the trials of life as a supposed lady.

Before the Duke's impressive abode, I open the gate slowly, so as not to make it creak too loudly, and approach the door, my eyes set on the remarkable lion on the knocker. I take it and thwack twice. Not once, for I would hate him to believe me to be Lady Dare again and therefore ignore the call. Or perhaps tonight he would not ignore it. Perhaps tonight he would be in the mood for...

What?

I bite my lip and step back, and with each silent second that passes, my anticipation lessens. How unfortunate. He is not home. My shoulders lax, my disappointment unstoppable, I walk away and reach the gate, but freeze when I hear the door opening. Short was the time with absent anticipation. It is back, more powerful than before. Unwilling to allow a repeat of my previous visit when I dawdled somewhat terribly, I whirl around fast, eager to capture even just a glimpse of the infamous Duke again.

"Oh," I breathe, finding not the Duke, but a manservant instead.

"His Grace wishes to see you."

Oh...

I am dawdling again.

"Miss Melrose?" he drawls, his head tilting in unwanted curiosity.

"You know my name."

"Indeed, I do."

"How?"

"His Grace."

"And how does *he* know?"

"His Grace wishes to see you." Translated: shut up and hurry up!

"He does," I say to myself as I swallow and walk up the path to the door. "And why do you suppose that is?" I step over the threshold as I lower the hood of my cape, and I am truly taken aback by the Duke's home. The entrance hall is certainly five times larger than any other houses on the square. The staircase grander and sweeping, the ceiling higher, the gold chandelier more extraordinary. I count thirty candles on the impressive piece, all lit, basking the expansive space in more light than I am used to at this hour. I expected it to be impressive within the walls of the disreputable house that stands proud on the edge of Belmore Square, but this is palatial.

"You tell me, Miss Melrose," he murmurs, walking on. "This way, please."

He is not happy, and, quite obviously, has a high desire for me to know. He should be assured, I am rather unhappy with myself, so we have one thing in common. What on earth am I thinking? The tingles have gone, as too has the anticipation, and in their place is a wariness I'm confused by.

"And what should I call you?" Each step I take is measured, the sound of my heeled boots clipping the beautifully polished wooden floor echoing off the rich crimson walls. We pass through a set of arched wooden doors with glass panels, and three more doors appear.

"Hercules," he says, so seriously, I wonder if he is actually joking.

Regardless, I laugh anyway, but soon shut up when he glares at me. "My apologies," I murmur. "I did not mean to—"

"Fear not, Miss Melrose," the giant of a man reassures me. "This way." I cannot help feeling wary of the look of foreboding impressed upon his crabby face as he motions me to walk on. I expect, like the Duke, and perhaps even me, he is wondering why in heaven's name I am here. Perchance the future holds that answer, for I am apparently quite oblivious—or uncaring— of the danger I am placing myself in.

Hercules points to a door, and I approach, taking the polished gold knob and turning. It creeps open, and I am faced with walls and walls of...

"Books," I murmur, immediately mesmerized by the floor-to-ceiling bookcases that are positively bursting at the seams. A desk sits before the heavily draped window, and two reading chairs sit before a roaring fire.

His study.

It is a man's domain.

"His Grace won't keep you waiting too long, Miss Melrose." The door closes, and I am alone. Alone with thousands of books. Goodness, there must be more titles here than Mr. Fuddy holds. I approach the nearest bookcase and start to recite the titles on the spines, my delight growing, for they are all travel books, or law books, or books bursting at the seams with world knowledge. I'm awed as I wander to the crackling fire and lower to the soft green seat, looking up when the door opens.

Lord above.

I shoot up on a sharp inhale. The impact of his looks never lessens. In fact, I am as struck by him now as I was in the royal park on our first encounter, when he all but trampled over me with his horse.

I must have woken him, for he is barely dressed, and his hair looks unacceptably but charmingly messy. His white muslin shirt is lacking the tie that will fasten it, leaving his chest half exposed, and his drawers fall just below his knees, leaving his calves bare. His state of undress is downright inappropriate, and I know not where to look. My eyes fall to the front flap of his drawers. *Perhaps not there, Eliza.*

I'm feeling rather hot, my cheeks burning. "Your Grace," I breathe, bowing my head, looking down at the floor. Why ever would he present himself to me half bare? It is confirmed beyond all doubt. The Duke is a heedless, unapologetic rake.

I peek up. The corner of his lip lifts, and I am baffled by it.

"My lady," he replies, closing the door. He does not seem at all concerned by his lack of modesty, because, make no mistake, he is a well-formed man. And his voice? It is rough like his face, which is blanketed in facial hair. Deep like the green of his eyes.

"I am no lady," I blurt, quickly looking away from him. I am unfamiliar with the rush of blood whooshing in my ears, making my hearing muffled and my thoughts rather fuddled. My mind has always been my own. Control has always been something *never* to surrender. Now? Now I am questioning everything.

I do, however, know one thing for certain. I am rather enjoying this odd breathlessness.

"And I am no gentleman," he whispers, remaining unmoving by the door, his shoulder resting on the wood so very indifferently.

"What is that supposed to mean?" I ask, watching as his eyes dance, as if he might be having fun. I fear he is. I, however, am feeling somewhat overwhelmed by the situation that I have come to find myself in. I laugh at the absurdity of my thoughts.

You mean the situation you walked right into, Eliza?

What was I hoping to find here at the Winters residence? Evidence of his supposed crimes? Answers to my endless questions? A kiss? Wherever they have sent King George for going stark raving mad, I think they should send me there also, for I am without question missing my common sense.

"It means what I say," he rasps, inciting a flurry of tingles inside me. I inhale and shift in my boots, though the full skirt of my dress and my cloak over it hides my fidgeting, I pray. Johnny Winters is a tingle *maker*. "I am no gentleman, my lady," he whispers, "so expect no chivalry or kindness."

"I believe I have already enlightened you to the fact that I am not a lady, Your Grace."

"Then what are you, Miss Melrose?" he asks, pushing away from the wood and stepping further into the room. "A whore? A harlot?" He nibbles the corner of his lip, in contemplation, I think. Is he really considering that? "An adventuress?"

Dangerous.

And not because he is suspected of murdering his family in cold blood. I believe I may have just crossed a line, so to speak. "How do you know my name?"

"How do you know mine?"

I narrow an eye. "I overheard someone in the park the day you returned to London. You?"

"I was curious about who was in my way that day, so I made inquiries."

I feel my lips purse. *In his way?* "So you're not dead," I say evenly, and I am sure I see him flinch.

"I am not dead," he replies quietly.

"And where have you been this past year?" My instinct is off on a tangent, digging for all of the information I can get.

"You are certainly full of questions. Am I on trial?"

"Should you be?"

His eyes narrow, and despite feeling a little uncertain, I lift my chin in feigned confidence. The mystery of the Winterses is a story desperate to be told and the only person in this world to tell it is before me. "Perhaps you have outstayed your welcome," he mumbles.

"I was welcome?"

"I invited you in, didn't I?"

"And now you are inviting me out," I say, my voice strong, eyeing the door past the Duke's broad shoulder. He does not wish to discuss his family. Hmmm.

"Why are you here, Miss Melrose?"

Good question. Why am I here? I cannot seem to rem— Ah! "I should like to know what you meant by your letter to me."

"Letter, my lady?"

"Note," I retort, my eyes falling to the exposed flesh of his chest. It is the first naked chest I have seen, aside from my brother, of course, and it is an impressive one at that. Must he brandish it so unethically? "And I am not a lady."

"Perhaps," he muses, "I should be the judge of that."

"And how will you make your judgment?" I ask, facing him with grit I am unsure I can uphold for very long.

"By how loud you scream when I pleasure you."

I inhale, stepping back. He really is an unrepentant, hedonistic rake! Provocative. Devastating in every sense of the word.

But I am not foolish like I expect many of his bed companions to be. Blinded by his unholy handsomeness and the body of a Greek god. It must be the reason their knees go weak for him, because I see no admirable qualities in his character, and I am not about to waste time trying to find any. I do believe I am looking at the most conceited, confident libertine, and despite being entirely opposed to conforming, I refuse to be subjected to such…such…such…

Excitement!

"Good evening, Your Grace," I mutter, walking forward, wondering why on earth I am addressing him so courteously when he is certainly far from cordial.

The Duke takes one careful, purposeful step to the side, allowing me to pass, and I take the doorknob, turn, and look down. His exposed legs come into my view, and the fire burning intensely across the room seems to heat my back. Or could it be the heat radiating from the Duke?

"You were leaving," he says, and I look up. Our eyes meet, and I am lost in the muted green tone of his stare. "My lady," he whispers.

"Your Grace," I murmur, pulling the door open. And I quickly slam it shut again. He's infuriating! "You lured me here."

He smirks. "Lured, did I?"

"Yes, lured." I face him, bold and unabashed. "Why else would you give a note to me if not to lure me?"

"And why would I want to lure you, Miss Melrose?"

Good question! And my head is beginning to hurt as I try to unravel *that* mystery. Will I ever? He seems to see me as a plaything. Something to tease and have fun with. Something that amuses him. Naturally. I have never in my existence met such a challenging, unreasonable man! To be fair, until arriving in London, I had hardly met *any* men. Winters is a big enough dose to see me through to my deathbed, thank you very much.

"Do you want to be lured?"

I snort. "Good night, Your Grace," I say, pulling the door open and marching through.

"Perhaps if you stay, I could indulge you."

My mouth falls open, but I refuse to turn back and allow him to see it. And how would he do that, I wonder? Indulge me? Pleasure me?

"Cat got your tongue?"

I stop, my words all jumbled in my mouth, and I fight furiously to untangle them. It's probably just as well I fail since none are very complimentary. I walk on.

"Sleep well, Eliza," he calls, provoking a flurry of tingles to attack me again, just by my name, my *real* name, being spoken by him. *Eliza.* "Be sure to dream of me."

"I fear it will be more a nightmare, Johnny." I slam the door and stand stock still, breathing heavily, like I could have just cantered for miles through the countryside. If he will insist on addressing me by my name, he must expect the same from me, for we are equals.

Equally daring.

Equally electric.

And together, it would seem, equally dangerous.

I hurry through the gardens, outraged, irritated and infuriatingly enamored, and make it to our house in no time at all. When I reach the door, I gaze at the shiny black wood for an age, vehemently trying to process the happenings of my visit with Winters. And how I wish I could return and re-experience such energy, for my heart is pumping wildly, my skin sizzling, and it is wholly addictive.

If I could be reassured that I might experience the thrill again, that would be infinitely appreciated. It would be something to anticipate in a world where nothing excites me. At least, nothing I have access to.

The prickles on my skin intensify somewhat rapidly, and I suspect it is not merely my thoughts instigating such an effect. Then I hear footsteps, and I know it to be true. My breath held, I peek over my shoulder. His green eyes shine bright in the darkness, and I turn, my back naturally pushing into the wood of the door. I find my eyes darting, checking we are alone. "Is there something I can help you with?"

As he steps closer, I notice a swirl of displeasure in those wonderfully green eyes of his. "Do me one kindness," he all but orders.

"And what might that be?"

"Under no circumstances must you venture out into the darkness alone again."

"Says who?" My chin lifts in an act of false bravado, and I am not without the intelligence to see that it displeases him tremendously, which, frankly, I don't particularly care for, despite suspecting I would probably do well to be considerate of his demeanor.

"Says me," he grates, stepping forward while my eyes take a peek at his athletic frame, that is now, thankfully, fully covered appropriately, albeit rather haphazardly, the buttons of his jacket askew. He must have been in a hurry. "And no more shimmying up and down drainpipes."

I gasp. He watched me? "You knew I was visiting?" Has he been spying as I have? Why? I know my reasons—a very attractive story and mystery, something to get my teeth stuck into —but why would he have an equal fascination with me?

"Yes, I knew."

I motion up and down his body. "And you still didn't bother to dress yourself?"

His lip curls. The nerve of this man! "Do not wander round alone in the darkness," he says again, and I conclude very quickly that it is because he knows not what else to say. Good. He is tongue-tied.

I snort, and it is wholly unattractive. If he did not yet believe I am no lady, then I expect he will now. "I believe you told me to expect no kindness or chivalry." I step forward, fueled by the revelation that's struck me, as his beautiful, rough square jaw pulses wildly. "Except you just escorted me home." My face is now close to his. So close, I can feel the heat of his breath. This is so utterly forbidden. Inappropriate. Wrong. Yet whatever we are to call it, I must confess it is rousing something odd inside me.

He knows not what to do with me as I stand before him, his tall body towering over me, stating facts that contradict his actions. I do believe I have rendered the wily Duke speechless. "Care to contest that, Your Grace?" His eyes, oh how they burn. They burn with infuriation, for I have questioned his actions. And they burn with something else, something unfamiliar and yet riveting.

"I care not," he murmurs, his gaze falling upon my lips.

"Then I do believe our matters for this evening have reached a satisfactory conclusion." The power I feel in this moment could never be rivaled. To have reduced a man of such a reputation to wordlessness is quite a feat, and I am proud for holding my own. "Good evening, Your Grace," I whisper, slowly turning away from him and taking hold of the drainpipe.

"Eliza," he warns as I hop up. "I demand you release it at once."

I ignore him and make fast work of climbing it, extending my leg and toeing the window open before hooking my leg over the edge and pulling myself through. I look out as I take the wood to push it down, seeing him glaring up at me, unimpressed. I scowl and slam the window shut.

And am attacked by merciless shakes. "Good heavens,"

I whisper, willing some feeling back into my legs to take me to my bed. I collapse, feeling boneless, breathless and nervous. It is in this moment I realize, without question, that I want to let him indulge me. Pleasure me. I cannot fathom a feeling more exhilarating than what I am feeling in this moment, this curiosity, as unexpected as it is, ruling me. My goodness, what just happened?

I fall to my back on the mattress and stare at the ornate ceiling, my hand resting lightly on my chest. I can still feel the pounds. My skin is still heated. And my mouth dry. I'm totally parched.

I get up, remove my boots, and pad down to the kitchen. As I pass my father's study, I hear rip-roaring laughter, and the irritating sound brings me to a stop. "Melrose," Lord Lymington slurs. "How does the fifteenth sound? Will you have tamed the shrew by then, because Frederick here is growing tired of her escapades."

"You have my word, Your Grace," Father says surely.

I stare, utterly dumbstruck, at the open space before me. *His* word? What about *my* word, for surely that is required also if I am to be wedded? I sneak back to the door. It is ajar, and I peek through the crack. Father is by the fireplace smoking, and Lymington is slumped in a chair by the roaring fire. I cannot see or hear anyone else, as my vision, unfortunately, is hampered.

"Good. It would be a shame to have to halt the progress of our deal," he mutters.

"That won't be necessary."

"Good. What is the time?" Lymington feels down his chest, patting for his pocket watch. It's all I can do not to snigger when I see him look at his quizzing glass, like it might enlighten him. *Idiot.*

I force my feet to move, to take me away before I unceremoniously burst in and declare my displeasure and embarrass my father in front of half of the male members of the *ton*. He is a good man, my father. Devoted, loving, semi-reasonable. I can only conclude that he's suffering a temporary loss of sanity. To pawn off his offspring. To laugh with these pompous idiots.

I guzzle down water ravenously and rush back to my bedroom before my temptations get the better of me, and I'm halfway up the stairs when I hear the front door open. "Eliza?" Frank says, his tone full of questions. "I thought you'd retired to your bedroom?"

I cringe but ensure all signs of guilt are wiped from my face before I face my brother. It is only a mild consolation that he is not among the guests in my father's study. "I had."

He shuts the door quietly, eyeing me with a curiosity I am not comfortable with. "And you're yet to undress?"

Damn it. "And I was under the impression that you were sharing after-dinner drinks and snuff with Father and his wonderful new friends."

"You divert well, sister."

"As do you. Where have you been?"

"Where have *you* been?"

My fingers become stiff, clawing around the wooden handrail of the staircase. "I simply have not yet got to the chore of undressing, that is all." I take no pleasure from lying to my brother. None at all. "I found myself lost in a book."

His eyebrow quirks. "Be careful, Eliza," he warns quietly, coming to the bottom of the stairs.

"Of what?"

"You are a desirable young lady here for her first season in London."

"And what of it?"

"I expect you will be in the sights of many unsuitable suitors. Just remember—"

"Do not tell me I'll die if I kiss a man before I am married, Frank."

"You will most certainly die if you kiss a man before you are married."

I laugh but quickly quieten myself down. "Oh, behave, will you? I fear, brother, that both you *and* Papa need to consider the possibility that no respectable lord or gentleman will willingly take on *me* and my *escapades*." I cannot bring myself to imagine that perhaps Frank might know of this deal. *All at a price.*

"Escapades?" he asks. "Why, Eliza, what *have* you been up to?"

I fidget, no matter how hard I try to hide my guilt. I am a fool unto myself. I have never been able to hide anything from Frank. He has an uncanny—and annoying—ability to see straight through me. "Me? I am not the one sneaking into our house at such an hour." *No, instead I used my initiative and scaled a drainpipe.*

Now, Frank laughs. "I am not sneaking, Eliza." He climbs the stairs, passing me. "I've simply met some friends at Gladstone's."

"Oh, the posh new gentleman's club?" I say, moving back to let him pass, my eyes following his smug form. "Quite a world apart from the old inn where you'd drink ale and shout raucously like a heathen." I catch a whiff of something. "Is that perfume?"

He stops. Silent.

"It is, isn't it?" I get closer, having a good, thorough sniff of my brother. The subtle hint of lavender on his jacket is unmistakable. "Do your friends wear ladies' perfume?"

"I can only assume it's come from one of Mother's friends after they greeted me earlier this eve." He continues on his way. "Good night, sister."

"Good night, brother," I say quietly, my mind racing. I have a strong urge to go to the dining room to smell each and every one of the ladies around the dining room table.

I do believe my brother is up to no good.

But with whom?

Could he be desiring a lady as unsuitable for him as I desire a man so unsuitable for me? Good God, the notion is both pleasing and worrisome, because with Clara falling for the stable boy also, Papa will drop dead with horror.

Chapter 7

I am awoken by the sounds of a commotion. Accusing shouts, yells of protest, and I sit up in my bed, somewhat disorientated, just as Mama bursts into my bedroom in her nightgown.

"It's a robbery," she gasps, dashing to the window and pulling back the draperies a tiny bit. "Right on Belmore Square!"

The shouts and yells continue as I shuffle to the edge of my mattress and join Mama, pulling my chemise down. "Who has been robbed and by whom?" I ask sleepily, looking down onto the street, where a young boy is being held by the scruff of his neck. "That's the stable boy," I say, taking in the rest of the scene, which is all rather messy and chaotic. Lymington is waving a hand around in quite a deranged fashion, and the poor boy cowers each time the Duke's hand comes close, like he is afraid he might be clipped around the ear at any moment.

"He has stolen the Duke's pocket watch."

My thoughts take me back to last night when I was unfortunate enough to overhear—and by no means eavesdrop—a wholly untasteful conversation. "His pocket watch?" I say quietly, watching, quite horrified, as a constable shakes the boy, as if by doing so, Lymington's pocket watch will be dislodged from wherever he is hiding it and drop to the ground. Of course, it won't.

I leave my bedroom and pace through the house, having frowns thrown at me from left and right by the staff. I am too outraged to consider the reason for their apparent shock. I burst into Papa's study and am immediately hit with the stale stench of alcohol mixed with an ungodly vile smell of tobacco. I go to the chair where I saw the Duke slumped last night and start feeling down the sides of the cushions.

"Eliza, what on earth are you doing?" Mother says from behind me.

I look back, continuing with my search down the back of the chair, to see she has now got her night coat on over her nightdress and a nightcap atop her head.

Decent.

I find nothing. "Damn it all to hell!" I mutter but then still. The thud. The thud I heard before Lymington left the dining room yesterday eve. I rush across the hall, dropping to my hands and knees and combing the floor under the table. Nothing. So I extend my search, not prepared to give up, certain—

Something glimmers at me from beneath the sideboard, and I crawl over, reaching under, my faced squished to the carpet.

"Eliza!" Mother shrieks.

"I've got it!" I yell, hoping the entire square will hear my calls for the boy's release. "I have the pocket watch!"

I jump up and make a mad dash for the front door, swinging it open. "Release the boy," I demand, holding up the pocket watch. I find Papa and Frank on the steps, and they look back, both of their foreheads wrinkled, so I explain. "The boy did not steal the Duke's pocket watch."

"He did!" Lymington insists, claiming the boy from the constable and shaking him. "I demand justice!"

"There *will* be justice," I murmur, taking the steps down to the cobbles and presenting the Duke, who looks damned indignant, with his pocket watch. "I believe you may have misplaced it in our dining room yesterday evening, Your Grace," I say as he lifts his quizzing glass and inspects the shiny silver piece. "This is yours, is it not?"

I see color creep into the Duke's cheeks, but I will not further his embarrassment, not because I pity him, but because

I simply cannot bring myself to shame my father by calling out the Duke. "An easy mistake to make, Your Grace," I say, dropping the watch into his hand. "I'm sure a few shillings to the boy will compensate him for his trauma."

"What?" Lymington blurts, looking up at me. I tilt my head, certain my eyes are projecting warning. "Oh, yes. Of course." He turns to the boy, who, poor thing, looks quite the frightened animal. I should assure him, it is not he who is the animal around here. The Duke holds out a shilling to the boy, and he accepts gratefully. One measly shilling? I clear my throat, and the Duke peeks at me.

"Oh God," my Father breathes quietly from behind.

I smile at the Duke, eyeing his coin purse, prompting him to delve back into the velvet pouch.

"How much does Mr. Fitzgerald pay you?" I ask the boy.

"Five shillings, my lady."

"I think ten will cover it."

The tight-fisted Duke nearly chokes, rendering him unable to contest my suggested donation.

"He has suffered quite an unfortunate injury, Your Grace," I say, flicking my eyes to the boy, my voice strong. "Haven't you?"

A moment's pause and a frown before he cottons on. "My neck," he spits out quickly, playing my game as he feels at his nape.

"His neck," I repeat on a nod. "Strained, I expect. I imagine his work as Mr. Fitzgerald's stable boy may be hindered for at least a week. Five shillings to cover his loss of earnings, and five for the inconvenience." I paint a smile on my face. "I would hate to see such a clumsy error aired in tomorrow's newspaper."

"Lord above, she'll bankrupt me," Father whispers as Lymington, with a face caught between graciousness and umbrage, coughs up, and the boy, after bowing his head in respect that the Duke is not worthy of, dashes off.

"Good day," I say, turning on my…bare feet? I look down. Bare feet. I feel at my stomach as I lift my eyes, finding Frank and Papa, who both look bewildered and are blinking rapidly, unmoving on the steps of our house. *Oh no.*

I am quite indecent, standing in broad daylight on the street in only my chemise. Smiling nervously, I look over my shoulder, finding a few people have gathered, and I fear it is not to witness the trial of the stable boy.

"Eliza, get inside the house," Papa hisses, but I hardly hear him. I cannot see much either now, for on the other side of the road, standing alone, is Johnny Winters, looking absolutely magnificent in a green velvet jacket that makes his eyes twinkle. The twinkle is wicked, and he stares at me, not in shock or horror as I expect the rest of my spectators are looking at me. No. His expression is entirely different. It's brooding. Lustful. And I am frozen.

On the street.

Half dressed.

In front of one too many members of the ton. My mind carries me back to yesterday evening, to his house, his study. To the feelings that overcame me. This man, this bold, rude, prohibited, unlawful, tainted man, makes my heart boom and my blood rush.

And it is utterly wonderful, I think, smiling secretly.

"Eliza!"

I jump, ripping my eyes from the Duke of Chester, being brought back down to earth with an enormous wallop. It seems in my desperation and urgency to serve justice, I neglected to remember to dress myself. How unfortunate.

I drop my eyes to my bare feet and disappear into our house, passing Mother in the main hallway. I risk a peek at her, smiling my apologies, for she will not hear the last of this from Papa. She nods, holding back her own smile of reassurance—or is that amusement?—as the door slams.

"My God, I will be a laughingstock!" Papa cries. "What were you thinking? Is it your sole purpose to ruin me, Eliza?" His head goes into his hands, his despair palpable. I find no joy in seeing my father so desolate, I must admit. "Good grief, how many times must I remind you that we are no longer in the countryside?"

Every hour, it would appear. "I'm sure your reputation will be perfectly intact," I say, looking at Frank, who is silent on the sidelines, but he, like Mama, is struggling terribly to hold back his amusement. Oh good. I am not the only one around here that is exasperated by the increasing need to impress. Father is worrying unduly. It is too early for many of the residents of Belmore Square to be awake, let alone dressed and out and about. With social events to attend most evenings, the nights are long and the days short during a London season. Although, admittedly, I felt the drapes at many windows twitching. "I think I will go to my room," I say, removing myself before Papa explodes with anxiety. Clara is at the top of the stairs in her nightdress, rubbing at her sleepy eyes. My little sister, since she was a babe in our mother's arms, has always slept like a log, even through the wildest of storms. The poor, oblivious thing has no idea that I just saved the *love of her life* from being imprisoned.

Naturally, upon arrival to my safe, private room, I go to the window and find the crowds have dispersed and Belmore Square now looks exactly how it should do at ten o'clock in the morning.

Quiet.

Come noon, carriages will appear, ladies will be leaving for their daily promenade in the royal park, and gentlemen will venture out for their regular trot and business meetings, before the eve arrives and partygoers emerge. What was Johnny Winters doing up and about at this early hour?

I hear a light knock on my door before it opens, and Mama

looks at me with much sorrow as I breathe out, cross my arms, and return my attention to the view across the square. "I cannot marry Frederick, Mama."

"Oh, my darling girl, I wish I could agree."

"Why can you not?" I ask, feeling her arm wrap around my shoulders and pull me into her side as she stands with me at the window. "I know ladies must marry suitably, but a *forced* arranged marriage is obsolete, Mama. You know that."

"Then do not make him force you."

"It is unfair and unethical." I look at her, and she smiles in that soft way she always used to but seems to have lost since our arrival for my first season here in London.

"You have always been partial to a moral battle. Do you remember when you declared you would be applying to attend Eton?" She chuckles. "Your father didn't bargain for a bright daughter, Eliza. A son, yes, but not a daughter. We could not afford the fees for Frank. Not then, so he missed out."

But they could now, and the truth is, if I were a boy, even a spare, I would be going to Eton, and perhaps following that, even Oxford. I would study any number of subjects. I would do something I loved.

Would. Would. Would.

"Come," Mother says, kissing my temple. "Let us dress. I should like to show you my new favorite shop in Mayfair. It comes highly recommended by Lady Tillsbury." She flounces out of my bedroom, as Emma enters and fills the bowl on my dresser with fresh hot water.

"Thank you," I murmur, and Emma, hesitant in her stance, pauses at the door, smiling back at me.

"It was a very honorable thing you did there, Miss Eliza. I must thank you."

"Honorability is pointless when you're a female, Emma. Especially a female of a certain status."

"Well, it was not pointless to me."

I tilt my head in question. "Do you know the stable boy, Emma?" I ask.

"He's my son, my lady."

"Oh." Holy hell, Clara is in love with Mama's maid's son? This gets more unfortunate by the minute.

Emma nods and leaves, and I wash and dress, silent and contemplative, thinking of many things I perhaps should not be thinking about—namely, the Duke of Chester—before meeting Mama downstairs. There is no need for me to inquire about my father's whereabouts. I know he's most likely drowning his sorrows—me—in alcohol already. Mother reaches for his study door and pulls it shut silently, glancing at me with a look to suggest I would do well to escape now, before nodding for Emma to open the front door.

Daylight streams in and my breath streams out, ready to face the world and the inevitable whispers of my morning capers. Picking up the bottom of her coat, Mama takes the steps and sets off down the street, head held high. I expect it is false bravado, but I am still appreciative of her apparent disregard. I follow, while attempting also to follow her approach to the unfortunate matter of me prancing around in an unacceptable amount of clothing, and ensure my smile remains fixed in place.

"Miss Melrose," Lord Hamsley greets, nodding as he passes me.

"My lord," I reply, hardly looking up.

"Miss Melrose," Mr. Simpson, resident of number four Belmore Square and a famed builder of ships, says, tipping his hat. "Good morning to you."

"Good morning, Mr. Simpson." I smile, though it is strained.

"Miss Melrose." Mr. Casper sings, more or less bowing before me. Mr. Casper is a lawyer who resides at number five and also father's confidant in all matters of business.

"Mr. Casper," I murmur, my eyes narrowing as I pass his delighted form.

Delighted by seeing me? "Whatever is wrong with everyone this morning?" I say to myself, looking back over my shoulder, seeing they, too, are looking back at me.

"I expect they are feeling quite regretful that you have ventured out this time *fully* clothed."

I swing round and find a rueful smile plastered across the beautiful face of Lady Dare. "Oh dear. You heard about that," I say, disliking, but very much unable to stop, the heat rising in my cheeks.

She laughs, a laugh I expect makes men weak at the knees, and fiddles with her gloves. Does it make Johnny Winters weak at the knees? Perhaps not, for I am privy to his adequately sturdy legs, because he, like me it would seem, likes to parade around half naked too. Bugger it all, he was there this morning, seeing me in all my mortifying glory.

I walk on, cross with myself and my annoying habit of taking action before putting my mind to it.

"I expect the whole of London has already heard." Lady Dare falls into stride beside me, her gloved hands now clasped, all fiddling ceased, and her body moves with a grace that should be impossible wearing dresses such as these. "I must warn you, Miss Melrose."

"Of what?"

"There is only room for one adventuress on this square."

I shoot her a shocked look. Is this wildly confident, unconventional woman threatened? "I'm not sure I understand."

Smiling brightly, revealing extremely white teeth, Lady Dare slows to a stop, prompting me to also, and turns her bright eyes my way. Her small nose wrinkles, her gloved hand reaching for my dress coat and tweaking a button that does not need to be tweaked. "How very odd," she says quietly. "I must be mistaken."

"About what, my lady?" I ask, my voice becoming tight. I am sure I do not like her persona, nor her tone, nor her look of false friendliness.

"Well, you see," she laughs, and it has an air of flirtation to it. Need I remind Lady Dare that she is, in fact, conversing with a fellow female who is immune to her tactics, and not any one of the gentlemen who reside here on Belmore Square, who I expect take on a rather pathetic form of dazzlement around her frosty beauty. "I thought, since you are an intelligent lady"—she looks me up and down, and it is, and is meant to be, haughty—"your public antics may have been a scheme to win the attention of many men."

"I can assure you, my intentions were nothing of the sort. I merely saw an injustice transpiring, and I was compelled to step in and halt it." Win the attention of many men? Never! But Lady Dare's assumptions certainly cast light on how her mind functions. I shall bear that in mind in future, when I see her wafting her skirt with a little too much oomph, perhaps with the intention of revealing a glimmer of her laced-edged pantalettes. *Tart.*

"Nearly naked." Her painted eyebrows lift as Viscount Millingdale trots past on horseback, smiling down at me. Me! Not the illustrious, notorious adventuress Lady Dare, but me. I shudder, the old man's eyes creeping all over me. Miss Austen may have had her tongue firmly stuffed in her cheek when she wrote it, but she was, it would appear, correct. Should a woman have the hardship of having any knowledge on any*thing*, she should disguise it, and disguise it well. It would appear revealing you have a brain could be fatal. Revealing your body while also revealing a brain? Christ, I am on course to get myself into all kinds of trouble, as well as killing off Papa.

But forgetting my semi-naked escapades for just a moment, let us resolve the problem at hand. Lady Dare's problem, I hasten to add, not mine. I inhale, taking on an air of indifference. "My lady," I say over a sigh. "You need not worry. I prefer to flaunt my mind over my body."

She cannot hide the fleeting wave of indignation that floats across her face. "I'm not sure I appreciate your insinuation."

"You shouldn't," I say, clipped and strong, passing her. I recant my previous thoughts. I do not admire, neither do I like Lady Dare. "Good day to you." I get a strong waft of lavender as I pass, and it brings me to a sharp stop before I can find my stride. God, no. *Frank!* Is there no man safe from her clutches? I should like to warn her to stay away, and yet, I admit, I would only be enticing her if I were to reveal any hint of my displeasure. That is a storm I shall have to ride out, for it won't last forever. Like every other man who has ever been caught in her web, my brother will be cast aside for the next victim.

I hope.

I *pray.*

And who is her next victim? I look across the square to the Winters house. I expect that ship has sailed. But will it sail again?

Chapter 8

I must hand it to Mother, she looks sublime in her new gown, the royal blue taffeta frills complementing her dark hair beautifully. She and Papa, who is still refusing to talk to me, leave ahead of us, since a carriage is not required for this evening's party, which is a stone's throw from our own house. Mr. Fitzgerald, it is rumored, has put on quite a spectacle at his home, and anyone who is anyone in London will be in attendance. It is no wonder Mama has lavished herself with a new gown, and Papa has splashed out on a new pair of breeches and a matching jacket in a blue velvet that complements Mama's dress. They look quite the expensive couple. I expect Frank will be sporting some new garb also, but since I am yet to encounter him today, I cannot confirm. I expect he is avoiding me, and so he should, the rake! What is he thinking, cavorting with the likes of Lady Dare?

Clara is looking pretty in pink this evening, but her mood is somber. She was thrilled, of course, that I saved her love from persecution, but quick on the heels of her joy came sorrow, for in that moment, she became privy to the impossibilities of loving an unsuitable someone. Her romanticizing over the stable boy was never going to end well, but—and I do not wish to appear coldhearted—the sooner she realized that, the better. The less hurt she will suffer.

"Must we go?" Clara says, sounding as grim as she appears. "I have no desire to pretend to be happy."

"We must," I say, brushing down the front of my silver-blue

dress, smiling at the irony of this situation and how the roles have reversed. Just a week or two ago, it was I who was reluctant and unwilling, and Clara who was full of beans. Perhaps now I have an ally in my sister, someone who understands my plight, though for different reasons, of course. "At least you do not have to endure the motions of being courted by a man you do *not* desire."

"Desire?" she says, accepting my arm when I hold it up for her to link. We leave the house and walk together around the square to Mr. Fitzgerald's home. "I do not desire him, Eliza. I love him!"

"If one loves, one tends to desire the person they love." I smile down at my dear, naïve sister.

"You mean pleasure," she whispers, her lips straightening to hide her grin. "Don't you?"

"What do you know of pleasure?" I swallow, thinking about the tingles that engulf me whenever I think about the Duke. And the throb I feel between my legs when I see him. *Just a myth.*

Clara rolls her eyes. "You and Frank think I'm stupid. Well, if I am stupid, so are you two." She drops her hold of me. "You, writing articles about that duke. What are you, obsessed? And Frank cavorting with that Dare woman."

I ignore her first accusation, naturally, and home in on her second. "What do you know of Frank cavorting?"

"I was worried about Lizzy Fallow, the harlot, but Lady Dare?" Her lips press into a straight line. "He is heading for trouble."

I stop and grab her shoulders. "Clara, for Christ's sake, what do you know of Frank cavorting with Lady Dare?" Has she seen them?

Her eyes narrow. "What happened to variety in your writing, because all I'm seeing these days are words about that murdering Duke."

I recoil. "There's not much variety around here." My eyes fall on the window of the Winters house and I get us moving again.

"He murdered his family, you know, Eliza," she says. "Burned them alive and fled London pretending to have perished with them."

"There is no proof of that, Clara."

"Except he looks as dangerous as he is claimed to be."

Ridiculous. The only danger the Duke of Chester appears to pose is a danger to my heart, for it feels like it could explode each time I encounter him.

"Eve Hamsley told me she overheard her father talking to Lymington, and he saw it happen!"

"What?" I whisper as we pass the Winters residence. "He saw Johnny Winters burn his family alive?"

"Indeed, he did. We should have taken the longer route," she says, increasing her pace and rushing past, as though Johnny might emerge at any moment and throw flames at us. God, how desperate I am to ask the Duke about his family. "Apparently the whole of the square will be in attendance this evening," she goes on as we round the gardens to Mr. Fitzgerald's home.

I laugh. "I can guarantee you, Clara, the whole square will *not* be in attendance."

"I am not lying!"

"Will the Duke of Chester be there?" I ask, cocking my head when we slow to a stop.

She waves my question off as if it is a stupid one. I suppose it is, but she isn't far wrong, because, it would appear that everyone *is* here. Except, of course, Winters. It would seem the wily Duke is being ostracized, at least by the gentry. The ladies? I bet they wouldn't mind an appearance from him.

I take a deep breath, remove my coat and hat and hand it to the waiting manservant, swoop up a glass of Champagne from a tray and float into the room, smiling. Inevitably, I am soon found by Frederick and the telling-off I have been bracing myself for ensues.

"I must insist you refrain from bringing shame upon my family's name," he blathers, and I inwardly roll my eyes. I also realize in this moment that the lack of scorn from my father is probably because he deems me the problem of another man, now that I am courting.

I purse my lips and smile tightly. "Excuse me, Frederick, but I have Champagne to drink and partygoers to insult." I walk away, shaking with anger, and it doesn't improve when I spot Frank entering, looking as dashing as ever. I come to a stop by Countess Rose, whose face does not appear as alarmingly ugly in candlelight as it does in daylight. It's a frightfully good thing, since Mr. Fitzgerald's house is packed to the rafters with people, all of whom are rather close to one another.

"Miss Melrose," the Countess croons, not having to say another word. Just the tone in which she spoke my name screamed disapproval. So she's heard of my escapades too, has she?

"Countess," I purr, half curtseying, making a sharp escape before I'm subjected to her sharp tongue, my target—my brother —in my sights. Unfortunately, he spots me before I can corner him and interrogate him and makes a hasty getaway, swiping up a drink and disappearing into a crowd of gentlemen. "Bugger it," I mutter.

"Bugger what?"

I groan under my breath, slap on a smile, and face Lady Dare. "How lovely to see you," I say through my teeth. "Wish I could stop and chitchat." I am making a hasty getaway to rival Frank's. I've done nothing but run away since I arrived, to avoid people. In fact, there is not a single person here whom I wish to converse with, only my brother, and since he is apparently avoiding me—the guilty git—I am questioning why on earth I am enduring this. I am certain I am no longer the prospective bride of the Earl of Cornwall after shaming him so thoroughly, so I may as well depart and do everyone a favor, as it seems I am not well versed in socializing. In fact, I am not well versed at much around here.

I drink my Champagne and go to the window, sighing as I look out onto the square. I cannot leave. I could never explain. Perhaps I could feign illness. After all, I didn't eat at lunch, nor at teatime, as I was bathing and, frankly, avoiding my father.

"Eliza?"

I still and tense at the sound of Papa's voice, and with a window before me, I have nowhere to run to. I find a smile and face him, bracing myself for a thorough dressing-down. "Yes, Papa?"

He regards me quietly for a few moments, making me shift uncomfortably, and I finally get tired of the awful silence and his quiet scrutiny. "Papa, I am sorry, I did not mean to embarrass you, but—"

"You understand, Eliza, my darling girl, that some of the freedoms that were bestowed upon you prior to our move to London cannot exist here."

I recoil, surprised. "Which freedom do you speak of, Papa, for I had many."

He smiles, and it is soft. "I am no longer only answerable to myself, Eliza. I have a business partner now."

He's talking about my stories. He knows. "I realize that, Papa."

A mild nod, a thoughtful pout, and he reaches for my cheek and strokes it. "My beautiful, headstrong baby girl." I try to smile and fail, and he retracts his hand. "I must find your mother." He backs away, leaving me feeling bereft, and I turn back to the window, but before I can let my tears of frustration fall, I spy something by the corner entrance of the gardens. Or some*one*. I gulp, and the tingles, God love those tingles, are back with a vengeance, my grievance forgotten.

He steps forward, bringing himself into the moonlight, his hands held behind his back, his eyes, which I can see with delightful clarity, smoky. Wicked. Dangerous.

Unfathomably irresistible.

I look behind me to the party guests. I could spend a week with these people, nonstop, and still not experience even a whisper of the exhilaration that I felt in just a second of the Duke's company. I am definitely, without question, going mad. I finish my drink, perhaps for a little added courage, and slip away, praying my absence will not be noticed anytime soon. If it is, I will lie and inform my interrogators that I came over all hot and faint and, to avoid embarrassing anyone should I be unfortunate enough to swoon, was forced to step outside and get some air. I nod my agreement to myself, ignoring the possibility that no one will believe me, since what the hell do I care if I embarrass anyone, and make my escape.

I close the door, lift my dress, and take the steps down to the street. I shiver, the nighttime air brisk and stinging, biting my skin, and I realize, in my urgency, I have completely forgotten my coat. "Bloody hell," I say, my teeth chattering, my skin becoming chicken-like, every hair standing on end. I am certain if it were not for the red staining them—the only makeup I will wear—my lips would be a rather unfetching shade of blue, but the second I look up and my eyes meet his burning stare, my frozen body is forgotten, and in the place of chills come sparks. Sparks that warm me to my bones.

The Duke shakes his head, scowling unhappily. "Eliza, you will catch your death," he says, striding toward me, removing his gray velvet jacket as he does. "What are you thinking?"

"There was no time to collect my belongings, and it would have provoked questions as to where I may be venturing alone and, worse, with whom." I let him drape his jacket around my shoulders, the move bringing him oh so very close. I am now frozen for an entirely different cause, and it would seem the Duke has been rendered inert also, his big, capable hands holding the tops of my arms. My nose is invaded by his manly scent, a heady intoxicating mix of Scotch and his natural fragrance, and my eyes are rooted to the vast expanse of his chest just a mere few inches away. I have absolutely no control of my mind or my body around this man. It's arousing. It's alarming. It's… dangerous.

I find myself stepping back, and his hands fall like stones to his side. I am immediately regretful of my move, not only because the absence of his touch physically pains me, but because I have provoked an unquestionable fleeting look of irritation on his otherworldly face. He was enjoying our closeness too.

"Worse, with whom?" he says, his irritation flaring. I find no joy in his apparent disgust, and a strong blush lands on my cheeks, surely sending them pink.

"I am promised to another man!" I blurt like a fool. "I mean—"

"Frederick Lymington is not a man, Eliza. He is a blithering idiot, and I do not wish to speak of him."

"Oh," I whisper, with a lack of anything more appropriate to say. He is not mistaken, though, as Frederick is somewhat of a blithering idiot. A judgmental one, too. "You do not like him?"

"I do not like anyone who speaks ill of me."

I laugh. "Then you mustn't like anyone," I say, but immediately regret it when anger replaces the irritation. "I mean—"

"Perhaps you should not speak at all," he suggests.

"Then why am I here, if not to speak?"

"You tell me, Miss Melrose. I was simply taking an evening stroll when I saw you running toward me half-dressed."

I stare at him in disbelief. I accept, he may not have directly ordered me to come to him, but his body language certainly did. And his eyes. They most certainly spoke to me, yet his intentions are ambiguous. However, whatever his motives for enticing me into his personal space, I should have resisted. I am surer than I have ever been that if my mother, or, God save me, my father, or any member of the ton, for that matter, were to become privy to my liaisons with the disgraced Duke, I would be persecuted. Perhaps even sent away in shame. *What a scandal!*

I ponder that for a moment. *Sent away.* From here. From all of this fluffy nonsense of matchmaking, suitors and status. Good heavens, I must shake those selfish thoughts from my mind without delay. "Then I shall leave you in peace, Your Grace, so you are no longer forced to endure the apparent trauma from my lack of dress," I say, unceremoniously flinging his jacket off my shoulders and pivoting, now too angry to suffer the effects of the cold on my skin. *The idiot!* Why I spent hours pondering this man is beyond me. I do, however, know that I shall waste no more of my contemplations on him.

"But half-dressed is apparently your favorite state of dress, if a man is to make assumptions based on a lady's behavior."

I halt, feeling my nostrils flare, and I swing around, ready to give this yellow-livered arrogant fool a piece of my mind. "I was simp— oh!" I crash into his body, ricocheting back. "Bugger it all," I murmur.

"A lady should not use such language."

"We have been over this, Your Grace. I am no lady."

"Perhaps that is a blessing."

"Trust me, it is not," I say over a laugh, putting more space between us once again. "Now, would you be so kind to inform me of why I am here."

"Because you're attracted to me, of course. I thought you were a bright woman, Eliza."

My eyes widen. "I told you, I am pr—"

"Yes, yes, I know. Promised to another." He shakes his head, exasperated. "Your challenge would be met with respect, if there was any sincerity in the reasoning for you brandishing such a ridiculous statement." On a huff, he scoops up his jacket and drapes it across my shoulders again before claiming my hand and leading my stunned form through the entrance of the gardens. His big hand envelops mine completely. A man has never held my hand before. It feels rather nice. Warm. Safe. Capable.

Capable of what?

Murder?

"What do you think you're doing?" I hiss, my sanity finding me, and I try in vain to prize his grip away, but his strength, of course, far outweighs mine. "You cannot manhandle me, you big ape!"

"Ape?" He laughs, and the sound is nothing short of breathtaking. Deep, rumbling, tingle-inducing. "I have been called many derogatory names in my time, Eliza, by many a man, but never an ape by a lady."

Men? Just men? "First time for everything," I mutter, completely at the mercy of his power, and yet I defiantly resist, digging my heels in, for what use it is. What do ladies usually call him then?

"There is," he says quietly. "Am I going to have to throw you over my shoulder?"

I gasp. "You would never."

Another laugh, and then in a collection of fast, expert moves, I'm suddenly whisked off my feet and draped over his shoulder. "My God," I yelp, bouncing up and down in time to his strides. He really is an ape!

"Are you referring to Him or to me?"

My jaw goes lax, my body tense from top to toe, vehemently fighting off those blasted tingles. "You are something else."

"But you like me, yes?"

"No, I absolutely do not."

He laughs again. "You, Eliza Melrose, are quite a delight."

"I wish I could say the same for you," I mutter. "Will you put me down!"

"It may have escaped your notice, but I am without a jacket, and it is bloody freezing. Forgive me, but I cannot hang around all night waiting for you to decide whether or not you can cope with the monstrous challenge of being in my company again. I have a roaring fire desperate for some companionship if you don't mind."

"I do mind."

"You are exasperating."

"But you like me, yes?" I say, with far too much cockiness for a woman in my physical position, an unstoppable grin finding me. It's quick to disappear when his hand squeezes my thigh over my dress, though.

And the tingles transform into explosions.

"For my sins, sweet Eliza, yes, I do happen to be rather taken."

"How unfortunate for you," I say on a swallow, staring at the swell of his rather pleasingly formed derrière. I did not anticipate such frankness, I must admit, and I wonder what I am to do with it.

"For both of us," he says, so quietly I expect he did not wish to be heard, and yet, I did hear him. And more than that, I heard the regret.

I am not blessed with more conversation, which I find a shame, for it was somewhat riveting. Neither am I blessed with the choice to walk for myself, which I find not to be so much of a shame. I feel weightless upon the Duke's shoulder. It is a pleasing feeling of uninhibitedness that I have come to forget in recent weeks, since Papa has moved us from the unassuming yet pleasant estate where I have lived since I was a babe in arms.

Naturally I am somewhat wary as I am carried through the gardens across Belmore Square, as I expect any one of the residents could peer out of a window and spy us, but, I remind myself, and it is undeniably a bloody good thing, most of the residents are in attendance at Mr. Fitzgerald's party, therefore otherwise engaged with matters of socializing.

"You were not invited to Mr. Fitzgerald's?" I ask casually, fishing for more information.

"I was not." The Duke stops rather abruptly on a quiet curse, and I conclude that he too, and it is a mild comfort, is concerned about the potential of being spotted.

"What is it?" I ask, trying to crane my head to see.

"Hush now," he orders harshly, moving, and we are suddenly surrounded by green.

"We're in the bushes!" I exclaim, wriggling upon his shoulder. It is terrible enough to be with him, least of all *on* him, and now we are unashamedly hiding in the bushes? For the love of everything, this is a disaster! I wish to assert that there would be nothing odd about taking an evening stroll with a companion, but, regretfully, I cannot. The Duke, quite clearly, is not Frederick. Whether walking with the Duke in a respectable fashion and with a chaperone, or being carted unceremoniously by him unchaperoned, just the mere fact I am in his company would be something of a scandal.

"You are very challenging, Eliza."

"As are you. Now put me down or, I swear, I will scream and have half of London descending to discover you man-handling—" my mouth snaps shut.

"Yes," the Duke says as Lady Dare floats by. She is dressed to kill in an exasperatingly striking purple gown that should but doesn't defy her skin tone. I feel sick to my stomach, and I fear how fabulous she looks in that fancy frock is not the cause for my overwhelming feeling of nausea. My mind's eye cruelly takes me back to the evening when I had the misfortune of seeing her calling upon the Duke. I am not comforted by the fact that he did not answer her call, for I have heard the rumors about the man whom I am currently draped over.

Rake.

One night with the Duke is something every available lady within a rather expansive radius, possibly stretching into Europe, or maybe even beyond, should like to experience, and many unavailable ladies, too, I expect. I do not wish to marry, but I also do not wish to surrender myself to a man who will steal my virtue and cast me aside for his next victim. He is the male equivalent of Lady Dare, except of a higher status. *They are made for each other!* My nose wrinkles. "I should like you to put me down."

"I should like you to stop fighting, but we do not all get our way, do we, Eliza?"

"It is Miss Melrose to you, Your Grace."

"Oh please," he mutters, getting us back on our way. "Do not insult me with formalities now." He once again squeezes my thigh, and I once again stiffen from top to toe. It is as if he has established that a mere touch will render me incapable of contesting his advances, and, unfortunately, he would be right. Bugger it all, fire races through me unstoppably and those darn tingles attack—they *attack*—and I am helpless. This is a catastrophe of the greatest proportions.

"Where are we going, anyway?" I mutter, continuing to bob up and down, at the mercy of his strength.

"To my home."

"Why?"

"I should like to talk to you."

"Talk?"

"What else would you suggest we do?"

"I do not like your tone, Your Grace," I say, although, I have to admit, I am feeling somewhat exhausted by this tiring back and forth game we seem to be playing. "From what I have heard, talking is not something a lady should expect from the rakish Duke of Chester."

"As you kindly keep reminding me, Miss Melrose, you are not a lady."

And to that, I have absolutely nothing to say. I have somehow managed to talk myself into a corner, and I know not how to talk myself out of it. So I shall, for my own sake, remain mute. It's disconcerting, for I could, according to my father, talk myself out of even the trickiest of situations. He has also claimed that my mouth would get me into trouble. He is correct.

Only once the Duke has got us into the privacy of his home

does he do me the kindness of setting me on my own, albeit unstable, two feet again. I am unable to look at him, for to look at him may be to ignite those newfound tingles, and I am truly fearful that they may lead me astray. I am apparently incapable of thinking sensibly when I am being indulged by his pleasing green eyes. So, yes, I shall avoid them at all costs.

I spend a stupidly long time brushing down the front of my dress after he removes his jacket from my shoulders, but he does not put it back on, rather hands it to Hercules, who, after brandishing an unmistakably concerned expression, silently leaves us with a nod. *Yes, I am foolish.*

"Where would you like me?" I ask, spending a pleasant while, because it is so worthy of my admiration, taking in the exquisite hallway of the Duke's home.

"Do not ask me questions like that, Eliza," he replies, striding away, leaving me behind. I must think before I speak. I am wholly at a disadvantage if that is a vital necessity when in the company of the Duke, because I have always had a terrible habit of letting my mouth work before my brain.

On a sigh, I follow the Duke into the same room I was escorted to on my last unexpected visit and find him standing by the blazing fire, his hand resting on the mantelpiece, his face thoughtful. Am I expected to await instruction? Should I sit? Speak?

Exasperated, and surprisingly staunch, I say, "And what now?"

He appears to jolt, and his eyes shoot to mine. I am caught off guard, and as a result, my resolute vow to avoid eye contact is foiled. Lord, have mercy on my soul, I am a slave to his hooded gaze. I am well aware that every thought I have about the Duke is sinful, not merely because he is a known rake and a man whom every mama would warn their daughter away from, despite his title. In addition, he is thought to have committed an unthinkable crime. Perhaps that is something that should be addressed, for the Duke simply must be wondering with untameable curiosity what the hell I am doing here, but as I move toward the chair, preparing myself to speak, he beats me.

"I suppose you are privy to the rumors about me." He looks away and pours himself a Scotch from the well-appointed cabinet that is home to an impressive display of various liquors. "Would you like a drink? Wine, perhaps?" He picks up a bottle. "This one here is French. I am told it complements fruit beautifully. You will try it."

"I see no fruit." The moment I utter the words, Hercules enters with a silver platter and places it on the table that sits between the two chairs by the stone fireplace. I am taken aback by the colorful array of exotic choices.

"You are told?" I mimic, making an extremely risky move and returning my eyes to the Duke. I find him to be holding up the bottle of wine still.

"I am yet to try it." He proceeds to pour me a glass before he sets it on the table with the fruit platter. With his hand resting on the glass, he looks up at me, his bent position bringing him alarmingly close again. My back presses into the soft material of the chair and my swallow is lumpy.

"Are you always so hospitable and offer such delights to all of your guests?" I ask.

"I am not, and I do not."

"Then what makes me so special, Your Grace?"

He can only smile as he unfolds his tall, athletic body and leaves me to breathe somewhat easier than when he is close. "Back to the matter at hand."

I frown and take some wine. "What was the matter at hand?" I ask, my mind scrambled, as I have come to expect around Johnny Winters.

"The rumors about me."

"And which rumors would they be?" I ask. "I have heard many."

"I do not doubt it for a moment," he says, appearing to hold back a roll of his eyes. "But I am explicitly referring to the supposed murder of my family."

I cough over my wine and shoot him a look that I expect can only be interpreted as horror. He shifts, as awkward as could be. I do not relish making him feel uncomfortable, but if he is to brandish such statements so freely, he cannot expect anything less of me. "What of it?" I manage to croak once I have wiped the trail of wine from my chin. A lick of my lips. His eyes rest there and there alone.

"Why are you here, Eliza?" he asks, turning those green pools of fire up to my gaze. "Are you curious about the rakish, wicked Duke like all the other single young ladies and their unbearable mamas?"

"You surely do not believe me to be a fool who trusts such nonsense?" I do hope he answers appropriately. I would be outright insulted if the Duke were to tarnish me with the same brush as many of those shortsighted, gullible females.

I am disheartened when he stares at me, unmoving, with his glass at his lips. He did. He thought me naïve and gullible. "Then whatever are you doing here?" he asks, sounding as flummoxed as he looks.

"I am here because I was dragged, Your Grace," I retort curtly. "For I certainly did not travel here"—I wave an arm around, splashing the fine wine everywhere—"of my own free will."

He snorts and takes an overdue sip of Scotch, coming closer. "What claptrap. You could have, with ease, I might add, walked away."

"Pardon me?" I stand. I do not appreciate his tall frame towering over my seated form. It is intimidating, and I am not to be intimidated. Not by him, not by anyone! "How do you propose I walk away with no legs to bloody walk on?" I slam my glass down, wondering if anyone has ever made me feel so wildly irate? I think not. But this man? He has an uncanny knack of swinging me from improperly submissive, to fittingly furious.

Damn it! I cannot keep up with him, nor my emotions, and in a demonstration of how out of control I am around Johnny Winters, I prod him in his chest, a move that the Duke appears to be amused by. Well, I am very glad he is finding this exasperating situation funny. If I were not a lady, I would slap that rakish grin clean from his maddeningly handsome face. Truth is, I could not have walked away, and not because I had no damn legs to walk on. Like now. Bugger it all to hell. I lower back to the chair and claim my wine, sipping casually. "Whomever you have fed this wine to, she is quite right. It's really very nice."

A slight curve of his eyebrow softens his features. "She?"

"I am intuitive."

"That you are, Eliza. That you are." He lowers to the chair opposite me and nods to the platter of fruit, and my heart sinks a little. He did not refute my claims. "Are you hungry?" he asks.

"You seem to be well-versed in what I am or what I want, so you tell me."

His look is warning me, but rather than challenge me and start a fresh bout with words, he reaches for the platter, plucks a piece of pineapple from the selection, and slips it past his lips in the most suggestive fashion. Eyes. On. Me. "I think you are hungry," he says, swallowing, and then he's on his knees coming toward me with another piece held up, and like a puppet on his strings, my mouth falls open. He is so tall; the front of his breeches meets my knees. Eye contact. Body contact. *I am doomed.* "It appears I have discovered the secret to shutting you the hell up." He pops the fruit in my mouth on a smirk. "Chew."

And I do, making my tastebuds tingle along with the rest of my body. He has the power of touch, and he is using it like a weapon. "Now," he says, returning to his chair, leaving me to find my equilibrium. "Let us return to the matter at hand once again."

"We have already established that I do not believe the rumors about you."

"Not *all* the rumors, though. Am I right?"

"You are right, albeit a moot point. Whether you are a rake or a respectable gentleman matters not."

"No?"

"No. I am merely here for the conversation."

He laughs lightly on a shake of his head, and I find myself, quite naturally, smiling myself. It is a true smile, and I remember not a moment in recent times that I have smiled so easily. It is not only heartwarming for that reason. The Duke, if handsome under normal circumstances, is devastating when he smiles. His green eyes glimmer, and I detect a rather adorable dimple on his right cheek. But my observations aside, he is, of course, correct. We need to get back, *again*, to the matter at hand, or at the very least establish the circumstances of the rumors. Yet I am somewhat stumped by how one should address such a sensitive subject. I am certain the Duke is not guilty of the crimes he's rumored to have committed. Of course, he cannot be. He would most certainly have been arrested immediately upon his return to London. "How do you find being a duke?"

"Tiresome. How do you find being a lady?" He hitches a brow, and I smile.

"Tiresome," I reply. "If you want the truth—"

"I do."

"I had expected to be safe from the ton for at least a few seasons."

"You mean safe from the single men in need of a wife?"

"Indeed. Sadly, I fear my fate was sealed before I had even packed my case to leave for London."

His head tilts, implying interest. "You did not choose Frederick Lymington as a husband?"

I laugh. He cannot be serious. "No, I did not. Frederick is about as far from my choice as I could possibly get."

"Who would be your choice?" the Duke asks, placing an

elbow on the arm of his chair and seeming to get comfortable. "If you had a choice?"

"I would choose no man at all, of course."

"You do not want to be married?"

"Not particularly."

"You do not want children?"

Frustrated, I sigh. "I do not know what I want, and if you want the truth, which you do because you have told me as much, I am somewhat exasperated by society's persistent and, might I add, infuriating insistence that a woman is unaccepted or odd if she chooses to remain independent of a man. Worse still, at the ripe old age of nineteen, and with hardly any life experience, I am expected to want to be a wife, a mother, a lady, and Lord knows what else, so long as it fits with the rigorous criteria set down by…whom? Who made all these rules?" I take a moment to take a breath. I had expected the Duke to appear bored to tears by my tirade, but, instead, and it is quite refreshing, he appears unperturbed. In fact, he is smiling rather fondly at me. "You don't think I'm odd?"

"Not in the least. In fact, I wholeheartedly agree with you."

"You do?" I am shocked to my core.

"I do," he says simply, and on this occasion, his touch on me is not required to shut me up. "Sad as it is, though, my sweet Eliza, my opinion matters not. You are expected to marry and marry well. You are expected to bear children and raise them to be good little lords and ladies." He pauses for thought, and I am not sure I am going to appreciate those thoughts. In fact, I am certain of it. "I expect most females of your background would be delighted at the prospect of becoming a lady. A true lady, by title. You will be a countess, Eliza, and that is a title that carries a lot of clout."

"Not as much as a duchess," I say without thought, flinching because of my own clumsy words. I have not the faintest idea where they came from. "I mean…"

His forehead has taken on a confused frown, and my mind is not working nearly fast enough to talk my way out of my clumsy mishap. "I will never marry, Eliza."

"Good for you," I say grimly. "And you will never be forced to, either, so I believe your life is in a better state of affairs than mine." I do not sip my wine, but rather down the entire glass, my thoughts, words and situation making me feel so very depressed.

"I doubt that," he says quietly. "Do you have any damaging rumors following you around?"

"What, like murder?" I ask on a laugh. "And why would anyone think you murdered your family?" It is a risky question, but we are still to establish the root of the rumors, and my inquisitive brain is apparently unprepared to let the matter of his family's death go. My mind once again goes to the letter I found and read, and I eye him, wondering, again, if he knows it was me who returned it. Of course he does. What I would like to know is who sent it. And why the whispers of the ton forced him to return.

Anger appears to rise in him again, and it makes me swallow down any further questions I have and the circumstances surrounding their deaths.

"Did you attend Eton?" I ask instead.

"Yes."

"And Cambridge?"

"Oxford."

I nod, naturally envious.

"Do not be jealous," he says, and I am startled that he has read my mind. "I did not fare well at Eton."

"How so?"

"How should one put it?" he says quietly, pouting.

"Plainly."

"The schoolmaster was not all too fond of me. Or the housemaster, for that matter, and, as a consequence, I was often put in the bill."

"The flogging list," I say. "So you were idle in lessons? Rude? Obnoxious? Disobedient?"

He tilts his head, looking thoughtful.

"Well," I say, sounding matter-of-fact. "If I were to be fortunate enough to attend Eton, Cambridge *or* Oxford, I indeed would not waste that time being indolent."

"I am certain of that, Eliza," he says quietly and thoughtfully, and a long silence falls upon us. It is not a silence I find to be arduous, but rather one that is peaceful. It's a pity I cannot say the same for the constant occasions where we catch one another's eye. In those moments, I feel an unfathomably strong urge to kiss him. It's a terribly unfortunate situation and, not for the first time, I tear my gaze from his and admire the endless books on every wall.

"May I choose one for you to read?" he asks.

I shoot him a surprised look, but I'm smiling too. "I am yet to read the last one you gave me."

"You do not need to read it, Eliza, because you have already read it."

"How do you know that?"

"Because you dream to travel and write, and any aspiring traveler has read *Gulliver's Travels*."

"Fair point. So it was used simply to conceal the note?"

He nods and sets his drink on the table before pushing his hands into the arms of his chair and rising. His move puts emphasis on a broad chest that needs no emphasis. Truly, this man is so handsome, it's disarming, and though I initially thought him to be an arrogant idiot, there is something rather charming about the disgraced Duke and, dare I say it, sweet. I watch his tall body roam his study, up and down at the foot of the bookcase, his long fingers dragging lightly across the spines of the books. Oh, to be one of those books.

Eliza!

"I think this one," he says, slowly pulling a red leather-bound book from the shelf and dusting it off.

"What is it?" I ask, too curious.

Opening it up, he wanders casually back to his chair and lowers as he pulls a piece of paper out and smiles at it. Of course, my enquiring mind is getting wholly out of control. "What are you reading?" I ask as he scans the paper.

"A poem." He places it on the table. "A dear friend wrote it. I knew not of the meaning, or perhaps I simply did not understand." The Duke regards me. "I think maybe now I do."

I tilt my head. "Would you like to read it aloud. I would be delighted to hear it."

"I think not."

"What is it about?"

"A woman."

"Oh?"

"A woman he met but briefly at a party here in London. He was deeply affected by the woman and was compelled to pen the poem." Going back to the book, he flicks through a few pages. "I think this will be a more suitable choice of reading material for my lady, who is not such a lady." He smirks at the words, and I, once again, find my jaw somewhat lax.

"And what is this supposed more suitable choice?" I ask, craning my head, not to see the book upon his lap, but the piece of paper on the table beside him.

"*Law and Order Volume III*," he says rather flippantly. "Let us discuss the legal system in our fine land, since I have learned you are rather passionate about justice and protecting the innocent."

A burst of laughter erupts unstoppably. "Well, Your Grace, I can, with the utmost confidence, I might add, advise you that there is absolutely no order in England, and the law, as it stands, is antiquated." I sit forward, keen to be heard. "How is it deemed a criminal offense to steal an apple, and yet a man can beat his wife black-and-blue and go unpunished? It's inexplicable.

I cannot fathom a world where material things come above one's life. A world in which a man can be hanged for stealing a loaf to feed his family because his employer pays him too little. A world in which a child—an eight-year-old child!—is sentenced to death for pilfering a pair of shoes because his feet are infected and sore from wandering the dank streets of London barefoot." I fall back in my chair and take a breath. "There is no order and there is definitely no law that I can respect. In addition to my many gripes and woes on the state of England's legal system, of which I'm certain you will soon tire of hearing, is the matter of newspapers, newspapers like my father's—freely printing whatever they so desire." I huff, and the Duke's eyebrows slowly lift. "That in itself is a crime—that they should be free to embellish stories, manipulate public opinion, or even manufacture stories completely, all to line the pockets of the rich or at least favor them. Any journalist can pen words and have half of London believing them. It is downright unfair. I cannot abide such absurdities." I sit back, disconcerted by my outburst, and watch with increasing nervousness as the Duke slowly closes the book, looking at me with quite stunned eyes, seeming to be in a trance.

"Are you feeling all right, Your Grace?" I ask, making him blink and jerk.

He shifts in his seat. Frowns. Sets the book aside. "Excuse me," he says, standing. "I…um…excuse me." He leaves rather quickly, the door slams behind him and I am alone. Just me and the crackling fire.

And the piece of paper.

I stand and pick up the piece, that is scrawled with words penned by a quill and a fine hand. "She walks in Beauty," I whisper, reading the poem, smiling sadly as I do. "George Gordon Byron," I say when I've reached the end. What a talent.

I hear whispers coming from beyond the door, whispers, that, make no mistake, are angry. "You are mad, Your Grace," someone hisses. Hercules. "You must halt this madness at once."

"I know I must!" the Duke barks. "And yet I cannot."

I blink rapidly and recoil, and the door swings open. The Duke appears, seeming somewhat edgy, his eyes burning with an air of determination I am not sure I should like.

"Stop what?" I ask, and he tilts his head, his face a picture of incredulity. I suppose it is rather a stupid question, and His Grace knows me not to be stupid. I realize attraction when it slams me in the face, even if I am not versed in the dance of flirtation. Young ladies of the ton may be persistently protected from the realities of marriage and what it brings, of how heirs are made, but I have not forever been a young lady of the ton and the Duke is privy to that small matter. I am not really an innocent. Innocent, but…not.

"I'm sorry," I say, finding it quite easy to apologize. "You know you must, and yet you cannot."

He nods mildly, his eyes falling to the paper in my hand.

"My apologies," I say quickly. "I did not mean to pry."

He frowns. "You should never apologize for being curious, Eliza."

"Is that what you are?" I question, all of my inhibitions apparently lost in this moment. "Curious?"

"Very."

"Why? I am but a young unladylike lady with too much to say."

"And yet I love what I am hearing."

I swallow. The Duke too has lost his inhibitions and I know not what to say to that. He likes me talking? "It's a beautiful poem," I blurt, setting the paper on the table again.

"It is."

I knew not of the meaning, or perhaps I simply did not understand. I think maybe now I do.

I bite my lip as my mind recalls some of the words, and

the Duke swallows hard. "I should like to dance with you," he declares.

"Pardon me?"

"The waltz, perhaps?"

"I do not have permission to dance the waltz."

He comes toward me with purpose, and I back up, alarmed. "Is it a crime?" he asks.

"No, do not be silly. It's merely inappropriate, for a debutante especially, to dance such an intimate dance."

"Suddenly she should like to abide by the rules which she strives to break." He steps closer.

"I do not strive to break rules." I am becoming increasingly breathless. The truth of it is, I know not how to dance, much as I have not the faintest idea how to be close to this man while maintaining my breathing. A man one should most certainly not be close to. And to waltz with him? Oddly, I do not want him to think I am incapable. "I strive to change the rules because the rules are ridiculous."

"Then you should like to dance the waltz with me, am I right?" Another step closer, and I am forced to tilt my head back to keep the Duke in my sights.

"You are familiar with the dance?" I ask.

"I spent much time in Paris, so, yes, I am familiar with the dance."

I must not inquire as to how many women he has shared such closeness with. Perhaps I am an idiot. It is not the dancing I should be concerned about. "I am here for conversation," I say, taking a sensible step away from the Duke and lowering to my chair.

"Would you prefer me to gain your mother's approval?"

I laugh lightly. "I do not need my mother's approval. I simply do not want to dance with you."

"Or be so close," he muses, lowering to his chair opposite me. "How is the wine?"

"Delicious."

"And the company?"

"Confusing."

"How so?"

"Because I can't fathom whether he wants to make me scream with pleasure or frustration." I cock him a wry smile, once again finding my composure now he is out of reach.

The Duke laughs under his breath and takes his drink. "You are frustrated?"

"Only, of course, because you confuse me."

"Better to be confused than scared, I'd say."

It is true, I suppose. I stand and meander to the bookcase, wandering the foot, reading the titles on every spine. I'm sure Mr. Fuddy would be envious of such a collection. I feel his eyes following me, and it is both thrilling and worrying. "Where have you been this past year?"

"Traveling. Tell me about your life in the countryside."

I hitch a brow to the books before me. "It was wonderful. Why have you returned to London?"

"I have business to tend to. Did you read the letter you returned to me?"

I purse my lips. "Of course not, it was private. What business?"

"Family business. How do you know the letter was private?"

"I assumed. Your family all perished, so what family business could you possibly have to tend to?"

"You ask too many questions."

So now he doesn't like what he hears? "As do you." I turn to face him, challenge him, and I slam right into his chest. "Goodness," I splutter as he takes the tops of my arms to steady me. "Must you be so close?" The heat that radiates through me is burning, and I peek up and find blazing eyes staring down at me, a swirl of something I don't recognize in his eyes. But these crazy sensations overcoming me? I recognize those. They are ever-present whenever the Duke and I are close. Touching.

My eyes drop to his lips. They part, and I get a glimpse of his tongue. My whimper is shallow as his mouth comes closer. Closer. Closer. Then he pauses just shy of his lips touching mine, and presses his together. "What is it?" I breathe.

"You," he groans, tightening his hold. "You…" His lips straighten, his look becoming rather grim. "You must leave." He releases me, and I exhale heavily.

"What?"

"Leave now, Eliza."

"I—"

"Leave!"

I jump with fright at his booming voice, startled, and, most disconcertingly, injured. I really have asked too many questions, and now he has demanded I leave? I raise my chin in an act of feigned confidence, because he looks truly angered in this moment, and walk to the door, not looking back. The warm, oddly comforting feel of his presence has been replaced by a frosty atmosphere I can't say I'm all too fond of. Damn him to hell. He should not entice me into his affections and then callously discard me. How can a man's manner sway so dramatically, from warm and welcoming, to irritation the most potent I have ever been unfortunate enough to bear? My eyes begin to sting, and it is infuriating. He is not worthy of my tears.

I rush past Hercules, who appears as stunned as I am, though I know not why, for I heard his hushed, angry whispers, and arrive outside, shutting the door with force. How dare he. How dare he make me feel so horrid.

The prompt termination of what was a rather pleasant, albeit challenging, evening is not my only complaint. I am now bloody freezing cold.

I wrap my arms around myself and hurry down the path and across Belmore Square with haste. I am surely in a dither. My reappearance at Mr. Fitzgerald's party would be questioned, for my cheeks are undoubtedly flush with both desire and anger, and my body is shaking with the effects of the cold night on my skin. The anger may be assisting with that too, and yet my options, unfortunately, are limited. I must return.

I choose my moment carefully and sneak back into the house, placing myself by the fire in the hopes that my teeth will stop chattering before someone engages me in conversation, but it would appear that luck is not on my side on this eve.

"Miss Melrose." The silky tone of Lady Dare would surely delight the ears of any man. Unfortunately, for I'm sure she would not treat me with such disdain if I were, I am not a man. My instinct has me not greeting her but searching the room for Frank, and I am relieved to discover his absence.

Inhaling, I face her. "My lady," I reply, all rather civilized. It's quite ridiculous. There was no denying the animosity shared between us this morn. "What a pleasure." Sarcasm drips from my tone, and I cannot help it. My recent dismissal from the Duke's home is not assisting in bettering my mood, granted. Regardless, I am not appreciating Lady Dare's obvious dislike of me. And to think I admired her from afar! It is true, she is a somewhat scandalous woman who cares not for protocol, a trait for which I once held her in high regard. Sadly, the notion has been squashed. She is rather unpleasant, and I care not for her flaunting habits. Perhaps now because the flaunting habits I speak of involve my brother.

And the Duke!

No. The Duke is a self-serving, bad-mannered idiot. She is welcome to him.

And what, do you suppose, Eliza, would you have done with him had he not demanded you leave his home? Kiss him? Lie with him?

I should laugh at myself. I wouldn't know how to do either. "Why, Miss Melrose, you look suitably wonderful," Lady Dare purrs, her crimson dress, which is naturally the brightest at the party, glowing spectacularly.

Is that sarcasm in *her* tone? "Very kind," I grate. I look nothing like the siren she is. In fact, I look noticeably dreary beside her in my blue simple gown.

"You look frightfully cold, Miss Melrose," she says as she reaches for my arm.

"I was forced to step outside for some air." I smile the sweetest smile I can muster, withdrawing from her outstretched hand.

"Be warned, Eliza," she says, wiping my sweet smile away. "One only ever gets one night with the Duke."

I balk. "Excuse me?"

"Every lady, and there are many, has only ever had one night. You will be no different. Or have you had your one night already?"

"I have no idea what you are talking about, my lady." *My God, how does she know?* "Excuse me. I'm being summoned by my mother." I edge past her, fighting back my guilty blush, leaving behind, I'm sure, a face full of thought. She can think all she likes. It shall never be confirmed. Though, of course, there is nothing to be confirmed. There have been *no* nights.

I leave the room and to my relief bump into Frank, but my relief wanes when I see he is engaged in conversation with Lizzy Fallow, another unsuitable candidate for my brother's affections, but perhaps the lesser of two evils. I look back and find what I hoped I would not, which is Lady Dare sporting a scowl as she too spies Frank with the pretty *younger* blonde. I predict a rather ugly outcome to this situation. I cannot imagine Lady Dare is familiar with rejection. First the Duke, and now Frank? Assuming the Duke has rejected her. *Has he rejected her?* Yes, on the evening I was witness to her calling upon him, but what of the nights since then? What do I care? And if she is right, and I know she probably is, then she, too, will only have been granted one night, although, and I'm certain of it after her backhanded warning just now, she wants more. Regardless, it is none of my business, but I do need to be careful of rumors that could cause me a headache with Papa, or anyone for that matter.

"Eliza, dear," Mother intercepts me, taking a worried scan of my thawing body. "I have been looking for you."

"Apologies, Mama. I came over a little hot and thought it best I step outside to take in some air."

"Oh?" Her hand is immediately on my forehead, her motherly concern shining past her newfound status. "Are you ill? Should I call for a doctor?"

"Worry not. The fresh air worked wonders."

"Oh good." Joining my side, she reinstates her smile. "Earl Lymington was looking for you too."

"Oh good," I groan, finding Frank and Lizzy Fallow again. Let us change the subject. "What do you think Mama?" I ask casually, setting us off on a circuit of the party again.

"I think your brother needs to marry suitably, and Lizzy Fallow is not suitable."

"I'm glad we can agree on that matter," I tease, earning a playful slap on my hand where it is resting on her forearm.

"Stop it, Eliza."

"Is it not enough that *I* am marrying suitably." Not that I want Frank to marry Lizzy Fallow, of course, she radiates supremacy without being supreme, but she's a good tool for my demonstration.

"Frank is our oldest and only heir."

"Therefore, the most important, which means I should be left to marry whom I choose."

Mother laughs. "And whom would you choose?"

"No one."

"Exactly," she sings. "We cannot have you single for an eternity, Eliza. People will—"

"What? Assume I am living in sin? Perhaps entertaining women instead of men. Or raising my skirt for any fellow who may flash me a suggestive smile?"

"You will go to hell."

"Good. Perhaps it's warmer there." I look over my shoulder, my nose rising higher. "What thinks you of Lady Dare?"

"I think she thrives on shocking people."

I think Mother is correct. One could call her an attention-seeker. "I caught her with her sights on Frank."

As expected, Mother gasps. "Say it isn't so."

"I cannot."

I hope Lady Dare is ready for the ugly side of my mother. She is a force to be reckoned with, and, naturally, I would not usually tolerate or encourage such behavior, especially when it is our futures in question, but, well. Lady Dare is all that needs to be said.

"I will soon solve that little problem," she seethes. "I can assure you."

"I'm sure." Speaking of problems. "Where has Clara got to?"

"Ah!" Mother chimes, as if she has just recalled something forgotten. "I thought she must have been with you. Was she not?"

I frown. "She was not."

"Then where the devil is she?"

"That's a fine question," I murmur, removing myself from Mother to seek her out, though I fear I have the answer. It would appear that all three of us are having dalliances with highly unsuitable members of society. "I will find her, Mama," I assure her.

"Oh, Lady Blythe!" Mother sings, delighted. "How wonderful you look this eve." She comes closer and hisses in my ear, "What was the name of her new novel again?"

"No idea, so perhaps talk about your twilight sneaky baking sessions."

"Hell," Mother spits, and I laugh.

"Is there anyone who isn't here?" Lady Blythe says. "It would seem the whole of Belmore Square is in attendance."

"Not the *whole* of Belmore Square," I blurt, once again my mouth taking on a mind of its own. "I mean…" I'm without words.

"Oh, you mean the wily Duke?" Lady Blythe purrs, and something in her eyes speaks to me. *Oh no, surely not?*

"You know him," I say, this time my words spoken with intention. I ignore the sharp nudge I receive from my mother.

Lady Blythe waves a hand in a manner that is meant to be flippant but is falsely so. "I knew his mother. She was quite unbearable."

"Unbearable, you say?" I ask, moving in closer, appearing much too fascinated by news of Johnny Winters's mother. "Aren't all mothers?" I wince as a result of yet another sharp nudge in my ribs, and my mother laughs loudly, making me flinch.

"Eliza," she says, her eyebrows forming sharp arches. "Earl Lymington wishes to speak with you."

"I look forward to it." I smile sweetly at my mother, whose jaw is as tight as the most unbearable corset one could find. The warning in her eyes is lethal but completely harmless. "Excuse me."

"Excused," she grates, turning her full attention back onto Lady Blythe. "I've nearly finished your book."

I breeze off on a roll of my eyes, joining Frank as Lizzy Fallow is summoned by Mrs. Fallow, who looks unimpressed by the prospect of my brother courting her daughter, for he bears no title. It is the one asset he is without, but it is the one asset every mama in search of a husband for their daughter is looking for. He is handsome. Tall. Impressively built, thanks to the years of manual labor between Father's old factory and our old country estate, not to mention plenty of exercise on various women, and now, thanks to Papa's hard work and sheer determination, he is the heir of a wealthy, successful industrialist.

It's a pity all of those impressive possessions and advantages fall short of what really matters around here. Not that

I am much bothered about that while Lizzy Fallow is the subject.

"I fear she does not approve of you," I say as I join him, nodding politely at Mrs. Fallow, who, rather unnecessarily, lifts her nose and ignores me. "It's probably a good thing, as Mama does not approve either."

He looks down at me tiredly. "Why are you not with Frederick?"

"Do you want me to die of boredom? Besides," I look at my brother accusingly. "I don't believe you are in a position to judge with whom I spend my time."

"It is expected, Eliza. You are courting."

"And what are you doing?" I ask, disgruntled. "You too should be courting. How is it that you can converse with whomever you choose, and I cannot?"

"Who else would you like to converse with? Apparently, you cannot abide anyone here." He laughs a little as he sips his drink, his eyes falling onto Lizzy Fallow. She tries desperately to hide her smile, her cheeks blushing as her eyes drop to her feet.

"She's flirting with you," I say, observing the unspoken between Frank and Lizzy Fallow.

"She is?" He shrugs. "I didn't notice."

"You're quite funny, brother."

"As are you. When will I get another story? Lymington is putting pressure on Papa and I need to get them off my back."

Another story? Lord, I have a few, but none I can tell. "I'm working on it. And what of Lady Dare?" I fire my question like a cannonball, and much to my horror, Frank snaps a rather concerned expression my way. Damn it, it is true!

"What of her?"

"Oh please." I sigh. "I do wish people around here would stop treating me like an imbecile." I take a glass of Champagne and hit it on the side of Frank's tumbler. "My acute observations should be celebrated."

"And what observations are they?"

"That you whiffed decidedly of lavender," I say, enjoying seeing my brother's eyes widening, "and I have since discovered that it is the delightful Lady Dare's scent of choice."

"You have, have you?"

"I have," I reply haughtily. "Whatever are you thinking, Frank? That woman is a man-eater."

"I know."

I cannot hold back my recoil. "You do?"

"Of course I do, Eliza. Fear not. I am not about to fall in love with her."

"Oh, well that's a relief." I return my attention to the room. "You would do well to avoid her."

"Thank you for"—he frowns down at me—"the advice, but what do you know of Lady Dare?"

I scoff. "There are whispers."

"I thought you did not care for whispers."

"I do not." I nod my respect to my brother. "But some whispers are very loud, so I would encourage you to be very careful, Frank."

His smile is as fond as I know him to be of me. "Must I return that sentiment?"

Keeping my face without reaction is a tricky endeavor, so I smile tightly and remove myself from my brother's company before he can detect anything untoward. Which, of course, there isn't. I can only thank the heavens that my brief encounters with the Duke have gone unnoticed.

I nibble my lip thoughtfully. "Miss Melrose," Mr. Fitzgerald says as I pass, and I smile my hello. It is quick to collapse upon arrival to the next room, where Frederick is hovering alone in a corner with not one person nearby that I might pull in to relieve me of the strain of making a conversation. "My lord," I say.

"Miss Melrose. I have been eager for your company all evening."

"I must apologize for my absence. I came over a bit queasy, if you must know." It is not an outright lie, so I shall not feel too guilt-ridden. I feel extremely queasy in this moment, truth be told, as I know not how long I can sustain this circus. My feet are twitching in my boots, desperate to carry me far away.

"You do," Frederick says, concern awash on his face, "look a trifle pale. Perhaps, with the permission of your father, naturally, I should escort you home."

"Perhaps," I murmur despondently, wondering if at all Frederick's suggestion is sensible. At least here I am somewhat distracted from the circling of my annoying thoughts, which I'm certain will escalate into a full spin upon finding myself alone searching for sleep.

Thoughts that not only revolve around the circumstances of the Duke's arrival in London, but thoughts that revolve around the way he looked at me. The words he said. The feelings overcoming me. His lips nearly upon mine and how secretly I'm devastated that he's denied me a kiss more than once.

God, what is this horrible feeling in my chest?

Father, naturally, is pleased to release me into the wild nighttime with Frederick and has Frank chaperone us. "Take Clara with you as well. Where has she been all evening, by the way?"

"Here, Papa!" she says, appearing from nowhere. "I was with Mama."

She lies, and yet I cannot call her out. But I will be giving her a stern talking-to. She needs to stop this silly infatuation with the stable boy.

Hypocrite!

The walk home is silent, and I immediately go to my bedroom and steal a peek out of my window across Belmore Square. It's past midnight, and the candles still glow in the window, the silhouette of someone casting shadows. I watch intently, wondering how we went from pleasant conversation to hostility.

"No," I whisper when I see Lady Dare crossing the square, my heart slowing, I admit. She knocks, and when he answers, my heart stops altogether.

I run to the bowl on my dresser and vomit violently before I weakly collapse into bed. My final thought before I drift off to sleep is...

Bugger it all, am I lovesick?

Chapter 9

The next morning, Clara bursts in and plonks herself on the edge of my bed. "Did you hear?" she asks.

"I have just this moment opened my eyes," I say, rolling over and punching my pillow to make it suitably plump. "Hear what and from whom?"

"Mr.—" Her nose wrinkles, and quick on the heels of that, a grimace. "Whatever is that awful stench?"

"Oh." The stench finds my waking sense of smell and wakes it fully. "That would be my vomit." I remove myself from the bed and go to the bowl, holding my breath as I place it outside my room. "Dalton!" I call. "Could I trouble you for a moment?" He appears, his usually friendly face twisting considerably when he sees what I am troubling him for. I can only smile my apologies as I pass him the bowl. "Thanking you kindly." I shut my door and find some perfume, flicking some drops into the air and opening a window. Good heavens, it is putrid. I should have dealt with it yesterday eve, but I was as weak as a kitten! In fact, I cannot say with any confidence that I feel much better. "You had better tell Dalton," I say to Clara over my shoulder, breathing in the fresh air, "to return the bowl without delay." I expect this is my penance for blatantly lying about my whereabouts yesterday evening. I feel plain dreadful, my hands braced against the window ledge the only thing holding me up.

"Should I get Mama?"

"That is not necessary." I unbend my body when I am

confident that I am in control of my heaves and go to face Clara to find out what the devil I am supposed to have heard, but my intentions are foiled when my attention is stolen by a figure across the square. A figure I have come unsuitably close to, and, disgracefully, have touched. I ignore how handsome he looks this morning. Handsome and together. Well dressed, as if he has some important business to attend to. I expect he is suitably satisfied after Lady Dare called upon him. He sent me away and invited her in. It would not be such an insult if I did not loathe the woman that he was rather quick to replace me with.

I am merely here for the conversation.

And the tingles.

My lips pressed into an angry line, I slam the window closed and return to my bed, feeling hotter. Sicker. "What are you blabbering on about, Clara?" I snap.

"Lizzy Fallow is said to be courting Viscount Millingdale."

"What?" I gasp, deeply shocked.

Clara, understandably, shudders. "He is so old! Goodness, Eliza, what if I am expected to marry a man fit for a coffin?" She looks at me with warranted horror. "I could not stand it!"

"If a man is fit to sire a son, he is fair game, so long as he carries clout and cash, but most importantly, a title." I imagine Mrs. Fallow is dancing with joy this morning. I saw the way in which she regarded my title-less brother. "Frank," I say. "Does he know?" Will he care?

"He is yet to rise." She frowns. "After he escorted you home, he returned to the party and became very drunk. Father was forced to summon Dalton to help carry him home."

"And where, may I ask, were you, because you were not with Mama as you told Papa?"

Clara's sudden shifting is worrying. "I was with Mama for the entire evening."

"I beg to differ."

"How would you know?" she asks with a smugness I'm sure

I shouldn't appreciate. "I saw you sneak out yourself. So where, may I ask, dear sister, did *you* go?"

"I already told you." I give my pillow a good thwack and slam my head down upon it. I regret my move immediately. My head is ringing, and, sadly, alcohol is not the cause. "I was unwell. I will just ask Mama if you were with her."

She pouts. "I won't tell if you don't."

I narrow my eyes, and she smiles, dipping to kiss my cheek but quickly thinking better of it, her nose wrinkling. "God, you whiff." She leaves with haste, shutting the door loudly behind her. It appears yesterday eve was quite a night for all involved. My thoughts turn to Lizzy Fallow. How must she be feeling? Dreadful, I expect. Frederick is hardly a ball of joy, but at least he can still walk without the aid of a stick. The poor thing. She is not my favorite person, but she is not as awful as Lady Dare, so I should call upon her later and offer my condolences.

Just as soon as this irritating wave of nausea has passed.

It did not pass that day. Nor the next day. Neither was it out of my system one week later. By day eight, I was becoming increasingly worried for my heart. Was it broken? Would I die of heartbreak? I must admit, it was with regret that when I left the Duke's house on that evening, I knew I would not find myself in his company again. It was with even more regret that I bore witness to another visitor on that very same evening, and it was with even more regret that I, with great reluctance, I must say, admitted that I had fallen for the Duke. How, I do not know. Attraction, I suppose, for he has not many other decent qualities.

I must stop lying to myself. He has many qualities that attract me. Acceptance, being one. A desire to indulge me in conversation is another. His ability to instigate those wonderful tingles is another.

Alas, all of those qualities, except, of course, his handsomeness, are now lost. He is a pig, and I am grateful to have been bed-ridden for this past week. My chances of bumping into him are nonexistent if I cannot leave the house. In truth, my sickness has been somewhat of a respite, the perfect excuse to avoid so-ciety, and, thankfully, Frederick. Though he has called upon me. Every bloody day at the same time. He even bought me flowers yesterday. Poor chap. It would seem he is very concerned. He would only be concerned if he cared.

There is a knock at my door and Emma enters with a bowl of fresh soapy water, Mother in tow. "Place it on the dresser, Emma," she orders, coming to the bed and feeling my forehead. "Hmmm," she hums. "The fever has passed."

"I feel better," I admit, shuffling to sit up. "I think perhaps today I can dress."

"And a walk. A walk should do you good."

I inwardly groan. "One step at a time, Mama."

"Everyone thinks you are dead, Eliza. We need to put their minds at rest."

"They care not if I am dead," I say over a laugh. "I expect Lymington already has a replacement lined up for Frederick." I hope he has. That would answer all my prayers. "I'm a bit stiff," I admit.

"Nothing a walk won't fix. Come now."

I endure her fuss, letting her help me bathe and dress. In fact, I quite relish her attentiveness and find it rather easy to ignore her motives. Mother could have quite easily passed the chore of tending to me on to our staff, but she has chosen to take care of me herself. Just as she always did. We had no governess. One maid was all we needed. "You are but skin and bones, Eliza," she whines as she pulls my stay to its tightest with ease. "A man should like a lady—"

"With a bit of meat on her bones?"

"Back to normal, I see," she remarks. "It's a pity your raging fever did not burn away your insolence, as well as the meat on your bones." She tugs at the fastener with a heavy hand, jolting me in warning.

My smile is unstoppable. "How is Frank?" He has not checked in on me since being taken to my bed, but Clara has, and she has kept me abreast of all things. Poor Lizzy Fallow has been sentenced to life and the wedding will go ahead.

"He is fine," Mother replies, clipped. "Now, what should we do with your hair?" she asks, turning me to face her and inspecting the mass of messy waves, her lips twisting in contemplation. "For this I shall need the assistance of Emma. Emma!" she hollers, and I wince.

"Mama, please." I feel like every sense is delicate, and why was she so dismissive of my inquiry into my brother?

Emma arrives, and the next hour is spent making me look presentable so I may be reintroduced to society—proof of life— and as I'm tugged and pulled around by Emma under Mama's instruction, I look out of the window, but my position only permits me to see the sky. Today, it is the most vivid of blues and the sun is shining. It would seem in this past week the weather has improved.

But what of the Duke's mood?

Not that I care, of course.

As I step out of our house, I feel a distinct change in the temperature. What a difference a week makes. I can't speak for the evening, but the daytime is rather pleasant, the need for a coat dress no more. So, in my dress, which is appropriately long-sleeved, and a bonnet, which is unfortunately decorated in the most lavish, colorful flowers Mother could find, a tactic, I'm sure, adopted solely to ensure I am seen, in order to put people's minds at rest that I am, in fact, alive and kicking, we walk down the street with the sun shining upon us. I cannot deny it, I am uncomfortable under the watchful eyes of all. They are probably keeping a close eye on me to see if I keel over, and

I notice also that no one approaches to greet me. They probably consider me contagious. Good. This bout of sickness really could be a blessing.

When we arrive at the promenade, the traffic is heavy, horses at every turn, and I conclude that, it would seem, the fair weather has brought out London's finest in droves.

I'm confused when Mother marches off in the opposite direction to the royal park. "Mother?" I call. "Has the park been relocated in the time I have been sweating like a pig in my bed?"

"Oh," Mother laughs in that sarcastic way in which she does, not appreciating my dry wit. "I have a new hat to collect." She does not let my question stop her in her mission.

I sigh, trudging after her. "And for what occasion would this one be for?"

"Lady Blythe is hosting quite a spectacle of a party on Wednesday evening of next week. I am for certain pleased you are now well enough to attend."

"Why? It is not like you need the occasion to marry me off," I say grimly. "Or has Lymington given up on trying to *tame the shrew* and started his search over?" Good luck to him. I cannot imagine there is a female in England who should be willing, not that she *needs* to be willing. After all, I was not, and that small matter keeps appearing in my mind. The deal that was made between Papa and Lymington. I should like to know for what my father sold me.

"Hold your tongue in public, Eliza," Mother grumbles, coming to a stop outside the milliner's shop. "It would be fair to say," she says quietly, her head tilted, "that there may be a considerable amount of sucking up to do in light of your recent absence."

"Why? I was ill."

"As was your father," she says under her breath, pushing her way into the shop. Her displeasure is soon exchanged for delight; however, my scowl remains. Papa was ill? Why did no one share this news with me? One would like to think that one's loved ones were worried about them. Perhaps they deemed the news too distressful, therefore could possibly hamper my recovery, therefore my reintroduction into London society. But, I digress, I am, as troublesome as it is, already promised to someone, so my reappearance on the social scene is of little importance. What the devil is going on?

I go after my mother, ready to interrogate her for the information to which I am certain I am entitled, since this is *my* life and happiness being used as compensation for whatever it is Father has received from Lymington, but she has taken on quite some speed, and doesn't that make me more suspicious. "Mother," I say, following her into the shop.

"Yes, darling?" she replies, smiling at me, as happy as could be. Florence Melrose has many talents. Moving fast is one of those talents. She's made it to the counter at the back of the shop already. She also has quite an impressive ability to adjust her facial expressions in the blink of an eye. Acting. That, too, she is quite a marvel at. She looks like a woman without the woes that I felt were just projected onto me. It would not be considered unusual to appear in public looking somber if one's husband was ill, and whilst I'm not particularly overjoyed with my father's recent shenanigans, he is a man with a soft heart. If he has been ill, I should like to know that he has made a full recovery.

I lift my dress to take the step to join Mother and ask her, quietly, of course, what is wrong with Father, but my boot barely leaves the floor when I hear the door behind me open and the hordes of patrons fall silent. A certain nippiness sweeps through the shop as I cast a wary eye across the shoppers. Every one of them is looking past me with a look of caution.

Curious, I turn to establish what has their worried attention.

And come face to face with the Duke of Chester. We are so close, I am forced to crane my head to get his face in my sights, however sure I am that it is a terrible idea, but, and it's frustrating, he is apparently a magnet to my eyes. His expression is taut. Angry. It is an anger I have been unfortunate enough to encounter before. I did not care for it then, especially since it was directed at me, and I care not for it now, when, again, the Duke's foul mood appears to be directed at me. Nonetheless, my body predictably reacts, and I am quickly tingling from the tip of my boots to the top of my fancy bonnet. And I feel hot. So very, very hot.

My eyes meet his, and they swirl madly, the green the greenest I have seen, perhaps because we are in daylight hours, and his jaw appears to tic. *Very* angry. I know not what to say, for there is an audience, and the Duke is quite stuck for words too. A distinct shuffling of feet ensues, and one by one, every man in the store leaves, giving the Duke a wide berth, therefore me too. It's ridiculous. He is of no danger to anyone. In fact, the only thing in danger at the moment is my heart. I hardly want to admit it, since we left on such terrible terms after our last encounter, but here I am struggling to keep my awe at his impressive presence in check.

"Come along, Eliza," Mother says, taking my elbow. "We will return another time."

I frown and find it in myself to tear my eyes from the Duke. Mother is looking all wide-eyed at him. Leave? I look down and discover no hat in Mother's possession. "We are here to collect your new hat, are we not?"

"We are."

"Then we should collect your new hat." I lift my chin and disregard the Duke, which is an extremely tricky challenge when my body is singing for his attention. What an inconvenience attraction is. Not normally, I expect. I expect *normally* it would be a blessing to have such responses to a man's closeness, if said man was a supposed potential suitor. Unfortunately for me, the Duke is not. Damn it all, he must be the only man alive with a dukedom who is deemed unbefitting. He is not a murderer, for the love of everything. Although, he quite obviously relishes the unsettling feelings he instigates in everyone he encounters who believes him to be so. The only crime Johnny Winters is guilty of is being a rake. And not just a rake, but a supercilious rake. "Come along, Mother." I reach the counter and smile at the daunted-looking runner. "When you are ready," I say, and he springs into action, clumsily finding Mama's hat and presenting it to her. His eyes, however, never stray far from the Duke lingering beyond, and I look over my shoulder and discover, amusingly, that the Duke has not moved a muscle. His eyes, on the other hand, have narrowed somewhat. On me.

I huff to myself and return my attentions back to the milliner as Mother stands like a statue beside me, she, too, keeping the Duke in her firm sights. What is this madness? What do these people think will happen? Murder? Arson? I collect Mother's hat on a smile of thanks, collect my mother also, and guide her unresponsive form from the shop. The Duke's eyes follow my path, his lips pressed straight into a very unimpressed line. "Good day to you," I say on a scowl as I pass him.

His tall, well-formed body turns to keep those narrowed eyes directed at me. He has a nerve to be treating me with such contempt, as it was he, after all, who pretty much threw me out into the cold and darkness, *and*, to add insult to injury, let Lady Dare, the outrageous adventuress, into his home. And what did they do? I flinch at the thought. I bet it did not involve conversation.

I do not show it, but I drink in air ravenously when we make it onto the street, wondering how I survived such a pressure pot in the store. "Wake up, Mama," I breathe, looking back into the shop. The Duke remains in place watching me, and it is all I can do not to curl my lip before I walk onwards. I'm suddenly parched. So much so, I am tempted to drag Mother into an ale house and down a tankard of beer to quench my thirst. To be fair, she looks like she needs a drink too.

"Well," Mother says, finally blessing me with life. "What a rude man he truly is!"

I frown. "He didn't even speak a word."

"He did not need to." She snatches her new hat and leaves, waving for the attention of Lady Tillsbury, surely to share the latest gossip, with a few added embellishments, of course. I sigh. I can see what is coming and, despite not holding the Duke in high regard at this very moment, and possibly—surely—never again, I must say, I greatly dislike the thought of the recent scene in the milliner's being embellished to paint the Duke in an even darker light. His world, it seems, is dark enough already without the help of the friendly folk of Belmore Square and beyond.

This misplaced sense of responsibility is irritating. What do I care if the Duke's reputation is tarnished beyond its current state of dishonor? After all, he, without too much encouragement, let it be said, thought little of tarnishing mine.

I rush after Mother. "Oh!" I yelp when I am seized from behind, and before I can blink or even scream my distress, I am against a wall with the body of a man holding me in place. "What are you doing?" I gasp, my chest pumping wildly. "This is not appropriate. How dare you manhandle me so!"

"I didn't care much for your look of utter contempt, Eliza."

The nerve of this man. "Then you should not have treated me with such," I hiss back, outraged.

"Where in God's name have you been this past week? I have been worried out of my mind!"

My eyes go round. He has been concerned for my well-being? It should *not* please me. "Where I have been is not a concern of yours."

"Apparently not, and yet, quite perturbingly, I have been concerned." The anger in him is tangible. The fire between our touching bodies is blazing hot. My heart is booming dangerously. "I thought perhaps..." His words drift off, as do his eyes to the heavens.

"You thought what?" But he need not answer, as realization arrives. "You thought our encounters had been discovered."

"I did indeed," he breathes, his head, his beautiful blond head, shaking in despair, despite surely knowing by this point he was mistaken. "I called upon your home and—"

"What?" I shriek, alarmed, and his lips straighten into an unimpressed line.

"I believe you heard me very well, Eliza. I called upon your home."

Goodness, Dalton must have known not what to do when faced with such a visitor. And my father? He must have been full of horror. No suitable men have called upon me since I have arrived in London for my first season. Not that they needed to, since Father had kindly taken care of business in that regard. But, and it is only just occurring to me now, the news of my courtship with Frederick Lymington did not, as one would expect, and as so often happens, have hordes of gentlemen deeming me worthy of pursuing. Why is that? Not one man? I know I am not a proper lady, not by status or title, but I am at least blessed with a good bone structure. That is thanks to my mother. My personality traits, traits I have inherited from my father, however, are not such a blessing. Furthermore, and an utter bone of contention, those traits are acceptable in my father, and yet not in me. Because he is a man. "And, when you called upon me, what did you say?"

"I asked if you were home. Your butler seemed rather alarmed and called for your father, whom, as I expected, and most certainly would assume, questioned me."

"He asked if we were acquainted?"

"He did."

Good grief. If indeed my father really is ill, this would explain everything. And does my mother know of this call from the Duke? "And…"

"Naturally, I told him we were not, but I should like to be."

I laugh under my breath. The Duke could be regarded as a brave, brave man. Or he simply does not care. I conclude it is the latter, for my father is not a man to be feared. Being angry has always been somewhat of an effort for him, which makes his grim mood and snappy words of late harder to accept.

Of course, I am not surprised by the brick wall the Duke was faced with, but I am rather surprised that he took such drastic action. Because he was concerned for me? I do not wish to tell His Grace that I was, in fact, feeling like death in my bed. He would drop me like a hot coal, I'm sure, and, save my soul, I am liking this closeness far more than I should. But I mustn't. *I mustn't!* "I did not wish to see you," I snap, wriggling.

He inhales. "Do not squirm like that Eliza. I cannot promise to control myself."

I still immediately, alarmed by the hardness of something pressing into my lower stomach. It's disturbing, if only because this dress is rather padded, so the Duke is quite clearly well-endowed.

Good heavens.

He takes a moment, his eyes low. Then he looks at my bonnet. "What is this?" he asks with a disapproving scowl.

I roll my eyes. "It is not of my choice."

"Then why are you wearing it?" he says. "My defiant, willful lady."

"If I were defiant, I would be fighting you off and screaming for assistance."

His eyebrows jump up. "I think I would like the thought of a physical altercation."

"Then perhaps you should wait upon Lady Dare to knock at your door."

His eyes widen. Mine narrow. "I do not care for that woman."

"Then why did you let her into your home on the eve you demanded I leave?"

"You were spying? Again?" he asks. *Guilty.* "Had you waited a few minutes, you would have seen Hercules escorting Lady Dare back out."

Oh? Well, that is pleasing.

Then his face comes so close, for a moment I am terrified he will kiss me. He must not!

"My mother," I whisper.

"She is far too busy fabricating the latest tale of my sins." His hot breath is drenching my face. "I expect by morn, I will have been brandishing a pistol at the milliner."

I cannot hide my amusement. "I am beginning to think you enjoy being the talk of the square."

"I enjoy your company far more."

"Well," I say on a laugh. "You are not going about the right way of gaining anyone's approval in that regard. We have had it confirmed that my father would probably rather die than allow me to so much as take a walk with you."

"Pity."

"It is," I murmur, my eyes falling to his lips. My thoughts are positively sinful. "We have done far more than simply take a walk together without a chaperone." I have been alone with this man. On *numerous* occasions. If anyone were to discover my transgressions, I would be ruined forever. Not that I care for the approval of the ton. I simply care for the well-being of my father. And the Duke? Well, he will go on about his business of intimidating and brooding. His reputation is of little consequence, since it is obliterated already.

"We have," he agrees, his face a picture of contemplation.

"But as I have told you on numerous occasions, Your Grace," I whisper. "I am promised to another."

"Yes, your father may have mentioned the nitwit."

I take my lip between my teeth.

"Do not do that, Eliza."

"Why?" Whatever am I saying? I must not encourage this madness. There can be no pleasant ending.

"Just…" He frowns, breaking his body away and raking a hand through his hair. "This is all rather unfortunate."

"What is?" I breathe, trying and failing to gather myself.

"I find I rather like your company."

"And that is a surprise?"

"Indeed, it is."

I think what the Duke is trying to say but also not say so not to insult me—my God, he isn't entirely without reason or feelings—is that he had only allowed for physical intimacy. He had not expected to actually *like* me. "So you really do like me?"

He looks up at me on a roguish grin that could melt me. "You have a kind heart, Eliza."

I snort. "I think perhaps you do too, under all of that brooding."

"Shhh," he hushes me playfully, and I roll my eyes.

"Why are you so determined to make everyone dislike you? Imagine if…you were liked."

His head cocks curiously. "Yes," he muses, so thoughtful. "Just imagine."

I look back toward the main promenade. "I really must go. I'm sure my mother will soon be finished detailing her brush with death in the milliner's shop."

"I must see you again." His tone is demanding, not pleading. "Tonight. We will…have pleasant conversation and drink wine from Italy."

Italy? Has he been to Italy? "And how do you propose I manage that?"

He reaches for his cravat on a scowl. "Do not play games, Eliza." He turns and strides away. "Find a way, but so help me God if I discover you have shimmied down any drainpipes again…"

"And what would you do, Your Grace?"

He looks back, his eyebrows high, daring me. "Try me."

I huff to myself. Mother is right. He is so very rude. And deadly handsome. And quite irresistible. Goddammit, I am so, so in love with him! "No, Eliza," I whisper to myself, an awful feeling of suffocation coming over me. Of all the men, trust me to become rather fond of the most unsuitable of the unsuitable. This is a disaster. For my own good, I should end this…this… this…whatever we are to call it.

I take a moment to gather myself before returning to the main promenade, where Mother, thankfully, is still holding Lady Tillsbury's rapt attention with tall tales. I can only imagine the extent of her embellishment, for I have been absent for quite some time. I find my teeth sinking into my lip, my shoulders rolling, and I peek back over my shoulder and see the Duke crossing the promenade, every one of his strides long and measured. He moves with such grace for a man of his stature, and as I cast my eye across the surrounding people, I see the eyes of women at every turn following his path. Their looks are longing. Their knees undoubtedly weak under their dresses. I expect each and every one is curious beyond acceptable about the rakish Duke. Desire and fear. What a delightfully potent mix. I can attest to that. Except my fear is reserved for something entirely different from every other person that fears Johnny Winters.

He has my heart and I am terrified I will never get it back.

Chapter 10

Supper is, as always, quite a casual affair. Frank is still missing, though no one, seemingly, wants to acknowledge that, and, in addition to my quiet speculation regarding my brother's where-abouts, I have been desperate to question Father, who appears in full health, might I add, about the Duke's recent calling. And my mother, actually. Is she oblivious, or has she learned a thing or two from all the other protective, ruthless mamas of the ton who'll go to alarming lengths to ensure the suitability of prospective callers? It's tricky to know for sure, but what I must remember is that any mention of the Duke will rouse questions that I do not want to answer and draw attention where it is not wanted, because, heaven help me, I absolutely must see him again. *Must.* I think I could possibly die if I do not. An exaggeration, I know, but still. I'm rather enamored.

This evening, I am told, Viscount Millingdale is hosting a more subdued dinner party, with only a select few guests. Much to Mother's delight, she and Father are among the select few.

"I should think so," Father laughs, helping himself to the potatoes. "After all, of the eighty banks in London, I chose his to take care of my fortunes. He also advertises his bank in my newspaper, for a heavily discounted rate, no less, therefore gaining him more business."

"You know as well as I do that money does not carry the same weight as a title, and Belmore Square is full of titles." Mother reaches for Clara's hair and removes a loose strand from her forehead, a move that appears to irritate my sister. She scowls and rolls her shoulder, effectively shrugging Mother off. "As was demonstrated by Mrs. Fallow's direct cut," she goes on, oblivious, or perhaps ignoring, Clara's testiness. What's got into her, I wonder? "She behaves as if she is in possession of a title herself."

Father looks at Mother with a fond smile, silently amused by her competitiveness, as he spoons some more potatoes onto his plate. "Porter and his wife will be accompanying us this eve."

Mother grimaces, because she, like me, finds the chief editor of Father's newspaper as unbearable as I do. "I do so hope Marion isn't sporting a darkened eye that we have to pretend *isn't* there again."

"It was an accident," Father says, his eyebrows lifting in warning. "And we have no reason to doubt Porter's explanation of Marion's unfortunate accident."

Mother huffs. I'm with her, though my doubt is, with great difficulty I admit, contained. "I shall require the carriage on the morrow."

"And where might my fine wife be traveling to?"

"The girls and I are going out for the day."

"We are?" I question.

"We are?" Clara says, speaking up for the first time since we arrived at the table. "I don't want to go out for the day."

Ignoring her, Mother sips her wine on a smile. "A lovely little outing will do us good. Some mother and daughter bonding. Yes. Lovely."

I eye her suspiciously. "And where are we going?"

"The theater and to the lovely new tea shop on Regent Street. Lady Tills…it's apparently very lovely."

And she's still hoping to win approval of at least one of the patronesses of Almack's. "Where's Frank?" I ask, the absence of my brother getting louder. I am yet to inquire into his feelings over the latest news concerning the old Viscount Millingdale and the young Miss Fallow.

"Your brother's whereabouts are a mystery each day," Father

says, looking worryingly thoughtful. "And sales are dropping with each day that passes."

"Oh, my dear, I have a story!" Mother sings, and I groan under my breath. Here we go. "That terrible Duke causing havoc in the milliner's today while Eliza and I were there collecting my hat."

"Havoc, you say?"

"Terrible havoc," she affirms, nodding.

Johnny might be right. I expect he'll have a gun by the time this story goes to press. For the love of God. It is hardly even a story. "I could write it," I say, looking at Papa tentatively.

"Absolutely not," he affirms, riling me. "Frank must write it."

"I'll write it," Clara chimes in, talking around her potatoes.

I ignore her. She doesn't want to write anything. "That's all well and good, Papa, but nobody knows of Frank's whereabouts," I say, my eyes passing quickly between my father and my mother, seeing them both fidgeting and both looking rather worried. What have I missed during my spell laid up? "Will someone please tell me where Frank is and what on earth is going on?"

"He's taken to the bottle," Mama says, waving a hand that is far too flippant for my liking. "And his backside has become stuck to a chair in the gentleman's club up in Mayfair."

Father slumps heavily back in his chair, rubbing at his forehead and exhaling loudly. "Whatever did I do to deserve such challenging children?"

There is an answer to that question, a valid answer, and yet I am reluctant to apply any more weight to my father's shoulders, for he looks fit to collapse under the strain of it all. So Frank has gone astray? Oh dear. It is worse than I expected. He must have really liked Lizzy Fallow. I pop a carrot in my mouth and chew thoughtfully. The poor man. I expect Lizzy Fallow is about as thrilled by the prospect of being wedded to the old, decrepit Viscount as I am about being married to Frederick Lymington. I must say, though, and with much relief, at least *my* unsuitable suitor can walk without the aid of a stick and can see without the assistance of a quizzing glass.

My attention turns to Clara, who looks no less forlorn. She is distracted, poking at her supper. It would appear I am not the only Melrose offspring in turmoil.

The moment Mama and Papa leave for this evening's party at Mr. Fallow's and Clara retires to the drawing room to do some embroidery, I make my escape. My face concealed by my cloak, I hurry through the darkness to Mayfair. Granted, the Duke demanded I visit him, and I am somewhat—*incredibly*— disappointed that I cannot, but there are more pressing matters to deal with.

I am sure to keep to the shadows, my shoulders hunched protectively, as I scurry through the streets. Once I arrive on Regent Street, I breathe easy for the first time since I stepped out of our house. I look at the gold plaque on the wall beside the door of the most renowned gentleman's clubs in Mayfair. Possibly even London. Gentleman being the operative word in this frightfully unfortunate situation. I am cloaked, certainly, disguised even, but I am not foolish enough to believe I can step into this establishment and fool all who set eyes on me that I belong here. So, once I've pondered my options, which doesn't take all too long, I resign myself to being as bold as the situation calls for. I drop the hood of my cloak, square my shoulders, and reach to ring the bell, thinking, really, this is no different to all the times I have ventured to the pub and coaxed my drunken brother out before he was unfortunate enough for Mother to find him, as she would, quite unceremoniously, drag him out by his ear.

I yelp when I am grabbed and hauled from the steps. I am carried away from Gladstone's and set gently on my feet where I am met with fierce green eyes and a twisted face. "There had better be a damn good reason for you wandering the streets at night, Eliza," he snaps, waving a pointed finger at me. "Actually, no. No reason would ever be satisfactory. What the hell are you thinking?" he hisses, starting to pace up and down before me, the impact of his boots on the ground making it shake. Furious. He is plain furious. I can't say I blame him. I realize the extent of my senselessness. But…"It's my brother," I begin to explain, hoping to settle his temper before he explodes, which, the longer I stand here, seems unlikely. He is positively livid.

"What of him?" he barks, squaring an expectant look at me.

"I'm worried for his well-being." I shake my head to myself. "I have not seen him for some days." I shall omit the reason for that. "I fear he is on a path to self-destruction, and I wish to stop it."

"He is a grown man."

"Nevertheless…" I pick up the bottom of my cloak. "I am worried for him so if you will excuse me, Your Grace."

I get precisely nowhere, the Duke blocking my path back to the door with his imposing body and moody expression that dares me to defy him. I dare. He knows I dare. "He is not in there, Eliza."

"What?" I look past him to the plaque, pointing. "Gladstone's. Mama said he was here at Gladstone's."

Johnny points across the road. "Your mama is incorrect. He is actually at Kentstone's."

"Kentstone's?" I question. "I've never heard of such a place."

"Not many have," he mutters in return.

"It's exclusive?"

"Something like that."

"Then I shall rescue him from there." I march across the street and approach the building.

"You are not entering that establishment."

"Says who?" I challenge with a strong voice, taking the steps up to the quite unassuming door.

"Me!" he barks, unceremoniously swooping me off my feet

and striding away. Once again, I am bobbing up and down upon his shoulder. "And every other person in the country, for that matter."

"It is but a gentleman's club, Your Grace," I sigh tiredly, not squirming or fighting, but accepting my position atop his shoulder which, I admit, I rather like. "I will be in and out very quickly. I hardly think all of this warrants such a strong reaction."

He growls. It's primal and, frankly, it makes me a little wary, as he sets me on my feet once more. "I will get him."

"You can't!" I protest, pulling my cloak into place. Frank will surely wonder what business the Duke could possibly have with him and undoubtedly refuse his request to step outside. The only option would be for Johnny to advise my brother of my presence outside the establishment, and that will lead to too many questions that I would rather not answer. It will also probably elicit suspicion. I need no one being suspicious of mine and the Duke's acquaintance. If the Duke is insistent on maintaining the *conversation* between us that he speaks of, then we must be practical. Frank will burst a blood vessel when he knows I am here. He will burst two if he learns who I am with, *without* a chaperone no less. My last thought has me pausing for a moment. "Did you follow me, Your Grace?"

"Of course I followed you. I was hardly going to leave you to venture into the darkness alone, now, was I?" He rolls his eyes. He does that a lot, a sign of how exasperating he finds me to be. Well, I find him rather exasperating too.

"I am quite capable of removing my brother myself—" A door flies open up the alleyway and a woman appears dressed in... "Bloody hell," I breathe, as the Duke steps in front of me, concealing me, I suspect. She was half naked! And not by accident! I find myself craning my head around the Duke's big body. My curiosity will be the death of me. His arm comes up, warning me to remain behind him.

"Oh," the woman says, amusement in her tone. "You need not resort to the filth of an alleyway with a baggage, Your Grace."

My mouth falls open, and I step out from behind the Duke, ready to protest her assumption. Once again, I get precisely nowhere, Johnny turning and slapping a hand over my mouth to silence me. "You must be quiet, Eliza," he whispers, his head tilting in that expectant way I am becoming familiar with. It prompts a lock of his dark blond hair to fall across his forehead, and my hand, damn my treacherous hand, twitches with the need to push it away. I am becoming all too attached to his touch, the contact between us.

The imploring in his gaze shoves me back into submission and I nod as well as I'm capable as he gently frees my mouth, his eyes never leaving mine, not for eight long seconds. I know of the exact amount of time because I count. "I will deal with this." He finally frees me of his burning eyes and faces the half-naked woman, who, apparently, knows him.

Your Grace.

He has been here before? Oh my. Perhaps naïvely, I assumed this establishment was a sophisticated gentleman's club, where gentry drank, chatted, discussed business and smoked. That woman, who seems to have misplaced her clothes, suggests otherwise.

Frank.

Oh, what trouble is he getting himself into? I cannot bear it. I pick up my cloak and hurry past the Duke and the woman, slipping through the door that, conveniently, is still ajar.

"Eliza!"

I am met with more half-naked women, their breasts being flaunted unashamedly, their faces painted heavily. Each and every one turns and looks at me. I feel somewhat overdressed, but there are more pressing matters at hand than my apparent state of decency. Hearing the thunderous pounds of the Duke's boots, I hurry on, following my nose and the smell of tobacco.

I arrive in a large, lavish room, it's dark, clouds of smoke hampering my vision farther, but I still see the women draped across the bodies of many men, fondling with them in one way or another. I quickly pick my jaw up off the floor.

"For Christ's sake, Eliza," Johnny yells, seizing my wrist. "This is not a place a lady should frequent."

"Obviously," I mutter, wrenching myself free of his grip. "But I am here now, so I may as well see to my business." I march on, scanning the endless well-dressed men, men held in the highest of regards, until I find my brother. He is slumped in a chair with a bottle of gin, and a woman is splayed across his lap, her generous breasts thrust alarmingly close to his face. He is barely conscious.

"Frank," I blurt, distraught to see him in such an indecent tangle.

He blinks, struggling to sit up, hastily knocking the woman off his lap. "Eliza?" He stands abruptly, albeit on wobbly legs. "What the d-d-devil…" he slurs, "are you doing h-h-here?"

"I am here to save you from this…this…" What am I to call it? I peek around. "…temptation!"

A rough laugh sounds from behind me, and I pivot to discover the Duke looking decidedly amused. I will soon wipe that smile from his face. "Before you are beyond being saved," I add, just loud enough for the Duke to hear. As anticipated, his humor disappears and is replaced with a belligerent snarl. I huff to myself. "I'll do you the kindness of waiting for you outside so you may at least make yourself decent in private," I declare to a rather startled-looking Frank. Decent? Private? "I trust you will not leave me alone and at the mercy of London by night for too long." And with that, I swivel and leave, feeling the eyes of many men follow my path to the front entrance of the club.

I can't say I can breathe easy once I am outside the confines of the stifling, scandalous palace of pleasure. A gentleman's club? What utter rubbish! I look left and right. This is not a place for a lady, not at this hour, anyway. Unless, of course, and as proven in the establishment behind me, you are a woman of a certain variety. Namely, brazen.

"Are you mad, woman?"

I look over my shoulder. The Duke is filling the doorway. He does not appear all too pleased by the situation. I snort. It hasn't escaped my notice that the woman in the alleyway recognized him. "I should like you to leave."

"I should like you to be caged, but, alas, I am not an unreasonable man."

"Ha!" He's an ass! "Where the hell is my brother?"

"Probably fastening his breeches." He rounds my quaking body and faces me. "I expect he will be a while. His coordination, courtesy of the gin, is awful."

"Why do you look so angered by this whole situation?" I ask. "I demand to know!"

"Because, Eliza, and it pains me to say it…" He comes close, his face as near as it could possibly be to mine, and I breathe in. It is shaky. "…I appear to have developed a somewhat unreasonable and misplaced concern for your well-being."

Oh? "Then lose it," I hiss. "And be gone!"

He snorts his thoughts on that. "I have never in my life met such—"

The door to the club swings open, and Frank appears, wobbling at the top of the steps. His eyes bounce between the Duke and me, his drunken mind undoubtedly taking far too long to enlighten him on who and what he is facing. "Eliza?" he says, closing one eye, as if trying to focus on me.

"Yes, yes." I climb the steps and circle an arm around his waist. "We already established it is I."

"You cannot be here!"

"Neither can you," I reply, feeling his weight lean into me. Oh, this won't do. I will never maintain the strength to be his leaning post the entire way back to Belmore Square. "It would be most helpful if you could please try to walk without my assistance."

"Eli...za!" he slurs, as he pushes himself away from me. "I am am am a-am...per...per...fect...fectly sober."

Johnny snorts his amusement, and if the situation were not of a catastrophically awful kind, I might stop and admire the vision of the eternally moody Duke having a jolly good time. *Ass.* "I beg to differ," I mutter, watchful for any signs that Frank might fall flat on his face. I do believe my earlier question, the one I asked myself, has been answered. This is how Frank has taken the news of Lizzy Fallow's imminent engagement to Viscount Millingdale. Namely, get blind drunk and pretend it hasn't happened. The trouble is, Frank cannot remain completely sozzled forever, as much as that may feel appealing to him at this present time. I do not even have the capacity to consider how I feel about how he clearly feels. Lizzy Fallow isn't Lady Dare, and that is all that matters to me.

"As I see it," the Duke says, speaking up, "you aren't getting very far without some assistance."

He is, of course, right. "Will you help me?" I ask.

"It would be my pleasure."

"Wait a minute." Frank raises an uncoordinated pointed finger and aims it at the Duke's face. "You're Johnny Winters."

"It's *Your Grace*," I point out to my intoxicated brother.

Frank snorts and I cringe. "I do not addr...ess murderers with re...re...spect."

"Perhaps you should," the Duke retorts, his lips straight as he takes a threatening step toward my brother. "Or this murderer might murder you too."

"Enough!" I cry, putting myself between them before fists start flying and, worse, duels are arranged at dawn. "No one is murdering anyone."

"Don't count on it, Eliza," the Duke hisses, looking rather deadly.

"Wait." Frank aims his pointed finger to the heavens as if enlightenment has just this minute made it past the fog of alcohol. I shrink. "You know each other?"

"No," I say on a laugh.

"Yes, actually," the Duke fires smugly.

I shoot him a threatening look that I fear will not threaten him in the least. Thankfully, he backs down, though I can see with worrying clarity that he does it with the greatest of reluctance. "I saw Miss Melrose on the street. I recognized her from Belmore Square and, as any gentleman would, asked if she was all right."

Good. That's good.

"Oh," Frank frowns and starts rubbing at his head. "I suppose I should call it a night."

"I think that is by far the best idea you have had for a while," I chirp, thrilled by Frank's announcement. "I have a story for you to write about a disgraced duke causing havoc in the milliner's." I smile at Johnny who rolls his eyes.

I sigh. "Let us get you home," I say to Frank.

"Did I ride here?"

"You could not have ridden here."

"That's funny," he slurs, swinging his eyes up and down the street, confused. "I'm certain I did."

"I think perhaps," the Duke says as he steps forward, casting a disapproving expression upon Frank, "your brother is getting confused over *who* has ridden what." He raises an eyebrow.

"You are a *dis*grace, Your Grace," I mutter, not as shocked as I should be. I have, without question, been subjected to considerably more than my innocent eyes and ears should take.

"Tell me something I don't know, Eliza."

"I think I'm a bit drunk," Frank chuckles, staggering toward me.

"Frank!" I shriek. I will be squashed against a brick wall!

"Give me strength." The Duke grunts and catches Frank,

steadying him, saving me from my imminent fate. "He obviously can't handle his drink."

"I fear he's in mourning," I say.

"Did someone die?"

"No, they did not." I look at my brother with all the pity I feel as the Duke kindly holds his limp body up. "As I understand it, I believe Frank may have formed a certain attachment to a certain lady who is now being married off to . . . how must I put it?"

"Plainly."

"Someone prehistoric."

"Oh."

"Indeed." I shake my head. "I do hope this doesn't mean he will return to inappropriate dalliances again."

"Inappropriate?" the Duke repeats, making me scowl to myself.

"You may know her." I pull my hood up and move to Frank's other side to help, not that I am much assistance. "Lady Dare," I mumble, moving in closer to my brother, trying in vain to support his ever-increasingly sagging form.

"Mama?" Frank mumbles. "Mama, can I have a bedtime story?"

I smile fondly. "Awww, he's dreaming."

"He's legless, Eliza." The Duke huffs and puffs, jolting Frank to get a more beneficial hold on him. "Keep to the shadows and your face down."

Unseen. I don't need to relay the plan to Frank. His chin is resting on his haphazardly fastened cravat, his face pointing to his feet as he mumbles and moans.

By the time we make it to the edge of Belmore Square, I am somewhat breathless, although, I must admit, I have hardly been helpful in the transportation of my drunken brother. In fact, I suspect the Duke considers me more of a hindrance judging by his constant long, loud draws for breath. Patience. He's searching for patience.

"You can leave him on the steps," I say. "I will have Dalton get him to his be—"

A small giggle sounds.

"What was that?" the Duke whispers, slowing to a stop, Frank now practically hanging down his front.

"I do not know." I release my useless hold and turn toward the gardens, hearing the sound again. It pulls me toward the entrance.

"Eliza," he hisses behind me. "Eliza, come back here immediately."

I frown as I step into the gardens. "Clara?" I call.

A gasp sounds, and fast-moving footsteps ring out. I see the shadow of a person dash across the cobbles and my little sister, very sheepishly, steps out from behind a large laurel bush. "Are you mad?" I blurt, taking her arm and guiding her toward the house.

"What the devil is going on now?" the Duke asks, his eyes following us. "Is that your sister?"

"Yes, I am!" Clara pipes up, full of indignation. She shrugs me off and plants her hands on her hips, pointing her interested attention the Duke's way. She looks at Frank. "I believe it is I who should be asking what the devil is going on."

"I have been rescuing Frank from an imminent fate worse than death," I declare. "And what have you been doing? You were with Governess enjoying some embroidery."

Clara snorts, and I don't suppose I can blame her. Neither of us enjoys embroidery. "What is *he* doing here?"

Naturally, I follow her lead. "You were with the stable boy," I fire accusingly.

"At least not a murderer."

"Clara!"

"For the love of God," the Duke mutters, carrying Frank over to the steps and releasing him somewhat carelessly. I rush over to assist, and Frank groans as his body sprawls out across the steps.

"Good night," Clara snaps, stepping over Frank's body and disappearing into the house. The Duke takes my hand, and I start, looking at him. I find an odd expression passing across his face. It looks like regret. Sorrow. His eyes are stuck to my lips, and I hold my breath as his face slowly comes toward mine. *My God. My God, my God, my God.* Is this it? Finally? Should I stop it? I cannot stop it, for I burn for his mouth on mine. To swallow down my words. Blind me to nothing but the pleasure he can give. I close my eyes and wait. And wait. Increasingly breathless. Anticipation killing me. His scent invading my senses. My heart pounding. But a few long seconds later, I am still without his lips on mine, and he releases my hand. The absence of his warmth is a cutting loss.

I open my eyes and find he has moved back, his forehead heavy, his gaze hard.

"Thank you for your help," I say quietly, hating the regret and pain I see in his stare.

He does not bless me with a reply, passing his attention to Frank on the steps. "Your father must have done something appallingly wicked in a previous life," he says quietly.

His statement makes me pause for thought, the tone of his voice so solemn, but, in truth, I cannot argue with him. Here we are, all three of my father's offspring, all behaving in the most inappropriate of ways and dallying with the most inappropriate of people.

"I must go," the Duke says, straightening his jacket, his focus set on his attire. "Goodbye, Miss Melrose." Without looking at me once more, he leaves, and with every step he takes, moving him farther and farther away from me, I feel my heart sinking more. His goodbye felt so…final.

Chapter 11

Blackmail, it would seem, was the only way forward. It was also the only way I could get Frank into the house without being detected and landing us *all* in Father's *or* Mother's black book. It matters not that I myself have some rather shocking secrets to hide. Revealing mine would be to reveal Clara's, and that is a weapon I shall use unashamedly. And did. She was quite eager to come back out and help me drag Frank to bed, and we managed to do so in the nick of time, notwithstanding losing various items of his clothing on our way—Frank, unfortunately, thought he was already in the privacy of his bedroom and started stripping. As luck would have it, Papa and Mama were jolly, a result of too much wine, I suppose, when they arrived home from their evening socializing at the Fallows. They were quite oblivious to my minor mishap of leaving Frank's cravat strewn on the stairs, where I found it this morning on my way to the dining room.

What a night!

It is not even past eight when I give up on sleep and take myself downstairs. My early appearance catches Dalton off guard, and he rushes to finish dressing the table and fetch coffee, spewing many unnecessary apologies. "It is all right," I assure him, pouring myself a cup and lowering to a chair at the unusually quiet table. "Try as I might, I cannot sleep, Dalton."

"Are you feeling better, Miss Melrose?"

"I fear I have taken enough rest in the past week to last me for one lifetime." I smile and sip, waiting until he has left the dining room before I rise and take myself to the window. To be expected at this hour, Belmore Square is without the hustle and bustle I am usually greeted with upon arrival to the dining room for breakfast. My eyes are drawn toward the Winters residence, my mind being pulled in a thousand directions. My resolve to sever my contact with the Duke. My conclusion to continue. My vacillation is driving me positively mad! But, and I don't mind confessing to it, I am, it would seem, rather attached to the broody oaf, yet, I hasten to add, perhaps in an attempt to ease my afflictions, I have seen softness in the hard, cold Duke. His smiles are like the sunniest of days, which, frankly, is ironic, because they are as rare as sunny days. His quick wit is refreshing. His touch is…

I sigh, sipping more coffee. It is true. I am falling in love. But what does it matter? He walked away yesterday evening, leaving me anticipating his kiss. "This is very unfortunate," I say quietly.

"What is?"

I whirl around and find Clara at the table. She must have crept down the stairs very quietly, for I heard not one creak. Hmmm. I narrow an eye on a pout. "You are awake very early."

"As are you," she retorts, pouring herself a coffee and plucking a bread roll from the basket that Dalton has just set down. She wanders over to the window and looks out across the square toward the Duke's house. "We are very lucky to be alive." She pops a piece of bread in her mouth and turns a cheeky smile my way. "After our encounter with the deadly Duke, that is."

"Oh please." I leave her at the window and drop to a chair. "There is more risk of our parents killing us than the Duke." I match her raised brows. "*If* they become privy to our mischiefs yesterday eve."

"Fear not, sister. Your secret is safe with me."

"What of your secret?" I blurt.

"What secret?" Frank's strained voice comes from behind, and

I turn in my chair to see him propped up against the door, dressed quite inappropriately in…not a lot.

"You look like death," I mutter.

His palm drags down his screwed-up face as he practically feels his way across the dining room to the table and plops into a chair. "Good grief, I feel it too, I assure you."

"You caused me untold inconvenience."

"And me!" Clara shrieks around her bread, joining us at the table.

"You?" I question. "You didn't have to carry him from…the gentleman's club."

"Neither did you," she points out, a rueful smile on her face. "As I saw it, it was, in fact, another who was carrying our dear, drunken brother."

"What?" Frank blurts, blinking rapidly.

"Nothing. Clara is being spiteful." I throw her a warning look and she shrinks into her chair. Good. "You can leave," I say flatly.

"What?"

This is not a conversation I should like to have in the company of my young sister. My tilted head is enough to spell out to Clara that I mean business, and since she has something rather outrageous to hide—although how outrageous is yet to be determined—she skulks off and leaves me to deal with our wayward brother. Good heavens, I am a hypocrite. Since when did I become the sensible, compliant one of the Melrose children? It matters not. My dalliances with the Duke are hardly dalliances. Clara's encounters with the stable boy, I pray, are innocent. Just two minors dreaming and planning a happily ever after that will never happen. Frank, however, is brazenly spreading his seed. It's shameful! I turn my attention back to my brother. "What are you thinking?"

His frown is heavy, his handsome face rough. "I don't remember. What was I thinking?"

"The gentleman's club," I remind him. "Kentstone's."

His look of horror is instant. "What do you know of Kentstone's?"

"Too much!"

His palms meet the table, his face coming threateningly close. He has nerve. "How much?"

"I know it is not a place a respectable gentleman, such as yourself, although I am doubting your eligibility, I might add, should be frequenting." Was he so drunk he does not remember the entire string of unfortunate events? How useful! "Does Mother know of its true happenings?"

His wince tells me no.

"What about Father?"

Another wince.

Well, it would seem I am in a fortunate position and have my brother backed into a corner.

"I was being pathetic," he mutters, his face grim.

"Be that as it may," I say, "you do not want a reputation as a rake. Well, not now we're in London."

His look is one of pure boredom, to be expected, I suppose. After all, his shenanigans in our old life were of no consequence or concern. It mattered not if anyone saw or heard him being pathetic. Nevertheless, I remain insulted. All of the lectures he has subjected me to, and he pulls a stunt like this? "You should make yourself presentable before Papa and Mama rise."

"I feel thoroughly scorned."

"Rather me than Father, I'm sure you'll agree."

Now, he scowls. I have him, and he cannot contest. "Fair enough." He pushes himself up from the table with effort and leaves me.

Goodness, I do hope Frank's memory does not find him. I will be done for! "As you should be," I say, frowning to myself. As an advocate for living as one wishes, regardless of the expectation placed upon me, I am being rather…judgmental. I should be relieved my siblings are walking the path of disgrace with me. Except I'm not. One wayward child—namely, me—is enough for our parents to contend with. They do not deserve three! Besides, Frank can choose whom he wishes to marry. Hopefully, Clara will be blessed with the privilege to choose too. So long as it's not the stable boy, naturally. I expect, just as soon as she is of age, Mother will be enticing every eligible bachelor across London into her clutches, giving Clara a pool of potential husbands to choose from.

I drift into thought but am soon pulled back when an urgent knock sounds at the door. It is wildly early. "Whoever could that be?" I ask myself, rising from my chair. I enter the hallway and find Dalton answering the door.

"I must speak with Mr. Melrose at once," the voice says. A distinct voice—one broken by excessive pipe smoking and—as rumor would have it—raucous bellowing at any of the gentleman's clubs he may be frequenting. I cannot confirm his behavior within the walls of any club, but I can confirm that he is a man who indulges excessively in all things, and one of those things is elaborate tales of London's happenings.

"Mr. Porter?" I say, passing Dalton.

"Ah, Miss Melrose. Fetch your father."

"I beg your pardon?" I retort, indignant. "I'm afraid he is sleeping. I'm sure," I say, catching a whiff of alcohol, "I need not enlighten you of the early hour." I expect by the way in which Mr. Porter has presented himself on this morning at our front door, he has not long stepped out of one of the clubs he is all too fond of. Thank goodness that club was not Kentstone's yesterday eve.

"You need not." He pats at his pocket watch. "It is of an urgent nature, Miss Melrose."

"I'll fetch my brother," I say, backing away. "I know him to be awake."

His head tilts in interest. "Is he well?"

I laugh under my breath. "That is debatable, Mr. Porter." I step back. "I suppose you ought to come in."

"Thank you," he says, shuffling into the hallway.

"You may wait in the dining room. Dalton has set out a fresh pot of coffee." My nose wrinkles, Mr. Porter's closeness not agreeing with my sense of smell. I step back. "Excus—"

"Porter?" Father says, appearing looking sleepy, his entire usually well-turned-out form in disarray. "What of this early hour?"

"My sincerest apologies for disturbing you so early, Melrose, but I'm afraid it's rather pressing."

Father frowns before motioning to his study across the hall. "Bring coffee, Dalton," he says, stalking off, leaving Porter to follow. *Bugger!* What is so pressing as to warrant a visit at this outlandish hour?

I watch Dalton leave Father's study after delivering coffee, and, shame on me, I soon have my ear pressed against the wood.

"And this comes from a reliable source?" Papa says.

"You know me, Melrose. I strive to achieve the utmost accuracy."

I snort to myself. Porter has never let the minor matter of the truth get in his way of a good story. *What is the story?* I can only imagine it is explosive to warrant Mr. Porter's early visit. I also know that on this occasion I have not written it.

I hear footsteps. I gasp and dash away from the door, just as Papa swings it open. "I need to find my son!"

"He came home last night, Papa," I say.

He appears relieved, his shoulders falling a fraction. "Dalton, get Frank, will you?"

"Immediately, sir," Dalton says, appearing and disappearing up the stairs. Father doesn't even bless me with a look before he's slamming the door. What the devil is going on?

Five minutes later, Frank trudges down the stairs, looking no better than when he left me not so long ago. "What's going on?"

he asks me, noting my position at the dining-room doorway opposite Papa's study.

I can only shrug. "Something about a story, I think. Mr. Porter arrived in a bit of a fluster."

"Oh?"

"Stinking of alcohol and stale nicotine."

Frank grimaces, looking to Father's study door as his hand rests on his stomach, which I expect is turning. "Oh joy."

"I would hold your breath, brother."

He heeds my advice and takes a long inhale before pushing his way into Father's study. "Porter," he says on an exhale, and I laugh, imagining him pulling in air again urgently. He still looks rather green. "Father."

"I'm glad you're home, son," Papa says softly before clearing his throat, getting back to business. "Now, tell me again, Porter."

The door knocks again, and I frown as I wonder who on earth *that* could be. I hurry forward, pull it open, and stand still and worried as Lymington looks me up and down on a curled lip before pushing past me and letting himself into Papa's study. I do not have one inkling what is going on, but I do not like it.

"Miss Melrose," Dalton says, looking at me with restrained interest. "A muffin, perhaps?" Translated: *I can see you are itching to eavesdrop but I must foil your intention.* Damn it.

"Thank you, Dalton," I say, wandering back into the dining room. I smile as I take a muffin and the moment Dalton has left the room, I'm up again and dashing across the hallway to Father's study. I press my ear up against the door.

"I have taken this newspaper from six sheets to twelve, Melrose. There is a certain pressure to fill those pages with something more than advertisements and notices."

"Yes, yes," Father mutters. "I am fully aware of the pressure placed upon us." There is a certain element of exhaustion in his tone. It should not be a surprise. I know of the hour he and

Mama arrived home from the party, and it is at least two hours before Father would usually awaken.

"And Frank doesn't seem to be producing any decent stories recently," Lymington adds. "He quickly lost his stride, didn't he?"

"Do you have any physical injuries?" Father asks.

"No," Frank answers, his voice tight. "I should like to know who this reliable source is."

"I do not disclose my contacts, Frank," Mr. Porter says. "Rule number one of journalism. So you do not recall the incident?"

"I do not," Frank sighs. "I remember walking home—"

"From where?" Lymington presses.

"Gladstone's."

I recoil. *Gladstone's?* But, of course, he cannot share his true whereabouts. The scandal would be catastrophic! And I seriously question whether Frank remembers *anything* after leaving Kentstone's. Regardless, whatever is all this about?

"And you were attacked," Porter states. "By Winters and an accomplice."

"Yes," Lymington agrees. "We all know he's capable."

"What?" I whisper.

"I wouldn't say *attacked*," Frank murmurs.

"Mugged?" Porter presses.

"Have you checked your possessions this morning?" Lymington asks.

"Yes," Frank replies, albeit quietly. Reluctantly. "Everything is accounted for. I don't recall much, if you want the truth. I fear it's hardly worth printing."

"Nonsense!" Lymington chortles. "You will write up the report immediately, Porter."

"What?" Frank asks, alarmed. "But I hardly remember a damn thing!"

"I have all the details I need," Porter says, smug. "My source."

"That is that. Now, Porter," Lymington says, "on the matter

of notices, I should like Miss Melrose's engagement to my son announced tomorrow."

I twitch like I could have been struck by a bolt of lightning. An announcement? No one makes announcements prior to the actual wedding. It's after. Always after!

"And when is the wedding?" Porter asks.

"Four weeks from this coming Saturday."

"Excellent," he says as I stare at the door in utter disbelief. I am yet to make amends with Frederick after my shenanigans. It appears I need not. "Good day, gentlemen." His voice gets louder. He's getting closer. *Bugger it*. I make a mad dash back into the dining room, just as Lymington and Porter emerge. Father goes upstairs, probably to return to bed, and Frank remains in the study.

Naturally, I go to him. "You lied," I say, my voice tight.

"What would you have me do, Eliza?" A nervous hand rakes through his hair. "Expose you? Expose me?"

"We cannot allow it! It could ruin Winters."

Frank laughs. "Come on, Eliza. The Duke is already ruined. What's the harm in one more rumor if it saves our skin? What do you care, anyway?"

"It's immoral!"

"You and your flaming morals." He comes closer, and I like *not* the questions in his eyes. "Tell me what happened last night," he demands. "Every detail."

Absolutely not! "I was worried about you. So I went to Gladstone's,"—My head tilts in quite an accusing fashion. Good, it's supposed to be!—"and, of course, you were not on the premises, but at a far less decent establishment across the street. I found you in a very compromising position with a...young lady." I scowl. "If I'd have known of the true happenings, I would never have stepped foot in there. I am scarred for life!"

He rolls his eyes. "You have found me in many compromising positions many times. Why is it a problem now?" he asks, and

I find my mouth snapping shut. That's a very good question. Why do I care? "Continue," he sighs.

"Try as I might," I go on, relieved he's spared me the need for an explanation, but I really must think hard about it. Perhaps it's because I'm worried for Papa's well-being. Or perhaps I simply cannot stand the thought of Frank in the clutches of Lady Dare. "I could not move your lumbering, drunken body, and the Duke happened to see my struggle and offered his assistance."

"And you accepted?"

"Would you rather me leave you in the gutter?"

"He helped you?"

"Yes!"

Frank's lips twist. "Well, this is all rather unfortunate, isn't it?"

"Not if we make sure we tell the truth of the matter."

"And then, dear sister, your reputation will be smeared."

"Don't forget yours. I was merely trying to save my brother from disgrace."

"And in doing so, you have risked disgracing yourself. For Christ's sake, Eliza. What are you thinking, putting yourself in the company of such a character without a chaperone?"

"I had a chaperone." I point out, a little too haughtily for a woman in my position. Frank gives me tired eyes. "Oh." I smile, and it is sickly sweet. "You mean a chaperone who was aware he was actually chaperoning."

"Ideally, yes."

"Well, the whole situation was not ideal," I reply, shaking my head in dismay, "so I was forced to think on my feet." It matters not that I am lying. The lack of the truth in this situation does not harm another. Porter's lies, however, most certainly will cause harm. I will not allow it. "He says he has a reliable source."

Frank laughs. "They all say that."

"Are you saying he's lying?"

"I don't know," Frank muses. "How else would he know that I was close enough to Winters to warrant a claim of mugging?"

"We must stop Porter."

"And how do you propose we do that?"

"I don't know," I admit. "But I do know that no one needs to be exposed. Except, perhaps, Porter and Lymington for being devious, immoral louts." What is their problem with Johnny?

"That's journalism, Eliza," Frank sighs, rubbing at his eye sockets. "And why Father will never allow you into the seedy world that's made him fortunes. It's no place for a lady."

"I've never been a damn lady."

"Fine. It's no place for a female, and you're definitely one of those, are you not?"

"I will find a way," I assure him on a scowl, "to prove it."

"Well, please do come wake me when you've figured it out." He leaves the study, and I look back over my shoulder to the glass cabinet in which Father keeps one copy of every edition ever printed. Some have my stories in. There are no lies in my stories, and never will be. Integrity is key. My nose wrinkles, and I go back to the dining room and pour myself a fresh coffee. What does one do to stop a story being printed? I ask myself the question repeatedly while I drum my fingers on the table. And it comes to me. I inhale, my fingers stopping. One creates a better story. A bigger story. A more scandalous story.

One that is true.

That could be trickier than it should be, as nothing true is as engrossing as an over-embellished pile of nonsense. Unless, of course, I share my dalliances with Johnny Winters. That's very true and would cause quite the scandal. I sigh.

And then out of nowhere, it comes to me. A solution. My brain works fast, my idea, frankly, genius! I shall do what I condemn Porter for doing. Embellish. Or, actually, completely fabricate something.

False news.

Perhaps integrity is not key, at least not on this occasion. And it's for a good cause, so I am forgiving of myself. My God, this could be the story of the century! But how the heck am I going to pull it off? I should not underestimate myself. I am, if anything, determined.

And falling in love.

MILLINGDALE BANK RUMORED TO CLOSE TOMORROW

Imagine if your fortune, every last shilling, was lost because of one bad business decision by the lord who owns the bank where it is stored. I have heard from quite the reliable source, that Lord Millingdale...

Chapter 12

The next morning, and for the first time in my existence, I intercept the delivery of our daily newspaper and breathe in deeply when I see the headline. Then I go to the window and look outside to see the residents of Belmore Square all flying out of their homes in a panic, some still pulling various items of clothing on, to head to Millingdale Bank and withdraw their money.

"Oopsie," I whisper, straining so hard to keep the satisfied grin from my face.

"Miss Melrose?" Dalton asks from behind me, forcing me to work harder in my endeavors.

I turn toward his voice, only once I can be certain I do not look as guilty as I am, and cock my head in question. "Yes, Dalton?"

"Would..." He frowns and goes to the door, pulling it open and looking out onto the square. I see Countess Rose hurrying past. "What in the devil's name is going on?"

"No idea, Dalton," I say, going to the dining room, my grin now uncontainable, and flick through the rest of the paper, searching for the other story, and after a few advertisements, one ironically for Millingdale Bank, I find no disturbing tale of the mugging of Frank Melrose. Well, that's all rather odd.

My confusion, however, is interrupted when I hear the high-pitched screech of my mother. I rush to the hallway and find her hands over her face. "Mama, what is it?" I ask, concerned. Are there tears in her eyes? Oh no. I am about to assure her that there is nothing to worry about, that all of their new money is safe, but I am halted when I spy a smile past the hand over her mouth.

She gasps, sniffs, and rushes forward, presenting me with two vouchers. "I made it," she breathes. "I have been approved!"

I frown and look down at her hand. "What is it?"

"A voucher for Almack's signed by Lady Tillsbury!"

My shoulders drop, but I just manage to stop my eye roll in its tracks. "I'm very glad your work stroking Lady Tillsbury's ego has paid off, Mama." I have to hand it to her, she's worked hard enough to secure herself entry into the sacred rooms, where only the most fashionable, wealthiest, most influential members of the ton will be seen. I pass her, my wondering regarding the absence of Porter's mugging report back. Frank. I need to speak with Frank this minute. Pray do tell me I didn't go to all the trouble of fabricating some false news and tricking Dalton into sending the story to the printworks under Papa's instruction for nothing.

"There is one for you too," she calls, sounding somewhat surprised. She is not alone.

I halt halfway up the stairs and turn. "What?"

"A voucher," Mother says, walking forward, waving it at me. "She has issued one to you, too."

"Why?"

Mother pauses for thought, and I wait with bated breath for what those thoughts might be. There's no explanation. Vouchers, subscriptions, tickets, blessings, whatever we are to call them, are like gold dust. They do not get handed out so frivolously. "I don't know," Mother says. "But I shall ask!" She whirls around and sings her way to the dining room, as I, confused for more than one reason now, look down at the newspaper in my hand.

"Frank," I say, rushing on and bursting into his room unannounced. He growls and pulls the bed sheets up over his head. "There is no story about the Duke."

"Then you should be delighted, I'm sure. Eliza saves the world again."

Delighted? No. I am perplexed.

"Now bugger off," he grumbles. "It's the crack of bloody dawn."

I glare at his bed, indignant. "I've heard the Millingdale Bank may collapse today."

The sheets are soon wafting through the air and Frank's sleepy form blinking rapidly. "What?"

"I cannot imagine the Fallows will be all too pleased about their daughter marrying a failed banker and a disgraced viscount."

"Are you serious?"

I smile, wink, making Frank frown hard, and pull the door closed. "You are most welcome, brother," I say to myself, having one last scan of the newspaper—just in case my eyes are failing me, for I am certainly lacking sleep—yet I find nothing. I frown, skimming once more. And the notice informing the whole of London that I, Eliza Catherine Melrose, will wed Frederick Lymington, is also absent. I can't say I'm sorry, not about either of the missing pieces in today's edition.

But I am wondering what the hell is going on.

I still haven't the foggiest by supper time. Father has been out on business all day, Frank with him, and Mother, undoubtedly with her vouchers signed by Lady Tillsbury fixed to her forehead for all to see, has been flouncing around the royal park. I was not invited, and I did not argue. She felt at my skin and hummed, in that considering way she does, when I told her I felt so much better. She concluded, thank heavens, that she thought it best I continued resting, if only so my ticket for the Almack's was not wasted, as she feared I may have got back on my feet somewhat too early after my weeklong illness. Dalton had a very high eyebrow as he polished the silver a few feet away, and I, naturally, ignored him.

I have paced around and around all day, peeking out of the window constantly, freezing when I have heard the front door, hoping it is Father coming home so I can perhaps prod gently for an explanation for the absence of the news I had been expecting, or, more to the point, dreading.

I sigh. I cannot murmur a word without looking as guilty as I am, but…I can interrogate Frank again. And I will. He must have become alert to *something* today that will explain.

My heart skips a beat when I hear a carriage rumble up the cobbles, and I dash to the window to see Father and Frank. *Yes!* Mother is coming down the street too, Clara plodding miserably behind her, and Emma carrying what I expect is another new dress.

The moment they are in the house, Dalton hands Mother something and she shrieks. "Bert!" she cries, waving the paper over her head. "My God, the society gods do so admire us today."

"What is it?" he asks, blinking rapidly.

"It has the royal seal! Oh my, we have been invited!" Mother looks on the verge of a heart attack. "The Prince's birthday!"

"Calm down, Florence," Father grunts, unimpressed. "You'll burst a blood vessel." He turns his attention onto me and narrows an eye. A suspicious eye. I find my spine straightening as if standing taller can convince him I am unaware of…anything.

"Good afternoon, Papa."

He hums, regards me closely a little while longer while I shift on my feet. "It's rumored Millingdale Bank is perfectly safe."

"Oh, thank God." I grin like an idiot.

"Quite." He goes to his study, calling for Frank to follow, and I relax, turning my attention onto my brother. He follows, shutting the door behind him. He looked tense too.

"Look, Eliza!" Mother shrieks on, making me flinch. "Oh, I shall have to buy another dress immediately." The invitation hits her chest, as if she is hugging it. "But first we must ready ourselves for the Almack's ball this evening." She's off, Emma in tow, singing at the top of her voice. "You look better, dear. I'm so glad you can come along."

That's funny, because I feel positively ill.

"What about me?" Clara gripes, and I know not why because she would rather shovel horseshit than socialize at Almack's.

"Perhaps in a year or two."

I look at Father's study door as my lips twist in contemplation, and then glance around to see if I am alone, which, much to my relief, I am. Creeping forward, I push my ear to the wood, but flinch when there's a rather aggressive bang at the front door. "For heaven's sake," I breathe, my palm on my chest where my heart booms with fright. Is everyone around here determined to kill me with fright?

"Melrose! Melrose, open up this minute!"

My teeth clench and my nose wrinkles in distaste, as I wonder what Lymington could possibly want, and so urgently? I know not, but I am positively dying with curiosity, so relieving Dalton of the task, I open the door. "Your Grace," I say, though it is through my teeth, which are still, quite painfully, gritting. He looks me up and down and, downright rudely, it must be said, pushes past me without an invitation to enter.

"Melrose!" he barks.

Father's study door swings open, revealing Frank. "Your Grace," he says, looking somewhat confused. And perhaps a little worried.

Frank too gets shoved aside by Lymington, this time by his walking aid. "What is the meaning of this?" he yells, waving his wooden stick in the air threateningly. "We had a deal. Age might be taking my sight, Melrose, but it is not taking my mind. We agreed it would be announced today! Where the hell is Porter?"

With eyes as wide as the Thames, I watch as Lymington stamps around Father's office and Father follows, trying to appease him. "Unfortunately, we cannot locate him at present, but

Frank here has our lawyer paying a visit to his home. He will be fired, mark my words."

Fired for forgetting to have a marriage notice printed? Surely not? I do not like Porter, be sure of that fact, but his lapse does not warrant Father's intended course of action.

There is another knock at the door, this one decidedly calmer and polite, and I open it again, still struck somewhat dumb.

"Miss Melrose," Mr. Casper says on a nod, his kind eyes smiling. "I am here to see your father."

"You had better come in," I say, opening the way to Father's lawyer as the shouts emanating from Father's office get louder. The whole street must be able to hear! "I fear it could get physical, Mr. Casper."

"Oh dear," he says, hurrying past me and disappearing into Papa's study. "Calm down, gentlemen," he placates, setting his work case on a chair by the fire. "I have spoken with Porter's wife, and she has helpfully shared his whereabouts."

"Well, where the flaming heck is he?" Father bellows as I wonder if I have ever seen him so distressed. I think not.

"In York."

"What?" Frank blurts.

"What?" Father mimics.

"York?" Lymington barks. "What business does he have in York? He should be here, seeing to this business!" Pointing his walking aid at Father, Lymington steps forward threateningly. If I was not so shocked by this whole unfortunate matter, I would laugh at the frail old man. Father could flick him over with his little finger! Of course, he would never, but something unsettling within is telling me the Duke's status is not the reason.

The deal.

"If," the old ogre goes on, "I do not see an announcement by morn, I will end you, Melrose. End you!"

"The date is set," Father says. "I have signed the contract, agreed to all of your terms! The arrangements are being made."

They are? Why do I not know of these arrangements? After all, it is me getting married. And what of this contract and terms. *What terms?* This is not simply my life being given away. It comes with certain terms, and I expect they are not of the traditional variety.

Lymington snorts. "Make it happen, Melrose. I don't mind ruining you if you fail." And with that, he storms out, barking an order for his manservant to follow.

"Oh dear me," Mr. Casper sighs. "I can't say I was confident this deal would run smoothly."

I am in Father's study before I can convince myself to consider my options. "I want to know of the terms." And the thoughts are tumbling out of my mouth too.

"Not now, Eliza," Father sighs, waving me off. He looks exhausted.

"Yes, now."

"Eliza," Frank warns.

"I'll be going," Mr. Casper says, making a hasty exit. My worry heightens. For a lawyer, a man trained to challenge people, he looked rather troubled at facing an argument.

I close the study door in demonstration. I am not moving until I have my answer. I can see with satisfying clarity when Father's face softens that he has grasped the strength of my determination. He's looking at me like he used to look at me as a girl, when I would present him with a detailed report on whatever interested me that day. "Eliza," he says, coming at me with open arms. "This is everything I've dreamed of for you. And Frank and Clara. A secure future!"

"Our future is secure," I point out. "You've made sure of that with your hard work, Papa. We do not need suitable husbands and wives to help us along the way to security." I give him my beseeching eyes. "Or happiness. I am happy as I am. I am happy with my family. I do not wish to be sent to Cornwall where I shall be eternally miserable."

He sighs, backing away. "When you have your own children, you will be far from miserable."

"*If* I should like children, and I know not if I do, I should like a man whom I actually like to sire them!"

"Please, Frank," Papa groans, "I beg you, talk some sense into that girl."

"I need no sense. It is you, Papa, who needs sense, as I cannot marry Frederick, and you should not make me."

"It's too late, Eliza." His shoulders drop, so heavy is the weight of his woes. I have a fun fact for my father. My woes are far heavier!

"What are these terms you speak of?" I ask.

"You will surrender all land and wealth upon your husband's death."

"No jointure?" I laugh and I cannot stop it, although, it should be noted, my amusement is not in humor. "So I don't even get paid for sustaining a marriage to a man whom I don't love?"

"You will, however, keep your title. You will remain in Cornwall."

"I'll be hidden in Cornwall," I blurt. "I am being used to bear an heir, that is all. They are ashamed of me and should wish to keep me locked up miles away from my home and family." This is worse than I ever imagined! "Frederick cannot secure a wife." I am more certain by the day that it is not actually Frederick's fault, despite him being quite bland and boring. I expect the reason he lacks a wife is because no one wants to be associated with his tyrant of a father. "I am a last resort for Lymington to secure the future of his dukedom!" I look at Frank, praying for some backup. He must know this will kill my spirit and destroy my contentment. *Please, Frank, please*, I pray, over and over. Alas, my brother stares down at his breeches, unable to face me. The coward!

"You shall be happy raising children," Father murmurs quietly. "You shall be happy taking our family into a status we are worthy of but lack due to that thing they call bloodlines."

My throat seems to clog up, my eyes stinging terribly. I know not what to say. How could he do this to me? To be married off without one say is terrible enough, but with so many unreasonable conditions attached too? This is madness!

"Now go ready yourself for this flaming Almack's ball before your mother bursts two blood vessels, and I will politely request, if I may, as your father, that you make an effort with your fiancé on this evening to ease the worry of Lymington."

Fiancé? "So he has officially asked for my hand?" I ask. "He came here and spoke to you?"

"He did, and he spoke rather fondly of you."

I tilt my head, watching my father carefully. "And is Frederick the only caller I have had?" Will he admit to Johnny Winters calling for me too?

He sighs. "You are the prettiest young woman this season, Eliza." But that is all he says. Nothing more. No firm confirmation of other callers, and yet it was a confirmation. I care not for any of them, except one. "Please, my darling girl, trust me."

"How can I trust you, Papa? You're condemning me to a life of misery, and for what?"

"The carriage will be here to collect you and your mother at eight." He looks away, and I wonder, for a fleeting moment, because that is how long it takes me to assume I am right, whether Lymington played a part in securing me a voucher to Almack's, just to be seen with Frederick in public, for it has been a while. To assure the ton we are happy and in love and all is well, when it absolutely is not.

I storm out, rushing up the stairs, and burst into my bedroom, falling onto the mattress. I cry. I cry so hard, the hardest I ever have.

*

I cannot match my mother's enthusiasm as much as I try to smile and praise her impeccably dressed form as she twirls around the drawing room and Emma follows, trying in vain to smooth down the endless frills on her new frock. I fear she could be trying forever and never succeed, for the dress is what one might describe as untameable. It is busy and bright and will certainly not be missed. Intentional, I expect, on Mother's part. "You look wonderful," I say, but my announcement is half-hearted and quiet, not that she notices, being so distracted by the task of containing endless flicks and frills.

"Thank you, Eliza." She comes to me and is forced to stretch her arms to reach me, for her dress only allows her so close. "I'm afraid," she says, pulling and pushing at the square neckline of my dress, "that you look somewhat underdressed."

"Or, Mother, perhaps it is you who is overdressed?"

Her fiddling hands falter and she looks at me with eyes that are bright, but not without the pity she feels for me. "Always so beautiful. You get it from me, of course." A cheeky wink.

"Did you speak with Lady Tillsbury?" I ask, my curiosity on that matter still raging.

"About what?"

"About why she would issue one of the rare and precious vouchers in my name when there are endless willing, and *available*, I may add,"—I smile sweetly—"young ladies itching to be swept off their feet at such a prestigious affair by any of the handsome eligible gentlemen. It was Lymington, wasn't it?"

"She was not at all too enthusiastic on discussing the matter, and, frankly, it matters not who recommended you. If only you could conceive the significance of being approved, Eliza."

"But I did not request to be approved, Mama, only you did, so, you see, this makes no sense to me at all, unless, as I have previously voiced, His Grace is acting in order to ensure everyone knows I am to wed Frederick." Because there is no other place more prestigious to be seen. Everyone will be talking about the event until the next one. And, as I know, the announcement he so vehemently wanted printed was, in fact, not printed.

"You are overthinking." Mother dismisses me with ease.

"If you say so." I sigh, glancing across at the doorway when I see Father and Frank pass the drawing room weighed down with arms full of papers. Frank nods, but Father does not even cast a look this way, neither does he speak. I am still in his black books, but that is fine, because he remains in mine.

Mother shrieks, "Frank, you're home!" and surrenders her tugging and pulling of me. Frank, quite reluctantly, I note, slows and casts a wary look our way, and I expect it is because he was hoping to avoid me. Yes, he is in my black books too, and it seems he shall be remaining in them, for he is a stubborn ass and will not confess his true feelings on this horrid situation I have been forced into.

I lift my nose and turn away from him to be sure he knows of my continued contempt. He had better not ever expect me to go out of my way and dig him out of trouble again. Or free the woman who he's obviously got his eye on from the horrid Viscount.

"You look wonderful, Mother," he says as Emma smooths my hair over my shoulder and tweaks the ends so it rests perfectly across the top of my breasts, before she starts artfully fixing a beautiful amethyst jeweled hair comb on the side.

"Tha—"

"And what about me?" I ask as I whirl around to face him, leaving poor Emma to, yet again, start over on the positioning of my jeweled hair comb. "Not that it matters, of course, for I am already engaged and destined for the delights of marriage and children with quite a catch." I tilt my head. "So why I'm being forced into this evening's festivities at a marriage market is beyond the capabilities of my small mind. It is a wasted voucher from whomever requested Lady Tillsbury issue it to me. Perhaps you, brother, should go in my place."

"The voucher is made out to you," he says quietly. "And I have business to attend to."

"Oh, have you located Porter?"

"Porter?" Mother asks. "What of Porter?"

"Nothing," Frank says, sighing. "He's merely visiting family in York."

"I'm surprised," I muse, holding still for Emma again. "What with the Almack's ball this eve and Prince Prinny's party on the horizon, there will be many stories to be had."

"Eliza, give me strength," Frank mutters. "I have not got time to hang around here being subjected to your sarcasm. We have a meeting with the Prime Minister."

"Oh, whatever for?" Mother says.

"Taxes," Frank mutters. "He's increasing the flaming taxes on newspapers."

Oh good. I can only hope this news means the rich, who are famously tight, will refuse to pay and Father's business will fail, meaning we can return to our home. I wince at my own spiteful thoughts, for he may be in my black books, but I do not wish failure on my father. I only wish for him to spare me this eternal misery. And, truly, if I wanted Father's business to fail, all I'd have to do is expose myself as the author of the most popular stories, because Lymington would surely be horrified and leave Father high and dry in this deal I keep hearing of, and since I am part of the deal, I cannot in good conscience damage Father to save myself. So, sadly, no one can ever know.

"Your carriage awaits, Mrs. Melrose," Dalton says.

"Come along, Eliza." Mother practically twirls her way out of the drawing room, and I follow. "Oh look," she whispers when I reach her. "Lady Rose."

"She doesn't look dressed for a soirée," I say, noting her lack of elaborate feathers reaching to the sky.

"That is because she has been blackballed."

"What? Why?"

"She was heard ridiculing Lady Blythe's latest novel."

"Lady Rose would read such stories?" I ask, surprised.

"No, that is the point. She is simply being spiteful. Unfortunately for her, Lady Blythe is a patroness too and has had the Countess's subscription revoked."

"Oh…" I breathe, somewhat amused, and I can tell Mother is too. "Remind me to never insult Lady Blythe."

Mother laughs, loud and over the top, taking the steps down to our carriage. "Good eve to you, Lady Rose," she sings, getting a sharp look shot her way for her trouble. "And will we have the pleasure of your company at Almack's?"

I sigh, going after Mother, as Lady Rose huffs off. "You are terrible, Mama."

"She had it coming, the old witch." She settles in her seat, patting down the puffs of her dress. "I see the way she looks at my family." Mother's eyes narrow. "And hear her tone when she addresses me. She does not think we belong on Belmore Square."

"We don't," I murmur, my eyes falling onto the Winters house.

I don't feel as though I belong anywhere.

The promises of luxury and glamour have not been exaggerated, for I see the ballroom, with its spectacular, glittering chandeliers and heavy velvet draperies, is quite the example of palatial as I admire it from the top of the grand staircase. It is true, what Mother said, I am certainly underdressed for such an occasion in such a venue as this, and yet I find the elaborate, feather and frill-loaded frocks worn by many of the ladies in attendance quite over the top.

I have been left in the care of Frederick, who is a seasoned pro attending such events and yet still somehow looks so very out of place, but Mother is not far, although her attention is fully devoted to socializing and not keeping a suitable eye on her daughter who is in the company of a man, despite said man being who he is, both to society and to me. She looks so happy, and not at all out of place amid the money and status of London, while I, however, feel as though this huge, impressive building is resting on my chest. Supper has been served and it is past eleven, but it feels like the time is ticking by at a mercilessly slow pace. How much longer can I stand this circus, and, God, it is frightening to think it, but I do not simply mean the circus of this evening. I look around again and, this time, I do not see a beautiful room. I see instead bare brick and iron bars and hear not the orchestra, but the torturous sound of water dripping loudly and people laughing wickedly.

Panic finds me and cruelly makes my heart beat faster.

"I should like to take some air," I say with a weak, breathless voice.

"Oh, that is not possible," Frederick replies. They are the first words he has spoken to me all evening. We have stood in silence the entire time, and it does not bode well for our future as husband and wife. "The doors are closed at eleven."

"Whatever do you mean? Are you saying I am imprisoned?" The thought makes my heartbeat quicken even more, and I am powerless to stop it.

"It's tradition. No one, after eleven, regardless of status, may enter."

I blink rapidly and swallow down the growing lump clogging my throat. "But I don't want to enter, I want to leave."

"Yes, but you will not be permitted reentry, you see, Eliza, so you cannot leave until Mrs. Melrose is ready."

I find my mother nearby giggling with some gentlemen of undeniably high social status, if their dazzling gold buttons are anything to judge by, and I wonder if she's already in the throes of lining up potential suitors for Clara. Regardless, she looks uncomfortably settled and quite far from wanting to leave. She will crawl out if she has to, I just know it, for she will not want to miss a moment of this glamorous gossiping gathering. I never knew of Mother's stamina until now, and, I must say, it would be impressive if it were not irritating on occasions—namely, when I am not benefitting from her distraction and endurance. "I'm sure if I explain, they will understand and permit me entry again."

"Forgive me, Miss Melrose, but not even a duchess or a viscountess, or anyone of such rank, for that matter, would question the orders and regulations, and you are not either a duchess or a viscountess, not even close, so I am afraid it is not possible, and, frankly, I would be most unimpressed if you were to so much as inquire, for the mere fact you have asked would raise gossip and risk disrepute on my family name."

I look at Frederick with my mouth agape and my forehead wrinkled heavily as he remains with his attention on the ballroom, where people dance and talk and laugh. "We can't have that, now, can we?" I say.

"We cannot."

That is all well and good, I think, but I am afraid the brewing panic attack that has caught me by surprise cannot wait. I am suffocating. "Will you catch me if I fall, Frederick?" I ask him.

"What?"

"I fear I am about to faint, so I will ask you again and hope for a swift response so I may get on with things. If I faint, will you catch me and save me the embarrassment?"

Frederick, the poor thing, looks quite alarmed. "I…um…" he stutters and stammers as he looks around.

"It is not a hard question, Frederick, and the answer is yes, you would, indeed, catch me, because it would pain you to see me injured if I fall headfirst to the floor."

"Of course," he murmurs as his body solidifies, bracing for my imminent collapse. "Or perhaps I should fetch Mrs. Melrose, who, I have noted quietly on several occasions, is rather tall and has good shoulders."

"Oh, for the love of God, Frederick, I must get out of here,"

I say, pushing past him and taking the stairs down to the ballroom, passing my oblivious mother, who is now chuckling with Lady Blythe.

I exit the ballroom, and make it to the entrance only to find it is guarded by two of the patronesses, one of them being Lady Tillsbury, and, I think to myself, how unfortunate that is, for I should like to question her about who requested a voucher be issued in my name. But first I must get that air. "I'm afraid," I say, somewhat breathless, "I must step outside and find some air."

The other lady, a rather plump woman with rosy cheeks and an unfathomably large nose, doesn't take too kindly to my request, that bulbous nose of hers lifting in quite an unfriendly way so she is, ironically, looking down her nose at me. "You are out of luck," she says, short and snappy. "The doors are closed, and I may not permit you entry should you leave."

I do not wish to rejoin the dreaded party, so her supposed problem is not such a problem, however, I am, for all my faults, a realist, and I realize I cannot place myself alone on the street, neither can I place undue worry upon my mother. This is a far from ideal situation that I know not how to deal with. "I see," I say, finding myself swallowing continuously, each one uncomfortably lumpy. "Then what do you suppose I—"

"I will tend to Miss Melrose," a quiet voice says, and Lady Tillsbury joins us, her smile soft as she regards me with soft eyes too, for everything about the Baroness of Shrewsbury is, as I have come to learn rather quickly from my observations, soft.

"Be that as it may," the plump lady says, "the rules are—"

"Thank you, Lady Weatherby." Lady Tillsbury's smile makes quite a remarkable transition from soft to cutting, and Lady Weatherby is unfortunate enough to be on the receiving end of it, something she seems to be quite regretful of if her plump form shrinking is a measure. She nods and departs, and Lady Tillsbury inhales and reinstates that softness. "Perhaps some water would solve this little problem of yours," she says, taking my arm and walking me to the edge of the hallway. "Or a waft of my fan, maybe." She produces a rather spectacular silk fan and flaps it out, holding it over her shockingly coy smile. "I suppose that is what it is for, after all." Her eyebrows lift just enough to tell me that Lady Tillsbury favors a fan for other reasons, and cooling off at these stifling events is not one of those reasons. *Oh my.*

"Men have the sword," I say, reciting a line I once read that has stuck with me forevermore, for it raised my eyebrow when I read the piece, *"women have the fan, and the fan is probably as effective a weapon."*

Lady Tillsbury chuckles, and that is soft too. What a desirable lady she is, and one, I expect, to be respected, not only for her rank, but perhaps for her wisdom too. "I fear," she says quietly so as not to be heard, as she loops arms with me and comes closer, "that you're a young woman with dangerous intentions."

"I have no intentions, least of all dangerous ones," I assure her, fairly confused by her rather bold statement, but somewhat worried too. What does she know of my intentions?

"You can be as promiscuous as you please, sweet Eliza, but, and I speak from experience, you must know, you should maintain a certain level of compliance."

"I do not understand."

"Of course, you are young. You have many years in which to learn what is necessary, and what is not." She stops and turns to me, and I know now her soft smile is because of my obvious perplexity, as I am certain my face must be a picture of confusion. "Sometimes in this world, Eliza, we, as women of the ton, must do what is expected in order for us to do what is *un*expected." She strokes my cheek fondly, and I gather a sense of motherly concern for my well-being. "You are here on a stranger's ticket, are you not?"

"Yes, I am," I say. "I know I look like a perfect stranger around these parts, too."

"I think not. I think you could fit right in, if you have patience and find your place."

"My place, apparently, is in Cornwall where I may never leave."

"Oh?" She recoils, and it is a relief to see such a reaction from the apparently composed character of Lady Tillsbury. It also tells me that perhaps Lymington did not order my entry, and actually, if he had, would she have obliged? Something tells me not. "Never?"

"Not ever," I confirm. "I find myself in this mess through no request or fault of my own, to serve as little more than a hatchery for the Lymingtons in order to guarantee the survival of their name."

"Oh, how frightfully disastrous." Lady Tillsbury is sporting her own frown as she looks past me, now thoughtful in her expression.

"Isn't it?" I agree, my heartbeat increasing once again, my panic revived.

"May I offer some advice?" she asks.

"Please do."

"A woman with her own mind is a dangerous creature, sweet Eliza."

"You don't have your own mind?"

"Oh, indeed I do, but I also have the sense to hide it. As I said, do what is expected in order to have the luxury to do the *un*expected."

I have no idea what she is talking about. "I think I should like that air now."

Lady Tillsbury whips out her fan and starts flapping it before my face. "I'm afraid, as Lady Weatherby was kind enough to mention, the rules, as stringent and unnecessary as they are, are, in fact, the rules, and one must be careful not to break them."

The fan is actually doing a rather fine job. I smile as she

continues to flap. "I'm surprised you do not have my mother trailing you."

She laughs. "Your mother is the sweetest, Eliza. I see where you get it from."

"She will be pleased you think so."

She waves a hand flippantly. "I understand she is searching for her place in this new world, a lot like yourself. She needs to be accepted to feel validated."

"Don't we all?" I ask quietly.

"Indeed we do," a man says.

I inhale too quickly and crick my neck with the speed of my head-turn toward the gruff voice. "Your Grace," I murmur, reaching for my nape and massaging the flash of pain away. "You are here." My voice rises into a rather alarmed shriek, that I expect might have pierced the eardrums of many partygoers.

"I am here," he mutters, not looking all too happy about that. "And you look a little pale again."

Now he mentions it, I am feeling a little suffocated once more.

"I am sure," the Duke says, his attention on Lady Tillsbury, who appears wholly unflustered by his presence, "given the circumstances of this unfortunate situation and the fact that we are perhaps at risk of causing quite a spectacle should Miss Melrose fall flat on her face, that an exception can be made on this occasion."

Lady Tillsbury can only smile. "I am sure," she says in a coy way women would, should they be delighted. I'm certain she is not delighted about being forced to break the rules, which leaves only one other explanation. Her fan comes up and wafts slowly as she bats her lashes. "Your Grace may have quite a valid point."

"I'm glad we agree," the Duke says in that low tone that sends most men into panic but ladies far and wide into bedlam. "I will escort her."

"You cannot!" I blurt.

"Why?" he asks. "You would rather me leave you to collapse?"

"I'm feeling much better, thank you."

"You are yet to master the art of lying, Miss Melrose," he snaps, taking my elbow and leading me to the door.

"I must not be alone with you," I hiss.

"I am terribly sorry to bear such bad news," he says, looking down at me with a scowl coating his handsome face, making it far less handsome than I like to see, "but you have been alone with me on a few separate occasions."

"Be that as it may, no one knew of those times."

"If it will settle you," he grunts, stopping and looking back at Lady Tillsbury.

"I didn't see a thing," she says on a smile, flapping her fan slowly. "Remember what I said, Miss Melrose."

Do what is expected in order to have the luxury to do the un-expected. My mouth falls open. It was Lady Tillsbury who ensured I was granted entry this evening? By Winters's order? Good grief, will women do *anything* he demands? I cock her a look, and she just smiles. "We won't be allowed to reenter."

"Yes, we will," he assures me, marching on. "Let us find that air you need before you fall at my feet." He peeks down at me. "We wouldn't want that, now, would we?"

"You are a disgrace."

"So I'm told."

We make it outside, and, I must say, regardless of the additional reason that I now have to panic—namely, the Duke—the fresh air is welcomed, and I drink it in urgently. "I could not bear it in there any longer."

"That is not surprising given the company you were being forced to keep." The Duke, hands linked behind his back, paces up and down before me, his face, which is pointing down at his boots, hidden, but I can detect the heaviness of his brow. He is thinking, so very deeply, I'm sure. I would love to know what his thoughts are but dare not ask.

"Why are you here?" I say instead.

"I am an annual subscriber."

I laugh under my breath. "You?"

"Yes, me. I can see you find that hard to believe."

"Of course I do! Of all the people in London who are likely to be blackballed, it would be you."

"Why is that, Miss Melrose?" he asks, looking up at me in question. "Because I'm a murderer? A rake? An ass?"

"All," I reply, lifting my chin. "All except a murderer."

"That's ironic, for I should like to murder you sometimes."

I recoil, offended. "That's rich. I risked my life to save yours."

"My life does not need saving. I am happy being—"

"Hated?"

His eyes narrow to dangerous slits and fire burns in their green depths that holds me mesmerized momentarily. Then he steps forward, snapping me out of my trance. "Do you hate me, Miss Melrose?"

My chest swells with the size of my inhale. "Or perhaps the patronesses approve you because they all want one night with the Duke."

"Undoubtedly," he whispers. "What about you, Miss Melrose? Do you want one night with the Duke?"

"No," I all but whisper, my body starting to tingle in that delicious way it does when the Duke is close by, and the more I feel these tingles, the more utterly intrigued I am by what other sensations he could ignite with a kiss.

"You do not lie well."

My back presses into the cold bricks behind me as he nears, his tall, athletic frame imposing and threatening. "I am not lying," I whisper, my voice surprisingly strong for my tense situation. His chest is only an inch from mine, and the pumping of both will have them brushing if he comes much closer.

"That is a pity."

"Why?"

"Because I have tried my damned hardest to stay away from you." His eyes drop unapologetically to my breasts and his hand smooths my dark locks where they rest, wickedly skimming my flesh with his fingertip.

"Your Grace," I whisper jaggedly.

"You don't want this?" he asks with a flick of his eyes to mine. His wicked tongue strokes the length of his bottom lip, and my body goes up in flames. *My God, what is this torture?* "You don't want me to kiss you?" His mouth descends and his breath spreads across my cheeks, his lips hovering over mine. Desire overcomes me. Tingles and throbs attack me. I fear if I did not have this wall behind me, I would crumple to the ground. I have experienced want before with this man—the intense, uncontrollable reactions in my body attacking me, but now, I fear, I have a craving on an entirely different level, and when the Duke's hips press forward and I feel his desire too, I succumb to the forbidden. Many thoughts run amok in my tangled mind, but one in particular is shouting the loudest. If I am to be punished so terribly, then I might as well make the crime one worth the punishment being imposed upon me, and secret meetings with a disgraced, handsome, forbidden duke is not a crime fit for my punishment. I shall make it fit. If I am to be imprisoned forever and die a death of unfulfillment, boredom and unhappiness, I should like some memories to take with me. I remember how aloof the Duke was just yesterday. How he looked at me with a confusing mix of admiration and scorn. But I also remember the way he has touched me. Burned for me. I have seen it in his deep green eyes. I cannot with good conscience leave my life not knowing what it is like to be kissed by him. I cannot!

"Yes, I do."

"Even if it will ruin you forevermore?"

Ruined. "I do not care about ruining myself. I care only for ruining my father. My family." I will be more ruined without it, I think, my eyes dropping to his lips, the feeling of him pressed into me like nothing I have felt before. The throb. The heat. My God.

He growls and forces himself away. "My want is sending me stupid, it would seem," he says, dragging a hand through his hair and, leaving me propped breathlessly against the wall, he begins to pace again. "I cannot bring myself to tarnish you." Disappointment engulfs me, but I know it should not. He shakes his head and appears to be angry, but I cannot fathom whether he is angry with himself or with me. "You should return to the ballroom before we are spied together alone."

"No," I say, adamant, and he looks at me alarmed. "I will not permit you to reject me again, Your Grace." I hold a finger up and wave it in his surprised face. "You have done it one time too many already." I prod him in the shoulder, but still manage to wonder what the hell I am doing. "You will kiss me, I demand it."

And like a lion pouncing, he's on me, covering my mouth with his and plunging his tongue deeply. God save my soul, my breath is stolen, and I am lost in the illicitness of our moment, my hands grappling at his shoulders as he swirls his tongue wildly, groaning as he does, his body forcing me harder into the wall. He is out of control, and I am helpless against his power, but I decide in this moment, here in the arms of the Duke, helpless feels most pleasing. I should not have worried. My body seems to know exactly what it should do, my tongue following his naturally.

"Damn it!" he barks, wrenching himself away and panting, roughly wiping his mouth with the back of his hand while looking at me with wild eyes and a snarl. I am breathless and heaving, my hand on my chest, my tongue aching and my thighs wet with the desire dripping from me unstoppably. He stares at me as I, too, stare at him, thinking how fascinating this man is. How desirable. How complex and…broken. I have never experienced anything like that kiss, and, it pains me to think, I might not ever again.

I swallow, refusing to break eye contact with him, and he growls once more. "I must have you again," he barks, coming at me again, kissing me violently. "My God, Eliza, you are the sweetest thing I have ever tasted."

I lose myself in the attention of his mouth and jolt with surprise when his palms cup my bottom, pushing me further into his hot body. I am overwhelmed by my need, my hands feeling at his cheeks, my whimpers of happiness falling freely, and I think how unfortunate it is that the Duke has given in to his wants in this moment, when we are far from privacy.

He slows our kiss and nibbles on my bottom lip before closing his eyes and resting his heavy forehead onto mine. "This is very unfortunate." On a sigh, he looks at me, and I see regret I am not sure I like lingering in his gaze.

I shrink. He didn't enjoy our kiss. But of course he didn't! I have never kissed a man, have no experience, and the Duke has taken many women on many nights. His smile is small and ironic, and I am unsure whether I like that either. He pities me?

I reluctantly move away and begin the quite impossible task of straightening out my flustered form, all the while keeping my eyes low so as to avoid his gaze. "I suppose I ought to return to the party." I take one step and am forced into stilling when he seizes my wrist.

"Why can you not bring yourself to look at me, Eliza?" he asks with a certain amount of irritation in his tone. "At least do me that honor before you leave."

"Why?" What more could he want in this moment than my surrender, and I do believe I have given him that only to be rejected once he got what he wanted. "I would have thought that to be quite obvious, Your Grace."

"To whom?"

I clench my teeth and take another step but make it precisely nowhere. The Duke eases me up against the wall again, takes my jaw, and forces my face to his, therefore forcing me to look at him. Once again, I am breathless, and once again, riddled with those sensations that apparently turn my brain to complete mush. I am awed by him, even now. Enamored.

"You will come to me this eve," he says in a demanding voice. Go to him? Why ever would I do that? He's stolen my first kiss. I will not allow him to steal any more from me. I have done enough damage as it is, but I can salvage the rest of my innocence. I will not only be one night.

I push him gently but firmly away just as the door swings open, and Lady Tillsbury appears, her eyes, full to the brim with knowing, passing between us, dancing, concluding correctly, although I shall never admit it. God damn me, what have I done?

I clear my throat and push my shoulders back. "I thank you for your graciousness," I say to her, shuffling past, exhaling heavily and closing my eyes tightly. My goodness, I can't even comprehend what has happened. All I know, and it is surely dangerous, is that I felt alive when he kissed me and crushed when he looked at me with regret.

I swallow and glance over my shoulder, seeing the Duke is wisely keeping his distance, although his eyes remain fixed on my shaky form, his expression sharp and as unforgiving as every one of his kisses. It is true, what I thought, for it would have been a travesty to die without the experience of a kiss from the Duke, but now I find myself in an even more unfortunate situation.

Wanting more.

Thankfully, Mother is steadfast in her ambitions to be accepted into the ton, consequently meaning she is still suitably distracted upon my return to the ballroom. The same cannot be said for

Frederick, who is standing alone on the edge of the dance floor with a glass in each hand, one water, one Champagne, looking lost. As I approach alone, no less, I can see him scanning my face for any signs that I have, in fact, fallen flat on my face and injured myself. Once he has given me a thorough checking over, and I'm sure it's the most he's looked at me since we were introduced, he appears to relax as he thrusts out the glasses.

"I thought it wise to be prepared for any eventuality," he says, "so I got you both."

I accept the water, as alcohol would not be wise when my thoughts are already foggy. "Thank you."

"You are welcome. Would you like to dance?"

I very nearly spit out my water. "What?"

"Dance," he says, motioning to the floor where endless couples twirl around. "Though, I must admit, I am somewhat of a novice."

"You have never danced before?" I ask.

"Never."

"Oh, well that's worrying. Will I have any feet left?"

"I will endeavor to refrain from stepping on your toes, Miss Melrose."

"Perhaps we should just watch," I suggest, feeling my skin start to prickle, and, sadly, it is not through nerves nor reluctance, but from wariness. I peek up discreetly and spy the Duke on the other side of the ballroom looking quite murderous, and I recall the Duke has, on numerous occasions, referred to Frederick with contempt and the odd curse word proceeding his name. Now I am wondering why. How well does the Duke know Frederick?

"I insist," Frederick says, taking my glass and discarding it before motioning to the floor. "It is high time."

"High time for what?" I ask, alarmed. What has got into him I cannot be sure, but this is not behavior I have come to expect from Frederick.

"Well, for us to dance. It's the perfect time and the perfect occasion, for the announcement of our engagement shall be published."

Oh? Has Porter returned from his trip to York, I wonder? Has Frederick's unbearable father made demands of Frederick?

I see the Duke once again and note his black look has not improved. He looks positively grim, and it's beginning to irritate me. Whatever has he got to look so annoyed about? With the greatest of reluctance, I step onto the dance floor full of nerves, and quite awkwardly, Frederick takes me in his hold, his chin high, every part of him as stiff as a board. I can say with confidence that my current position is by far the most uncomfortable I have ever been, and when Frederick starts moving us, it is so very jerky.

I catch sight of the Duke again and roll my eyes at the gaggle of determined women hovering unapologetically nearby, just waiting to be invited onto the floor by him, every one of them positively dying to experience the dangerous Duke in some form. I expect he won't entertain their unashamed hints, but then, with his eyes still burning into me, he holds his hand out without so much as looking toward whom he's inviting onto the floor. I however, do.

Lady Dare, delighted, curtseys and they are soon twirling around in a very close, intimate hold. They can also dance very well, which is more than can be said for the clumsy mess of bodies I am currently tangled up in. I'm humiliated. Injured. I am many things I suppose I ought not to be, and yet as I watch Johnny in all his expert ways, thrilling another woman, I feel a horrid bout of jealousy grip me. I cannot bear witness to this, and I am certain my feelings must be plastered all over my face, so I vehemently rip my gaze away from the perfection of the Duke's dancing and concentrate on making it out of this mess with my feet still intact.

"Oh," I hiss, as Frederick steps on my toe. "Ouch!" I yelp as he tramples on my other foot.

His lips press into a straight line, and he carries on, looking past me, his chin still high, as he turns me. I see Johnny and the intention in his eyes a second before he crashes into us.

"Apologies," he grunts, a definite curl to his lip as he twirls Lady Dare off in another direction.

"He did that on purpose," Frederick cries, outraged, releasing his hold of me and straightening himself out. "Father is indeed right, he is a menace." Lymington seems to have quite an aversion to Johnny Winters. "I should have him thrown out."

"You absolutely should," I agree, scowling fiercely.

"And for his blatant disregard for the dress code."

I find the Duke on the floor again, and I notice for the first time that he is wearing black trousers. They are the only ones in the room, every other gentleman wearing knee breeches. He looks rather lovely, although I would never admit it.

"Yes, I agree, he should be removed at once." I pat Frederick's shoulder. "Why don't you go and make sure of that."

Nodding to himself and pulling his jacket in, Frederick walks off to see to his grievance, and I sag in relief.

"Eliza," Mother coos, beckoning me. "You danced with Frederick, how lovely."

"Did you laugh?" I ask seriously, my watchful eye on Frederick who is now speaking with a barrel of a man whose breeches are so tight, his gut hangs over the waist. They are both looking at the Duke, who is still twirling a delighted Lady Dare around the floor.

"I did nothing of the sort!" Mother protests.

"You're a terrible liar," I say, not so much as having to look at her to determine that whenever Mother lies, her voice rises just one octave.

"Oh, what is going on?" she asks, moving in close, her attention now caught by Frederick and the fat man who is interrupting

Winters's and Lady Dare's flawless waltz. He speaks quietly in the Duke's ear, the Duke replies, and then he's off around the floor again, apparently unbothered. "I see my quiet word with Lady Dare has had the desired effect and she has moved her sights onto another," Mother muses.

"What!" I blurt, making Mother's eyebrow lift. "I mean, good. Yes, very good."

"Eliza?" she questions, somewhat suspicious.

"Ah, here's Frederick," I say, escaping her, thoroughly scorning myself for being so transparent. I loop my arm through his and let him walk us away from my curious-looking mother. "Let us get a drink," I suggest. "Did you deal with the Duke?"

"Not quite."

"What did he say?"

"I'm afraid such language cannot be repeated in front of a lady, for your ears will surely bleed."

"What a horror he is," I muse, my eyes following him around the floor with Lady Dare, who is so obviously in her element. How many kisses has she shared with the Duke? How many tingles? How many butterflies? I look at Frederick, my *suitor*, and wonder for the first time if he is a better match after all. Safe. At least with Frederick, I will not be constantly questioning myself. I will not doubt myself. But that kiss, my first kiss, was so very intoxicating. And yet my only kiss. All kisses could feel that amazing for all I know. Wouldn't that be a marvelous thing? In a moment of pure compulsion and utter recklessness, and maybe revenge because he surely twirled Lady Dare around the room to spite me, I drag Frederick, much to his distress, into a dark corner.

"What are you doing?" he cries, alarmed.

"Quiet, Frederick," I order, peeking around, making sure we cannot be seen. And then I slam my lips on his and kiss him, waiting, hoping, praying for the sparks to find me and consume me, but I am devastated to find that I feel nothing, and it isn't because his mouth appears to be sewn shut.

"Eliza!" Frederick yells, outraged, shoving me back. "We must not!"

No, we mustn't, because it was plain underwhelming, and I should like *not* to feel such disappointment ever again. "My apologies, Fred—" I am cut short when the Duke appears behind Frederick, almost a head above him, looking positively furious. His jaw is twitching, his eyes are wild, not with desire, I should mention, and his body looks poised to kill. "Finished dancing?" I ask, narrowing my eyes on him, goading him.

"What?" Frederick questions in plain confusion, a look, I have come to realize, that is frequently on his face. Yes, the man looks persistently confused, or, now I'm thinking about it, alarmed. "Nothing," I mutter as the Duke moves away, not before landing me with a look of pure threat. Why is he so confusing? And what on earth does this mean?

Chapter 13

Mother did not shut up the entire way home, though, I noted, her words were somewhat slurred. In actual fact, she was well and truly drunk, something that Papa too observed, when she unceremoniously threw herself into his arms upon our arrival. She sang about her wonderful evening, detailing the many stories of gossip, which, thankfully, did not include my encounter with the Duke, but did include, much to my despair, news of Winters knocking Frederick over on the dance floor. Such an embellishment! I am sure Mother was born to be a journalist. Father certainly raised a brow at the news but avoided my eyes when I looked at him in question. *Yes, the Duke barged my betrothed off the dance floor.*

You will come to me this eve.

I snort at my thoughts. Never.

On that conclusion, a conclusion I am sure is sensible, I undress, laying my lavender gown over the back of the chair, but I falter, frowning, when I catch the sound of rustling in the silk. In nothing but my pantaloons, I stand, rummaging through the material—thank goodness not as much material as some of the dresses being worn this eve—until I find a piece of paper. My heart begins to clatter, though I beg it to stop, for all these reactions, now to a silly piece of paper too, are quite unnerving. I unfold it and read the neatly scrolled words.

I await your arrival with bated breath and, be assured, if you fail to call upon me, I will not think twice about

collecting you myself. The choice is yours, Eliza. I rather think the former option will be less conspicuous, don't you?
Yours, JW

My heart leaps, my lips press together, and a flurry of tingles marches through me, forcing me to lower my bottom to the mattress, as I vehemently fight with my thoughts.

Go.

Do not go.

I stand and walk to the window and look out across the square, pulling the draperies across my body to conceal myself. A few carriages pass, delivering partygoers back to their homes, the sound of hooves hitting the cobbles echoing in the darkness. So dark. But still I see him, standing on the corner of the gardens. My heart stops as he steps into the moonlight, and I am certain it is an intentional move to ensure I see his serious face. It's expressionless, impassive, and his gloved hands are joined before him, his tall body rigid in its stance. If I didn't know him, I would be scared of him.

When he steps back into the shadows, I know I am being summoned. I go to my mirror, releasing my hair from the jeweled comb, and it tumbles over my shoulders. I comb through it, thoughtful, staring into my eyes. My mind cannot be my own, for it is thinking quite unthinkable things. *The Duke.* My senses scream, my breasts ache, and the flesh between my thighs throbs. *That kiss.* My lips part, and my heart booms, and all of these feelings, untimely in their arrival as they are, for I should *not* go to him, are quite thrilling.

If I go to the Duke now, we will both bend under the pressure of our desires, despite how angry I have been, and I am certain to be ruined forever. Perhaps we should just talk. Converse. I know I have many questions again, the pile seeming to build each day.

I pull on a chemise, a cloak, slip on my boots, and I leave my bedroom quietly, creeping through the house like a mouse. I am sure to avoid all the stairs that creak, as well as the floorboards. My surreptitiousness, to be expected, I suppose, lengthens the time of the short journey considerably, and by the time I have made it outside, the Duke is crossing the cobbles, a dark, angry look plastered across his handsome face. He spots me and stops abruptly, and I see the darkness lift somewhat.

"I had feared," he says as his shoulders lower, as if he was tense but now not, "that you had jilted me."

"I am here," I say, lowering the hood of my cloak. "Only here."

Worried, and not unduly, I suppose, he moves in and lifts it back into place as he glances around. "And what is that supposed to mean?"

"It means I am here, not in your home or your bed, and I have no intention to be."

"I always get what I want, Eliza, so we will see about that."

"We will," I retort sharply, quite unappreciative of his reminder of his rakish ways, and I can see he regrets his words. His hands still, holding each side of my hood, and his green eyes, eyes I am sure I could get lost in, turn onto mine.

"Let us not begin our evening on a bad note." He steps back, creating space between our bodies that crackles and sizzles no matter how much I try to shut off all my senses.

"Our evening began hours ago, and it has been a constant and consistent stream of bad notes."

"Perhaps you will write about it in tomorrow's newspaper."

I inhale sharply and move back, desperately, though very slowly, trying to locate some words. Some defense. "Pardon me?" is all I can muster.

"Just imagine," he whispers, pouting in contemplation. "If I knew your mind well enough, paid enough attention, listened with a keen enough ear, to know your words when I am blessed to be reading them."

I swallow, damning him to hell. It is as if he knows exactly what to say in order to win my affections, and yet I do not know why he would when he has not long ago rejected me. "Imagine indeed," I counter quietly, unable to confirm it. Damn him, he must never tell. Lymington will soon put an end to my writings if he should discover Porter and Frank have been claiming work that is actually mine. "Maybe your imagination is wild," I retort, but he only smiles. "I am not interested in one night," I blurt, eager to move the conversation along.

"You want more?"

Another swallow. A man who knows my mind. A man who cares for it. A man who would encourage it. "It matters not, because I cannot even have one night without being ruined forever."

"And you care about being ruined?"

"Do you care about me being ruined?"

"Enormously."

"Then why are you here?"

He shies away from my question. "Come." Grabbing my hand, he turns and walks through the entrance to the gardens, pulling me along with him. "Keep to the shadows."

"What are you doing?" I hiss, helpless in the face of his strength, my feet working fast to keep up with him.

"Taking you for some conversation."

I am halted on the edge of the gardens opposite the Winters residence by the Duke's solid arm being held out.

"Wait," he hisses.

"What is it?"

"I have a caller."

I crane my head to see and let out a long groan, that, when the Duke scowls down at me, is as loud as it was long. "Is there a woman on Belmore Square who happens to have escaped your charms?" I ask as I watch Lady Blythe knock at his door. "Perhaps she is seeking some inspiration." Or more inspiration.

I think he must have charmed every woman he has met into bed, which speaks volumes for the female population. We are braver than men. Tougher than men. I cannot imagine any lord or gentleman around here putting themselves in a room alone with the Duke of Chester for fear of what may happen to them, and yet every woman, it would seem, is willing to open her legs for him. And I wonder, for the first time, what I am doing here with him. Bugger it all, I am here because he thrills me. Excites me. He makes me feel alive in a world where I would otherwise feel dead. But he is a very desirable man. If any one of the women I have seen lusting after him has experienced his softer side, then it is no wonder they persistently call upon him. I positively detest the thought! In fact, I feel quite sick. I am just another conquest, although, I remind myself, I am yet to give myself to him. I do not want to marry Frederick, but perhaps one day, if by some miracle I manage to escape it, I might wish to marry someone else, then what? I would be tainted. No man should wish to consider me. I am all at sixes and sevens, to be sure, for I am having wild thoughts that are so very out of character for me. I do not wish to marry. That is the entire bloody point! Conversation, he said. My problem is, I cannot seem to talk to him or even be in the same space as him without having extreme alarming reactions to him. I look down at my hand in his. How lovely it looks.

"I'm afraid I am making a grave mistake," I murmur, more to myself than to the Duke, who is watching and waiting for Lady Blythe to leave so he can lure me into his cave.

Whatever am I thinking even being here? It matters not that I have been kissed. No one knows. No one saw. I can stop this madness.

I back away and make it precisely one step before I am scooped from my feet and carried onward. "Oh no," he says, his jaw rolling. "Not again, Eliza."

"I demand you release me."

"Stop thinking," he orders, opening his door and carrying me inside, "is all I ask, as I believe you may be *over*thinking."

I am placed on my feet, and he steps back, not, I expect, to give me space, but to take some respite from the heat of our bodies when they are close, for they surely burn. "There appears to be a lot to think about."

"I agree," he says, motioning to his study with a gentlemanly sweep of his arm. "After you."

I look across the hallway and see Hercules with a tray, eyeing me with worry, as I walk on wobbly legs and enter the warm space where the fire rages and candlelight offers a glow, that, dare I say it, is quite romantic. I lower to one of the chairs when the Duke indicates it and shake my head when he holds up a bottle of wine. He ignores me and pours two glasses anyway.

"Why did you kiss Frederick Lymington?" he asks, scowling heavily as he passes me a glass. His fingers brush mine, a tactical move, I'm sure, one to remind me that while Frederick stirs nothing within me, the Duke stirs everything. I jerk, splashing the wine. "Careful," he murmurs, taking my hand to his mouth, his body bending as he does to bring him closer, and licking it clean. Eyes on mine.

I begin to shake, and it does not go unnoticed. "I kissed him because I was mad with you." I look away from him and immediately scorn myself for it.

"Why were you mad with me?"

"Your obvious distaste after you kissed me, that is why."

"Distaste? For you, Eliza?"

I look at him.

"Never," he whispers softly, removing the glass from my hand and setting it on the table. "I have only distaste for myself." He reaches for my cloak, pulls the tie loose, and pushes it from my shoulders. His eyes drop to my breasts. "My God," he whispers, lowering to his knees before me, resting his forehead on my stomach. I can feel his shakes. Hear my heart pounding. Smell the need dripping from us both.

Power. Heavens, it is potent within me. I can bring him to his knees, this feared, ill-reputed heathen. Bend him, break him. I know better than I know anything that he can do the same to me. But I can sense his reluctance, which is somewhat confusing. His letter was quite assured, as was his kiss. Oh, his kiss. "Is something the matter?" I ask quietly, and he laughs, a laugh of true humor, and, perhaps, a little despair. It's quite unexpected.

"Yes. You in that chemise," he says, shaking his head and blinking rapidly, "is what's the matter." On a loud curse, he stands, drinks back his wine, and pulls at his cravat in quite an irritated fashion, as he starts to pace up and down. "I am not the kind of man a lady should build her dreams on, Miss Melrose."

I balk at him. He says that now? "I suppose you brought me here merely to share that news with me, did you?"

Another curse. I may join him imminently, for I am growing progressively cross too. He wants me. He doesn't. He does. He doesn't. Fair enough, I am not without my own dawdling, I must confess, but the Duke is leaps ahead of me and, frankly, it's becoming tiresome.

He curses under his breath. "If you want me to speak frankly—"

"I do." I smile sweetly when a scowl is thrown at me.

"I am, apparently and none too reassuringly, unable to stop imagining all of the ways in which I can pleasure you."

My back straightens. "Maybe you should try to resist thinking such lurid thoughts."

"You cannot expect me to resist when you present yourself to me in such a manner." He waves a hand up and down my body.

Is he suggesting this is all my doing? "As I understand the situation, it is you who has instigated this, from the stranger's voucher for Almack's, to the kiss outside. From the letter, to me being here at this very moment, to you removing my cloak just now."

"I'm questioning myself, trust me on that, Eliza," he mutters, raking a nervous hand through his hair. "I find you unhealthily irresistible. Your smart mouth, your ambitions, your stubbornness." He sighs. "To name but a few of your appealing qualities. But you shall be disgraced if you surrender to me, and I do not wish to tarnish your prospects." He frowns, in utter confusion, as if surprised by his own reasoning.

"Then let me put us both out of this misery." I dip and collect my cloak, throwing it over my shoulders. "I think we can both agree it is for the best, and I would ask you kindly to refrain from temptation again." I walk to the door, pull it open, and jump when it is slammed shut over my shoulder. I whirl around. His eyes land on me, heavy with confliction, content, and, God save me, intent.

He groans, removing my cloak once again, and I inhale, pushing myself into the wood. His forehead takes on a mild sheen as he stares at my breasts. "This won't only be one night, Eliza," he says, his voice strong but rough. "Once I've had you, I will not give you up."

I am hardly able to breathe, let alone speak.

"And I fear we will both be ruined." His hand, which is shaking terribly, reaches forward slowly and tentatively, and for my sins, I will him to hurry. My heart is pumping dangerously, every inch of my skin singing for his touch, but I can see his remaining lingering reluctance as well as I can feel my own, because we may not only have one night, but we certainly will not have acceptance.

"Your Grace, if I may share—"

"Do not speak, Eliza," he warns as his hand comes closer and his eyes appear to smoke further. "I need silence in this moment."

"Why?"

"So I can hear your desperate breathing. It tells me you want this as much as I do."

"I do," I whisper. I do not think wild horses could drag me away from this moment. Not my conscience. Not my fear. Not my worries.

"I cannot marry you, Eliza. And I will not be forced to, not by your brother or your father, be sure of that."

I can only nod, and he smiles, as if he feels sympathy for me, but it soon drops when his fingertip brushes my neck. "Forgive me," he whispers as I close my eyes and release a quiet whimper. His fingertip. Just his fingertip! But that fingertip must be magic because when he drags it lightly over my flesh, something quite incomprehensible happens. I convulse. I jerk. I shudder. So much so, I'm forced to reach for his arms to cling to, and as his eyes burn into me, I see his reluctance diminish.

"I have never in my life wanted anything as badly as I want you, Eliza." His body moves in and squashes the space so I am forced to look up at him. How can something so beautiful, I wonder, be so broken and dark? But I can see glimmers of light here and there.

His hand cups my breast and, all too sharply, I suck back air, daring to flatten my palm on his chest, still, as I was the first time I encountered him, amazed by the fine form of his physique. Stepping back and leaving me at the mercy of my unstable limbs, he removes his jacket and drops it to the rug. Tugs his cravat off and drops that, too. Then, his crisp white shirt. I'm certain that if I were capable of tearing my beguiled eyes from his bare chest, I would find a look of power and certainty.

"Have you touched a man's naked torso before, Eliza?" he asks.

He knows I have not, so I do not waste my breath answering him.

He watches me so very closely as he slowly moves his fingertip to my lips and presses the pad of his finger against my soft flesh, and his head tilts in thought, lengthening his neck. It is taut and inviting. A wicked bang lands between my thighs, making me shift. Oh my goodness, he looks too sensual. I feel hot, even standing here in this sheer cloth. His finger moves to my hair and he twirls a lock around it, and I wonder what he could be thinking, for his face is tight and expressionless.

Then, quite unexpectedly, he grabs the front of my chemise and pulls me onto his mouth, and it catches me by surprise. There is, however, nothing I can, or want to do to stop him. His voracious invasion is impossible to resist and without thought or instruction, I naturally surrender to its power. I find his naked shoulders and delight in my first experience of a man's bare flesh under my palms. He moans, the sound deep and rumbling, in between firm swirls of his tongue, and I taste the sharp edge of gin. I suppose it could be said that he has lost control, for his actions certainly suggest it, and his kiss is almost clumsy, but then he pulls back and gasps in my face, searching my eyes as his hands lie upon mine on his shoulders. "I do believe, and I must apologize sincerely, that I have crossed the line." He heaves and wipes his mouth with the back of his hand roughly. He has kissed me before, but it is not our kiss to which he refers. He was clothed and we were not in the privacy of his home.

I look at my hands on his naked flesh. "I cannot be sorry in this moment, Your Grace."

He smiles very lightly, and it is exquisite on his hard face. "Eliza, to you I am simply Johnny." He cups my cheek and I find myself unable to resist nuzzling into it. "And I hope you may never regret it."

I don't know what to say, so I say nothing, instead choosing to continue with my fitful breaths as he holds me in place.

"Are you ready to be disgraced?"

I swallow and nod as he, brimming with need, slowly comes closer, his green eyes passing from my mouth to my eyes constantly until his lips are lightly brushing over mine, but, this time, contrary to our last kiss, it is relaxed and tender, less urgent and rushed. Not a stolen kiss, but one without urgency. He holds the nape of my neck over my hair and begins walking backward, which, in turn, encourages my steps. I care not where he is taking me, and I cannot see to know, my eyes remaining closed as we kiss deeply, but as my body becomes warmer, I conclude we are nearing the fireplace. It is true, the Duke is quite the talented kisser, overwhelmingly good. One night would never be enough, so I am truly glad he has expressed his expectations in that regard. I feel in this moment, this exquisite, tender, understanding moment, that I need nothing but this feeling of raw abandon ever again.

His hand leaves my neck and grasps the hem of my chemise, lifting it and breaking our mouth contact to get it past my head so I'm forced to release his shoulders and lift my arms. I am naked, completely bared to him, but I lack the ability to pay too much time or concern to that fact, as his passion and energy consume me.

"Are you all right?" he asks, breathing down on me, his groin pressing into my stomach.

"Yes," I gasp, clenching my eyes shut, trying to comprehend what is happening. "Yes, I am very all right."

His hands encase my cheeks. "Open your eyes, Eliza."

I do as I am bid and the moment I am looking into his bright green ones once again, he kisses me sweetly. "I must be gentle with you."

"Why?"

"You are pure and untouched, are you not?"

I reach up and rest my palms on his torso, smiling at his gentlemanly approach. Which, frankly, does not suit him. "Of course, but I am not confident this urge within me will permit your gentleness." I feel as though I could ravage him. Every sense is screaming for me to attack.

He withdraws and smiles, and, God help my heart, it sings

at the beautiful sight. "I should indulge in you, and it should be slow so I may appreciate every second of this moment." He reaches for my stomach and circles my bellybutton, and my body instinctively bends. "Your skin is so soft, Eliza. So creamy. So pure. I hardly want to tarnish it."

"You must," I insist. "I will go mad if you do not."

"Mad, you say?"

"Johnny, please," I beg. "Please, torture me no longer."

He lazily removes his trousers and undergarments. And then I am staring at it, mouth agape, despite my best efforts to remain unaffected by his pulsing length of hard flesh. *My God, however will it fit?*

"You will stretch," he says quietly, and I shoot him a startled look. "I will be slow. You will adjust and accept me." He drops to his knees and holds my bottom with his big palms. "But first, I must prepare you."

I have not one moment to consider his statement and what he could possibly mean. Reaching forward with his mouth, he kisses me softly at the apex of my thighs, and I cry out and grapple for his shoulders, an unbearable ache falling into my stomach. My body, which appears to have a mind of its own, starts to jerk and shake. "Johnny," I whisper as I brave looking down at him, just in time to see his tongue dash out and lick me. I cry out once more, the sound piercing, and my legs lose their strength. I crumple to the floor, and he catches me in his arms before he lays me upon the rug before the fire. I look up at him with nothing but awe. *You cannot love him, Eliza!*

"Don't do it, Eliza," he says quietly. "You must not."

I look away in a terrible effort to hide my guilt. How can I love this man? *I beg you tell me how!* He is a horror. Rude and obnoxious. It should be impossible to feel anything other than contempt and disdain, and yet, and I cannot stop it, I do not. It is a matter of sense, if you ask me, for I have seen a softer side to the feared man, and I wonder if he has meant to expose that to me? I am not certain of much as I lie here sacrificing myself to him, except, perhaps, for one thing. I can love him because he smiles at my words rather than gasps. He looks at me with fascination rather than confusion or contempt. "What are you talking about?" I ask, a ridiculous question if ever there was one asked.

"You are not brainless, Eliza, so please, I beg you, do not pretend to be."

"What do you expect of me?" I ask, my frustration creeping up on me. His hand moves to mine and guides it to his groin. I suppose that answers my question.

"Hold me," he whispers, his voice hoarse and desperate. His words drive me into action, as does my lingering annoyance, and I slowly open my hand and take him in my hold. A small hitch of breath escapes the second the hard heat of his flesh touches me. I feel the pulse. I dare not look down, so I keep my eyes on his strained face, finding it soothing.

"Move your hand," he hisses, his head dropped, but try as I might, I am frozen beneath him. "Eliza," he says, almost brusque and short.

"I know not what to do," I confess, overwhelmed, thinking how ironic it is that one can feel desire, one can sense it, but to sate it is another matter entirely. "I apologize," I murmur, lying like a stupid idiot, unmoving and incapable.

His smile, one which is unmistakably sympathetic, makes me feel so very small and stupid. I am not like his former lovers, full of confidence, I'm sure of it, and without the need for instruction to pleasure him.

"I wish to be a memorable lover," I say, unable to prevent my thoughts falling out of my mouth. I cringe as a result.

"You are already memorable, Eliza," he says softly as he positions himself over me, astride my waist, his hard, hot penis being flaunted without apology. I am engrossed, even more so when he rises to his knees and takes himself in a firm grip.

I flick my eyes briefly to his face, seeing him looking down, his lips parted. It's a pleasurable sight, which only leaves me wondering what's to come. "Let me show you," he says, stroking himself slowly up and down. My stomach spins, my legs shifting beneath him, tingles exploding between my thighs. "Are you all right?" he asks, resting a palm by my head, his face suspended over me.

"Yes," I nod as I speak, not quite certain the word will leave my mouth past my thick tongue, and then I feel something firm and hot slip across my flesh and I yelp, my hands flying up to his chest. He's staring at me, and my eyes refuse to leave him, even though I desperately want to clench them shut and hold my breath. "Ready?"

I nod again, and he pushes forward gently, slowly breaching my entrance and sliding into me on a loud exhale of air. Pain sears through me, making me quietly whimper and dig my nails into his flesh. I know my face is etched with discomfort, and there's nothing that I can do to stop it. The pain is quite something, and I know not how to handle it, nor do I want to complain and displease him.

"Eliza," he grunts. "Jesus, Eliza, you're so very tight." The strained expression on his face tells me he's in pain, too. "Am I hurting you?"

"No!" I yelp.

"I don't want to hurt you." He's braced on his arms, as still as could be.

"It hurts a little," I admit quietly, inhaling back the pain. "But I do not want you to stop."

He eases back gently, and the pain subsides somewhat, much to my relief. "It will become easier if you can tolerate it." He retreats carefully and rocks gently back inside, and the way he gazes down at me, as if I am the most exquisite thing he has seen and this is the most exquisite feeling he has experienced, does not help me with my fight to keep my feelings controlled. I never imagined that closeness with a man could be this intimate. I suspect it is not for many, just a transaction, if you will, an expected necessity, and I wonder with alarming worry how many women truly share this kind of connection with their husband, for if it was a guarantee that one would have this inexplicable experience each time she pleased him, no woman would be averse to being married at all. Except it is not a guarantee. Possibly not even a possibility. I fear this, what is happening now, is rare and it should be savored. Cherished.

I find my hips lifting, wanting him to plunge deeper, now the pain has abated a little. He falls to his elbows and places his mouth upon mine, easing back and pushing in a little further, circling his groin. "Does it feel good, Eliza?"

"Yes," I breathe.

"I am inclined to agree." He teases my mouth with little dashes of his tongue across my lips, and it is maddening. So, bold and unabashed, I attempt to capture his lips and kiss him as deeply as he has kissed me, but he pulls away. "Slowly," he whispers, swaying in and out perfectly, gazing down at me and blinking lazily to match his gentle thrusts, stretching me gently, and I know his tactics are succeeding because the pain is becoming less each time he enters me, and, as if they simply cannot, his eyes never move from mine. This is special, I know it, and yet I am aware of how dangerous my thoughts are. I feel muscles within me, muscles that I never knew existed until I met the Duke, contract around him, sensitizing me to each delicious pump of his hips, pushing me higher and higher. I begin to tense, and it feels essential, as if I am protecting myself from something. But what?

"You are trembling, Eliza."

"I can't stop it!" I cry, becoming a little fraught by the unfamiliar bombardment of sensations.

"You should not try, either." He gasps, his moves taking on an edge of urgency. "You must let it claim you."

"What? Let what claim me? And where will it take me?"

"To heaven, my sweet lady. It'll take you to heaven, and you may never want to come back to earth."

I yelp, jacking underneath him, my body feeling so hot, like it could burst into flames at any moment. What is he speaking of? I shake my head under his mouth, not feeling in the slightest bit concerned. I'm too distracted by the heaviness between my legs, getting heavier with each gentle thrust. I never realized it could be like this.

"Oh, Eliza!" His mouth is ripped from mine and his chest swells, muscles roll, his veins pump beneath his skin, everything taut, including his face.

I grapple at his shoulders, my head shaking wildly. The pain has gone. My God, it's disappeared and…"Johnny!"

His drives slow, but become firmer—more accurate and measured, and he kisses me softly. I become lightheaded, and my eyes start rolling and my hands, which are now grasping his mass of blond hair, shake too, but I don't stop. I can't stop. An unknown pressure builds inside, and it must release.

"Yes, Eliza!" He pulls away once again and props himself on his strong arms, pumping, banging into me, leaving me with no mouth to devour. His jaw is ticking, his eyes deadly serious. He pleasures me with more and more and more. I feel out of my mind, and it is so utterly wonderful. His pace picks up and so does the pressure. My hands brace on his forearms and push, taking me further up the rug.

I yelp, "Oh God," unable to be utterly ashamed using the Lord's name in vain, for I am unable to stop anything happening in this moment. Nothing.

Everything is frantic, an urgency I can't explain overcoming me. His breathing, my breathing, his grunts, my whimpers, the sweating, the tensing, both of us chasing the end, but whereas Johnny appears to know what to expect, where we are going, I do not, and I am becoming increasingly wary of it.

His handsome face becomes blurred. The room beyond starts to spin, and something powerful, and so far out of my control, sparks, sizzles and explodes, and my body bends so harshly, I swear it could break.

Even if it breaks me.

My body isn't my own, and neither, apparently, are my thoughts, for I am thinking the unthinkable.

Keep me. Please, do not let me go. Marry me. Love me. Let me bear your heirs and be a good wife.

He then roars, the most carnal sound, and I am stretched further, but rather than rejecting the additional invasion, my body welcomes it, feeling like it could be pulling him in further to me. Making us one. Heat overcomes me, and I sigh, my useless arms flopping behind my head, and he collapses onto me, panting into my ear as his skin slips across mine.

"I know not what to say," I gasp, dazed, dizzy, and rather enjoying this aftermath. My heart has never beaten so strongly. I have never felt so alive. Exhausted but alive.

He licks the shell of my ear, causing a shudder to ride through me. That, too, is delicious. "This moment requires no words, Eliza, so let us not waste them."

I could not agree more. The Duke, who has taken many lovers, a rumor I know to be true, is, it would appear, somewhat stuck for words, too, and that is such a very thrilling feeling. His weight atop of me, albeit heavy, feels incredible, so we remain breathless and sprawled on the rug before the fire, as naked as a newborn babe, and it is so very peaceful as my fingertips gently graze across his skin instinctively.

"I know what to say," I murmur. "I should like to thank you." I smile when I feel him, the notoriously stoic Duke, grinning against my neck. I take the back of his head and encourage him to face me so I may see the delightful sight. And it is so very delightful. What I am seeing here, this blinding vision, is so far removed from the clipped, brooding, arrogant Duke who has wholly charmed me, without really even trying. "I wish you would smile more."

"I save my smiles only for those who are worthy of them." He rests his weight on his forearms and brings his face close to mine, nose to nose, forehead to forehead. And he smiles once more. "Fortunately for you, Eliza Melrose, my wanton, wild sweetheart, you are worthy."

"Why, thank you, Your Grace."

His grin is twisted and adorable and…bugger it all.

I *am* in love.

God damn me. I *am* in love. It's unstoppable, really. How any man could make me feel this way and not expect to win my heart is unthinkable. "You are most welcome," he says. "Of course, I must remind you that I do not offer them freely, so should you be inclined, I would not be opposed to hearing the charms of your clever mouth from dawn until dusk, if you so wish."

I nod my head, making his nod, too. I feel incredibly calm and serene, and I am certain it's the loveliest of feelings.

"Now, are you going to tell me how long you have been secretly writing for your father's newspaper? And perhaps why here in London your only pieces have been about me?"

My nose wrinkles, and he taps the end with his fingertip.

"You should be grateful. If anyone else had written it, it would not have been accurate, and you'd probably have been damned more so than you have been already."

"I have no doubt."

"Anyway, I must disappoint you," I say, feeling somewhat smug. "I have actually written a piece that doesn't feature your fine self."

"Oh?"

"The Millingdale Bank report," I declare, and he frowns.

"That was definitely claptrap."

"It was. I made it up to divert from another report that was supposed to publish." I pause, bracing myself. His head tilts in question. "Lymington and Porter were reporting a mugging."

"Who mugged who?"

"You mugged my brother," I say tentatively.

"When did I mug your..." he fades off, frowning.

I nod, my lips pressed together. "Lymington really does not like you," I say, digging a little. "And I have heard you call Frederick many unpleasant names."

He nods, thoughtful. "But the report didn't publish."

"Porter went missing."

"He did?"

"He left Town abruptly to visit friends."

"Interesting."

"Is it? Why?" What's going on?

"Let's not bore ourselves with your father's newspaper's politics." He shifts his hips and the satisfying fullness disappears. I hiss and close my legs but Johnny, on his knees looming over me, pulls them apart. His face twists a little, and, curious of that look, I peek down to see blood staining the inside of my legs.

"I should bathe you," he says, slowly rising and taking my hand, and then, both of us still bare and exposed, he leads me out of his study and up the stairs.

"Hercules," I say, my eyes stuck to his powerful back.

"Has retired for the evening, so you need not worry."

I nod as I am led into a room. His bedroom. The bed is huge and high, the elaborate woodwork glossy, and the rich claret draperies are heavy and, thankfully, drawn. I notice steam rising into the air and see a bathtub in the corner of the room, full of hot water. It must have been drawn only very recently. By request of Johnny? I'm sure. He helps me in and is patient as I grow accustomed to the hot water, my skin becoming red, and, much to my shock when I have finally come to rest on my bottom, he steps in and lowers himself behind me, taking a cloth and starting to squeeze water, very gently and lovingly, across my back. "You are washing me," I say quietly, and his motions falter, only momentarily, though, before he continues.

"I am."

I frown. "Because you've dirtied me," I say, worried about the silent yet alarmingly loud conclusion I have drawn from his actions. "It is, isn't it?" I turn in the bath to face him, taking the cloth from his hand. "You feel compelled to clean me after tarnishing me. Do you not realize, Johnny, that nothing can wipe away what just happened? It cannot be scrubbed away like it never happened, not from my body and most definitely not from my mind."

He stares at me, a look I am certain I do not appreciate, for it holds sympathy, and I want none of that from him. "I cannot bear," he says, his voice soft, but he is obviously struggling to keep it that way, "the idea of ruining you, Eliza. I cannot stand it."

"Ruined?" Have we not gone over this over and over? He must shake this misplaced guilt. "If this is how ruined feels, then I must insist you ruin me every day for the rest of my life." I wish for the world to know of this moment. I wish every woman to learn of the heights of pleasure he has taken me to, of the softness he has shown me, of the gentleness of his heart. I withdraw, as I have just comprehended the spew of words I have spoken, and what he must be concluding is not going to benefit me. I drop my eyes to his wet chest. "I'm sorry."

"How many times must I tell you?"

"Only once, Your Grace," I say curtly. "I am not likely to forget it now, am I?" I stand, completely unabashed, and water pours from my body as I step out of the bath, but his grasp around my wrist halts me.

"If I could have it any other way," he says as I look at him, hating his pained expression, "I would."

"You are not chained to this life. Only by yourself."

"That is not true. I could never marry you, Eliza. I have told you this."

"I am not asking for marriage. I am asking for more than marriage"—*something like love*—"and I, mistakenly it would seem"—*and in a moment of utter stupidity*—"thought that perhaps you were the only man in this godforsaken world who could give me more than nuptials. Now, if you will excuse me, I have another man waiting in the wings who *does* want to marry me." *But whom I do not and cannot love.* "Goodbye." What the heck am I saying? I want to marry Frederick about as much as I want to leave the Duke in this moment.

"I forbid you to leave."

I laugh and wrench my wrist free as my skin begins to pimple and my teeth start to chatter. "You don't own me."

"You speak spiteful words to hurt me."

"You do not want me, so why you hurt is a mystery."

"Eliza!" he bellows, the sound of rushing water surrounding it. I ignore the ferocity of his tone and hurry downstairs to his study. I cannot punish myself in such a way. I cannot! I cannot pretend to claim I knew of the pleasure I would experience here on this eve, and, more than that, I never appreciated the risk I was taking. Not of being caught or ruined.

But falling in love, because I'm certain this rather awful pain in my heart can only be that. One night, I stand a better chance of forgetting. Any more, I might not survive the aftermath. I cannot have his body, his mouth, his words and his mind, if I do not have his heart.

"Eliza!"

"To hell with you." I wrestle into my chemise and toss my cloak over my shoulders as he falls into the doorway, a dripping wet, very angry form of a man. Bare. I rip my eyes away from the pleasing sight before my heart can betray me any further.

"I'm already in hell, Eliza, so believe me when I say it, nothing could worsen my position."

"Then it matters not if I leave or if I stay." I step forward and tilt my head with expectancy. "Please excuse me."

"I am not releasing you from my company."

I laugh. "You speak as if you have a right over me. Need I remind you that you want *not* that responsibility."

"Loving is painful, Eliza."

His family. He speaks of his family. The family the world believes he burned to death. "You will punish yourself like this? Deprive yourself of light and remain in the darkness and you will not tell me why."

"Because being associated with a Winters will certainly lead to your demise!"

I recoil, and he roars, turning and grabbing at his hair.

"I never made any promises, Eliza. If you have allowed your feelings to go further, then that is not my problem but your own." He turns and his face is the most expressionless it has ever been.

He has shut down. I wish I could as well. "Johnny, let me help you," I plead, placing a hand on his chest, but he takes it and whirls me around fast, easing me against the wooden paneling.

He appears carnal. Furious. His hot breaths are rushed and his burning, naked skin searing the material of my cloak. "Do not speak words as if you are well-informed of my plight."

I stare into his hard gaze. "Then tell me."

"I cannot."

"Then let me go."

He does not, but instead slams his wet, hungry mouth upon mine and kisses me with urgency and desperation, growling like a bear, and, predictably, I fold under the promise of more pleasure. More escape.

Until he stops, panting, his eyes clenched shut, and pushes himself away on a yell of frustration. "Go," he demands harshly. "Go now before I ..."

How has this happened? I was leaving and he was trying to stop me, and now he is kicking me out? "Before you what?" I ask, goading him, so very furious, not only with him, but with myself for handing him the cards. For putting him in the position of power. *Damn me!*

His nostrils flare and, so slowly it looks as if he is struggling to even move, he turns his naked body toward me. "Before I murder you like I did the rest of my family."

The sting is very real. He wants me to hate him. He need not try to make that happen. I do hate him. I hate him for making me feel these feelings and for denying them himself. My throat swells and my eyes sting with unfallen tears and like the coward he is, he looks away. Ashamed.

"You have killed nothing except my spirit." I turn and run away from him.

And—I hope, I pray—away from these unexpected, painful feelings.

Chapter 14

Needless to say, I did not sleep one wink that night. Nor the next. Or the three that have followed. In fact, I fear I may never find rest again. The days are quite torturous, spent taking lessons on piano, learning a language I'll never use and walking with a man I will never love, but my suffering pales in comparison to the nights. Sleepless, endless nights.

My mind is elsewhere, no matter how much I so wish it not to be, and yet for every second of respite I get from thinking about him, about that night, I pay for it with hours of torturous flashbacks. How could I? What an idiot I must be. By succumbing to the Duke's charms, all I have done is make my future more difficult. Harder to accept. Harder to sustain. And on top of it all, I have no desire to write about…anything. I feel like a shell, floating through my days, an empty vessel that will never find fulfillment ever again.

Just imagine if I knew your mind well enough, paid enough attention, listened with a keen enough ear, to know your words when I am blessed to be reading them.

I could never have imagined that, something so wonderful. And yet I had it, albeit briefly.

It is the evening of the royal ball for the Prince Regent's birthday celebrations, and my mood is low, along with my enthusiasm. Although why I need it, I do not know, for Mother has it in abundance, enough for the whole of Belmore Square, I expect. That was, until the flounce on her dress fell off.

As I sit in the drawing room gazing out of the window, I listen to her wail about the disaster, Emma following her with a needle and thread trying to get hold of the dress so as to repair it.

Unfortunately for Father, he chooses this precise moment to arrive home.

"It is broken!" she cries, thrusting the masses of silk toward him.

"And what do you suppose I should do about that, Florence? I have had a horrid day at work, and I should like a moment's peace in my study, so please do not disturb me with trivial matters of faulty flounces." The door slams behind him, and I stand, concerned, thinking he looked rather ashen, quite anxious, in fact, his expression matching his words.

"Well," Mother murmurs, sounding wholly injured, as she passes her dress to Emma. "That was rather uncalled for."

What does she expect Father to do with a damaged dress? I can't say I'm all too fond of the melancholy that has become her as she stares at Father's office door. It has been noted, not only by Mama but by myself, too, that Father is becoming increasingly grumpy in recent weeks. I know sales have dropped a little, for I have heard Lymington moan on and on about it, but since Porter is still absent and Frank has been let go, that doesn't look likely to change. Yes, Frank has been let go. Sadly, my story about Millingdale Bank collapsing failed to spoil the arrangement between the Viscount and Lizzy Fallow. What it did instead was get my brother in trouble for reporting false news. I saw the pain on Father's face. And Frank would never have betrayed me, so he accepted his dismissal with a nod and nothing more. I know he's relieved. I know Father is more anxious than ever. He knows too that Frank did not write that story, but what can he say? Do?

Mama looks down at me and smiles ever so mildly. "You look brighter today," she says. "I don't know what has gone on in recent weeks, Eliza, and I do not wish to, but I have noted your spirits have dipped."

Dipped? Or plummeted? I return her smile, wondering which statement is most untrue.

Out of sight out of mind? Or, *absence makes the heart grow fonder?*

He's definitely not out of my mind. And I hate him more today than I did the eve he threw me...

I walked out.

"I am all right, Mama," I assure her.

"I do not believe you, Eliza. I may have adopted a certain—"

"Ruthlessness?"

Her lips purse. "I want us to be accepted. Your father has worked so hard, he deserves the recognition and respect some seem unable to offer. It's new versus old, and old is powerful by name, not by mind."

"So why the incessant need to marry me off to Frederick?" I ask. "If title means nothing and mind everything, because I know I have the latter."

"In abundance, my dearest. In abundance. Sadly, once you make a deal with Lymington, you do not renege on it."

The deal. "Why?"

"Well—"

Frank bowls through the door, and Mother loses her sadness at the sight of her son. "Francis, ho—"

"Not now, Mother," he snaps, passing her without so much as a fleeting look and, appearing as anxious as Father, disappearing into the study too. Our poor mother recoils, injured, and flinches when the door slams. I take no pleasure from the sadness that washes over her, so, as a matter of duty and compassion, and because I'm not a complete ass, I go to her, taking her arm and huddling close into her side. I need not say a thing. She looks down at me and smiles ever so mildly.

"I suppose I ought to fix that dress," she says, patting the top of my hand.

"I will help you," I reply, following her back into the drawing room where Emma is struggling to find the end of the length of flounce amid the masses of silk layers, but I am wondering the whole way why Frank looked so harassed and went to Papa's study if he no longer works for the newspaper? I feel as though I am constantly asking what on earth is going on, for one reason or another.

I drop to my knees and start rummaging, and, on a laugh that truly thrills me, Mother joins me, chuckling when I disappear under the dress. "Oh, Eliza, I have lost you!"

"Are you surprised?" I ask, fighting with the endless layers. "Ah, I have it." I flap the material back over my head and present it to Emma on a smile. "Perhaps double stitch."

"I should make a complaint," Mama grumbles, taking my hand and gazing at me fondly. I can see it in her eyes. Regret. She is lonely here, lonely at all the busy, chaotic, gossiping parties. She wants her husband back, but she will not make that confession. No. She loves the freedom Papa's riches have offered her, yet she quietly acknowledges that the money that's brought a release of hardship, has taken freedom from her children. But she would never say it. Never admit. She would never betray Papa's hard work in such a way. But I'll wager she'll continue to bake in the dead of night for a long time, possibly even forever. "What are you wearing?" she asks instead.

"My blush gown, I expect."

"Perfect."

I roll my eyes and stand, leaving the room. "You speak as though I have masses of eligible bachelors to impress."

"You have your fiancé to impress."

Another roll of my eyes at the mention of my betrothed. I am to be wed in a fortnight. I have often wondered why such a monumental event should happen so quickly, almost rushed, and I think now, when it is I facing the challenge of nuptials, I know. It is undoubtedly to ensure the hesitant party has less time to scarper. I am the hesitant party in this instance, and I should like to scarper. Every minute of the day, when, of course, I am not thinking about the wily Duke and our *one* night together, I want to pack a bag and disappear into the night.

Or disappear back to the Duke's house, for that was most certainly as good as disappearing from a world I do not want to be a part of.

No, Eliza!

I reach Father's study door and hear hissed whispers coming from beyond, but, much to my annoyance, Dalton appears with a tray of tea and I am forced onward. I make it halfway up the stairs and peek over my shoulder. Dalton has gone, so I rush back down and squish my front against the door, very carefully so as not to alert anyone of my presence, and listen.

"Dead!" Father yells. "One minute he's writing a piece on your attack, the next he's dead. You know what this looks like, don't you Frank? Murder!"

I back away from the door, stunned. Porter is dead? How? I have not a moment to think or even to barge in and ask. The front door knocks, Dalton appears, looking particularly rushed on this eve, and Mr. Casper, looking worryingly similar in expression to my father and brother, appears.

Without Dalton's gesture or instruction, he heads straight for Father's study and bursts in, practically knocking me from his path in the process.

"Speak!" Father demands.

"I'm afraid it is true, Melrose. Porter is, indeed, dead. Murdered."

"For the love of God, Casper, how did he die?"

"He…" Casper coughs, his reluctance obvious. "He was found with his gut sliced."

My mouth falls open and Dalton, who I'm sure is in an utter panic because of where I am and what I am hearing, not because it's truly shocking but because this is a conversation not to be heard by anyone, tries in vain to move me along. Naturally, I deny him. I'm raging with curiosity and…fear.

"Who would do this?" Casper asks. "Who is capable of such a malicious crime."

I can't say I like the silence that ensues. It tells me, for one thing, that Frank and Father are considering that question, when they should be blurting a resounding, *I don't know.*

So…do they think they know?

"The Duke," Father says, so flatly. So sure.

I gasp, horrified, and it sends me back a few paces.

"Winters?" Frank says. He sounds dubious, and it is reassuring, I must admit. "Surely not."

"After all, he was the victim of the backlash Porter's story could have fashioned."

"The Duke has an alibi, Melrose," Casper says, and, unsure if I can cope with these pendulum emotions, I find myself exhaling in untold relief.

"We can all get ourselves one of those with the right amount of cash," Father grumbles. "Who is this alibi?"

"Lady Dare," Casper says, and, naturally, with his answer comes a jolt of my body. "She has confirmed," he coughs, "that she and the Duke were…"

I step back from the door, pain I never knew could exist searing my heart. He was with her? I reach for my throat, feeling as though it could be closing. "After me?" I whisper, not wanting to believe it, but, because I am not a complete idiot, though many would challenge me on that matter, I can't see how I *cannot* believe it.

"Then who the bloody hell has killed my best journalist and chief editor!" Father bellows.

The sound of shuffling footsteps coming closer to the door

is my key to leave, so I hurry up the stairs to my room. Porter? His gut sliced?

Naturally, as I always do, I immediately go to the window and look across the square. If there were any lingering feelings hanging around for the arrogant, confusing Duke, they are surely gone with the news of his recent dalliance with Lady Dare.

Surely.

Chapter 15

The palace is alive, bright and happy. It is everything I am not, and the sheer effort it is taking me to simply stand here and breathe is more than I can bear to suffer. Lymington is waffling on to Countess Rose about something or other, I do not care to know what, and Frederick has not strayed far from my side. If I did not know better, I would think he was guarding me, but I do know better. The man is a social catastrophe and, most lucky for me because my company requires no effort on his part, that appears to mean that I have the privilege of his persistent presence. Lucky for Frederick, I'm not in a talking mood, so he can remain comfortably stuck for words.

But then he surprises me and speaks for the first time since I arrived and he claimed me from my mother to join his awful father. I could see Mother's poorly concealed guilt as she smiled politely at Frederick and sent me off with her blessing. "Would you like a drink?" he asks.

"No, thank you, I am not thirsty," I reply, catching the murmur of a name that is surely going to win my attention.

"I have my doubts," Lady Rose says, her white-gloved hand lifting her Champagne to her lips. "Winters is at the top of my suspect list."

"It's just that small matter of evidence," Lymington muses, pouting in thought, as if he's contemplating where he might find some of that evidence.

"Indeed," she replies. "His name and presence are a constant black cloud over Belmore Square."

I laugh out loud, and I absolutely did not mean to, but…oh please. The Duke casts a black cloud? I step forward to speak, but jump when Frederick more or less dives in front of me to block my path. I look up at him in question. "Excuse me, Frederick."

"Please, Eliza," he begs.

"Please what? Keep suitably silent?" I move him aside with physical force and find the stuffy, crabby faces of Countess Rose and Lymington. "I believe it is, in fact, the importunate mutterings of old, decrepit members of the ton who cast the shadows over Belmore Square. Need I remind you that the Duke of Chester has an alibi?" I have no idea why I am defending his honor. I shouldn't be wasting my breath. But still, injustice is injustice, and, well…I can't bear injustice.

Lymington's eyes narrow dangerously on me. "You will shut your mouth," he hisses. "Before I shut it for you."

"Father!" Frederick gasps, startling me as much as he does Lymington.

"And you can shut yours too. Come, dear," he lifts his nose and motions for the Countess to lead on. "We must wish the Prince well for his birthday." One more warning look flicked my way before the Duke is off with the Countess, both holding each other up.

"What's going on?" Frank asks, joining Frederick and me.

"I believe I need a drink," Frederick says, wandering off, looking a bit pasty.

"I think Frederick just defended my honor," I say.

"Good for him." Frank seems genuinely impressed. I am, too, I have to admit. "God, isn't this hideous?"

"I have every reason to find this eve hideous," I say, scanning the crowds, "but I am struggling to understand *your* grievance." I motion to the room full of eager, ruthless mothers, many of whom, unsurprisingly, have their sights set on my handsome, most eligible brother, their daughters waiting in the wings to be shoved his way. "You have the pick of the bunch."

Frank hums noncommittally, and I follow his line of sight to the other side of the ballroom. I spot Lizzy Fallow with Viscount Millingdale. "I tried, Frank," I whisper.

Frank does not answer me, so I peek at him, seeing a solemn look as he follows the path of the couple across the ballroom. And then to Lizzy Fallow, whose sad eyes are low, as if she dares not look up from her feet. My God, is he…?

"Frank, are—"

"My lady," Frank says, bowing his head as Lady Blythe breezes toward us, cutting my intended question dead in its tracks. "How wonderful you look on this eve."

"And how wonderful *you* look," she replies, coy, turning her deep brown eyes my way. "Eliza Melrose," she says with a little too much interest for my liking. "As do you."

"Lady Blythe." I smile tightly. Has she been calling upon Johnny again recently? "Your dress is spectacular."

"You're too kind. Now, tell me," she casts her eyes over Frank and me, "have you read my latest novel and, if so, what did you think?"

I swallow, coming over a little hot. Lady Blythe is clearly feeling a little insecure after Lady Rose disparaged her latest offering to the literary world. More fool Lady Rose, I say. Lady Blythe soon used her influence as a patroness to put the old Countess in her place, although, if Mother has heard the whispers right, and I suspect she has on this occasion, and also hasn't embellished them, Lady Rose overturned the decision and has had her subscription reinstated. Still, Lady Blythe had her fun. I'm not about to be her next game. There is only one right answer to her question, unless, of course, I should like to be banished from the ton. I pause for thought. I absolutely should like to be banished from the ton.

"Actually, I—"

"I do believe I spotted it on Eliza's nightstand," Frank says, interrupting me, a blatant move to halt *my* blatant move. His look dares me to say the words that'll turn Lady Blythe's face from friendly to fierce. "And I'm sure I heard her mention that it was utterly wonderful," he adds.

Lucky for Frank, I am all out of fight. "Truly wonderful," I grate, smiling through my teeth at Lady Blythe. She's delighted, of course, and, thankfully, she doesn't interrogate me on the plot, characters or anything else, for that matter, relating to her new masterpiece. Her head cranes, looking past me, and her smile drops. "Oh, God save me, she's spotted me."

Both Frank and I turn and find Mrs. Fallow flapping a deranged hand in the air.

"Viscount Millingdale is in for a treat," Lady Blythe says quietly, "if Lizzy Fallow is as irritating as her mother." She whirls off, all smiles, leaving Frank and me alone once more.

My eyebrows jump up. "Irritating?"

Frank looks past me to Lizzy Fallow. "Yes, irritating," he says quietly and contemplatively.

"Are you telling me, Frank, or yourself?" I ask.

He blinks rapidly and seems to snap out of a trance. "Pardon me?"

"Oh dear," I breathe, prompting my brother to quickly reinstate his cheeky smile. I thought right.

"What?"

"Do not *what* me, Francis Melr—" My words tangle in my throat, clogging it terribly, when I catch sight of Johnny Winters entering the ballroom. His eyes immediately find mine, and, I'm certain of it, I stop breathing. My heart, God damn that pathetic muscle in my chest, turns, and my body begins to shake. He looks... oh, he looks like he could have just fallen from that place he took me to. Heaven. He is a god clad in the finest claret velvet jacket and cream trousers, his shirt, as ever, as crisp and white as snow, matching his cravat and gloves. Everything is perfect. Even his forbidding expression.

"Eliza?" Frank questions.

"Yes," I squeak, turning away from the Duke. *Whatever is he doing here?*

"You look a bit pasty."

"You know, I do feel a bit queasy," I admit. "Too many bubbles, I'm sure." My palm finds my stomach and circles. "I think I'll step out into the courtyard for a moment to catch some air."

"I'll come," Frank says, looking a bit concerned.

"No, no." I rest my hand on his forearm. "You must save Mama from Countess Rose." I nod toward our mother, who looks about ready to punch the old lady on the nose. I wish she would.

Before Frank can contest, I make my escape. I hurry down a corridor, turn left, then right, then left again. "Damn it," I mutter, in a fuddle. It is this way, I am certain of it. And yet after a few more turns, I am still lost in the labyrinth of corridors.

I turn back, deciding I should retrace my footsteps as best I can remember, but I am halted by the looming, tall, hard frame of a man. The tingles tell me who it is before I look up, as does the familiar scent invading my nose.

"Lost?" he asks, his voice flat and without the warmth I unearthed and so loved.

No, Eliza, remember where he's been! "Excuse me," I say, stepping to the side to pass him, but, quite smoothly and without urgency, he moves with me, remaining before me, remaining in my way. My jaw becomes tense as I stare at his broad chest, refusing, for it'll be my undoing, to look at his face. "Excuse. Me."

"Look. At. Me."

"No."

"Do it, Eliza. Do it now."

"No."

He growls and takes my jaw, directing my face to his. So I slam my eyes closed, defying him at every turn. Protecting myself. "Let me go," I order. "Or, I swear, I will scream."

"You will definitely scream, Eliza," he growls, pushing me with the gentlest of thrusts, but with unmistakable power, up against a wall. "Be sure of that."

Even now, with his body pressed close to mine, a flurry of flashbacks overcoming me, and his breath spreading across my face, I remain in my darkness.

"Why won't you look at me?"

"Go back to Lady Dare," I hiss. "I'm certain she'd be willing to scream for you."

"For the love of God." He kisses me chastely, and I gasp and flip my eyes open. The moment mine meet his, the pain subsides, not because he's loosened his grip, but because, worrying to me, his eyes ease me. *He* eases me. It is with great regret that I must admit, Johnny Winters appears to be the cure for most of my disagreeable feelings. "Better," he grunts.

And then he kisses me again, this time long and deeply, and I am instantly lost in the force of it, his greedy tongue tussling chaotically with mine. I whimper, every grievance and gripe forgotten.

"I must have you." His hand goes beneath the skirt of my gown and hoists it up, and he tugs my pantaloons down. I gasp, my head falling back, as he frantically kisses my neck, biting and sucking, wrestling with his trousers. "Tell me you want me," he demands.

"I do." Oh, how I do! I yelp when I feel the familiar sensation of his wet, naked flesh between my thighs, and on a strangled bark and a yell from me, he thrusts inside me and pushes me up the wall. "Heavens above," he breathes, burying his face in my neck. "Are you all right?" he whispers, as every muscle within me tightens and pulls him closer.

"I am fine," I assure him, dizzy with pleasure.

And he starts to move, slowly at first, stretching me again, but his pace soon increases and as our pleasure builds, so does the urgency for us both to reach that incredible place at the end of this path. Pound after pound, he gives it to me, and cry after cry, I accept it. He looks at me, his stare unmoving, as our bodies bang and clash. My vision starts to fog and his face becomes distorted, and when it hits me between my thighs, comparable only to a cannonball striking me there, my knees become weak and my legs wobbly so I can no longer hold myself up.

"Dear God," I whisper, flopping against him. "I..." I just manage to hold my tongue before I say something I may regret.

"You what?" he pants, still swelling inside me, pinning me against the wall with his hard body.

"Nothing," I whisper.

"It is not nothing," he says, looking down at me and nuzzling, encouraging my face from where it is hiding in his chest. "Tell me, Eliza. Speak the words you dare not say, because I need to hear them."

"Why?" I whisper.

"I *need* to hear them."

He needs. He knows what I want to say and he *needs* to hear it. But why, when he has persistently told me not to love him? Maybe not outright, but in his own way. I stare at him, not knowing the outcome of this, not knowing what impact my words will have, but I must say them. I must tell him. I would hate to live with the regret of not expressing what he means to me. He means freedom. Happiness. Light. "I love you," I say quietly, almost nervously. "I have tried, but I cannot stop myself from loving you, and I know not where that leaves me. In hell, I suppose. I don't know, but it is a rather unpleasant notion to think that you could never love me back."

His smile is sad, and he kisses me on my forehead, breathing me deeply into him. "I have a confession."

My heart sinks. Oh God. I should have kept my stupid mouth shut. "If you are considering telling me that you have had dalliances with a certain resident of Belmore Square since enticing me into your bed, then you are wasting your breath. I already know." I gently push him back again, and I wince when he slips free from me. "I need not a reminder of your rakish ways, but I suppose I ought to be grateful, since your encounter with her proves you are not responsible for the death of Mr. Porter."

"Oh Christ," he mutters. "I was not with Miss Dare, Eliza. I was with you the night Porter was murdered, but I couldn't very well share that, unless, of course, you want every member of the ton to know and judge." His head tilts, and my mouth falls open.

"You weren't?"

"No." He scowls at me. "I've not shared my bed with another because, rather unfortunately, I have been unable to think of much more than our night."

What is that inside? Satisfaction? Happiness? "Really?"

"Yes, really. And…"

"And?" I ask, my heart soaring.

"And, Miss Melrose," he says, his shoulders dropping, his hand raking through his unruly hair. "Unfortunate as it is, how could I not love you?"

My heart squeezes. Does that mean he does? I'm scared to ask. But I must. For my sanity, I must. "Does that mean…?" My lips press together as my hope soars.

"I love you."

Something inside bursts. I think it might be my heart with happiness. "You love me?"

"Yes, so you may," he says, waving a hand flippantly, "do what I expect you're positively bursting to do."

I expect he expects me to squeal and throw myself into his arms. I could, but I won't. "I am bursting to kiss you," I whisper.

His eyebrow quirks in interest. "Just kiss me?"

He knows I am bursting to do much more, to smother him with my mouth and drag him to the nearest bed, and he could never complain, since it is he who's unearthed this insatiable thirst in me. Not that he would ever complain, I'm sure. And my thirst is only for him. I sigh and rest my hands upon his velvet jacket, looking up at him. "What are we to do?" I ask. "I am to be married to another."

He hums, thinking. "This needs some careful consideration."

"You had better hurry up, because I am due to wed in only a fortnight."

His nose wrinkles, and he kisses me delicately on the corner of my mouth. "Our love affair must not be discovered."

"Are you suggesting we sneak around for all time?" I pull away. Forgive me, but that felt *not* like careful consideration. "Wait. Are you suggesting I still marry Frederick and take you as a lover?"

He shrugs, and it is sheepish. My God, that's exactly what he is suggesting! "I see no other way to protect you."

"Protect me?" I wail, sounding somewhat deranged. "I do not need protecting. And from what, anyway? The ton?" I throw my arm out toward where the festivities are happening. "The small-minded nitwits out there?" I had been awfully hurt when I believed another woman had been indulged in the delights of Johnny's attention. Had his lips upon hers. His body touching hers. And to think he, apparently, and leaving me even more hurt, would be happy to share me with another man? No. I will not and cannot accept this...this... madness!

He squeezes his eyes closed. "No, I—"

"I care not for their opinion. I care not for the disdain or con—"

"The truth!" he yells, angered, and I recoil, shocked. "I'm protecting you from the truth!"

I watch his chest pump with his impatient heaves. "What truth?"

He growls, frustrated. "Christ."

"Johnny, what truth do you speak of? You must tell me."

He shakes his head. "The repercussions, Eliza. The truth. I will not have you treated as I have been."

"To hell with them!"

"You certainly are sending a lot of folks to hell, Eliza."

"Yes, and myself it would seem too! You want to share me? You won't help me understand this madness. One of the many reasons why I love you is that you do not treat me as though I am stupid." I feel my throat swelling. "To hell with you too." I walk away, roughly wiping at my face, willing the tears away.

"You already sent me there, Eliza!" he calls after me. "A one-way ticket!"

My emotions make me tremble as I weave the corridors once more, with no direction at all, no thought for my route either, my thoughts scattered, so when I make it back to the ballroom, I am surprised I actually found it with such little effort.

"There you are!" Frank says, rushing over. "I went to the court-yard, and you were not there. Are you all right?"

"I am fine," I say, scanning my brother's face. His lips look rather…red. I reach up and run my thumb across the bottom one, looking at the pad, seeing the remnants of some lip stain.

"Strawberry juice," he blurts, roughly wiping his mouth. "Damn stuff. Are you sure you are fine?"

"Quite sure." I brush off his concern, my own concern taking over. "Funny, it looks rather similar to the shade of stain Lizzy Fallow is wearing on this evening."

Frank takes my elbow and leads me further into the room, just as Johnny emerges, his eyes deep pits of burning anger. "You look as guilty as I expect you are," I say, looking away from the Duke.

"That mouth of yours gets you in enough trouble," Frank mumbles. "Do not let it get me into trouble too."

"I might include it in my report tomorrow."

Frank stops and drops his hold. "You can't because I no longer work for *The London Times* and Porter is dead, so both of your covers are blown. Plus, need I remind you that if Lymington finds out a woman has been writing some of the most popular stories, he will give Papa hell?"

I will protect you from the truth! "You need not," I murmur. "Do you realize what you are getting yourself into?" Listen to me. I am in the same situation, albeit reversed. *Damn it all.*

Frank looks past me, and I turn to see Johnny watching us. "Can you hear yourself?"

He is right, of course. "I can."

"What is going on, Eliza?"

"That is a very good question, Frank." I sigh, seeing Frederick's head swinging back and forth. "I should like to speak to my fiancé." I head toward him with a forced smile on my face.

"Are you all right, Miss Melrose?" His concern is very real, the dear man.

"What a wonderful evening," I say, linking arms with him. "Shall we?" He tenses with contact.

I see the Duke circling like a wild lion around his prey, his eyes on me. What a nerve. He wants me to marry another man? Share me? He doesn't look like a man who would like to share as he eyes Frederick as though he could very well harm him if he so much as sniffs me. The fool. He should think before he speaks. I have a good mind to marry Frederick to spite him, but that, I realize, would be ridiculous. "Do you want to marry me, Frederick?" I ask.

He blinks rapidly, surprised, and looks away. "Of course I want to marry you."

"Do you really, Fr—" I'm jolted in my side and knocked a good few feet, but a pair of large, familiar hands catch me and my body solidifies, if only to stem the tingles attacking every inch of my skin. I freeze in his hold, breathing raggedly into his shoulder. I must move. I cannot move. "My apologies, Miss Melrose," Johnny says in a low voice, close to my ear as he steadies my unsteady frame. He pulls away, his smile knowing as he stares at me, and I peek around us, seeing the stunned faces of many partygoers, including Frederick, all watching us. "I did not see you."

I straighten myself and try with everything I have to find my composure. "Apology accepted," I whisper. "I am fine."

I look at Frederick, who is hovering to the side, his face a picture of dread as he stares at the Duke, perhaps wondering if he will be murdered should he step in and check his betrothed is all right. "If you'll excuse us," I say, prompting a poorly concealed growl from Johnny. "Good eve."

"Is it?" he mutters, narrowing his eyes.

I quickly turn away from him, undoubtedly displeasing him further, but what does he expect from me in this moment, and everyone gets back to the business of partying so I am soon free from the looks of judgment. My God, what is he thinking? He cannot expect to dictate what I must do and how I must do it. Marry Frederick. Take a lover. Accept all of these injustices with a smile and no fight. "I need some air."

"Again?" Frederick says. "Didn't you just get some?"

"I need more." I leave the room and, this time, I really do find air. Luckily, I also find Clara so I have some company and that will lessen the risk of being dragged off by an angry Duke. "You look thoroughly flustered," she says, eyeing me. "The Duke of Chester is here, by the way."

"He is?" I reply, sounding indifferent.

"Yes. I saw him while I was fetching some lemonade."

"And you're still alive?" I gasp theatrically, and she throws a filthy look at me, her nose lifting.

"You'll go to hell, Eliza Melrose."

"I can't," I say, sighing, positively done with this eve. "There are too many people there I do not wish to se…oh no," I murmur as Lady Dare flounces out of the ballroom scanning the crowds. I just know she is looking for me, and I expect what she has to say should not be said in front of my sister. "Must go," I squeak, picking up my dress and hurrying away before I am spotted. I am too late, damn me, and Lady Dare—how the hell does she move so quickly in such a dress?—intercepts me.

"Are you late for something?" she asks, her smile as false as I've ever seen.

"Yes, actually, I believe my brother wishes to speak with me." Why in God's name would I mention Frank to this trollop? "If you'll excuse me." Of course, she doesn't budge and, regrettably, I know it is because she is not done with me. "Lady Dare, we are all quite busy, so would you be so kind as to spit it out."

"As you wish. I will warn you, Miss Melrose, if you know what's good for you, to keep your eyes off the Duke." Her friendly smile, albeit utterly false, has been lost and in its place is quite the look of threat. "I have seen the way in which you look at him."

Deny it!

But…

If I know what's good for me? I could laugh. I know what's good for me, yet, somehow, I think that will be wasted on Lady Dare. How does she know? And what does she care? After all, she is hardly showing signs of being the devoted type. But, and it is a shock to be sure, I do care. I gasp to myself. Am I jealous? Christ, I am. I'm jealous that Johnny so much as looked at this woman, let alone…

I stop that direction of thinking rather sharply. *Deny it!* "And if I don't?" I ask, cringing. I must learn to control my mouth.

I'm protecting you from the truth, Eliza.

What is the truth? Is *she* the truth he speaks of? Should I pry more? God, I am forgetting that I am supposedly marrying Frederick Lymington in a fortnight, and I do not need Lady Dare complicating matters further with her gossip, even if what I share with her in a fit of jealousy isn't really gossip.

Once you make a deal with Lymington, you do not renege on it.

The deal.

"If you don't," Lady Dare says, lifting her dress, "I will offer you the same kindness that I offered Annabella Tillsbury." She flounces away, and I am left with my mouth hanging open, my brain working fast to try and piece it together.

Yours, A

A is Lady Tillsbury? The letter Johnny received warning him of the story I wrote was from Lady Annabella Tillsbury? It has to be. She showed me some kindness at Almack's, and she also helped us return to the rooms when it is always forbidden. And she issued the voucher in my name to the ball at Johnny's request.

I lift my dress, intending to find Johnny and hit him with all of my questions, but I only make it a mere two paces before I am halted by the sight of Frederick appearing, searching for me. Uncharitably, I divert so as to avoid him, and I catch sight of Johnny, who has Lady Dare biting at his ankles, demanding attention. I watch in fascination as she talks to his uninterested form, and I see clearly that he is growing tired of her presence as he scans the room. He's looking for me, and when he marches away from Lady Dare and disappears down a corridor, I go after him, checking to make sure I am not being watched. I hear his boots hitting the ground in even strides. "Johnny," I call. "I'm here."

He turns, and the second I catch sight of his face, I realize I am in trouble. "What were you thinking?" he barks, stopping me in my tracks with his furious words. "I was protecting you, Eliza, and you could have just ruined everything!"

I wilt, thoroughly scorned. "I couldn't bear to listen to her speak about you in such a way." My defense is rather pathetic. Now is not the time to be possessive, but, and I doubt I should share, I could have said a lot more. Wanted to say a lot more!

"You will stand it like I must stand watching you with that nitwit Lymington."

He did not look like he was standing it very well when he bumped into me. Neither when he barged Frederick and I on the dance floor at Almack's. But now is perhaps not the time to point this observation out to him. "What are you protecting me from, Johnny? I demand to know the truth."

He waves a deranged hand at nothing in particular. "I'm protecting you from all of them."

"I do not need protecting from them."

He sighs, rubbing at his creased forehead. "But me...?" He looks like a man ruined as he paces up and down. "*You*," he says with extreme emphasis, "must control your mouth, Eliza."

I snort. "That's rich. You claim to love my mouth."

"Your smart mouth, not your out-of-control mouth."

"My mouth is my mouth. Take it or leave it."

"If you insist." He's on me like a lion, kissing me ferociously, and I am once again breathless. Consumed. My insides swirl more as he explores my mouth as if he knows it inside out in *every* way, because he does. It was quite refreshing to know Frank and my father had been paying enough attention to figure out I was writing again. That they know me so well, and my writing style is so familiar to them. But the Duke? He knows me. Understands me. "Imagine if," I say around his kiss, "I knew it was Lady Tillsbury who wrote to you advising you of my article about your arrival in London." I break away and look him directly in the eye, but before I can ask, he answers my unspoken question.

"Only ever one night, but with you..." He strokes my cheek softly. "An eternity with you will never be enough, Eliza."

I sigh, clasping the front of his jacket and looking up at him. I fear he is right. I also fear it would feel like an eternity to wait for the moments we may steal and be together. "Why do you hate Frederick so?" I ask. "He is but a harmless man."

He laughs lightly. "Why do you think?"

"You greatly disliked him before becoming fond of me." There's more to this. I know it.

"I…" He drops his eyes to my throat, frowning. "I never expected to fall in love, Eliza. I didn't think I was capable. I have only ever let down those whom I love, you see, and I am scared of…" He shakes his head. "You must give me the time I need to make this all right. I promise I—"

The shrill cry of a woman reaches us from the ballroom, and we both dart our eyes down the corridor. The entire palace seems to fall still and quiet. "What was that?" I ask as Johnny breaks away.

"Stay there," he orders, sounding all too edgy for my liking, as he disappears down the corridor toward the ballroom. I follow, ignoring him, and when I emerge, I see all the guests hurrying toward the grand entrance. I scan the space for Johnny, not seeing him, so I follow the crowds.

"Eliza, there you are," Frank mutters, taking my arm.

"What is happening?"

My brother doesn't answer, just frowns, as we leave the ballroom and join the other guests at the front of the palace.

"It's Frederick Lymington," someone says, on their tippytoes to try to see past everyone.

"What?" I question, shrugging Frank off and pushing my way through the crowd. I break out the other side and gasp my horror when I find Frederick lying unconscious on the ground. He has a lump as big as an egg on his head, and he starts to groan and writhe as a few of the Prince's footmen move in to assist, helping him to sit up. "Frederick, what happened?" I ask, rushing to his side, alarmed by the size of the lump, which seems to be growing by the second.

"Colleen?" he says, squinting, reaching for my shoulder. "Colleen, is that you?"

"Who is Colleen?"

"Shut up, Frederick!" Lymington barks. "Isn't it obvious what's happened," he goes on, smacking people with his walking aid to move them from his path. "He's been attacked."

Frederick reaches for his forehead and winces. "Ouch."

"By whom?" I ask.

Lymington points his stick. "By him."

I hear gasps, and I turn to find Johnny behind me looking as dark as a man could look. "What?" I whisper, knowing it not to be true. I was with Johnny just now, and I recall seeing Frederick unharmed and on his feet, as I went after the Duke. What is this madness? "Prove it," I blurt.

"If you insist." Lymington bends with some effort and picks up something from the ground, waving it. "I believe this is yours," he says to Johnny, who instinctively reaches up to his pocket and pats at where the handkerchief should be. Then he looks down at his chest on a frown before darting his wary eyes to mine.

My God, he's being framed! "No," I say quietly, turning to Lymington. "That could be anyone's handkerchief."

Lymington snorts and, so smugly, I just know he's got something up his sleeve, he pulls one corner taut, showing it to the crowds. The initials JW stitched in gold to match the buttons of Johnny's velvet jacket stare back at me. "I believe we now have the evidence we need to prove that *this* man is a danger to society. He tried to kill Frederick, and he killed Porter in an attempt to halt the rumors of him attacking Frank Melrose. He must be hung for his crimes!"

"Seize him!" the Prince barks, prompting his men to all move in and circle Johnny.

"No," I whisper, as I am grasped and pulled away by Frank. "What are you doing?" I protest. "I must defend him!"

"Eliza, you must stop it this instant before you are arrested for treason."

"I do not care!" I yell. "Johnny could not have harmed Frederick."

"How can you be so sure, Eliza? It's there as plain as the nose on my face."

"I…" *You must give me the time I need to make this all right.* God damn it. But it's all so horribly wrong right now. "I just know it to be true!"

Frank whirls me around, keen to remove me, and as he pushes me through the crowds, my tears flow. We make it outside and I watch, horrified, as they escort Johnny away. He does not wriggle and fight. Why? Why is he accepting this?

He looks back at me and the expression on his face pains me. It's a mix of anger and sadness, and he smiles softly, as if trying to reassure me. It won't work. Frank pulls me on, the pain in my heart unbearable. I would never have survived this new world without Johnny. Now he's gone?

I already feel as though I am slowly dying.

Chapter 16

Father has been holed up in his office throughout the night, various men coming and going, but one man has remained. Lymington. I despise him. I have sat at the top of the stairs trying to listen to the conversation, but they are talking in whispers. I cannot get any closer either, as Dalton, though he's aware of my interest, or perhaps because he has been told to, is keeping close guard on Father's study. Frank has remained in the drawing room too, on hand to be summoned whenever Father needs him. I am unsure as to whether I should be comforted by my brother's banishment, or wary. God damn it, what damning tales are being concocted in there?

I cannot sit here without speaking up. I cannot allow them to condemn Johnny. I am proof that he did not attack Frederick, and I must confess, no matter what.

I stand and pace down the stairs, and, having heard me I expect, Frank comes out of the drawing room, looking as tired and as drained as I feel. "Go to bed, Eliza," he says once again.

"I cannot allow this."

Rolling his eyes, he scrubs a hand down his face, turning and going back into the drawing room. "What is it with you and this misplaced desire to prove that the Duke is innocent in all the things?"

"Because, brother, it is the right thing to do."

"The right thing for you to do is to shut up."

I recoil, indignant and march right up to Frank.

And punch him in his bicep.

"Owwww!" he yelps, feeling at his arm.

"You shut up," I order. "The right thing for you to do is step away from Lizzy Fallow. The right thing for Clara to do is steer very clear of the stable boy. The right thing for me to do is..."

"Clara and the stable boy?" Frank asks.

Damn my runaway mouth. "The Duke has been framed, and I for one cannot stand by and watch as an innocent man is hung for crimes he did not commit. There's something untoward going on here, Frank, and I intend to find out what." Pivoting, I march to Father's study and thump on the door.

"Clara and the stable boy?" he bellows, making me flinch.

"What of Clara?" Mother appears, and I turn to see her looking between us.

"Nothing," I hurry to reassure her, just as the door to Father's office swings open behind me.

"What of Clara?" Father asks.

Bloody hell.

I look at Frank as though he is mad and perhaps stupid, which is rich, I know.

"What?" Clara appears beside Mother, and I silently will her to leave.

"Nothing," I say.

"Nothing," Frank adds.

"Then leave me in peace," Papa grumbles. "Florence, will you please contain our children whilst I deal with business?" He points a look at Mother, and her nostrils flare dangerously.

"Only if you contain that monster in your study."

Father recoils, as do Frank, Clara, and I. "Florence?"

"I am done with this madness," Mama hisses. "Done, I tell you, Burt!" She gathers us up in her wide embrace, as though we were small children again, and ushers us to the drawing room, leaving Father standing somewhat struck dumb in the doorway to his study.

"Mama?" I say quietly when she's plonked herself in the

chair in the window, her head going into her hands. "Are you all right?"

Dalton appears with a glass of wine and sets it on the table beside her chair, and Emma takes it and places it in Mother's hand. "Thank you," she says, before taking a very long sip. "I am not." She looks to the ceiling, as if looking to God for forgiveness for confessing it. "My beautiful, bright, wonderful children."

I look to Frank and Clara, who each look to me, too, all of us bemused.

"I want only the best for you all," she says, taking another sip. "I hope you can forgive me."

"For what?" I ask, stepping forward. "What must we forgive you for?"

"I fear my own desires to be accepted by the ton has played a part in this mess."

I go to Mama and kneel before her, taking her hand, positively hating her forlorn expression, and Frank circles the back of her chair, resting a reassuring hand on her shoulder. She smiles up at him and down on me as Clara perches on the arm of the chair. "You always told us everything can be fixed," Clara says.

"It can." She nods. "I must believe it can, or I might lose you all forever."

"What are you talking about?" I ask.

"It seems your father and I have got ourselves in a bit of a sticky situation and we know not how to get ourselves out of it."

I don't like the sound of that.

Mother looks at me and smiles, though it is strained. "You must talk to Frederick, my darling."

"Why?"

"Ask him about Colleen."

I inhale and stand. "Colleen?"

"Who the hell is Colleen?" Clara asks.

"Will you please watch your mouth, young lady?" Frank barks, making Clara roll her eyes.

"Where will I find Frederick?"

"I not long saw him in the gardens looking quite the beaten man."

I leave the house with haste, with no chaperone or voicing a request for one, hurrying to the gardens and weaving the path to the bench in the middle. I find Frederick with his head low. Mama is right. He looks quite the beaten man. "May I join you?" I ask tentatively, prompting him to lift his head with some effort.

As predicted, he scans the vicinity for who might be escorting me, but I ignore his silent question, and obvious worry, and join him. "That was all very unfortunate, wasn't it? How is your head?"

"Sore."

I nod, thinking he might have a headache for some time. The bump is huge. "Can you remember what happened?"

He frowns, shaking his head, and I believe him. "One minute I was enjoying a lemonade, the next my head was pounding." He reaches up and feels at his impressive lump, wincing.

"Who is Colleen, Frederick?"

He darts a surprised look my way, and I smile. "You said her name numerous times when you were coming round."

He sighs, looking so very flattened. "She is the love of my life, Eliza. I am sorry. I feel as though I have tricked you."

God bless him. I take his hand and squeeze, and today he does not freak out or try to stop me touching him. In fact, he squeezes it back. "*You* have not tricked me, Frederick. Your father forced this upon you?"

He shifts, uncomfortable, and removes his hand from mine. "I have already said too much."

Good God, he is afraid. It pains me, because Frederick is not the only one who is afraid of Lymington. "I understand," I say, standing. He has not really said much, but enough. "I'm sorry we are both in this ghastly situation. You're quite a catch, Frederick. For the right woman."

He laughs, and it's the kind of laugh on Frederick that he should always laugh because it changes his vacant face to one of fulfillment. "And you. For the right man." He shakes his head and sighs heavily. "Eliza, I must tell you, if I do not marry you, my father will destroy Colleen's family. They're merely farmers. They hardly survive as it is." He looks at me, pleading in his eyes. "Please, Eliza, you must marry me, or she will be left destitute. I could never live with myself."

My God, what a mean man his father truly is. Frederick and I have more in common than we would both like. "You need not worry, Frederick," I assure him quietly, offering a small smile before walking quickly back to the house.

I march straight to the study and enter without knocking and scan the room, not at all liking what I am seeing. Lymington is comfortable in a chair by the fire, Father is pacing by the bookcase, and a man, a reporter, I expect, is at Father's desk scribbling down notes. Tomorrow's headlines, I'm sure.

"Get rid of her," Lymington barks at my father without so much as looking at me.

"Eliza, please," Father begs, coming to me as I throw Lymington the most contemptuous glare I can muster. "Now is not the time for your contribution." He takes my arms gently, and as I regard him, I see the dark circles under his eyes. I know them not to be through tiredness alone, but perhaps through worry too. "I have a deadline I must meet."

"But you mustn't," I say, hoping to take away the strain upon his shoulders. "I don't know how his handkerchief came to be at the scene of the crime"—I absolutely do know how it came to be at the scene—"but the Duke of Chester could not have harmed Frederick."

"Eliza," Father sighs, closing his eyes to gather patience. His exhaustion may play in my favor because he looks without the energy to fight my persistence. "He murdered Porter in cold blood. His family, for Christ's sake, and now an attempt on Frederick, too. The man needs to be stopped and the truth told."

I look at Lymington, and I can't say I like the thoughtfulness on his old, pale, crabby face. He knows. He must know about Johnny and me. Why else would he set him up like this?

I'm protecting you from the truth, Eliza.

"Why did you promise me to Frederick?" I ask my father outright as I return my attention to him. "What did *he* give you in return?"

"Eliza," Father warns softly.

"I paid for machinery," Lymington barks, struggling up from his chair, using his stick to help. "I paid for the machine that has made *The London Times* the biggest in the country."

I gasp. "You told us all you used the last of the family's money."

"We had no money, Eliza! Nothing! We were on the brink of ruin, the business failing."

"So you sold me?" I whisper.

"I bought us a better life."

"For you!" I yell. "A better life for you, but for me?"

"Oh shut up," Lymington mutters. "You should be honored. My son comes from good stock."

"Why would you pay for a wife for him? Let him marry whom he chooses and desires." I refrain from mentioning Colleen out of loyalty to Frederick and nothing else. I would hate his father to cause him more hardship.

"I have to pay because it's the only way to secure our future. He needs an heir! One simply has to hope that the babe doesn't bear its mother's insolence."

"Or its grandfather's cruelty," I snipe. "Why do you hate the Duke of Chester so? You told lies to discredit him, tried to have damaging news printed about him, and now you say he attacked Frederick?"

"Eliza!" Father physically shakes me. "Enough!"

I take no pleasure in Papa's distress. None at all. "You cannot allow this to happen, Papa. You cannot print more lies about the Duke."

His eyes clench shut, his face ashen. "I owe His Grace a great deal, Eliza."

"My money is the only reason you could purchase a machine to increase print runs."

"Pay him back, Papa. Give him back the seven hundred pounds and be gone with him!"

"That wasn't the deal," Papa breathes.

And now we are indebted to him forever.

"I'm sorry, Eliza."

I take a breath, swallowing hard, my reality hitting me so much harder than it ever has before. That is it, then. There is no happy end here for the Duke and me. I cannot change my fate or society's expectations. "I will marry Frederick without further protest or defiance," I say, spitting out the words as though they are poison in my mouth. "I will be a good wife. I will give him as many heirs as the Duke wishes, boys and girls. I will live in Cornwall without complaint. But only if you guarantee Johnny Winters's freedom and declare him an innocent man. Not just from the crimes you claim of this eve, but from all those he has been accused of before."

Papa looks so utterly confused. "I know you don't want to do this. You've fought me the entire way. You do not want to marry Frederick, so why would you do all of that for him?"

"Because that man tried to seduce your daughter," Lymington scathes, and I look at him in shock. He did know. All of this to force me into marriage? To guarantee I will wed Frederick? "And she has fallen for it, like all the other brainless females he's charmed into bed."

"My God," Father whispers, falling to his chair heavily. "Eliza?"

I don't refute him, it would be a pointless endeavor, and this brainless female is done. "You will leave the Duke to live in peace. You will never print his name in your newspaper ever again. If you do, I will run away, and if I am blessed to have them, I will take my children with me, never to be found." I could scream from the rooftops of the Duke's innocence. No one will believe me. *Or* a disgraced duke. Not over a respected businessman and the *noble* Duke of Cornwall. So, really, this is the only way. And, actually, I love Johnny too much to subject him to the wickedness of society, because, with me, his life will not improve, but worsen.

"You act with integrity," Lymington says. "Though, I hasten to add, it is wasted."

"Why?" I ask.

"I take no pleasure in sharing this with you, Miss Melrose."

I laugh. I doubt that to be true if his smug smile is a measure. "Sharing what?"

"His attempts to seduce you were in a fit of revenge. You see," Lymington goes on, hobbling over to the fireplace. "Winters and Frederick went to Eton together, and that Winters was always picked ahead of my son in the Wall Game. I knew the housemaster, you see, and…well…"

"You had him flogged for being a better player than Frederick?"

His nose lifts, and it is all I can do not to march over and punch him on it. "Of course not! I had him flogged for causing a grave injury to Frederick during a game."

"It can't have been that grave. He is still alive! And from what I have heard, the game is a rather raucous affair and many players come off with many injuries!"

Lip curling, Lymington waves his stick at me, dismissing me. "Be warned, girl," he seethes. "Every flog that man endured was deserved."

"He was a boy!"

"Why do you care? Have you not yet realized that you have been but a pawn in his game to seek revenge upon me?"

"What?" I breathe, a horrible pain searing me, my mind not helping me understand this news. Father places a hand upon my arm, moving to stand before me, as if protecting me from the wrath of Lymington.

"Enough, Your Grace." And yet he still honors him with his title.

"Be wise, Melrose," Lymington warns. "Winters has been acting in revenge and nothing more, and the sooner your defiant, wayward daughter realizes that, the better for us all. And by that, I mean the better for you."

I see my father's body shrink in defeat before me and I exhale, my heart hurting more than it ever could. Johnny was merely using me in a mean fit of revenge? It's almost too much to withstand, to believe, and yet all I can hear are Johnny's choice words when referring to the Lymingtons. He hates them. I should withdraw my demand to free him of the condemnation, but what does it matter? Whether I was a pawn or not, I am not to be with him and I, quite honestly, am too tired to fight any more. For the Duke. And for myself.

"My conditions still stand, so I suppose you ought to decide what is more important, Your Grace. Damning an already disgraced duke or continuing your family name." I quickly think of something else. "And Frank must have his position back," I order, making Papa's eyebrow quirk. "Good evening," I murmur, dejected, as I leave Father's study, passing a silent Frank and my mother, who's looking the saddest I have ever seen her. I can assure her, she is not as sad as I am. I have always been dealing with a force far more powerful than I am. Now, it has finally overcome me.

Chapter 17

The following two weeks pass by in a blur of wedding plans and despair. Frederick has called three times. The first time was to finalize the wedding contract in Father's study, which was followed by a visit to me in the drawing room where, quite awkwardly, because neither of us truly want this, he presented me with an elegant ring. It felt heavy upon my finger. Still does. I had smiled tightly, told him it was beautiful, and excused myself with claims of a headache. I stood at the window watching as the residents of Belmore Square went about their usual business. And I saw him, the Duke, leave his house, starting his life as a free man, while I began mine as a prisoner. My heart had cracked, and tears pinched the back of my eyes as I whipped the draperies across. They have been closed since, sparing me the torture of seeing the outside world.

The second time Frederick called, he brought flowers for my mother and me. Tulips for her, roses for me. Bright red ones. I have to commend him on his efforts to make the best of our dismal situation. But this, me and him, the wedding, is merely a transaction. A business deal.

I accepted the flowers, passed them to Emma without so much as sniffing them, thanked him, and left the room. This time, after Mama saw him out, she came after me, and as I looked at her, I saw the despair and helplessness I know she feels. Guilt. It was emblazoned upon her face. And her words, *once you make a deal with Lymington, you do not renege on it*, rang loud in my ears. He bought my parents wealth and recognition,

266

and they paid with happiness. Not just mine, but all of ours. Frank is subdued, Clara is avoiding us all, and Papa is in his study drinking himself into an early grave.

Now is the third time for Frederick to call upon me, and, unfortunately, it appears that his father isn't leaving room for me to avoid him this time.

"Eliza would love nothing more than to promenade with you," Lymington says as Dalton helps Papa into his jacket and hands him his hat. "I'm sure Mrs. Melrose will accompany you while Mr. Melrose and I discuss business at Gladstone's."

"I'm afraid not," Mother pipes up as she breezes past. "I have been invited to Lady Tillsbury's luncheon."

I smile at Mother's aloofness, but while her attempt is admirable, and undoubtedly driven by guilt, she cannot save me.

"Do any of the women in your life know their place, Melrose?" Lymington mutters.

"I will chaperone my sister," Frank says, and before I know it, I am in my room with Emma helping me get ready. As I place myself in front of the mirror and fix my bonnet, Emma goes to the draperies and pulls them open before leaving my room to help Mother. I wander over and look down onto the square but pull back on a skip of my heart when I see him on the edge of the gardens, as still as an ice sculpture, looking up at my bedroom window. His expression is fierce. My swallow is lumpy.

"Eliza," Frank calls.

"Coming," I whisper, preparing myself to leave the safety of our house for the first time in weeks. I pat down my dress, exhale, and walk on. Clara is waiting at the bottom of the stairs with Frank. "Oh, how lovely," I say, descending the stairs. "All the Melrose children together for a walk in the park to celebrate my demise."

Clara looks mighty inconvenienced. "All of our demises, actually, sister."

"Oh, is the stable boy no more?"

"Ask our brother." She barges him as she passes, and I cock my head in question to Frank.

"I suppose this means there will be no stain upon your lips in the near future?"

"You suppose right," he says, sweeping a hand out in gesture for me to walk on. "I couldn't have you in the depths of misery alone now, could I?" He takes the steps behind me.

"So what now? You carry on being a rake?" I come to an abrupt stop at the bottom of the steps and Frank bumps into me, jolting me forward. My eyes narrow as Lady Dare breezes across the cobbles in a vivid blue silk dress, her eyes set firmly on my handsome brother.

"Maybe," he muses, pulling my stare to him. I find his attention on the adventuress Lady Dare, and my heart sinks. I saw how he looked at Lizzy Fallow. It is not how he looks at Lady Dare. I do not like this.

"How lovely you look, Miss Melrose." Frederick appears, smiling awkwardly and sheepishly.

I smile, pull on my gloves and march through Clara and Frank. "Thank you, Frederick. As do you." I notice he is not pointing out my lack of formalities toward him, and I conclude he would simply like to make this whole hideous process as easy as possible. I thank him for that. I let my eyes fall to the same spot where I saw the Duke from my window. Regrettably, he is gone. I should have liked him to see me relatively composed.

We walk, Frederick and I leading, Frank and Clara following, toward the park. I look back, checking Frank and Clara are not close enough to hear me before I speak. "Where is Colleen, Frederick?" I ask.

He, too, looks back, nervous, but he settles when he sees we are safe from prying ears. "In Cornwall, Miss Melrose." He smiles fondly. "I expect she has some smudges on her face from plowing the fields with her father today."

"Find her and run away to Scotland." If Frederick leaves, surely I cannot be held to the deal?

He throws a stunned look at me but quickly reins it in. "I'm not sure I understand, Eliza."

"Oh, you do, Frederick. And I am certain more than I am certain of many things that you have considered it on more than one occasion." As the golden gates to the park appear in the distance, the sound of charging hooves approaches, the ground vibrating under my feet. It's a familiar sound, one I remember from the countryside, and far too reckless to be any of the gentlemen of the ton taking their morning rides.

I look up and see them. Three horses, two black, one white, heading our way. The highwaymen. For the first time in days, my blood rushes with excitement. Chaos ensues, people screaming and running, and I stand there, silently encouraging the wild horses, mesmerized by the majestic creatures cantering toward me.

"Hell," Frank blurts, grabbing Clara and pulling her close. "We need to move."

"I'm fine where I am," I declare, following their path, watching them come closer and closer and closer. The promise of something interesting to write about is suddenly monopolizing my brain.

"Eliza," Frank yells, just as I am barged from the side. I look up and find Johnny glaring down at me. "What is it with you and wild horses?" He takes the bare skin of my elbow and speaks to Frank. "If you remain on the edge of the path, you should be safe. Now, excuse me a moment while I borrow your sister. I would ask her *betrothed*, but he appears to have scarpered."

Frank frowns as he searches the vicinity for Frederick, and Clara chuckles as I am hauled away into a nearby alleyway with absolutely no regard for potential spectators. It matters not that everyone is most likely distracted by the highwaymen. He has a rather bad habit of manhandling me, and I can't say I appreciate it. "Let go of me, you big oaf."

"An oaf is what I am, and I, where you are concerned, Eliza, do not mind remaining as such, but you will shut your mouth for a mere moment and hear me out." His hand seizes my jaw and holds me still as his body, oh, his glorious, hard, familiar warm body, holds me against the wall. His mouth comes close. His eyes flick from mine to my lips, back and forth, as if he simply cannot decide which to focus on. He settles on my eyes. His narrow. So do mine. "Promise you will hear me to the end."

"I promise nothing to a man who has hoodwinked me into his bed with false promises of—"

"Of what, Eliza? I have promised you nothing. In fact," he goes on, his jaw becoming progressively tighter, "I do believe I explicitly informed you of my desire to *not* promise you a damn thing."

"That may be so, but I distinctly remember you telling me you loved me. That was cruel, Your Grace."

"It was not cruel, because it was the truth. And you may not call me *Your Grace*."

"Of course. Because there is nothing graceful about you, is there, *Your Grace*."

"You infuriate me." And he slams his mouth on mine, kissing me hard, and I am a slave to it. "And yet I cannot resist your allure, Miss Melrose." And I his, it seems. "Now, listen to me and listen good."

"Or else?"

"Do not test me."

"You have a nerve."

"Indeed I do." He pushes away from me and straightens out his jacket.

"Did you entice me into your affections to exact revenge upon Frederick?"

Jaw ticking, his frown deepening into a scowl, he thinks for a long, hard time. I have no idea why, unless, of course, he is considering lying. "Yes." He spits out the word as if it's poison on his tongue.

"Then I am afraid I must depart." Why I am speaking so politely I do not know, for I am raging on the inside. But I must not allow him to see my inner turmoil. My hurt and anguish. I have already given this monster my innocence. I refuse to lose my self-respect to him also. Or, at least, any more of it. "Excuse me." I refrain from touching him, scared of where that may lead me, and move past him.

"Eliza, wait."

I keep moving. *Just keep moving!*

"Eliza, you cannot walk away!"

"Yes, I can!" I shout, whirling around, suddenly quite dizzy with rage. "This may have been a fun game to you, but in the process I have surrendered what little bit of freedom I had for the sake of *your* freedom, and for what? To learn that you have taken advantage of me. Stolen from me. Forced me into a marriage to a man I am not meant to be with!"

"Then do not marry him."

"I am not the only one backed into a corner here, Your Grace. Besides, if I do not marry him, they will lock you up and even after everything you have done to me, I cannot with good conscience pardon that." Turning, I walk away, barely holding on to my emotions, but I do, if only to save myself the inevitable questions from Frank upon my return to him.

"I won't give up, Eliza. Where you're concerned," he yells, unbothered by being heard, "I have no boundaries."

He's never lived by boundaries. Now should be no different. This isn't simply about keeping Johnny out of prison but keeping my father away from financial ruin too.

I edge my way out onto the promenade and see two of the horsemen circling a few rather terrified-looking gentlemen, who have their coin purses held out with shaking hands. But what of the third?

I turn and find Frank, stock still and silent, nose-to-nose with a handsome white stallion, staring, as the horseman stares down at him. He looks lost in a daydream, and I wait with bated breath for either one of them to move, but it is the horse that breaks the staring standoff, rising to its back legs on a yowl, knocking Frank to his backside.

I freeze on the spot when I hear the horseman laugh, and stare, taking in the form of the rider upon the steed as I walk forward and help my brother to his feet before facing the horse and finding the rider. "Good day to you, Miss...?" My head tilts, and though I can only see her eyes, the triangle of material covering the rest of her face, her hat pulled low, I can see now with perfect clarity her lashes, which are longer than a man's should be. And when those eyes sparkle, I know she's smiling at me. She kicks her horse, and they gallop off, the two black stallions following.

"In broad daylight in the middle of Park Lane!" Frank splutters.

"Very bold, don't you think?" I ask, thoughtful. A woman. A highway*woman*. What a story that would make. I glance back to see Johnny has emerged from where he dragged me and is looking quite furious. I don't give him too much of my time. "Where's Frederick?" I ask, searching for him.

"He ran that way," Clara says, pointing toward Belmore Square. "I expect he's messed his breeches too."

I should scold her, but I don't. Frederick lacks in many areas, for me at least, but I cannot blame him for being scared out of his wits. Even Frank looked terrified. "I think I've had enough drama for one day," I say quietly, watching the highwaymen disappear into the distance.

"Indeed," Frank muses, he, too, watching, his look thoughtful. "Did you notice something funny about that horseman?"

"You mean that he was, in fact, a she?"

He gasps and turns to me. "My God, you are right!" he says, almost delighted. "A horsewoman, not a man?" He winces at the sound level of his own voice and glances around. "I must return home immediately and have the report written for tomorrow's edition."

"No, no!" I say, grabbing at his arm. "I have already written the story in my head." I scowl at him but soften it when I realize something. He's excited. I cannot take that away from him. "I cannot wait to read it."

He grins and cups my head roughly, planting a hard, loud kiss on my forehead. "Come along, sister, we have work to do."

I look at Clara as Frank strides off, and she rolls her eyes. "You two have fun." And she's gone like a shot, making the most of Frank's distraction.

"Clara, come back!" I call, in complete vain. She is like a greyhound, and I fear I know exactly where she is going. "Oh dear," I say on a sigh, looking back, seeing the Duke has now gone.

Chapter 18

Frank spent the rest of that day writing the report, checking it over, assessing it, asking me to check it too. I have never seen him so invested in a story. Or enthusiastic. Or...enthralled. I am uncertain in this moment whether it is a good thing, or a terribly bad thing. Time, I'm sure, will tell. One thing I know is that while he is distracted by a compelling story that's got his creativity flowing, he is not thinking about Lizzy Fallow or Lady Dare.

On the morning of my wedding, I wake with a deep ache in my stomach and a head that feels heavy upon my shoulders. It is the weight of my thoughts, I'm certain. For a fleeting moment, I wonder—and perhaps hope—if Frederick will have the front to show up at our wedding after leaving me at the mercy of the highwaymen, but I know Frederick, and, unfortunately, the man has as much to lose as I and he would never defy his father. I would like to think that is purely a result of respect. Alas, it is not. No. It is fear. God, how I wish he would listen to my reckless suggestion and run away to Scotland to marry Colleen after he has found her. Save us both from this life sentence.

I look at myself in the mirror. My eyes are empty. My lips straining to curve as Emma fixes the flowers in my hair and Mother fusses around me, distracting herself from having to look me in the eye. I have never seen her look so tentative. I have never seen my father look so tired. And I have never felt so hopeless. Clara is twirling and singing across the room, oblivious, and it makes me want to poke her in the eye. I expect wherever she disappeared to the other day in the royal park is the reason for her wistful obliviousness. How I wish she would open her eyes and see the impossibilities that face her, as they do me.

"Have you seen Frank?" I ask, going back to gazing at the woman reflected back at me, in her best dress made of the softest muslin, that is squeezing against her ribcage, making it tricky to breathe, and lace sleeves that are itching her skin. I inhale and push air out.

"He is dressing," Mama says. "The carriage has arrived."

"Then I suppose we ought to be going." I walk to the door in even, determined strides and pull it open. Frank is coming out of his room, and he looks up at me. Then, quickly looks away, unable to face me.

"You look beautiful," he murmurs, eyes low.

"Thank you." Though all this effort is wasted on a man who will not appreciate the effort. Not because he is a bad man, of course, but because he does not love me. To feel bitter is probably unreasonable, and yet I cannot help it. I shake my head to myself for having such thoughts, for I never considered or desired to be loved by a man. Now? Now I am angrier than ever that I allowed myself to feel things and dream of things so far out of my reach. I have had a taste of the dream and that only makes reality harder to face. To lie with a man because I desire to and not because it is my duty. That thought brings me full circle back to now. My wedding day. And after the day, comes night. I have not received any kind of talk from my mother regarding what will be expected of me on this eve. Because she knows I have engaged in the act already, because I am certain Papa will have shared the shocking news with her. She is, for want of a better phrase, feigning ignorance of my transgressions. Not one person in this house can look me in the eye. Well, Clara can, but she is a fool in love with the stable boy.

I hate that she, too, will face the horrors of reality as soon as she is launched into society, just as I have.

Frank rushes out and I take the stairs, pass Father outside his study, and leave the house, eyes forward, not wishing to see the hordes of Belmore residents who have come out to see the blushing bride.

"You look beautiful, Eliza," Father says, joining me.

"Thank you, Papa," I murmur, and he flinches, appearing to struggle with my acquiescence.

"Eliza, I do not know wh—"

"There's no need," I say with a strong voice, walking on. "Let us get this over with." I brace myself to board the carriage, before I break out in a run and ruin everyone I love—my father, my mother, Frank, Clara...and the Duke. I wince, lifting my dress to step up.

"Eliza!"

I freeze and every hair on my body stands up on end.

"Eliza, wait!"

I look across the gardens and see Johnny running this way. What on earth?

"Get down from that carriage," he orders, sounding out of breath. "Now, Eliza, I demand it." He comes to an abrupt halt and grabs my hand, pulling me down. "You are not getting married today."

I feel all eyes on me. "What in God's name are you doing?" I ask. This is all very gallant, but, good heavens, is he determined to ruin us both? Johnny's mouth falls open, ready to speak, but a carriage, traveling at quite an impressive and perilous speed, rounds the corner into the square, tilting precariously on two wheels.

I recognize the elaborately decorated carriage immediately, as does Father, who I would expect to appear alarmed but instead looks plain tired by the sight of the Lymingtons' transport.

"What took you so long?" Papa says, looking to Johnny for an answer.

"What's going on?" I murmur, frowning, noticing Johnny's back visibly straightening, his chest, which is impressive under normal circumstance, puffing out farther, his eyes narrowing to slits as Lymington struggles down from his carriage, followed by Frederick.

"It took longer than expected to find Porter's wife," Johnny mutters.

"Find me the constable!" Lymington barks to no one in particular, pointing his stick at Johnny. "I want this man arrested!"

"Wait," I cry, alarmed, stepping forward. "That was not part of the deal!"

"Stand back, Eliza," Johnny warns, his arm coming out to restrain me. "I will deal with this."

"Deal with what, exactly?" I ask, my eyes darting back and forth between the men. Short of circling each other, which I highly expect to begin soon, they may as well be foaming at the mouth like hungry lions.

"Would you like to explain?" Johnny asks Lymington. "Or would you prefer me to undertake that honor?"

"Explain what?" I ask.

"About this," Frederick says, holding up a newspaper in his hand, waving it in the air for all to see, before he walks toward Johnny and passes it across to him and then joins me. "I think I will take your advice, Eliza," he says quietly.

"What advice?"

Frederick smiles as my brother slams the door of Lymington's carriage shut. "I'd prefer to hear the Duke of Chester's take," Frank says.

"What the hell is happening?" Lymington barks. That's a damn fine question, and I would be grateful if someone would please enlighten me.

"I believe we might be witnessing your demise," Frank chirps, all too happily.

"I am thoroughly confused," I confess.

"I was feeling somewhat that way myself," Frederick says. "Until Winters explained."

"Explained what?"

"I feel it only right the man himself gets to enlighten the crowds," Frederick muses, rocking back on his heels, like he is settling in for quite a show.

Out of patience and feeling my hope soar—hope that I am unsure is wasted—I march to Johnny. "I demand answers."

"Make your demands in the bedroom, my darling," he whispers, loud enough for only me to hear. My mouth falls open. My God, he's crazy. I look at my father who looks...happy? And to my mother, who has moved to her husband's side and is looking up at him in question. Papa pats her forearm, his smile growing.

"Arrest him!" Lymington barks again.

"Oh, do shut up," Johnny mutters, opening up the newspaper as he starts a leisurely pace up and down the cobbles.

"He murdered his family! Burned them alive in a fit of fury for bringing shame upon his name."

"Yes, that's exactly what this report says, Lymington. The one written by Porter some months ago. Do you recall it?"

"I...I...I..."

"You...you...you? You must recall, since it was you who fed Porter the *facts*. I use the word loosely." Johnny snarls, moving in, and Lymington leans back. "Are you afraid, Lymington? Because you should be. You murdered my family."

"What?" I whisper.

"Well," Johnny says, his jaw uncomfortably tight, "my father, at least."

"You're talking rubbish!"

"Am I?" Johnny frees Lymington from his deadly glare for just a second and pulls a piece of parchment from his trousers, holding it up. "A letter written from Porter to Burt Melrose. Lymington here ended Porter when he returned from visiting a friend in York. A friend who confirmed Lymington was close to bankruptcy not too long ago." Johnny waves the letter. "His wife found this letter addressed to Melrose in his desk spilling every detail."

"Arrest that man," Father orders with grit, pointing at Lymington. "He murdered the Duke of Chester in cold blood."

That is well and good, but we still do not know why.

"I will have you all banished!" Lymington protests. "What is the meaning of this?"

"You," Johnny says, sounding as accusing as he appears, "knew my father was about to revolutionize printing with his invention. You saw an opportunity, so you stole his idea and murdered him. Then you sold his invention to the Germans, claiming it as your own, but you didn't want the credit, did you? Because to take the credit would have raised suspicion. So in exchange, you took a machine and gave it to Melrose in a dirty deal that would see your bank account go from empty to bulging. And as a bonus, you got to control the press too. Spill your lies about my family. Make sure the Winters could never return and claim what is rightfully theirs."

"My God," I whisper as the constable moves in and seizes Lymington. "Frederick, do something!" he wails, but Frederick simply shakes his head, in disappointment, I suppose. "Frederick?"

"Goodbye, Father." Looking at me, Frederick bows his head, a small smile tickling the corner of his mouth, and I know, I just know, where he is heading. I nod in return, sending him on his way with my silent blessing and best wishes.

"Ah, finally they have arrived," Johnny says as the sound of horses' hooves clip-clop into the square.

"What? Who?" I turn, along with everyone else, to see two black stallions pulling a carriage into the street.

The carriage rumbles to a stop, and the silent anticipation is palpable as we wait with bated breath for whoever is inside to emerge.

The door swings open with force and a man appears. A man, make no mistake, that could only be Johnny's brother. "God, it's good to be back," he declares, hopping down, his smile stretched wide across his handsome face.

"Brother," Johnny murmurs, going to him. They hug fondly. "You must be weary after your travels."

He smirks, smacking Johnny on the shoulder. "Yes, indeed, so weary." He does not look in the *least* bit weary.

I stare on, shocked, which is quite a feat on my part, for I knew the rumors to be untrue. They were never murdered, but that is not my issue in this moment of clarity. Yet regardless of my silent conclusions, I cannot fathom how the rest of Belmore Square must feel to see a member of the Winters family, who is supposed to be dead. Dead! But as I cast a look around, I suddenly can. Shocked would describe it well.

"May I present to you Miss Eliza Melrose," Johnny says, pulling me close. "Eliza, this is my little brother, Lord Sampson Winter."

"Also known as the best-looking brother," he adds cheekily, bowing dramatically. "Enchanted, I'm sure. My brother has told me much about you, Miss Melrose."

"He has?" I blurt.

"Oh, much," he adds, and my cheeks burst into flames.

"How delightful."

Johnny smiles mildly and goes to the carriage, reaching inside, and a gloved hand appears, laid upon his. "Mother," he says, and she appears, his mother, the illustrious, beautiful Wisteria Winters. Utterly breathtaking. Dark hair, green eyes that are a perfect match for Johnny's, and a sculptured face that would be the envy of women far and wide. My God, she's quite simply a celestial being.

Smiling demurely, she steps down onto the cobbles and pats Johnny's cheek affectionately before casting her eyes across the silent crowd, a somewhat pointed look tarnishing her soft features. And behind her, another woman appears, a younger woman, who I suppose is around my age.

"Mother, Taya, this is Eliza Melrose," Johnny says, presenting my useless form to them. "Eliza, my mother, Lady Wisteria Winters, and my sister, Lady Taya Winters."

"So you're the one who's dragged me back to London," Wisteria Winters says quietly, her smile sedate.

"I…"

"The truth has dragged you back, Mother," Johnny says, and she smiles at him, so fondly, before she takes a few steps forward, reaching a now quiet Lymington who is still being held by the constable, looking rather stunned. She looks him up and down in a way no woman should look at a man. "I would not wish for my worst enemy to sustain the miseries bestowed upon us by the Lymingtons."

My eyes bat back and forth between them and my hand around Johnny's tightens, as Sampson and Taya take a leisurely wander around Lymington, their expressions cold, their demeanor hard. The Winters clan. Sampson is fashioned quite differently from his older brooding brother, he seems playful and cheeky, but is equally as handsome, if more boyishly. And the sister? Beautiful like her mother, but fierce like her brothers. My God, what a force.

"You're heathens!" Lord Lymington barks, looking rather flustered, his stick wobbling. "Do not listen to the rubbish they spew."

"No, fine sir," Sampson leans into his ear, his lip curled. "We are nobility, and your lies and deceit will not chase us away again."

"Jesus," I whisper.

"That's what I said," Frank says from beside me.

I swing my eyes to his. "You know everything?"

"I had no choice but to listen." He nods to Johnny. "He's quite a determined fellow, don't you know."

"I *do* know." I follow his gaze and find it's rooted on Johnny's sister, Taya. "Tread carefully, brother," I warn, not imagining Johnny taking all too kindly to a union between Frank and his sister, or, more fittingly, any dalliances.

"Come," Johnny says, claiming me and leading me on, but bringing us both to a stop when Papa coughs loudly. "Bugger it all," he whispers, looking to the heavens.

"What?"

"We cannot leave."

"Why ever not?"

"Because part of the deal I made with your father included a traditional courtship."

"Wonderful. So now I am simply part of another deal."

"You speak as if you are troubled by that when I know it not to be true."

"*You* speak with too much confidence." My nose wrinkles as Johnny turns me back and walks me over to my father.

"Mr. Melrose," he says politely, practically handing me over to my father. What is this craziness? "If I may, I should like to call upon your daughter tomorrow."

"Tomorrow?" I blurt, outraged. How must I survive until then?

"You may," Papa says, ignoring me. "My daughter has work to do."

"I do?"

"You do. I believe there's a rather interesting story about two families at war to be told."

I inhale. "What?"

"That was also part of the deal," Johnny says.

"An easy part," Father adds, and my heart soars, both for Papa and for Johnny. But...

"There was a hard part to this deal?"

"Yes, there was a very hard part." He looks at Johnny, and I hear Mama exhale, almost dreamily. "We'll get to that later."

We definitely will, but for now…"You know, if I am to write a story accurately," I say, my conniving mind working fast, "I must do my research."

"Oh?" Papa says, head tilted.

"Yes, I believe I must sit with His Grace and take notes."

Johnny looks at Papa and shrugs. "She has a point."

"Always does," Papa agrees over a small laugh as he wraps an arm around Mother's shoulder, the other around Clara, and leads them toward the house. "Frank will chaperone."

My shoulders drop, Frank grins, and Johnny rolls his eyes.

But it is better than tomorrow.

Chapter 19

When we arrive at Johnny's house, Wisteria Winters goes upstairs with Sampson carrying her bags, and Taya settles in the drawing room. "You can wait here with my sister," Johnny says to Frank, pointing to a chair, and, a surprise unto me, Frank doesn't protest, which only makes me somewhat warier. I watch him move quietly across the room and lower himself to a chair as Johnny's sister eyes him carefully. I'm about to voice my concerns, but Johnny leads me to his study and shuts the door, before guiding me to a chair and encouraging me to sit. Then, once he has placed a kiss upon my face, he pours wine into two glasses and joins me.

"Where would you like me to begin?" he asks, all rather businesslike, taking his seat once he's filled my hand with one of the glasses, and crossing one leg over the other.

"From the beginning, I suppose." I sip my wine, something telling me I should brace myself. What a ridiculous thought. When with the Duke, I should always be bracing myself. I pause for thought and lower my glass to my knee. "But first," I say, "I have a question."

"You may ask me anything and I will answer you truthfully."

"I should think so," I retort, indignant, and he smiles. "It will take you a lifetime to pay me back for the distress you have caused me."

"Then it's a fine thing we have a lifetime ahead of us, isn't it?"

I fight to hide my surprise and my delight. "You're assuming I bless you with the opportunity to win back my affections."

"Oh, Eliza," he purrs, relaxing back in his chair, his eyes burning me with the intensity of his stare. "How you thrive on the thrill of the chase."

I pout, sipping my wine. "Which leads me to my question," I muse. "Your planned seduction."

He smiles. "It was far more difficult than it should have been. I expected to have the deed done and dusted on our first encounter. Alas, I found myself quite taken by a rather smart mouth."

I balk at his honesty. "Well, I'm sorry to disappoint."

"You could never disappoint me, Eliza. Only if you reject me again."

"I might yet."

He nods mildly, his eyes never leaving mine, and rises to his full, wonderful height, strolling casually over to me. He rounds the back of my chair and his closeness alone has my body tensing. Then I feel his mouth at my ear, and I inhale slowly, closing my eyes. "Are you certain of that?" he whispers, his tongue wickedly licking the shell of my ear. I moan, ready to abandon the story, despite being desperate for every detail, and ravage him to death.

But he pulls away abruptly, leaving me a panting mess in the chair, my wine splashing up the glass. "Now, from the beginning," he says, smiling in satisfaction as he takes his seat once more. "Are you ready, Eliza?"

"I am," I breathe, composing myself. But…am I?

"Once upon a time," he begins, swallowing, perhaps to gather strength to tell his tale, "there were two dukes. One from Cornwall, one from Chester." *His father. Lymington.* "One duke was notoriously cunning, the other notoriously kindhearted. The families had long been rivals—and the rivalry was only enhanced when both dukes fell in love with the same woman." He smiles, but it is far from fond, and I stare at him wide-eyed. "The problem was, the girl was promised to the cunning duke."

"Lymington."

He nods.

"But she loved your father." I state it as the fact I know it must be.

Another nod, and he stands and starts wandering the room. I'm certain he's trying to walk off the anger. "Lymington challenged my father to a duel, and Papa met him on the common. Little did Lymington know, my father was a talented gunman and won fair and square, although he did not kill him, but merely injured his knee. He's needed a walking aid ever since."

"Good God," I whisper.

"Yes." His jaw twitches. "The rivalry only worsened. Fast forward many years and endless questionable business deals, Lymington was on the verge of bankruptcy. My father, ever the mad scientist,"—he smiles fondly now, but I detect sadness too—"had invented many pieces in his time, but this new piece was sure to revolutionize printing. We were due to attend a party at the Duke of Tillsbury's estate. All of us." He frowns. "Except Papa. He never did like socializing."

"Annabella Tillsbury," I whisper.

"Her husband. Lymington saw an opportunity and took it."

"No."

He swallows. "Mother did not feel well, so decided to remain at home, too, and Taya and Sampson insisted on watching over her. I, however…" The pain on his face is very real. The party boy. The wayward rebellion. I see his guilt. "I got home in time to save my mother and siblings, but my father…" He shakes his head, a sorrow as strong as I have ever seen settling in his expression. "I took my family to our estate in Cambridge to recuperate. I suspected Lymington had a hand in it but could not prove it. I decided to remain out of London for the safety of my mother, brother and sister. A few months later, I heard Lymington had invested in a newspaper. I started to piece it all together. The invention of Father's. The steam printing. And then a story released claiming we had all died and it was me who was responsible." His jaw tics. "I knew then he was responsible, I just did not know how to prove it. I've been plotting my revenge ever since."

I rub my head, which is beginning to ache. "I was part of your revenge."

"*Was*, Eliza. Not now."

"You've been through so much." My head is pounding, and it feels somewhat wrong for me to admit that, even if only to myself.

"All of the horrors have led me to you, though, sweet lady." He comes to me and clasps my shoulders, dipping to get his face close to mine. "I cannot be sorry for that kindness from the Fates."

I smile and lean in, kissing him freely. "I love you."

"I know you do," he answers, letting me indulge in his mouth. "Do you forgive me?"

"I forgive you."

"Good. I am glad we are friends again." He breaks away, rises, and walks to his antique, mahogany desk and pulls out the chair, resting his hands on the back of it. "I believe you are now furnished with all of the details you need to tell the people the truth."

I get up, walking over and lowering myself to the seat. He picks up the quill, dips it in ink, places it between my fingers, and pulls a piece of parchment toward me. "Write," he orders gently, pushing his lips into my neck, biting softly at my flesh. "And when you are finished, I will show you how the story ends."

I inhale, my hand shaky, and start with the date, as he kisses my neck, my throat, my cheek. "I'm afraid I must insist on knowing the end before I can even think to write this story," I whisper as he nips and bites at my flesh.

His moving hands falter, his mouth pausing on my cheek, and then I am seized and thrown on his desk. The quill leaves my hand, ink flies, and a pile of papers waft into the air. "I just do not know what I am going to do with you," he says, his palms spreading across my lower back pulling me close to him.

"I'm sure you do," I whisper, scanning his handsome face, my hands in his hair.

He smirks, dipping and dotting kisses over every inch of my face, working his lips down my front. "It may take longer than one night." His hand disappears up my dress and I shudder, tingles invading me. "Are you ready for the end?" he asks, shoving my dress up and ripping my pantaloons down.

"Ready."

He pushes into me on a gruff bark, and I cry out, holding on to him tightly, my nails sinking into his back, my face nuzzling into the crook of his neck.

And I smile into his skin at the thought of many more nights with the Duke.

My duke.

Acknowledgments

As ever, so much thanks to my publishers Orion and Grand Central for giving my stories a home. *One Night with the Duke* was at times a total stress-fest to write—who knew the word "stress" wasn't even in use then, which is bloody ironic as I seem to cause my characters much stress, as they do me! But the joy and pleasure I got from creating this new world far outweighed those moments of tearing my hair out. I hope you enjoy this new direction. It's something a little different but hopefully with all the JEM traits you have come to love.

Thank you for reading.

JEM x

Don't miss the next book in the sizzling
Belmore Square series!

A GENTLEMAN NEVER TELLS

Available in ebook in Summer 2023

About the Author

Jodi Ellen Malpas was born and raised in the Midlands town of Northampton, England, where she lives with her husband, boys and Theo the Doberman. Her novels have hit bestseller lists for the *New York Times*, *USA Today*, *Sunday Times*, and various other international publications, and can be read in more than twenty-four languages around the world.

Find out more at:
JodiEllenMalpas.co.uk
Facebook.com/JodiEllenMalpas
Twitter @JodiEllenMalpas